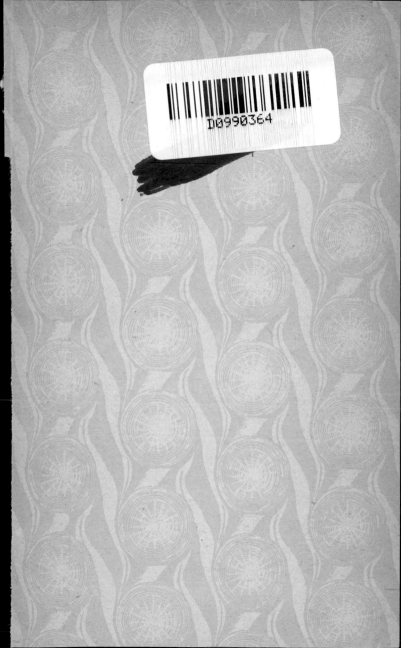

Everyman, I will go with thee, and be thy guide,
In thy most need to go by thy side.

This is No. 845 of Everyman's Library

EVERYMAN'S LIBRARY

ROMANCE

THE DECAMERON
OF GIOVANNI BOCCACCIO
INTRODUCTION BY EDWARD
HUTTON · IN 2 VOLS. · VOL. 1

GIOVANNI BOCCACCIO, born in Paris in 1313, the illegitimate son of a Florentine merchant and a French woman. Spent his youth in Florence; met 'Fiammetta' at Naples in 1336, returning to Florence in 1341. Met Petrarch, 1350. Died in poverty 21st December 1375.

THE DECAMERON
OF GIOVANNI BOCCACCIO

VOLUME ONE

LONDON: J. M. DENT & SONS LTD.
NEW YORK: E. P. DUTTON & CO. INC.

J. M. DENT & SONS LTD.
Aldine House · Bedford St. · London

Made in Great Britain
by
The Temple Press · Letchworth · Herts
First published in this edition 1930
Last reprinted 1950

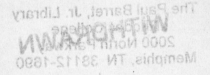
Y 15/39 m

INTRODUCTION

THE facts concerning the life of Giovanni Boccaccio, the author of the *Decameron*, may be very briefly noted.

His father was Boccaccio di Chellino da Certaldo, who between the years 1310 and 1314 was in business in Paris, where Giovanni was born, out of wedlock, in 1313, his mother being a French girl, whose name, from which his own would seem to be derived, was Jeanne. Probably as a tiny child he was brought to Florence, whither his father returned in 1314 and where he almost at once married Margherita di Gian Donato de' Martoli, who presently brought him a legitimate son, Francesco. Giovanni's boyhood was spent in Tuscany, partly at Certaldo, his father's native place, partly in and about Florence and especially perhaps in the hills about Fiesole and Settignano, the scene of the *Decameron* and of other works, where at Corbignano Margherita had brought her husband a small property.

Still a boy, he was sent to Naples to learn business, and there in that brilliant city, at the age of twenty-three, in 1336, as scholarship has now practically decided, he met "Fiammetta" Maria d'Aquino, that is, the bastard daughter of the King, Robert the Wise, on Holy Saturday in the church of S. Lorenzo of the Franciscans. His love for this lady is as famous as Petrarch's love for Laura, and for twelve year', till she died in the Black Death of 1348, he could think of little else : it was for her and about her he wrote all his early works, among them the *Amorosa Fiammetta*, the earliest of psychological novels.

With a growing devotion for literature, while in Naples he won his father's consent to abandon business and take up the study of canon law, which on his father's ruin and his own return to Florence in 1341 he finally abandoned for letters.

The works he had begun in Naples, such as the *Filocolo*, the *Filostrato*, the *Teseide*, he completed in Florence and added to them the *Ameto*, the *Fiammetta* and the *Ninfale Fiesolano*. Whether he returned to Naples we do not know.

Even before he left Naples Fiammetta had found a new lover, and in the Black Death of 1348, as is generally believed, she died. That frightful pestilence, which brought the Middle Age to an end, killed three out of five people in Florence, in Siena, in Naples, throughout Europe generally and even in England. It left him really alone in the world. He has immortalised it in the Proemio of the *Decameron*, many of the stories of which were by then already written and which he now put in order and furnished with its incomparable form and setting.

Till now the inspiration of his life and work had been his love for Fiammetta : the rest of his days were to be filled with another passion—his friendship for Petrarch. His work as a creative artist was at an end : the savage satire, the *Corbaccio*, was finished immediately after the *Decameron*, and he now turned, spontaneously at first and then more and more under the influence of Petrarch, to study. He writes his *Life of Dante*, presents Petrarch with a copy of the *Divine Comedy* and is lent in return at his own request a manuscript of Homer.

Boccaccio first met Petrarch in the spring of 1351 in Padua, whither he had gone in the name of Florence to recall the poet from exile. There, as Petrarch's guest, he was a witness of his enthusiasm for " sacred studies," his disregard of Italian literature ; and we now see Boccaccio, most unfortunately as we may think, giving up all work in the vernacular, and setting all his energy on work in the Latin tongue, on the study of antiquity and the acquirement of learning.

As a creative artist, as the author, to name only the best, of the *Decameron*, Boccaccio was the master of a world Petrarch could not enter ; he takes his place with Dante and Chaucer and Shakespeare. It is seldom, however, that a great creative artist is also a great scholar. Boccaccio certainly was not, and though it is easy to underrate his Latin works, which were the cyclopædias and dictionaries of the early Renaissance, he achieved nothing that was beyond the reach of an industrious compiler, except this, that it was he who with love and self-abnegation recovered for us the poems of Homer. This priceless gift Italy and Europe owed to Boccaccio, for though Petrarch supplied the Greek text, which no one in Europe could read, it was Boccaccio who took the ruffian Leon Pilatus into his house, kept him, tended

him, humoured him, while this barbarous Calabrian spelled
out the immortal text, which he could only half understand,
and at length finished the long task of a complete transla-
tion of Homer.

The remainder of Giovanni's life is full of melancholy,
with only his friendship for Petrarch and his occasional
meetings with the poet or his family to brighten his days.
He was poor, he was afflicted with a superstitious fear of
death and the hereafter, which Petrarch was only in part
able to dissipate, and he seems to have been neglected.
At any rate, it was only in his last days that, alone in his
house in Certaldo, half-starved with cold in winter, he was
invited to fill the first *Cathedra Dantesca* in Florence, which
seems to have been founded to relieve his miseries; and to
lecture on the poem he had always defended, even in the
face of his beloved friend Petrarch, the *Divine Comedy*.
He delivered his first lecture in October 1373 at the age of
sixty. But he was not able, as it proved, to complete the
seventeenth canto of the *Inferno* before he fell sick and
returned to Certaldo really to die. In the summer of 1374
Petrarch passed away, and in December of the following
year on the twenty-first of the month, in the old house at
Certaldo, Giovanni Boccaccio also breathed his last.

We have already noted that all Boccaccio's early works
in Italian were inspired by and written for his adored mistress,
Fiammetta, and in the very opening page of the *Decameron*
we see that even after writing six works in prose and verse
about her, even now she is dead, he cannot forget her. The
great proem opens with her unspoken name and closes too
in the same fashion. Moreover, of those seven ladies and
three youths who are the protagonists of the *Decameron*,
it is only she named Fiammetta who lives. The others
are without any personality—mere lay figures. As for Boc-
caccio himself, you will not find him in all those hundred
stories.

It is strange that the work which best represents his
genius, his humour and wide tolerance and love of man-
kind, should in this be so opposite to all his other works in
the vulgar tongue, which are inextricably involved with his
own personal affairs, his view of things, his love, his contempt,

his hatred. He speaks to us there once or twice, it is true, but always outside the stories, and his whole treatment of the various and infinite plots, incidents and characters of this great work is as impersonal as life itself.

The *Decameron* is an absolute work of art, as " detached " as a play by Shakespeare or a portrait by Velasquez. The scheme is formal and immutable, a miracle of design, in which almost everything can be expressed. To compare it with the *Arabian Nights* is to demonstrate its superiority. There you have a sleepless king, to whom a woman tells a thousand and one stories in order to save her life which this same king would have taken. You have, then, but two protagonists and an anxiety which touches but one of them—the fear of death on the part of the woman, soon forgotten in the excitement of the stories. In the *Decameron*, on the other hand, you have ten protagonists—three youths and seven ladies— and the horror which is designed to set off the stories is a universal pestilence which has already more than half dispeopled the city of Florence, and from which they are fled away to the exquisite seclusion and delight of a great villa garden on the slopes under Fiesole, where they spend their time in telling stories in order to pass the time in safety and forget.

The *mise en scène* is so well known as scarcely to need describing, but the proem in which it is set forth is one of the most splendid pieces of descriptive narrative in all literature and absolutely convincing. Boccaccio evokes for us the city of Florence in the grip of the Black Death of 1348. We see the streets quite deserted or horrible with the dead, and over all a dreadful silence broken only by the more dreadful laughter of those whom the catastrophe has freed from all human constraint, while fear has seized upon such of the living as disaster has not driven mad.

On a certain Tuesday morning seven young women have met by chance after Mass in the church of S. Maria Novella ; and the eldest, Pampinea, proposes that they should leave the beautiful, dangerous, depopulated city for the country and there live on one of their *poderi* " like honourable women, shunning alike death and the evil example of others."

While they are discussing this plan, there come into the church three young men, one of whom is a kinsman of Pampinea, and to the girls' joy, for they are fearful of being alone and undefended, the young men readily agree to accompany them, and the next day at dawn they set out.

Arrived at the villa, they enter among the gardens, and again it is Pampinea who proposes that one among them should be elected chief for a day so that each may be in turn in authority. Pampinea herself is first chosen and is crowned with bay leaves. Later, towards evening, they hie them to a meadow and at the queen's command range themselves in a circle on the grass, and there she proposes that each should tell a story in turn during the heat of each day for solace and forgetfulness and to pass the time. This was found pleasing to all, and so Pampinea turned to Pamfilo, who sat at her right hand, and bade him begin. Thus opens the series of immortal tales which compose the *Decameron*.

Such, then, is the incomparable design which the *Decameron* fills, beside which the mere haphazard telling of *The Hundred Merry Tales* seems barbarous, that of *The Thousand and One Nights* inadequate. That Boccaccio's design has indeed ever been bettered might well be denied, but in *The Canterbury Tales* Chaucer certainly equalled it. If the occasion there is not so dramatic, nor the surroundings at once so poignant and so beautiful, the pilgrimage progresses with the tales and allows of such a dramatic entry as that of the Canon and the Canon's Yeoman at Boughton-under-Blee. That entry was most fitting and opportune, right in every way, and though there is no inherent reason why the *Decameron* itself should not have been similarly broken in upon, the very stillness of that garden in the sunshine must have made any such interruption less acceptable.[1]

The true weakness of the plan of the *Decameron* in comparison with that of *The Canterbury Tales* is not a weakness of design but of character. Each of Chaucer's pilgrims is a complete human being : they all live for us more vividly than any other folk, real or imagined, of the fourteenth century in England, and each is different from the others —a perfect human character and personality. But in the protagonists of the *Decameron* it is not so. There is nothing or almost nothing to choose between them. Lauretta is not different from Filomena and may even be confused with Dioneo or Filostrato.

[1] The only interruption of the *Decameron*, if so it can be called, is the introduction of Tindaro and Licisca at the beginning of the Sixth Day. The diversion, however, has very little consequence.

We know nothing of them ; they are without any character
or personality, and indeed the only one of them all who stands
out in any way is she called Fiammetta, and that because she
never appears, but Boccaccio intervenes to tell us something
of her or to describe her beauty.

In Chaucer the tales often weary us, but the tellers never
do ; in Boccaccio the tales never weary us, but the tellers
always do. Do we there touch upon a fundamental difference
between English and Latin art ? In Latin art we have as a
rule an affair of situation, that is to say, the narrative or drama
rises out of the situation rather than out of the characters
of the persons, while even in the most worthless English work
there is an attempt to realise character, to make it the funda-
mental thing in the book, from which the narrative proceeds
and by which it lives and is governed.

In dealing with the *Decameron*, then, we must, more or less,
leave the narrators themselves out of the question : they are
not to be judged, they are but the *décor* or, if you will, the means
or excuse for the story ; they are really puppets who can in
no way be held responsible, so that if now and then an especially
licentious story is told by one of those virtuous ladies, it is
of no account—the tales are altogether independent of those
who tell them.

But if these young and fair protagonists soon pass from our
remembrance in the infinitely vivid and living stories they
tell, the setting, the background of that plague-stricken and
deserted city, the beauty and languorous peace of those
delicious gardens in which we listen, always remain with us,
so much so that tradition has identified the two palaces which
are the *milieu* of the whole *Decameron* with two of those villas,
the glory of the Florentine contado.

The first of these palaces—that to which they came on that
Wednesday morning—was, Boccaccio tells us, no more than
" two short miles from the city." There on the brow of a
hill was a palace, with a fine and spacious courtyard in the
midst and with loggias and halls and rooms, all and each one
in itself beautiful and ornamented tastefully with jocund
paintings. It was surrounded too with grass plots and
marvellous gardens and with wells of coldest water . . .
This " estate " has always been identified with Poggio Gher-
ardo, which now stands above the road to Settignano, then,
no doubt, a mule track, about a mile from that village and
some two miles from the Porta alla Croce of Florence. In the

fourteenth century it must have been, as Boccaccio describes it, equi-distant from the roads, the Via Aretina Nuova by the Arno, and the road to Fiesole from Florence.

Poggio Gherardo is not much more than a stone's throw from Corbignano, the *podere* which Margherita brought to Boccaccio's father as part of her dowry and where it appears likely that Giovanni spent part of his boyhood.

But Poggio Gherardo is not the only palace of the *Decameron*. At the close of the second day, Madonna Neifile being crowned queen, proposed that they should visit a new place " if we would avoid visitors," and indeed she had a spot in her mind. She led them " westward by an unfrequented lane to a beautiful and splendid palace" which tradition assures us is the Villa Palmieri. This villa standing as it does on the lower Fiesolan slope, certainly accords with Boccaccio's description " on a low eminence somewhat from the plain." [1]

Nor are these two palaces the only places mentioned in the setting of the *Decameron* that we may identify. It was an afternoon of spring, six days had almost passed and the tales had been short that day, when, the gentlemen being at dice, Madonna Elisa called her friends to her and said : " Ever since we have been here I have wished to show you a place, not far off, where I believe none of you have ever been ; it is called La Valle delle Donne. . . . It is yet early ; if you choose to come with me, I promise you that you will be pleased with your walk." After a walk of nearly a mile they came to the place where there burst forth a fair crystal stream. The little plain in the valley was an exact circle, about half a mile in circumference, surrounded by six hills of moderate height. The rivulet came through two of the hills, and coming into the plain beneath a waterfall formed a pool not deeper than a man's breast and so clear you could see the gravelly bottom. "There the ladies all came together and . . . finding it commendable . . . did, as it was very hot and they observed themselves secure from observation, resolve to take a bath."

This delicious spot,[2] called to this day the Valle delle

---

[1] Villa Palmieri is nearly as beautiful, though not so secluded, as it was so long ago ; only while the gardens with their pergolas of vines, their hedges of jasmine and crimson roses, their carved marble fountains remain, the two mills which he speaks of are gone, having been destroyed in a flood of the Mugnone in 1409, less than sixty years after he wrote of them.

[2] The place has been drained to-day, and is now a garden of vines and olives in the *podere* of Villa Ciliegio.

Donne, may be reached from the " unfrequented lane " by which they all passed from Poggio Gherardo to Villa Palmieri.

> "Where the hewn rocks of Fiesole impend
> O'er Doccia's dell, and fig and olive blend . . .
> Here by the lake Boccaccio's fair brigade
> Bathed in the stream and tale for tale repaid."

The hundred tales that were thus told in the shade of those two beautiful gardens may doubtless be traced to a large number of sources—Egyptian, Arabian, Persian and French ; but their origins matter little. Boccaccio was almost certainly unaware of them, gathering his material as he did from the tales he heard in Naples and up and down Italy. Certainly to the Contes and Fabliaux of France a third part of the *Decameron* may be traced, much too to Indian and Persian sources and a little to the *Gesta Romanorum*. But we might as well accuse Chaucer or Shakespeare of a want of originality, because they took what they wanted where they found it, often indeed in Boccaccio, as arraign the author of the *Decameron* for a dependence he was quite unaware of on sources such as these. He has made the tales his own.

The *Decameron* is a world in itself, and its effect, upon us who read it, is the effect of life, which includes, for its own good, things moral and immoral. The book has the variety of the world and is full of an infinity of people, who represent for us the fourteenth century in Italy, in all its fullness almost, though, as in Shakespeare's plays, the religious temperament is not to be found.

The book deals with man as life does, never taking him very seriously or without a certain indifference, a certain irony too, and laughter. Yet it is full of courtesy, of luck, of all sorts of adventures both gallant and sad. In its details, at any rate, it is true and even realistic, crammed with observation of those customs and types which made up the life of the time. It is dramatic, ironic, comic, tragic, philosophic and even lyrical ; full of indulgence for human error, an absolutely human book beyond any work of Dante's or Petrarch's or Froissart's. Even Chaucer is not so complete in his humanism, his love of all sorts and conditions of men. Perfect in organism, in construction, and in freedom, each of these tales is in some sort a living part of life and a criticism of it. Almost any one could be treated by a modern writer in his own way, and remain fundamentally the same and fundamentally true. What licentiousness there is might seem to be due rather to the French sources of some of the tales than to any invention on the part of Boccaccio, who softened much of their original grossness, and later came to deplore it.

But it is in its extraordinary variety of contents and character that the *Decameron* is chiefly remarkable. We are involved in a multitude of adventures, are introduced to innumerable people of every class, and each class shows us its most characteristic qualities. Such is Boccaccio's art : for the stories were not originally, or even as they are, ostensibly studies of character at all, but rather anecdotes, tales of adventure, stories of illicit love, " good stories " about the friars and the clergy and women, told for amusement because they are full of laughter and are witty, or contain a brief and ready reply with which one has rebuked another or saved himself from danger. Whatever they may be, and they are often of the best, of the most universal, they are not, for the real lover of the *Decameron*, the true reason why he goes to it again and again, always with the certainty of delight.

The book is full of people, of living people—that is the secret of its immortality. Fra Cipolla, Celandrino, poor Monna Tezza his wife, whom at last he so outrageously gives away, Griselda, Cisti the Florentine baker, the joyous Madonna Filippa or Monna Belcolore should be as dear to us as any character in any book, not by Shakespeare himself. They live for ever. And yet it must be confessed that while the book is a mirror of the world, and doubtless as true to the life of its time as any book that was ever written, it lacks a certain idealism, a certain moral sense, which, even from a purely æsthetic point of view, would have given it a balance, a sense of proportion, which it has sometimes seemed to me it needs.

It is true that Boccaccio deals with life and with life alone. It is true that life then, as now, made little of sexual morality. But with Boccaccio sexual immorality usurps or seems to usurp a place out of all proportion to its importance in life. It is here that Boccaccio is most conventional, for here his comic genius is seen at its best. The unreality of this most real book lies in the fact that this is his most frequent theme. His *spose* are all beautiful young women who live in the arms of beautiful youths ; they are nearly all adulteresses.

Griselda indeed might seem to be the only faithful wife among them. Consider, then, the wife of Pietro di Vincolo, who sells herself, fresh and lovely as she is. Consider the pretty Prunella the Neapolitan. She, like the rest, is not only without regret but without scruple. They all seem to have her extraordinary astuteness, her readiness of the devil.

There is Sismonda the wife of the rich merchant Arriguccio Berlinghieri ; there is Isabella who loves Leonetto and Monna Beatrice who to her adultery adds contempt of her husband. . . . But why go on ? They are all sisters. Lydia is even more wily, Bartolommea more shameless.

And if the women are thus, the husbands are fools. Yet Boccaccio well knows how to draw the honest peasant, the hard-working artisan, the persistent and adventurous merchant, and a harder thing, the man of good society, such as Federigo degli Alberighi, when he will. As a writer of comedy he is one of the greatest masters ; and it must be remembered that as a master of comedy he was to some extent at the mercy both of it and of his audience. This must excuse him for his too persistent stories about adulteries. The deceived husband was always a comic figure ; it is possible that he always will be. This being so, we shall not judge the women of Boccaccio's day by his tales, and it might seem that we should discount in the same way his stories about the clergy.

Like every other comic master he naturally finds some of his choicest material among them, who always have been, are now and ever will be a never-failing source of amusement. But here we must go warily, for Boccaccio's treatment of the clergy might almost be said to exhaust what little moral indignation he possessed. " I have spoken the truth about the friars," he tells us with immense relief in the conclusion to his work ; and if he had not time, courage, or opportunity to tell us the truth about the monks, nuns and the secular clergy, he has left us, it must be confessed, some very remarkable evidence. His whole attitude of attack is different when he exposes the clergy ; moreover, while we have no evidence at all in support of his supposed representation of the married woman as universally adulterous —and it may be questioned whether he intended to leave us with any such impression—we have ample support from the best possible sources as to the general looseness of discipline among the clergy both secular and religious. Even if we discount the indictment of St. Catherine of Siena as exaggerated, we cannot altogether so dispose of the evidence of Grosseteste Bishop of Lincoln or of Pope Alexander VI. Consider, then, what such a beast as the priest of Varlungo must have been in a village ; consider the rector of Fiesole. It is true too that we should not recognise in any one of Boccaccio's friars the brother of St. Francis or St. Dominic. Consider them, then : Fra Cipolla is a lovely rogue, of the best ; who more cunning than Fra Alberto da Imola ; who more eagerly wily than Fra Rinaldo ; who more concupiscent than Fra Rustico ? The only son of St. Francis illumined with light and piety is the confessor of Ser Ciapelletto, and he has no name, and is, I fear, quickly forgotten.

But here again we must discount what we read. Scandal is more noisy than virtue. We know that the secular clergy, the monks and friars too were not generally but only exceptionally corrupt : that had it been otherwise, the revolt would have appeared not when it did and where it did and for quite other reasons, but in Italy in the fourteenth century, in a country still able to produce numberless saints, and, under the direct influence and direction of the clergy, to cover almost every church with the purest and the loveliest art in the world.

No one has thought to condemn the morality of the thirteenth century because of Dante's *Inferno* ; nor should we think to indict the fourteenth out of the stories of the *Decameron*. The *Divine Comedy* and the *Decameron* in their immense energy bear witness together to the essential soundness and sanity of the great age which gave them birth.

The *Decameron*, moreover, though widely read and enthusiastically received, was censured very strongly in its own day, and we find allusions to this in the proem to the Fourth Day and in the Conclusion to the work. Nor did it escape the knife of the Church, though it was never suppressed. It is probably the greatest though not quite the first prose work in the Tuscan tongue. Written in a very beautiful but complicated style it is often lacking in simplicity. Yet who would attack it ? It has justified itself, as every work of the sort must do, by its appeal to mankind.

The original manuscript has disappeared and the oldest we possess seems to be that written in 1368 by Francesco Mannelli, though the later Hamilton MS. now in Berlin is the better of the two. More than ten editions were, however, printed in the fifteenth century and some seventy-seven in the sixteenth. There is not a *novelliere* in Italian literature for many centuries who has not inspired himself with the *Decameron*.

Its fortune abroad was almost equally good. Hans Sachs, Molière, La Fontaine, Lope de Vega, to mention only the greatest names, were in its debt ; and in England our greatest poets have drawn from it, once the form and often the substance of their work. One has only to name Chaucer, Sidney, Shakespeare, Dryden, Keats, Tennyson to suggest England's debt to Boccaccio. And although our prose literature produced no great original example of this sort, possibly because the Bible so early became a part of English literature, still its influence was shown by the popularity of translations from it, so that according to Ascham " a tale of Bocace was made more account of than a story out of the Bible."

The sixteenth century exhibits many translations of some of Boccaccio's stories, but it was in 1620 that the first practically complete *Decameron* appeared in English, translated inaccurately but very splendidly, apparently from the French version of Antoine le Macon. Isaac Jaggard published it in two parts in folio with wood-cuts. The titles bore no translator's name. Five editions in all were published during the seventeenth century.

The first really complete translation to appear in English was that of Mr. John Payne, printed for the Villon Society (1886), but the first complete translation to pass into general circulation was that of Mr. J. M. Rigg, which is rendered with careful accuracy and much spirit and is here reprinted in the *Everyman's Library*.

EDWARD HUTTON.

LIST OF WORKS :

Dates given of first editions :

> Filocolo, Venice, 1472. Filostrato, 1480 (?). Teseide, Ferrara, 1475.
> Ameto, Rome, 1478. Amorosa Visione, Milan, 1521. Fiametta,
> Padua, 1472. Ninfale Fiesolano, Venice, 1477. Decameron,
> Venice, 1471. Corbaccio, Florence, 1487. Vita di Dante, Venice,
> 1477. De Genealogiis. De Montibus, Sylvis, Fontibus. De
> Casibus Virorum Illustrium. De Claris Mulieribus.

> Works, 17 vols. Moutier, Florence, 1827 et seq. Letters of Boccaccio,
> 1877. Lives by Edward Hutton (1910) and T. C. Chubb (1930).

CONTENTS

VOL. I

xix

CONTENTS

PAGE

DISTANT VIEW OF THE VILLA DI POGGIO GHERARDO

Beginneth here the book called Decameron, otherwise Prince Galeotto, wherein are contained one hundred novels told in ten days by seven ladies and three young men.

PROEM

'TIS humane to have compassion on the afflicted ; and as it shews well in all, so it is especially demanded of those who have had need of comfort and have found it in others : among whom, if any had ever need thereof or found it precious or delectable, I may be numbered ; seeing that from my early youth even to the present I was beyond measure aflame with a most aspiring and noble love [1] more perhaps than, were I to enlarge upon it, would seem to accord with my lowly condition. Whereby, among people of discernment to whose knowledge it had come, I had much praise and high esteem, but nevertheless extreme discomfort and suffering, not indeed by reason of cruelty on the part of the beloved lady, but through superabundant ardour engendered in the soul by ill-bridled desire ; the which, as it allowed me no reasonable period of quiescence, frequently occasioned me an inordinate distress. In which distress so much relief was afforded me by the delectable discourse of a friend and his commendable consolations, that I entertain a very solid conviction that to them I owe it that I am not dead. But, as it pleased Him, who, being infinite, has assigned by immutable law an end to all things mundane, my love, beyond all other fervent, and neither to be broken nor bent by any force of determination, or counsel of prudence, or fear of manifest shame or ensuing danger, did nevertheless in course of time abate of its own accord, in such wise that it has now left nought of itself in my mind but that pleasure which it is wont to afford to him who does not adventure too far out in navigating its deep seas ; so that, whereas it was used to be grievous, now, all discomfort being done away, I find that which remains to be delightful. But the cessation of the pain has not banished the memory of the kind offices done me by those who shared

[1] For Fiammetta, *i.e.* Maria, natural daughter of Robert, King of Naples.

by sympathy the burden of my griefs ; nor will it ever, I believe,
pass from me except by death. And as among the virtues
gratitude is in my judgment most especially to be commended,
and ingratitude in equal measure to be censured, therefore, that
I shew myself not ungrateful, I have resolved, now that I may
call myself free, to endeavour, in return for what I have received,
to afford, so far as in me lies, some solace, if not to those who
succoured me, and who, perchance, by reason of their good
sense or good fortune, need it not, at least to such as may be
apt to receive it.

And though my support or comfort, so to say, may be of
little avail to the needy, nevertheless it seems to me meet to
offer it most readily where the need is most apparent, because
it will there be most serviceable and also most kindly received.
Who will deny, that it should be given, for all that it may be
worth, to gentle ladies much rather than to men ?   Within their
soft bosoms, betwixt fear and shame, they harbour secret fires
of love, and how much of strength concealment adds to those
fires, they know who have proved it.   Moreover, restrained by
the will, the caprice, the commandment of fathers, mothers,
brothers, and husbands, confined most part of their time within
the narrow compass of their chambers, they live, so to say, a
life of vacant ease, and, yearning and renouncing in the same
moment, meditate divers matters which cannot all be cheerful.
If thereby a melancholy bred of amorous desire make entrance
into their minds, it is like to tarry there to their sore distress,
unless it be dispelled by a change of ideas.   Besides which they
have much less power to support such a weight than men.
For, when men are enamoured, their case is very different, as
we may readily perceive.   They, if they are afflicted by a
melancholy and heaviness of mood, have many ways of relief
and diversion ; they may go where they will, may hear and
see many things, may hawk, hunt, fish, ride, play or traffic.
By which means all are able to compose their minds, either in
whole or in part, and repair the ravage wrought by the dumpish
mood, at least for some space of time ; and shortly after, by
one way or another, either solace ensues, or the dumps become
less grievous.   Wherefore, in some measure to compensate the
injustice of Fortune, which to those whose strength is least, as
we see it to be in the delicate frames of ladies, has been most
niggard of support, I, for the succour and diversion of such of
them as love (for others may find sufficient solace in the needle
and the spindle and the reel), do intend to recount one hundred

Novels or Fables or Parables or Stories, as we may please to
call them, which were recounted in ten days by an honourable
company of seven ladies and three young men in the time of
the late mortal pestilence, as also some canzonets sung by the
said ladies for their delectation.   In which pleasant novels will
be found some passages of love rudely crossed, with other
courses of events of which the issues are felicitous, in times as
well modern as ancient : from which stories the said ladies,
who shall read them, may derive both pleasure from the enter-
taining matters set forth therein, and also good counsel, in that
they may learn what to shun, and likewise what to pursue.
Which cannot, I believe, come to pass, unless the dumps be
banished by diversion of mind.   And if it so happen (as God
grant it may) let them give thanks to Love, who, liberating me
from his fetters, has given me the power to devote myself to
their gratification.

Beginneth here the first day of the Decameron, in which, when the author has set forth, how it came to pass that the persons, who appear hereafter, met together for interchange of discourse, they, under the rule of Pampinea, discourse of such matters as most commend themselves to each in turn.

As often, most gracious ladies, as I bethink me, how compassionate you are by nature one and all, I do not disguise from myself that the present work must seem to you to have but a heavy and distressful prelude, in that it bears upon its very front what must needs revive the sorrowful memory of the late mortal pestilence, the course whereof was grievous not merely to eye-witnesses but to all who in any other wise had cognisance of it. But I would have you know, that you need not therefore be fearful to read further, as if your reading were ever to be accompanied by sighs and tears. This horrid beginning will be to you even such as to wayfarers is a steep and rugged mountain, beyond which stretches a plain most fair and delectable, which the toil of the ascent and descent does but serve to render more agreeable to them ; for, as the last degree of joy brings with it sorrow, so misery has ever its sequel of happiness. To this brief exordium of woe—brief, I say, inasmuch as it can be put within the compass of a few letters—succeed forthwith the sweets and delights which I have promised you, and which, perhaps, had I not done so, were not to have been expected from it. In truth, had it been honestly possible to guide you whither I would bring you by a road less rough than this will be, I would gladly have so done. But, because without this review of the past, it would not be in my power to shew how the matters, of which you will hereafter read, came to pass, I am almost bound of necessity to enter upon it, if I would write of them at all.

I say, then, that the years of the beatific incarnation of the Son of God had reached the tale of one thousand three hundred and forty-eight, when in the illustrious city of Florence, the fairest of all the cities of Italy, there made its appearance that deadly pestilence, which, whether disseminated by the influence of the celestial bodies, or sent upon us mortals by God in His

4

just wrath by way of retribution for our iniquities, had had
its origin some years before in the East, whence, after destroying
an innumerable multitude of living beings, it had propagated
itself without respite from place to place, and so, calamitously,
had spread into the West.

In Florence, despite all that human wisdom and forethought
could devise to avert it, as the cleansing of the city from many
impurities by officials appointed for the purpose, the refusal
of entrance to all sick folk, and the adoption of many precautions
for the preservation of health ; despite also humble supplications
addressed to God, and often repeated both in public procession
and otherwise, by the devout ; towards the beginning of the
spring of the said year the doleful effects of the pestilence began
to be horribly apparent by symptoms that shewed as if
miraculous.

Not such were they as in the East, where an issue of blood
from the nose was a manifest sign of inevitable death ; but in
men and women alike it first betrayed itself by the emergence
of certain tumours in the groin or the armpits, some of which
grew as large as a common apple, others as an egg, some more,
some less, which the common folk called gavoccioli. From the
two said parts of the body this deadly gavocciolo soon began
to propagate and spread itself in all directions indifferently ;
after which the form of the malady began to change, black
spots or livid making their appearance in many cases on the
arm or the thigh or elsewhere, now few and large, now minute
and numerous. And as the gavocciolo had been and still was
an infallible token of approaching death, such also were these
spots on whomsoever they shewed themselves. Which maladies
seemed to set entirely at naught both the art of the physician
and the virtues of physic ; indeed, whether it was that the
disorder was of a nature to defy such treatment, or that the
physicians were at fault—besides the qualified there was now
a multitude both of men and of women who practised without
having received the slightest tincture of medical science—and,
being in ignorance of its source, failed to apply the proper
remedies ; in either case, not merely were those that recovered
few, but almost all within three days from the appearance of
the said symptoms, sooner or later, died, and in most cases
without any fever or other attendant malady.

Moreover, the virulence of the pest was the greater by
reason that intercourse was apt to convey it from the sick to
the whole, just as fire devours things dry or greasy when they

are brought close to it. Nay, the evil went yet further, for
not merely by speech or association with the sick was the
malady communicated to the healthy with consequent peril of
common death ; but any that touched the clothes of the sick
or aught else that had been touched or used by them, seemed
thereby to contract the disease.

So marvellous sounds that which I have now to relate, that,
had not many, and I among them, observed it with their own
eyes, I had hardly dared to credit it, much less to set it down in
writing, though I had had it from the lips of a credible witness.

I say, then, that such was the energy of the contagion of the
said pestilence, that it was not merely propagated from man to
man, but, what is much more startling, it was frequently
observed, that things which had belonged to one sick or dead
of the disease, if touched by some other living creature, not of
the human species, were the occasion, not merely of sickening,
but of an almost instantaneous death. Whereof my own eyes
(as I said a little before) had cognisance, one day among others,
by the following experience. The rags of a poor man who
had died of the disease being strewn about the open street, two
hogs came thither, and after, as is their wont, no little trifling
with their snouts, took the rags between their teeth and tossed
them to and fro about their chaps ; whereupon, almost
immediately, they gave a few turns, and fell down dead, as if
by poison, upon the rags which in an evil hour they had
disturbed.

In which circumstances, not to speak of many others of a
similar or even graver complexion, divers apprehensions and
imaginations were engendered in the minds of such as were left
alive, inclining almost all of them to the same harsh resolution,
to wit, to shun and abhor all contact with the sick and all that
belonged to them, thinking thereby to make each his own
health secure. Among whom there were those who thought
that to live temperately and avoid all excess would count for
much as a preservative against seizures of this kind. Where-
fore they banded together, and, dissociating themselves from
all others, formed communities in houses where there were no
sick, and lived a separate and secluded life, which they regulated
with the utmost care, avoiding every kind of luxury, but eating
and drinking very moderately of the most delicate viands and
the finest wines, holding converse with none but one another,
lest tidings of sickness or death should reach them, and diverting
their minds with music and such other delights as they could

devise. Others, the bias of whose minds was in the opposite
direction, maintained, that to drink freely, frequent places of
public resort, and take their pleasure with song and revel,
sparing to satisfy no appetite, and to laugh and mock at no
event, was the sovereign remedy for so great an evil : and that
which they affirmed they also put in practice, so far as they
were able, resorting day and night, now to this tavern, now to
that, drinking with an entire disregard of rule or measure, and
by preference making the houses of others, as it were, their
inns, if they but saw in them aught that was particularly to
their taste or liking; which they were readily able to do, be-
cause the owners, seeing death imminent, had become as reckless
of their property as of their lives ; so that most of the houses
were open to all comers, and no distinction was observed
between the stranger who presented himself and the rightful
lord. Thus, adhering ever to their inhuman determination to
shun the sick, as far as possible, they ordered their life. In
this extremity of our city's suffering and tribulation the vener-
able authority of laws, human and divine, was abased and all
but totally dissolved, for lack of those who should have adminis-
tered and enforced them, most of whom, like the rest of the
citizens, were either dead or sick, or so hard bested for servants
that they were unable to execute any office ; whereby every
man was free to do what was right in his own eyes.

Not a few there were who belonged to neither of the two said
parties, but kept a middle course between them, neither laying
the same restraint upon their diet as the former, nor allowing
themselves the same license in drinking and other dissipations
as the latter, but living with a degree of freedom sufficient to
satisfy their appetites, and not as recluses. They therefore
walked abroad, carrying in their hands flowers or fragrant
herbs or divers sorts of spices, which they frequently raised to
their noses, deeming it an excellent thing thus to comfort the
brain with such perfumes, because the air seemed to be every-
where laden and recking with the stench emitted by the dead
and the dying, and the odours of drugs.

Some again, the most sound, perhaps, in judgment, as they
were also the most harsh in temper, of all, affirmed that there
was no medicine for the disease superior or equal in efficacy to
flight ; following which prescription a multitude of men and
women, negligent of all but themselves, deserted their city,
their houses, their estates, their kinsfolk, their goods, and went
into voluntary exile, or migrated to the country parts, as if

God in visiting men with this pestilence in requital of their
iniquities would not pursue them with His wrath wherever
they might be, but intended the destruction of such alone as
remained within the circuit of the walls of the city ; or deeming,
perchance, that it was now time for all to flee from it, and that
its last hour was come.

Of the adherents of these divers opinions not all died, neither
did all escape ; but rather there were, of each sort and in every
place, many that sickened, and by those who retained their
health were treated after the example which they themselves,
while whole, had set, being everywhere left to languish in almost
total neglect. Tedious were it to recount, how citizen avoided
citizen, how among neighbours was scarce found any that
shewed fellow-feeling for another, how kinsfolk held aloof, and
never met, or but rarely ; enough that this sore affliction
entered so deep into the minds of men and women, that in the
horror thereof brother was forsaken by brother, nephew by
uncle, brother by sister, and oftentimes husband by wife ; nay,
what is more, and scarcely to be believed, fathers and mothers
were found to abandon their own children, untended, unvisited,
to their fate, as if they had been strangers. Wherefore the sick
of both sexes, whose number could not be estimated, were left
without resource but in the charity of friends (and few such
there were), or the interest of servants, who were hardly to be
had at high rates and on unseemly terms, and being, moreover,
one and all, men and women of gross understanding, and for
the most part unused to such offices, concerned themselves no
further than to supply the immediate and expressed wants of
the sick, and to watch them die; in which service they them-
selves not seldom perished with their gains. In consequence
of which dearth of servants and dereliction of the sick by
neighbours, kinsfolk and friends, it came to pass—a thing,
perhaps, never before heard of—that no woman, however
dainty, fair or well-born she might be, shrank, when stricken
with the disease, from the ministrations of a man, no matter
whether he were young or no, or scrupled to expose to him
every part of her body, with no more shame than if he had
been a woman, submitting of necessity to that which her
malady required ; wherefrom, perchance, there resulted in
after time some loss of modesty in such as recovered. Besides
which many succumbed who, with proper attendance, would,
perhaps, have escaped death ; so that, what with the virulence
of the plague and the lack of due tendance of the sick, the

multitude of the deaths, that daily and nightly took place in the city, was such that those who heard the tale—not to say witnessed the fact—were struck dumb with amazement. Whereby, practices contrary to the former habits of the citizens could hardly fail to grow up among the survivors.

It had been, as to-day it still is, the custom for the women that were neighbours and of kin to the deceased to gather in his house with the women that were most closely connected with him, to wail with them in common, while on the other hand his male kinsfolk and neighbours, with not a few of the other citizens, and a due proportion of the clergy according to his quality, assembled without, in front of the house, to receive the corpse ; and so the dead man was borne on the shoulders of his peers, with funeral pomp of taper and dirge, to the church selected by him before his death.   Which rites, as the pestilence waxed in fury, were either in whole or in great part disused, and gave way to others of a novel order.   For not only did no crowd of women surround the bed of the dying, but many passed from this life unregarded, and few indeed were they to whom were accorded the lamentations and bitter tears of sorrowing relations ; nay, for the most part, their place was taken by the laugh, the jest, the festal gathering ; observances which the women, domestic piety in large measure set aside, had adopted with very great advantage to their health.   Few also there were whose bodies were attended to the church by more than ten or twelve of their neighbours, and those not the honourable and respected citizens ; but a sort of corpse-carriers drawn from the baser ranks, who called themselves becchini [1] and performed such offices for hire, would shoulder the bier, and with hurried steps carry it, not to the church of the dead man's choice, but to that which was nearest at hand, with four or six priests in front and a candle or two, or, perhaps, none ; nor did the priests distress themselves with too long and solemn an office, but with the aid of the becchini hastily consigned the corpse to the first tomb which they found untenanted.   The condition of the lower, and, perhaps, in great measure of the middle ranks, of the people shewed even worse and more deplorable ; for, deluded by hope or constrained by poverty, they stayed in their quarters, in their houses, where they sickened by thousands a day, and, being without service or help of any kind, were, so to speak, irredeemably devoted to the death which overtook

[1] Probably from the name of the pronged or hooked implement with which they dragged the corpses out of the houses.

I—B 845

them. Many died daily or nightly in the public streets; of many others, who died at home, the departure was hardly observed by their neighbours, until the stench of their putrefying bodies carried the tidings; and what with their corpses and the corpses of others who died on every hand the whole place was a sepulchre.

It was the common practice of most of the neighbours, moved no less by fear of contamination by the putrefying bodies than by charity towards the deceased, to drag the corpses out of the houses with their own hands, aided, perhaps, by a porter, if a porter was to be had, and to lay them in front of the doors, where any one who made the round might have seen, especially in the morning, more of them than he could count; afterwards they would have biers brought up, or, in default, planks, whereon they laid them. Nor was it once or twice only that one and the same bier carried two or three corpses at once; but quite a considerable number of such cases occurred, one bier sufficing for husband and wife, two or three brothers, father and son, and so forth. And times without number it happened, that, as two priests, bearing the cross, were on their way to perform the last office for some one, three or four biers were brought up by the porters in rear of them, so that, whereas the priests supposed that they had but one corpse to bury, they discovered that there were six or eight, or sometimes more. Nor, for all their number, were their obsequies honoured by either tears or lights or crowds of mourners; rather, it was come to this, that a dead man was then of no more account than a dead goat would be to-day. From all which it is abundantly manifest, that that lesson of patient resignation, which the sages were never able to learn from the slight and infrequent mishaps which occur in the natural course of events, was now brought home even to the minds of the simple by the magnitude of their disasters, so that they became indifferent to them.

As consecrated ground there was not in extent sufficient to provide tombs for the vast multitude of corpses which day and night, and almost every hour, were brought in eager haste to the churches for interment, least of all, if ancient custom were to be observed and a separate resting-place assigned to each, they dug, for each graveyard, as soon as it was full, a huge trench, in which they laid the corpses as they arrived by hun-dreds at a time, piling them up as merchandise is stowed in the hold of a ship, tier upon tier, each covered with a little earth, until the trench would hold no more. But I spare to rehearse

with minute particularity each of the woes that came upon
our city, and say in brief, that, harsh as was the tenor of her
fortunes, the surrounding country knew no mitigation ; for
there—not to speak of the castles, each, as it were, a little city
in itself—in sequestered village, or on the open champaign, by
the wayside, on the farm, in the homestead, the poor hapless
husbandmen and their families, forlorn of physicians' care or
servants' tendance, perished day and night alike, not as men,
but rather as beasts.   Wherefore, they too, like the citizens,
abandoned all rule of life, all habit of industry, all counsel of
prudence ; nay, one and all, as if expecting each day to be their
last, not merely ceased to aid Nature to yield her fruit in due
season of their beasts and their lands and their past labours,
but left no means unused, which ingenuity could devise, to
waste their accumulated store ; denying shelter to their oxen,
asses, sheep, goats, pigs, fowls, nay, even to their dogs, man's
most faithful companions, and driving them out into the fields
to roam at large amid the unsheaved, nay, unreaped corn.
Many of which, as if endowed with reason, took their fill during
the day, and returned home at night without any guidance of
herdsman.   But enough of the country ! What need we add,
but (reverting to the city) that such and so grievous was the
harshness of heaven, and perhaps in some degree of man, that,
what with the fury of the pestilence, the panic of those whom
it spared, and their consequent neglect or desertion of not a
few of the stricken in their need, it is believed without any
manner of doubt, that between March and the ensuing July
upwards of a hundred thousand human beings lost their lives
within the walls of the city of Florence, which before the deadly
visitation would not have been supposed to contain so many
people ! How many grand palaces, how many stately homes,
how many splendid residences, once full of retainers, of lords,
of ladies, were now left desolate of all, even to the meanest
servant ! How many families of historic fame, of vast ancestral
domains, and wealth proverbial, found now no scion to continue
the succession ! How many brave men, how many fair ladies,
how many gallant youths, whom any physician, were he Galen,
Hippocrates, or Æsculapius himself, would have pronounced
in the soundest of health, broke fast with their kinsfolk, com-
rades and friends in the morning, and when evening came,
supped with their forefathers in the other world !
Irksome it is to myself to rehearse in detail so sorrowful a
history.   Wherefore, being minded to pass over so much thereof

as I fairly can, I say, that our city, being thus well-nigh depopu-
lated, it so happened, as I afterwards learned from one worthy
of credit, that on a Tuesday morning after Divine Service the
venerable church of Santa Maria Novella was almost deserted
save for the presence of seven young ladies habited sadly in
keeping with the season. All were connected either by blood
or at least as friends or neighbours ; and fair and of good
understanding were they all, as also of noble birth, gentle
manners, and a modest sprightliness. In age none exceeded
twenty-eight, or fell short of eighteen years. Their names I
would set down in due form, had I not good reason to with-
hold them, being solicitous lest the matters which here ensue,
as told and heard by them, should in after time be occasion of
reproach to any of them, in view of the ample indulgence which
was then, for the reasons heretofore set forth, accorded to the
lighter hours of persons of much riper years than they, but
which the manners of to-day have somewhat restricted ; nor
would I furnish material to detractors, ever ready to bestow
their bite where praise is due, to cast by invidious speech the
least slur upon the honour of these noble ladies. Wherefore,
that which each says may be apprehended without confusion, I
intend to give them names more or less appropriate to the
character of each. The first, then, being the eldest of the
seven, we will call Pampinea, the second Fiammetta, the third
Filomena, the fourth Emilia, the fifth we will distinguish as
Lauretta, the sixth as Neifile, and the last, not without reason,
shall be named Elisa.

'Twas not of set purpose but by mere chance that these ladies
met in the same part of the church ; but at length grouping
themselves into a sort of circle, after heaving a few sighs, they
gave up saying paternosters, and began to converse (among
other topics) on the times.

So they continued for a while, and then Pampinea, the rest
listening in silent attention, thus began :—" Dear ladies mine,
often have I heard it said, and you doubtless as well as I, that
wrong is done to none by whoso but honestly uses his reason.
And to fortify, preserve, and defend his life to the utmost of
his power is the dictate of natural reason in every one that is
born. Which right is accorded in such measure that in defence
thereof men have been held blameless in taking life. And if
this be allowed by the laws, albeit on their stringency depends
the well-being of every mortal, how much more exempt from
censure should we, and all other honest folk, be in taking such

means as we may for the preservation of our life ?　As often
as I bethink me how we have been occupied this morning, and
not this morning only, and what has been the tenor of our con-
versation, I perceive—and you will readily do the like—that
each of us is apprehensive on her own account ; nor thereat do
I marvel, but at this I do marvel greatly, that, though none of
us lacks a woman's wit, yet none of us has recourse to any
means to avert that which we all justly fear.　Here we tarry,
as if, methinks, for no other purpose than to bear witness to
the number of the corpses that are brought hither for interment,
or to hearken if the brothers there within, whose number is
now almost reduced to nought, chant their offices at the canoni-
cal hours, or, by our weeds of woe, to obtrude on the attention
of every one that enters, the nature and degree of our sufferings.

" And if we quit the church, we see dead or sick folk carried
about, or we see those, who for their crimes were of late con-
demned to exile by the outraged majesty of the public laws,
but who now, in contempt of those laws, well knowing that
their ministers are a prey to death or disease, have returned,
and traverse the city in packs, making it hideous with their
riotous antics ; or else we see the refuse of the people, fostered
on our blood, becchini, as they call themselves, who for our
torment go prancing about here and there and everywhere,
making mock of our miseries in scurrilous songs.　Nor hear
we aught but :—Such and such are dead ; or, Such and such
are dying ; and should hear dolorous wailing on every hand,
were there but any to wail.　Or go we home, what see we there ?
I know not if you are in like case with me ; but there, where once
were servants in plenty, I find none left but my maid, and
shudder with terror, and feel the very hairs of my head to stand
on end ; and turn or tarry where I may, I encounter the ghosts
of the departed, not with their wonted mien, but with something
horrible in their aspect that appals me.　For which reasons
church and street and home are alike distressful to me, and the
more so that none, methinks, having means and place of retire-
ment as we have, abides here save only we ; or if any such
there be, they are of those, as my senses too often have borne
witness, who make no distinction between things honourable
and their opposites, so they but answer the cravings of appetite,
and, alone or in company, do daily and nightly what things
soever give promise of most gratification.　Nor are these secular
persons alone ; but such as live recluse in monasteries break
their rule, and give themselves up to carnal pleasures, persuading

themselves that they are permissible to them, and only forbidden
to others, and, thereby thinking to escape, are become unchaste
and dissolute. If such be our circumstances—and such most
manifestly they are—what do we here ? what wait we for ?
what dream we of ? why are we less prompt to provide for our
own safety than the rest of the citizens ? Is life less dear to
us than to all other women ? or think we that the bond which
unites soul and body is stronger in us than in others, so that
there is no blow that may light upon it, of which we need be
apprehensive ? If so, we err, we are deceived. What insensate
folly were it in us so to believe ! We have but to call to mind
the number and condition of those, young as we, and of both
sexes, who have succumbed to this cruel pestilence, to find there-
in conclusive evidence to the contrary. And lest from lethargy
or indolence we fall into the vain imagination that by some
lucky accident we may in some way or another, when we would,
escape—I know not if your opinion accord with mine—I should
deem it most wise in us, our case being what it is, if, as many
others have done before us, and are still doing, we were to quit
this place, and, shunning like death the evil example of others,
betake ourselves to the country, and there live as honourable
women on one of the estates, of which none of us has any lack,
with all cheer of festal gathering and other delights, so long as
in no particular we overstep the bounds of reason. There we
shall hear the chant of birds, have sight of verdant hills and
plains, of cornfields undulating like the sea, of trees of a thousand
sorts ; there also we shall have a larger view of the heavens,
which, however harsh to usward, yet deny not their eternal
beauty ; things fairer far for eye to rest on than the desolate
walls of our city. Moreover, we shall there breathe a fresher
air, find ampler store of things meet for such as live in these
times, have fewer causes of annoy. For, though the husband-
men die there, even as here the citizens, they are dispersed in
scattered homesteads, and 'tis thus less painful to witness.
Nor, so far as I can see, is there a soul here whom we shall
desert ; rather we may truly say, that we are ourselves deserted ;
for, our kinsfolk being either dead or fled in fear of death, no
more regardful of us than if we were strangers, we are left alone
in our great affliction. No censure, then, can fall on us if we
do as I propose ; and otherwise grievous suffering, perhaps
death, may ensue. Wherefore, if you agree, 'tis my advice,
that, attended by our maids with all things needful, we sojourn,
now on this, now on the other estate, and in such way of life

continue, until we see—if death should not first overtake us—the
end which Heaven reserves for these events. And I remind you
that it will be at least as seemly in us to leave with honour, as in
others, of whom there are not a few, to stay with dishonour."

The other ladies praised Pampinea's plan, and indeed were
so prompt to follow it, that they had already begun to discuss
the manner in some detail, as if they were forthwith to rise
from their seats and take the road, when Filomena, whose
judgment was excellent, interposed, saying :—" Ladies, though
Pampinea has spoken to most excellent effect, yet it were not
well to be so precipitate as you seem disposed to be. Bethink
you that we are all women ; nor is there any here so young,
but she is of years to understand how women are minded
towards one another, when they are alone together, and how ill
they are able to rule themselves without the guidance of some
man. We are sensitive, perverse, suspicious, pusillanimous
and timid ; wherefore I much misdoubt, that, if we find no
other guidance than our own, this company is like to break up
sooner, and with less credit to us, than it should. Against
which it were well to provide at the outset." Said then Elisa :—
" Without doubt man is woman's head, and, without man's
governance, it is seldom that aught that we do is brought to a
commendable conclusion. But how are we to come by the
men ? Every one of us here knows that her kinsmen are for
the most part dead, and that the survivors are dispersed, one
here, one there, we know not where, bent each on escaping the
same fate as ourselves ; nor were it seemly to seek the aid of
strangers ; for, as we are in quest of health, we must find some
means so to order matters that, wherever we seek diversion or
repose, trouble and scandal do not follow us."

While the ladies were thus conversing, there came into the
church three young men, young, I say, but not so young that
the age of the youngest was less than twenty-five years ; in
whom neither the sinister course of events, nor the loss of
friends or kinsfolk, nor fear for their own safety, had availed
to quench, or even temper, the ardour of their love. The first
was called Pamfilo, the second Filostrato, and the third Dioneo.
Very debonair and chivalrous were they all ; and in this troub-
lous time they were seeking if haply, to their exceeding great
solace, they might have sight of their fair friends, all three of
whom chanced to be among the said seven ladies, besides some
that were of kin to the young men. At one and the same
moment they recognised the ladies and were recognised by

them : wherefore, with a gracious smile, Pampinea thus began :—" Lo, fortune is propitious to our enterprise, having vouchsafed us the good offices of these young men, who are as gallant as they are discreet, and will gladly give us their guidance and escort, so we but take them into our service." Whereupon Neifile, crimson from brow to neck with the blush of modesty, being one of those that had a lover among the young men, said :—" For God's sake, Pampinea, have a care what you say. Well assured am I that nought but good can be said of any of them, and I deem them fit for office far more onerous than this which you propose for them, and their good and honourable company worthy of ladies fairer by far and more tenderly to be cherished than such as we. But 'tis no secret that they love some of us here ; wherefore I misdoubt that, if we take them with us, we may thereby give occasion for scandal and censure merited neither by us nor by them." " That," said Filomena, " is of no consequence ; so I but live honestly, my conscience gives me no disquietude ; if others asperse me, God and the truth will take arms in my defence. Now, should they be disposed to attend us, of a truth we might say with Pampinea, that fortune favours our enterprise." The silence which followed betokened consent on the part of the other ladies, who then with one accord resolved to call the young men, and acquaint them with their purpose, and pray them to be of their company. So without further parley Pampinea, who had a kinsman among the young men, rose and approached them where they stood intently regarding them ; and greeting them gaily, she opened to them their plan, and besought them on the part of herself and her friends to join their company on terms of honourable and fraternal comradeship. At first the young men thought she did but trifle with them ; but when they saw that she was in earnest, they answered with alacrity that they were ready, and promptly, even before they left the church, set matters in train for their departure. So all things meet being first sent forward in due order to their intended place of sojourn, the ladies with some of their maids, and the three young men, each attended by a man-servant, sallied forth of the city on the morrow, being Wednesday, about daybreak, and took the road ; nor had they journeyed more than two short miles when they arrived at their destination. The estate [1] lay upon a little hill some distance from the nearest

---

[1] Identified by tradition with the Villa Palmieri (now Crawford) on the slope of Fiesole.

highway, and, embowered in shrubberies of divers hues, and
other greenery, afforded the eye a pleasant prospect. On the
summit of the hill was a palace with galleries, halls and cham-
bers, disposed around a fair and spacious court, each very fair
in itself, and the goodlier to see for the gladsome pictures with
which it was adorned ; the whole set amidst meads and gardens
laid out with marvellous art, wells of the coolest water, and
vaults of the finest wines, things more suited to dainty drinkers
than to sober and honourable women. On their arrival the
company, to their no small delight, found their beds already
made, the rooms well swept and garnished with flowers of every
sort that the season could afford, and the floors carpeted with
rushes. When they were seated, Dioneo, a gallant who had
not his match for courtesy and wit, spoke thus :—" My ladies,
'tis not our forethought so much as your own mother-wit that
has guided us hither. How you mean to dispose of your cares
I know not ; mine I left behind me within the city-gate when
I issued thence with you a brief while ago. Wherefore, I pray
you, either address yourselves to make merry, to laugh and
sing with me (so far, I mean, as may consist with your dignity),
or give me leave to hie me back to the stricken city, there to
abide with my cares." To whom blithely Pampinea replied,
as if she too had cast off all her cares :—" Well sayest thou,
Dioneo, excellent well ; gaily we mean to live ; 'twas a refuge
from sorrow that here we sought, nor had we other cause to
come hither. But, as no anarchy can long endure, I who
initiated the deliberations of which this fair company is the
fruit, do now, to the end that our joy may be lasting, deem it
expedient, that there be one among us in chief authority,
honoured and obeyed by us as our superior, whose exclusive
care it shall be to devise how we may pass our time blithely.
And that each in turn may prove the weight of the care, as well
as enjoy the pleasure, of sovereignty, and, no distinction being
made of sex, envy be felt by none by reason of exclusion from
the office ; I propose, that the weight and honour be borne
by each one for a day ; and let the first to bear sway be chosen
by us all, those that follow to be appointed towards the vesper
hour by him or her who shall have had the signory for that day ;
and let each holder of the signory be, for the time, sole arbiter
of the place and manner in which we are to pass our time."

Pampinea's speech was received with the utmost applause,
and with one accord she was chosen queen for the first day.
Whereupon Filomena hied her lightly to a bay-tree, having

often heard of the great honour in which its leaves, and such as
were deservedly crowned therewith, were worthy to be holden ;
and having gathered a few sprays, she made thereof a goodly
wreath of honour, and set it on Pampinea's head ; which wreath
was thenceforth, while their company endured, the visible
sign of the wearer's sway and sovereignty.

No sooner was Queen Pampinea crowned than she bade all
be silent. She then caused summon to her presence their four
maids, and the servants of the three young men, and, all keeping
silence, said to them :—" That I may shew you all at once,
how, well still giving place to better, our company may flourish
and endure, as long as it shall pleasure us, with order meet
and assured delight and without reproach, I first of all constitute
Dioneo's man, Parmeno, my seneschal, and entrust him with
the care and control of all our household, and all that belongs
to the service of the hall. Pamfilo's man, Sirisco, I appoint
treasurer and chancellor of our exchequer ; and be he ever
answerable to Parmeno. While Parmeno and Sirisco are too
busy about their duties to serve their masters, let Filostrato's
man, Tindaro, have charge of the chambers of all three. My
maid, Misia, and Filomena's maid, Licisca, will keep in the
kitchen, and with all due diligence prepare such dishes as
Parmeno shall bid them. Lauretta's maid, Chimera, and
Fiammetta's maid, Stratilia, we make answerable for the ladies'
chambers, and wherever we may take up our quarters, let them
see that all is spotless. And now we enjoin you, one and all
alike, as you value our favour, that none of you, go where you
may, return whence you may, hear or see what you may, bring
us any tidings but such as be cheerful." These orders thus
succinctly given were received with universal approval. Where-
upon Pampinea rose, and said gaily :—" Here are gardens,
meads, and other places delightsome enough, where you may
wander at will, and take your pleasure ; but on the stroke of
tierce,[1] let all be here to breakfast in the shade."

Thus dismissed by their new queen the gay company saun-
tered gently through a garden, the young men saying sweet
things to the fair ladies, who wove fair garlands of divers sorts
of leaves and sang love-songs.

Having thus spent the time allowed them by the queen, they
returned to the house, where they found that Parmeno had
entered on his office with zeal ; for in a hall on the ground-floor
they saw tables covered with the whitest of cloths, and beakers

[1] The canonical hour following prime, roughly speaking about 9 a.m.

that shone like silver, and sprays of broom scattered everywhere.
So, at the bidding of the queen, they washed their hands, and
all took their places as marshalled by Parmeno. Dishes,
daintily prepared, were served, and the finest wines were at
hand ; the three serving-men did their office noiselessly ; in a
word all was fair and ordered in a seemly manner ; whereby
the spirits of the company rose, and they seasoned their viands
with pleasant jests and sprightly sallies. Breakfast done, the
tables were removed, and the queen bade fetch instruments of
music ; for all, ladies and young men alike, knew how to tread
a measure, and some of them played and sang with great skill :
so, at her command, Dioneo having taken a lute, and Fiammetta
a viol, they struck up a dance in sweet concert ; and, the
servants being dismissed to their repast, the queen, attended
by the other ladies and the two young men, led off a stately
carol ; which ended they fell to singing ditties dainty and gay.
Thus they diverted themselves until the queen, deeming it time
to retire to rest, dismissed them all for the night. So the three
young men and the ladies withdrew to their several quarters,
which were in different parts of the palace. There they found
the beds well made, and abundance of flowers, as in the hall ;
and so they undressed, and went to bed.

Shortly after none [1] the queen rose, and roused the rest of the
ladies, as also the young men, averring that it was injurious to
the health to sleep long in the daytime. They therefore hied
them to a meadow, where the grass grew green and luxuriant,
being nowhere scorched by the sun, and a light breeze gently
fanned them. So at the queen's command they all ranged
themselves in a circle on the grass, and hearkened while she thus
spoke :—

"You mark that the sun is high, the heat intense, and the
silence unbroken save by the cicalas among the olive-trees. It
were therefore the height of folly to quit this spot at present.
Here the air is cool and the prospect fair, and here, observe, are
dice and chess. Take, then, your pleasure as you may be
severally minded ; but, if you take my advice, you will find
pastime for the hot hours before us, not in play, in which the
loser must needs be vexed, and neither the winner nor the on-
looker much the better pleased, but in telling of stories, in
which the invention of one may afford solace to all the company
of his hearers. You will not each have told a story before
the sun will be low, and the heat abated, so that we shall be

[1] The canonical hour following sext. *i.e.* 3 p.m.

able to go and severally take our pleasure where it may seem best to each. Wherefore, if my proposal meet with your approval—for in this I am disposed to consult your pleasure—let us adopt it ; if not, divert yourselves as best you may, until the vesper hour."

The queen's proposal being approved by all, ladies and men alike, she added :—" So please you, then, I ordain, that, for this first day, we be free to discourse of such matters as most commend themselves to each in turn." She then addressed Pamfilo, who sat on her right hand, bidding him with a gracious air to lead off with one of his stories. And prompt at the word of command, Pamfilo, while all listened intently, thus began :—

NOVEL I

Ser Ciappelletto cheats a holy friar by a false confession, and dies ; and, having lived as a very bad man, is, on his death, reputed a saint, and called San Ciappelletto.

A SEEMLY thing it is, dearest ladies, that whatever we do, it be begun in the holy and awful name of Him who was the maker of all. Wherefore, as it falls to me to lead the way in this your enterprise of story-telling, I intend to begin with one of His wondrous works, that, by hearing thereof, our hopes in Him, in whom is no change, may be established, and His name be by us forever lauded. 'Tis manifest that, as things temporal are all doomed to pass and perish, so within and without they abound with trouble and anguish and travail, and are subject to infinite perils ; nor, save for the especial grace of God, should we, whose being is bound up with and forms part of theirs, have either the strength to endure or the wisdom to combat their adverse influences. By which grace we are visited and penetrated (so we must believe) not by reason of any merit of our own, but solely out of the fulness of God's own goodness, and in answer to the prayers of those who, being mortal like ourselves, did faithfully observe His ordinances during their lives, and are now become blessed for ever with Him in heaven. To whom, as to advocates taught by experience all that belongs to our frailty, we, not daring, perchance, to present our petitions in the presence of so great a Judge, make known our requests for such things as we deem expedient for us. And of His mercy richly abounding to usward we have further proof

herein, that, no keenness of mortal vision being able in any
degree to penetrate the secret counsels of the Divine mind, it
sometimes, perchance, happens, that, in error of judgment, we
make one our advocate before His Majesty, who is banished
from His presence in eternal exile, and yet He to whom nothing
is hidden, having regard rather to the sincerity of our prayers
than to our ignorance or the banishment of the intercessor,
hears us no less than if the intercessor were in truth one of the
blest who enjoy the light of His countenance. Which the
story that I am about to relate may serve to make apparent ;
apparent, I mean, according to the standard of the judgment of
man, not of God.

The story goes, then, that Musciatto Franzesi, a great and
wealthy merchant, being made a knight in France, and being
to attend Charles Sansterre, brother of the King of France,
when he came into Tuscany at the instance and with the support
of Pope Boniface, found his affairs, as often happens to mer-
chants, to be much involved in divers quarters, and neither
easily nor suddenly to be adjusted ; wherefore he determined
to place them in the hands of commissioners, and found no
difficulty except as to certain credits given to some Burgundians,
for the recovery of which he doubted whether he could come by
a competent agent ; for well he knew that the Burgundians
were violent men and ill-conditioned and faithless ; nor could
he call to mind any man so bad that he could with confidence
oppose his guile to theirs. After long pondering the matter,
he recollected one Ser Ciapperello da Prato, who much frequented
his house in Paris. Who being short of stature and very
affected, the French who knew not the meaning of Cepparello,[1]
but supposed that it meant the same as Cappello, *i.e.* garland,
in their vernacular, called him not Cappello, but Ciappelletto
by reason of his diminutive size ; and as Ciappelletto he was
known everywhere, whereas few people knew him as Ciapperello.
Now Ciappelletto's manner of life was thus. He was by pro-
fession a notary, and his pride was to make false documents ;
he would have made them as often as he was asked, and more
readily without fee than another at a great price ; few indeed
he made that were not false, and great was his shame when
they were discovered. False witness he bore, solicited or
unsolicited, with boundless delight ; and, as oaths were in

[1] The diminutive of ceppo, stump or log : more commonly written
cepperello (cf. p. 30) or ceppatello. The form ciapperello seems to be
found only here.

those days had in very great respect in France, he, scrupling not to forswear himself, corruptly carried the day in every case in which he was summoned faithfully to attest the truth. He took inordinate delight, and bestirred himself with great zeal, in fomenting ill-feeling, enmities, dissensions between friends, kinsfolk and all other folk ; and the more calamitous were the consequences the better he was pleased. Set him on murder, or any other foul crime, and he never hesitated, but went about it with alacrity ; he had been known on more than one occasion to inflict wounds or death by preference with his own hands. He was a profuse blasphemer of God and His saints, and that on the most trifling occasions, being of all men the most irascible. He was never seen at church, held all the sacraments vile things, and derided them in language of horrible ribaldry. On the other hand he resorted readily to the tavern and other places of evil repute, and frequented them. He was as fond of women as a dog is of the stick : in the use against nature he had not his match among the most abandoned. He would have pilfered and stolen as a matter of conscience, as a holy man would make an oblation. Most gluttonous he was and inordinately fond of his cups, whereby he sometimes brought upon himself both shame and suffering. He was also a practised gamester and thrower of false dice. But why enlarge so much upon him ? Enough that he was, perhaps, the worst man that ever was born.

The rank and power of Musciatto Franzesi had long been this reprobate's mainstay, serving in many instances to secure him considerate treatment on the part of the private persons whom he frequently, and the court which he unremittingly, outraged. So Musciatto, having bethought him of this Ser Cepparello, with whose way of life he was very well acquainted, judged him to be the very sort of person to cope with the guile of the Burgundians. He therefore sent for him, and thus addressed him :—" Ser Ciappelletto, I am, as thou knowest, about to leave this place for good ; and among those with whom I have to settle accounts are certain Burgundians, very wily knaves ; nor know I the man whom I could more fitly entrust with the recovery of my money than thyself. Wherefore, as thou hast nothing to do at present, if thou wilt undertake this business, I will procure thee the favour of the court, and give thee a reasonable part of what thou shalt recover." Ser Ciappelletto, being out of employment, and by no means in easy circumstances, and about to lose Musciatto, so long his mainstay and support, without the least demur, for in truth he had hardly any choice

made his mind up and answered that he was ready to go. So
the bargain was struck. Armed with the power of attorney
and the royal letters commendatory, Ser Ciappelletto took leave
of Messer Musciatto and hied him to Burgundy, where he was
hardly known to a soul. He set about the business which had
brought him thither, the recovery of the money, in a manner
amicable and considerate, foreign to his nature, as if he were
minded to reserve his severity to the last. While thus occupied,
he was frequently at the house of two Florentine usurers, who
treated him with great distinction out of regard for Messer
Musciatto; and there it so happened that he fell sick. The
two brothers forthwith placed physicians and servants in
attendance upon him, and omitted no means meet and apt for
the restoration of his health. But all remedies proved un-
availing; for being now old, and having led, as the physicians
reported, a disorderly life, he went daily from bad to worse like
one stricken with a mortal disease. This greatly disconcerted
the two brothers; and one day, hard by the room in which Ser
Ciappelletto lay sick, they began to talk about him; saying
one to the other :—" What shall we do with this man? We
are hard bested indeed on his account. If we turn him out of
the house, sick as he is, we shall not only incur grave censure,
but shall evince a signal want of sense; for folk must know
the welcome we gave him in the first instance, the solicitude
with which we have had him treated and tended since his illness,
during which time he could not possibly do aught to displease
us, and yet they would see him suddenly turned out of our
house sick unto death. On the other hand he has been so bad
a man that he is sure not to confess or receive any of the Church's
sacraments; and dying thus unconfessed, he will be denied
burial in church, but will be cast out into some ditch like a dog;
nay, 'twill be all one if he do confess, for such and so horrible
have been his crimes that no friar or priest either will or can
absolve him; and so, dying without absolution, he will still
be cast out into the ditch. In which case the folk of these
parts, who reprobate our trade as iniquitous and revile it all
day long, and would fain rob us, will seize their opportunity,
and raise a tumult, and make a raid upon our houses, crying :—
' Away with these Lombard dogs, whom the Church excludes
from her pale;' and will certainly strip us of our goods, and
perhaps take our lives also; so that in any case we stand to
lose if this man die."

Ser Ciappelletto, who, as we said, lay close at hand while they

thus spoke, and whose hearing was sharpened, as is often the
case, by his malady, overheard all that they said about him.
So he called them to him, and said to them :—" I would not
have you disquiet yourselves in regard of me, or apprehend loss
to befall you by my death. I have heard what you have said
of me and have no doubt that 'twould be as you say, if matters
took the course you anticipate ; but I am minded that it shall
be otherwise. I have committed so many offences against
God in the course of my life, that one more in the hour of my
death will make no difference whatever to the account. So
seek out and bring hither the worthiest and most holy friar you
can find, and leave me to settle your affairs and mind upon a
sound and solid basis, with which you may rest satisfied."
The two brothers had not much hope of the result, but yet they
went to a friary and asked for a holy and discreet man to hear
the confession of a Lombard that was sick in their house, and
returned with an aged man of just and holy life, very learned
in the Scriptures, and venerable and held in very great and
especial reverence by all the citizens. As soon as he had entered
the room where Ser Ciappelletto was lying, and had taken his
place by his side, he began gently to comfort him : then he
asked him how long it was since he was confessed. Whereto Ser
Ciappelletto, who had never been confessed, answered :—
" Father, it is my constant practice to be confessed at least
once a week, and many a week I am confessed more often ;
but true it is, that, since I have been sick, now eight days, I
have made no confession, so sore has been my affliction."
" Son," said the friar, " thou hast well done, and well for thee,
if so thou continue to do ; as thou dost confess so often, I see
that my labour of hearkening and questioning will be slight."
" Nay but, master friar," said Ser Ciappelletto, " say not so ;
I have not confessed so often but that I would fain make a
general confession of all my sins that I have committed, so far
as I can recall them, from the day of my birth to the present
time ; and therefore I pray you, my good father, to question
me precisely in every particular just as if I had never been
confessed. And spare me not by reason of my sickness, for I
had far rather do despite to my flesh than, sparing it, risk the
perdition of my soul, which my Saviour redeemed with His
precious blood."

The holy man was mightily delighted with these words, which
seemed to him to betoken a soul in a state of grace. He there-
fore signified to Ser Ciappelletto his high approval of this prac-

tice ; and then began by asking him whether he had ever sinned
carnally with a woman. Whereto Ser Ciappelletto answered
with a sigh :—" My father, I scruple to tell you the truth in
this matter, fearing lest I sin in vain-glory."   " Nay, but," said
the friar, " speak boldly ; none ever sinned by telling the truth,
either in confession or otherwise."   " Then," said Ser Ciappel-
letto, " as you bid me speak boldly, I will tell you the truth of
this matter.   I am virgin even as when I issued from my
mother's womb."   " Now God's blessing on thee," said the
friar, " well done ; and the greater is thy merit in that, hadst
thou so willed, thou mightest have done otherwise far more
readily than we who are under constraint of rule."   He then
proceeded to ask, whether he had offended God by gluttony.
Whereto Ser Ciappelletto, heaving a heavy sigh, answered that
he had frequently so offended ; for, being wont to fast not only
in Lent like other devout persons, but at least three days in
every week, taking nothing but bread and water, he had quaffed
the water with as good a gusto and as much enjoyment, more
particularly when fatigued by devotion or pilgrimage, as great
drinkers quaff their wine ; and oftentimes he had felt a craving
for such dainty dishes of herbs as ladies make when they go
into the country, and now and again he had relished his food
more than seemed to him meet in one who fasted, as he did,
for devotion.   " Son," said the friar, " these sins are natural
and very trifling ; and therefore I would not have thee burden
thy conscience too much with them.   There is no man, however
holy he may be, but must sometimes find it pleasant to eat
after a long fast and to drink after exertion."   " O, my father,"
said Ser Ciappelletto, " say not this to comfort me.   You know
well that I know, that the things which are done in the service
of God ought to be done in perfect purity of an unsullied spirit ;
and whoever does otherwise sins."   The friar, well content,
replied :—" Glad I am that thou dost think so, and I am
mightily pleased with thy pure and good conscience which
therein appears ; but tell me : hast thou sinned by avarice,
coveting more than was reasonable, or withholding more than
was right ? "   " My father," replied Ser Ciappelletto, " I would
not have you disquiet yourself, because I am in the house of
these usurers : no part have I in their concerns ; nay, I did but
come here to admonish and reprehend them, and wean them
from this abominable traffic ; and so, I believe, I had done, had
not God sent me this visitation.   But you must know, that my
father left me a fortune, of which I dedicated the greater part

to God ; and since then for my own support and the relief of
Christ's poor I have done a little trading, whereof I have desired
to make gain ; and all that I have gotten I have shared with
God's poor, reserving one half for my own needs and giving
the other half to them ; and so well has my Maker prospered
me, that I have ever managed my affairs to better and better
account." "Well done," said the friar ; "but how ? hast
thou often given way to anger ? " "Often indeed, I assure
you," said Ser Ciappelletto. "And who could refrain there-
from, seeing men doing frowardly all day long, breaking the
commandments of God and recking nought of His judgments ?
Many a time in the course of a single day I had rather be dead
than alive, to see the young men going after vanity, swearing
and forswearing themselves, haunting taverns, avoiding the
churches, and in short walking in the way of the world rather
than in God's way." "My son," said the friar, "this is a
righteous wrath ; nor could I find occasion therein to lay a
penance upon thee. But did anger ever by any chance betray
thee into taking human life, or affronting or otherwise wronging
any ? " "Alas," replied Ser Ciappelletto, "alas, sir, man of
God though you seem to me, how come you to speak after this
manner ? If I had had so much as the least thought of doing
any of the things of which you speak, should I believe, think
you, that I had been thus supported of God ? These are the
deeds of robbers and such like evil men, to whom I have ever
said, when any I saw :—' Go, God change your heart.' " Said
then the friar :—" Now, my son, as thou hopest to be blest of
God, tell me, hast thou never borne false witness against any,
or spoken evil of another, or taken the goods of another without
his leave ? " "Yes, master friar," answered Ser Ciappelletto,
"most true it is that I have spoken evil of another ; for I had
once a neighbour who without the least excuse in the world
was ever beating his wife, and so great was my pity of the poor
creature, whom, when he was in his cups, he would thrash as
God alone knows how, that once I spoke evil of him to his wife's
kinsfolk." "Well, well," said the friar, "thou tellest me thou
hast been a merchant ; hast thou ever cheated any, as mer-
chants use to do ? " "I'faith, yes, master friar," said Ser
Ciappelletto ; "but I know not who he was ; only that he
brought me some money which he owed me for some cloth that
I had sold him, and I put it in a box without counting it, where
a month afterwards I found four farthings more than there
should have been, which I kept for a year to return to him, but

not seeing him again, I bestowed them in alms for the love of
God." "This," said the friar, "was a small matter ; and thou
didst well to bestow them as thou didst." The holy friar went
on to ask him many other questions, to which he made answer
in each case in this sort. Then, as the friar was about to give
him absolution, Ser Ciappelletto interposed :—" Sir, I have yet
a sin to confess." "What ? " asked the friar. " I remember,"
he said, " that I once caused my servant to sweep my house on
a Saturday after none ; and that my observance of Sunday
was less devout than it should have been." " O, my son," said
the friar, " this is a light matter." " No," said Ser Ciappelletto,
" say not a light matter ; for Sunday is the more to be had in
honour because on that day our Lord rose from the dead."
Then said the holy friar :—" Now is there aught else that thou
hast done ? " " Yes, master friar," replied Ser Ciappelletto,
" once by inadvertence I spat in the church of God." At this
the friar began to smile, and said :—" My son, this is not a
matter to trouble about ; we, who are religious, spit there all
day long." " And great impiety it is when you so do," replied
Ser Ciappelletto, " for there is nothing that is so worthy to be
kept from all impurity as the holy temple in which sacrifice is
offered to God." More he said in the same strain, which I pass
over ; and then at last he began to sigh, and by and by to weep
bitterly, as he was well able to do when he chose. And the
friar demanding :—" My son, why weepest thou ? " " Alas,
master friar," answered Ser Ciappelletto, " a sin yet remains,
which I have never confessed, such shame were it to me to tell
it ; and as often as I call it to mind, I weep as you now see me
weep, being well assured that God will never forgive me this
sin." Then said the holy friar :—" Come, come, son, what is
this that thou sayst ? If all the sins of all the men, that ever
were or ever shall be, as long as the world shall endure, were
concentrated in one man, so great is the goodness of God that
He would freely pardon them all, were he but penitent and
contrite as I see thou art, and confessed them : wherefore tell
me thy sin with a good courage." Then said Ser Ciappelletto,
still weeping bitterly :—" Alas, my father, mine is too great a
sin, and scarce can I believe, if your prayers do not co-operate,
that God will ever grant me His pardon thereof." " Tell it
with a good courage," said the friar ; " I promise thee to pray
God for thee." Ser Ciappelletto, however, continued to weep,
and would not speak, for all the friar's encouragement. When
he had kept him for a good while in suspense, he heaved a mighty

sigh, and said :—" My father, as you promise me to pray God
for me, I will tell it you. Know, then, that once, when I was
a little child, I cursed my mother ; " and having so said he
began again to weep bitterly. " O, my son," said the friar,
" does this seem to thee so great a sin ? Men curse God all day
long, and He pardons them freely, if they repent them of
having so done ; and thinkest thou He will not pardon thee
this ? Weep not, be comforted, for truly, hadst thou been
one of them that set Him on the Cross, with the contrition
that I see in thee, thou wouldst not fail of His pardon." " Alas !
my father," rejoined Ser Ciappelletto, " what is this you say ?
To curse my sweet mother that carried me in her womb for
nine months day and night, and afterwards on her shoulder
more than a hundred times ! Heinous indeed was my offence ;
'tis too great a sin ; nor will it be pardoned, unless you pray
God for me."

The friar now perceiving that Ser Ciappelletto had nothing
more to say, gave him absolution and his blessing, reputing him
for a most holy man, fully believing that all that he had said
was true. And who would not have so believed, hearing him
so speak at the point of death ? Then, when all was done, he
said :—" Ser Ciappelletto, if God so will, you will soon be well ;
but should it so come to pass that God call your blessed soul to
Himself in this state of grace, is it well pleasing to you that
your body be buried in our convent ? " " Yea, verily, master
friar," replied Ser Ciappelletto ; " there would I be, and nowhere
else, since you have promised to pray God for me ; besides
which I have ever had a special devotion to your order. Where-
fore I pray you, that, on your return to your convent, you cause
to be sent me that very Body of Christ, which you consecrate
in the morning on the altar ; because (unworthy though I be)
I purpose with your leave to take it, and afterwards the holy
and extreme unction, that, though I have lived as a sinner, I
may die at any rate as a Christian." The holy man said that
he was greatly delighted, that it was well said of Ser Ciappelletto,
and that he would cause the Host to be forthwith brought to
him ; and so it was.

The two brothers, who much misdoubted Ser Ciappelletto's
power to deceive the friar, had taken their stand on the other
side of a wooden partition which divided the room in which Ser
Ciappelletto lay from another, and hearkening there they
readily heard and understood what Ser Ciappelletto said to the
friar ; and at times could scarce refrain their laughter as they

followed his confession ; and now and again they said one to another :—" What manner of man is this, whom neither age nor sickness, nor fear of death, on the threshold of which he now stands, nor yet of God, before whose judgment-seat he must soon appear, has been able to turn from his wicked ways, that he die not even as he has lived ? " But seeing that his confession had secured the interment of his body in church, they troubled themselves no further. Ser Ciappelletto soon afterwards communicated, and growing immensely worse, received the extreme unction, and died shortly after vespers on the same day on which he had made his good confession. So the two brothers, having from his own moneys provided the wherewith to procure him honourable sepulture, and sent word to the friars to come at even to observe the usual vigil, and in the morning to fetch the corpse, set all things in order accordingly. The holy friar who had confessed him, hearing that he was dead, had audience of the prior of the friary ; a chapter was convened and the assembled brothers heard from the confessor's own mouth how Ser Ciappelletto had been a holy man, as had appeared by his confession, and were exhorted to receive the body with the utmost veneration and pious care, as one by which there was good hope that God would work many miracles. To this the prior and the rest of the credulous confraternity assenting, they went in a body in the evening to the place where the corpse of Ser Ciappelletto lay, and kept a great and solemn vigil over it ; and in the morning they made a procession habited in their surplices and copes, with books in their hands and crosses in front ; and chanting as they went, they fetched the corpse and brought it back to their church with the utmost pomp and solemnity, being followed by almost all the folk of the city, men and women alike. So it was laid in the church, and then the holy friar who had heard the confession got up in the pulpit and began to preach marvellous things of Ser Ciappelletto's life, his fasts, his virginity, his simplicity and guilelessness and holiness ; narrating among other matters that of which Ser Ciappelletto had made tearful confession as his greatest sin, and how he had hardly been able to make him conceive that God would pardon him ; from which he took occasion to reprove his hearers ; saying :—" And you, accursed of God, on the least pretext, blaspheme God and His Mother, and all the celestial court." And much beside he told of his loyalty and purity ; and, in short, so wrought upon the people by his words, to which they gave entire credence, that they all con-

ceived a great veneration for Ser Ciappelletto, and at the close
of the office came pressing forward with the utmost vehemence
to kiss the feet and hands of the corpse, from which they tore
off the cerements, each thinking himself blessed to have but a
scrap thereof in his possession ; and so it was arranged that
it should be kept there all day long, so as to be visible and
accessible to all. At nightfall it was honourably interred in a
marble tomb in one of the chapels, where on the morrow, one
by one, folk came and lit tapers and prayed and paid their
vows, setting there the waxen images which they had dedicated.
And the fame of Ciappelletto's holiness and the devotion to
him grew in such measure that scarce any there was that in
any adversity would vow aught to any saint but he, and they
called him and still call him San Ciappelletto, affirming that
many miracles have been and daily are wrought by God through
him for such as devoutly crave his intercession.

So lived, so died Ser Cepperello da Prato, and came to be
reputed a saint, as you have heard. Nor would I deny that
it is possible that he is of the number of the blessed in the pre-
sence of God, seeing that, though his life was evil and depraved,
yet he might in his last moments have made so complete an
act of contrition that perchance God had mercy on him and
received him into His kingdom. But, as this is hidden from us,
I speak according to that which appears, and I say that he
ought rather to be in the hands of the devil in hell than in
Paradise. Which, if so it be, is a manifest token of the super-
abundance of the goodness of God to usward, inasmuch as He
regards not our error but the sincerity of our faith, and hearkens
unto us when, mistaking one who is at enmity with Him for a
friend, we have recourse to him, as to one holy indeed, as our
intercessor for His grace. Wherefore, that we of this gay
company may by His grace be preserved safe and sound through-
out this time of adversity, commend we ourselves in our need
to Him, whose name we began by invoking, with lauds and
reverent devotion and good confidence that we shall be heard.

And so he was silent.

NOVEL II

Abraham, a Jew, at the instance of Jehannot de Chevigny, goes to the court of Rome, and having marked the evil life of the clergy, returns to Paris, and becomes a Christian.

PAMFILO's story elicited the mirth of some of the ladies and the hearty commendation of all, who listened to it with close attention until the end. Whereupon the queen bade Neifile, who sat next her, to tell a story, that the commencement thus made of their diversions might have its sequel. Neifile, whose graces of mind matched the beauty of her person, consented with a gladsome goodwill, and thus began :—

Pamfilo has shewn by his story that the goodness of God spares to regard our errors when they result from unavoidable ignorance ; and in mine I mean to shew you how the same goodness, bearing patiently with the shortcomings of those who should be its faithful witness in deed and word, draws from them contrariwise evidence of His infallible truth ; to the end that what we believe we may with more assured conviction follow.

In Paris, gracious ladies, as I have heard tell, there was once a great merchant, a large dealer in drapery, a good man, most loyal and righteous, his name Jehannot de Chevigny, between whom and a Jew, Abraham by name, also a merchant, and a man of great wealth, as also most loyal and righteous, there subsisted a very close friendship. Now Jehannot, observing Abraham's loyalty and rectitude, began to be sorely vexed in spirit that the soul of one so worthy and wise and good should perish for want of faith. Wherefore he began in a friendly manner to plead with him, that he should leave the errors of the Jewish faith and turn to the Christian verity, which, being sound and holy, he might see daily prospering and gaining ground, whereas, on the contrary, his own religion was dwindling and was almost come to nothing. The Jew replied that he believed that there was no faith sound and holy except the Jewish faith, in which he was born, and in which he meant to live and die ; nor would anything ever turn him therefrom. Nothing daunted, however, Jehannot some days afterwards began again to ply Abraham with similar arguments, explaining to him in such crude fashion as merchants use the reasons why our faith is better than the Jewish. And though the Jew was

a great master in the Jewish law, yet, whether it was by reason
of his friendship for Jehannot, or that the Holy Spirit dictated
the words that the simple merchant used, at any rate the Jew
began to be much interested in Jehannot's arguments, though
still too staunch in his faith to suffer himself to be converted.
But Jehannot was no less assiduous in plying him with argument
than he was obstinate in adhering to his law, insomuch that
at length the Jew, overcome by such incessant appeals, said :—
"Well, well, Jehannot, thou wouldst have me become a
Christian, and I am disposed to do so, provided I first go to
Rome and there see him whom thou callest God's vicar on
earth, and observe what manner of life he leads and his brother
cardinals with him ; and if such it be that thereby, in conjunc-
tion with thy words, I may understand that thy faith is better
than mine, as thou hast sought to shew me, I will do as I have
said : otherwise, I will remain as I am a Jew." When Jehannot
heard this, he was greatly distressed, saying to himself :—" I
thought to have converted him ; but now I see that the pains
which I took for so excellent a purpose are all in vain ; for, if
he goes to the court of Rome and sees the iniquitous and foul
life which the clergy lead there, so far from turning Christian,
had he been converted already, he would without doubt relapse
into Judaism." Then turning to Abraham he said :—" Nay,
but, my friend, why wouldst thou be at all this labour and great
expense of travelling from here to Rome ? to say nothing of the
risks both by sea and by land which a rich man like thee must
needs run. Thinkest thou not to find here one that can give
thee baptism ? And as for any doubts that thou mayst have
touching the faith to which I point thee, where wilt thou find
greater masters and sages therein than here, to resolve thee of
any question thou mayst put to them ? Wherefore in my
opinion this journey of thine is superfluous. Think that the
prelates there are such as thou mayst have seen here, nay, as
much better as they are nearer to the Chief Pastor. And so,
by my advice thou wilt spare thy pains until some time of
indulgence, when I, perhaps, may be able to bear thee com-
pany." The Jew replied :—" Jehannot, I doubt not that so it
is as thou sayst ; but once and for all I tell thee that I am
minded to go there, and will never otherwise do that which
thou wouldst have me and hast so earnestly besought me to do."
" Go then," said Jehannot, seeing that his mind was made up,
" and good luck go with thee ; " and so he gave up the contest
because nothing would be lost, though he felt sure that he

would never become a Christian after seeing the court of Rome.
The Jew took horse, and posted with all possible speed to
Rome ; where on his arrival he was honourably received by his
fellow Jews.　He said nothing to any one of the purpose for
which he had come ; but began circumspectly to acquaint
himself with the ways of the Pope and the cardinals and the
other prelates and all the courtiers ; and from what he saw
for himself, being a man of great intelligence, or learned from
others, he discovered that without distinction of rank they were
all sunk in the most disgraceful lewdness, sinning not only in
the way of nature but after the manner of the men of Sodom,
without any restraint of remorse or shame, in such sort that,
when any great favour was to be procured, the influence of the
courtesans and boys was of no small moment.　Moreover he
found them one and all gluttonous, wine-bibbers, drunkards,
and next after lewdness, most addicted to the shameless service
of the belly, like brute beasts.　And, as he probed the matter
still further, he perceived that they were all so greedy and
avaricious that human, nay Christian blood, and things sacred
of what kind soever, spiritualities no less than temporalities,
they bought and sold for money ; which traffic was greater and
employed more brokers than the drapery trade and all the
other trades of Paris put together ; open simony and gluttonous
excess being glosed under such specious terms as " arrangement "
and " moderate use of creature comforts," as if God could not
penetrate the thoughts of even the most corrupt hearts, to say
nothing of the signification of words, and would suffer Himself
to be misled after the manner of men by the names of things.
Which matters, with many others which are not to be mentioned,
our modest and sober-minded Jew found by no means to his
liking, so that, his curiosity being fully satisfied, he was minded
to return to Paris ; which accordingly he did.　There, on his
arrival, he was met by Jehannot ; and the two made great
cheer together.　Jehannot expected Abraham's conversion
least of all things, and allowed him some days of rest before he
asked what he thought of the Holy Father and the cardinals
and the other courtiers.　To which the Jew forthwith replied :—
" I think God owes them all an evil recompense : I tell thee, so
far as I was able to carry my investigations, holiness, devotion,
good works or exemplary living in any kind was nowhere to be
found in any clerk ; but only lewdness, avarice, gluttony, and
the like, and worse, if worse may be, appeared to be held in
such honour of all, that (to my thinking) the place is a centre

of diabolical rather than of divine activities. To the best of
my judgment, your Pastor, and by consequence all that are
about him devote all their zeal and ingenuity and subtlety to
devise how best and most speedily they may bring the Christian
religion to nought and banish it from the world. And because
I see that what they so zealously endeavour does not come to
pass, but that on the contrary your religion continually grows,
and shines more and more clear, therein I seem to discern a
very evident token that it, rather than any other, as being
more true and holy than any other, has the Holy Spirit for its
foundation and support. For which cause, whereas I met your
exhortations in a harsh and obdurate temper, and would not
become a Christian, now I frankly tell you that I would on no
account omit to become such. Go we then to the church, and
there according to the traditional rite of your holy faith let me
receive baptism." Jehannot, who had anticipated a diametric-
ally opposite conclusion, as soon as he heard him so speak, was
the best pleased man that ever was in the world. So taking
Abraham with him to Notre Dame he prayed the clergy there
to baptise him. When they heard that it was his own wish,
they forthwith did so, and Jehannot raised him from the sacred
font, and named him Jean ; and afterwards he caused teachers
of great eminence thoroughly to instruct him in our faith, which
he readily learned, and afterwards practised in a good, a virtuous,
nay, a holy life.

NOVEL III

*Melchisedech, a Jew, by a story of three rings averts a great danger
with which he was menaced by Saladin.*

WHEN Neifile had brought her story to a close amid the com-
mendations of all the company, Filomena, at the queen's behest,
thus began :—

The story told by Neifile brings to my mind another in which
also a Jew appears, but this time as the hero of a perilous
adventure ; and as enough has been said of God and of the
truth of our faith, it will not now be inopportune if we descend
to mundane events and the actions of men. Wherefore I pro-
pose to tell you a story, which will perhaps dispose you to be
more circumspect than you have been wont to be in answering
questions addressed to you. Well ye know, or should know,

loving gossips, that, as it often happens that folk by their own folly forfeit a happy estate and are plunged in most grievous misery, so good sense will extricate the wise from extremity of peril, and establish them in complete and assured peace. Of the change from good to evil fortune, which folly may effect, instances abound ; indeed, occurring as they do by the thousand day by day, they are so conspicuous that their recital would be beside our present purpose. But that good sense may be our succour in misfortune, I will now, as I promised, make plain to you within the narrow compass of a little story.

Saladin, who by his great valour had from small beginnings made himself Soldan of Egypt, and gained many victories over kings both Christian and Saracen, having in divers wars and by divers lavish displays of magnificence spent all his treasure, and in order to meet a certain emergency being in need of a large sum of money, and being at a loss to raise it with a celerity adequate to his necessity, bethought him of a wealthy Jew, Melchisedech by name, who lent at usance in Alexandria, and who, were he but willing, was, as he believed, able to accommodate him, but was so miserly that he would never do so of his own accord, nor was Saladin disposed to constrain him thereto. So great, however, was his necessity that, after pondering every method whereby the Jew might be induced to be compliant, at last he determined to devise a colourably reasonable pretext for extorting the money from him. So he sent for him, received him affably, seated him by his side, and presently said to him :—" My good man, I have heard from many people that thou art very wise, and of great discernment in divine things ; wherefore I would gladly know of thee, which of the three laws thou reputest the true law, the law of the Jews, the law of the Saracens, or the law of the Christians ? " The Jew, who was indeed a wise man, saw plainly enough that Saladin meant to entangle him in his speech, that he might have occasion to harass him, and bethought him that he could not praise any of the three laws above another without furnishing Saladin with the pretext which he sought. So, concentrating all the force of his mind to shape such an answer as might avoid the snare, he presently lit on what he sought, saying :—" My lord, a pretty question indeed is this which you propound, and fain would I answer it ; to which end it is apposite that I tell you a story, which, if you will hearken, is as follows :—If I mistake not, I remember to have often heard tell of a great and rich man of old time, who among other most precious

jewels had in his treasury a ring of extraordinary beauty and
value, which by reason of its value and beauty he was minded
to leave to his heirs for ever ; for which cause he ordained, that,
whichever of his sons was found in possession of the ring as by
his bequest, should thereby be designated his heir, and be entitled
to receive from the rest the honour and homage due to a superior.
The son, to whom he bequeathed the ring, left it in like manner
to his descendants, making the like ordinance as his predecessor.
In short the ring passed from hand to hand for many genera-
tions ; and in the end came to the hands of one who had three
sons, goodly and virtuous all, and very obedient to their father,
so that he loved them all indifferently. The rule touching the
descent of the ring was known to the young men, and each
aspiring to hold the place of honour among them did all he
could to persuade his father, who was now old, to leave the
ring to him at his death. The worthy man, who loved them
all equally, and knew not how to choose from among them a
sole legatee, promised the ring to each in turn, and in order to
satisfy all three, caused a cunning artificer secretly to make
two other rings, so like the first, that the maker himself could
hardly tell which was the true ring. So, before he died, he
disposed of the rings, giving one privily to each of his sons ;
whereby it came to pass, that after his decease each of the sons
claimed the inheritance and the place of honour, and, his claim
being disputed by his brothers, produced his ring in witness of
right. And the rings being found so like one to another that it
was impossible to distinguish the true one, the suit to determine
the true heir remained pendent, and still so remains. And so,
my lord, to your question, touching the three laws given to
the three peoples by God the Father, I answer :—Each of these
peoples deems itself to have the true inheritance, the true law,
the true commandments of God ; but which of them is justified
in so believing, is a question which, like that of the rings, remains
pendent." The excellent adroitness with which the Jew had
contrived to evade the snare which he had laid for his feet was
not lost upon Saladin. He therefore determined to let the Jew
know his need, and did so, telling him at the same time what
he had intended to do, in the event of his answering less circum-
spectly than he had done.

Thereupon the Jew gave the Soldan all the accommodation
that he required, which the Soldan afterwards repaid him in
full. He also gave him most munificent gifts with his lifelong
amity and a great and honourable position near his person.

NOVEL IV

*A monk lapses into a sin meriting the most severe punishment,
    justly censures the same fault in his abbot, and thus evades
    the penalty.*

THE silence which followed the conclusion of Filomena's tale
was broken by Dioneo, who sate next her, and without waiting
for the queen's word, for he knew that by the rule laid down at
the commencement it was now his turn to speak, began on
this wise :—Loving ladies, if I have well understood the intention
of you all, we are here to afford entertainment to one another
by story-telling ; wherefore, provided only nought is done that
is repugnant to this end, I deem it lawful for each (and so said
our queen a little while ago) to tell whatever story seems to
him most likely to be amusing. Seeing, then, that we have
heard how Abraham saved his soul by the good counsel of
Jehannot de Chevigny, and Melchisedech by his own good
sense safe-guarded his wealth against the stratagems of Saladin,
I hope to escape your censure in narrating a brief story of a
monk, who by his address delivered his body from imminent
peril of most severe chastisement.

In the not very remote district of Lunigiana there flourished
formerly a community of monks more numerous and holy than
is there to be found to day, among whom was a young brother,
whose vigour and lustihood neither the fasts nor the vigils
availed to subdue. One afternoon, while the rest of the con-
fraternity slept, our young monk took a stroll around the
church, which lay in a very sequestered spot, and chanced to
espy a young and very beautiful girl, a daughter, perhaps, of
one of the husbandmen of those parts, going through the fields
and gathering herbs as she went. No sooner had he seen her
than he was sharply assailed by carnal concupiscence, insomuch
that he made up to and accosted her ; and (she harkening)
little by little they came to an understanding, and unobserved
by any entered his cell together. Now it so chanced that, while
they fooled it within somewhat recklessly, he being overwrought
with passion, the abbot awoke and passing slowly by the young
monk's cell, heard the noise which they made within, and the
better to distinguish the voices, came softly up to the door of
the cell, and listening discovered that beyond all doubt there

was a woman within. His first thought was to force the door open ; but, changing his mind, he returned to his chamber and waited until the monk should come out.

Delightsome beyond measure though the monk found his intercourse with the girl, yet was he not altogether without anxiety. He had heard, as he thought, the sound of footsteps in the dormitory, and having applied his eye to a convenient aperture had had a good view of the abbot as he stood by the door listening. He was thus fully aware that the abbot might have detected the presence of a woman in the cell. Whereat he was exceedingly distressed, knowing that he had a severe punishment to expect ; but he concealed his vexation from the girl while he busily cast about in his mind for some way of escape from his embarrassment. He thus hit on a novel stratagem which was exactly suited to his purpose. With the air of one who had had enough of the girl's company he said to her :—" I shall now leave you in order that I may arrange for your departure hence unobserved. Stay here quietly until I return." So out he went, locking the door of the cell, and withdrawing the key, which he carried straight to the abbot's chamber and handed to him, as was the custom when a monk was going out, saying with a composed air :—" Sir, I was not able this morning to bring in all the faggots which I had made ready, so with your leave I will go to the wood and bring them in." The abbot, desiring to have better cognisance of the monk's offence, and not dreaming that the monk knew that he had been detected, was pleased with the turn matters had taken, and received the key gladly, at the same time giving the monk the desired leave. So the monk withdrew, and the abbot began to consider what course it were best for him to take, whether to assemble the brotherhood and open the door in their presence, that, being witnesses of the delinquency, they might have no cause to murmur against him when he proceeded to punish the delinquent, or whether it were not better first to learn from the girl's own lips how it had come about. And reflecting that she might be the wife or daughter of some man who would take it ill that she should be shamed by being exposed to the gaze of all the monks, he determined first of all to find out who she was, and then to make up his mind. So he went softly to the cell, opened the door, and, having entered, closed it behind him. The girl, seeing that her visitor was none other than the abbot, quite lost her presence of mind, and quaking with shame began to weep. Master abbot surveyed her from

head to foot, and seeing that she was fresh and comely, fell a
prey, old though he was, to fleshly cravings no less poignant
and sudden than those which the young monk had experienced,
and began thus to commune with himself :—" Alas ! why take
I not my pleasure when I may, seeing that I never need lack
for occasions of trouble and vexation of spirit ? Here is a fair
wench, and no one in the world to know. If I can bring her to
pleasure me, I know not why I should not do so. Who will
know ? No one will ever know ; and sin that is hidden is half
forgiven ; this chance may never come again ; so, methinks, it
were the part of wisdom to take the boon which God bestows."
So musing, with an altogether different purpose from that
with which he had come, he drew near the girl, and softly bade
her to be comforted, and besought her not to weep ; and so
little by little he came at last to show her what he would be at.
The girl, being made neither of iron nor of adamant, was readily
induced to gratify the abbot, who after bestowing upon her
many an embrace and kiss, got upon the monk's bed, where,
being sensible, perhaps, of the disparity between his reverend
portliness and her tender youth, and fearing to injure her by
his excessive weight, he refrained from lying upon her, but laid
her upon him, and in that manner disported himself with her
for a long time. The monk, who had only pretended to go to
the wood, and had concealed himself in the dormitory, no
sooner saw the abbot enter his cell than he was overjoyed to
think that his plan would succeed ; and when he saw that he
had locked the door, he was well assured thereof. So he stole
out of his hiding place, and set his eye to an aperture through
which he saw and heard all that the abbot did and said. At
length the abbot, having had enough of dalliance with the girl,
locked her in the cell and returned to his chamber. Catching
sight of the monk soon afterwards, and supposing him to have
returned from the wood, he determined to give him a sharp
reprimand and have him imprisoned, that he might thus secure
the prey for himself alone. He therefore caused him to be
summoned, chid him very severely and with a stern countenance,
and ordered him to be put in prison. The monk replied trip-
pingly :—" Sir, I have not been so long in the order of St.
Benedict as to have every particular of the rule by heart ; nor
did you teach me before to-day in what posture it behoves the
monk to have intercourse with women, but limited your instruc-
tion to such matters as fasts and vigils. As, however, you have
now given me my lesson, I promise you, if you also pardon my

offence, that I will never repeat it, but will always follow the
example which you have set me."

The abbot, who was a shrewd man, saw at once that the monk
was not only more knowing than he, but had actually seen what
he had done ; nor, conscience-stricken himself, could he for
shame mete out to the monk a measure which he himself merited.
So pardon given, with an injunction to bury what had been
seen in silence, they decently conveyed the young girl out of
the monastery, whither, it is to be believed, they now and again
caused her to return.

NOVEL V

*The Marchioness of Monferrato by a banquet of hens seasoned
with wit checks the mad passion of the King of France.*

THE story told by Dioneo evoked at first some qualms of shame
in the minds of the ladies, as was apparent by the modest blush
that tinged their faces : then exchanging glances, and scarce
able to refrain their mirth, they listened to it with half-sup-
pressed smiles. On its conclusion they bestowed upon Dioneo
a few words of gentle reprehension with intent to admonish
him that such stories were not to be told among ladies. The
queen then turned to Fiammetta, who was seated on the grass
at her side, and bade her follow suit ; and Fiammetta with a
gay and gracious mien thus began :—

The line upon which our story-telling proceeds, to wit, to
shew the virtue that resides in apt and ready repartees, pleases
me well ; and as in affairs of love men and women are in diverse
case, for to aspire to the love of a woman of higher lineage than
his own is wisdom in man, whereas a woman's good sense is
then most conspicuous when she knows how to preserve herself
from becoming enamoured of a man her superior in rank, I
am minded, fair my ladies, to shew you by the story which
I am now to tell, how by deed and word a gentlewoman both
defended herself against attack, and weaned her suitor from
his love.

The Marquis of Monferrato, a paladin of distinguished prowess,
was gone overseas as gonfalonier of the Church in a general
array of the Christian forces. Whose merits being canvassed
at the court of Philippe le Borgne, on the eve of his departure
from France on the same service, a knight observed, that there

was not under the stars a couple comparable to the Marquis
and his lady ; in that, while the Marquis was a paragon of the
knightly virtues, his lady for beauty and honour was without
a peer among all the other ladies of the world. These words
made so deep an impression on the mind of the King of France
that, though he had never seen the lady, he fell ardently in
love with her, and, being to join the armada, resolved that his
port of embarkation should be no other than Genoa, in order
that, travelling thither by land, he might find a decent pretext
for visiting the Marchioness, with whom in the absence of the
Marquis he trusted to have the success which he desired ; nor
did he fail to put his design in execution. Having sent his
main army on before, he took the road himself with a small
company of gentlemen, and, as they approached the territory
of the Marquis, he despatched a courier to the Marchioness, a
day in advance, to let her know that he expected to breakfast
with her the next morning. The lady, who knew her part and
played it well, replied graciously, that he would be indeed
welcome, and that his presence would be the greatest of all
favours. She then began to commune with herself, what this
might import, that so great a king should come to visit her in
her husband's absence, nor was she so deluded as not to surmise
that it was the fame of her beauty that drew him thither.
Nevertheless she made ready to do him honour in a manner
befitting her high degree, summoning to her presence such of
the retainers as remained in the castle, and giving all needful
directions with their advice, except that the order of the banquet
and the choice of the dishes she reserved entirely to herself.
Then, having caused all the hens that could be found in the
country-side to be brought with all speed into the castle, she
bade her cooks furnish forth the royal table with divers dishes
made exclusively of such fare. The King arrived on the
appointed day, and was received by the lady with great and
ceremonious cheer. Fair and noble and gracious seemed she
in the eyes of the King beyond all that he had conceived from
the knight's words, so that he was lost in admiration and inly
extolled her to the skies, his passion being the more inflamed
in proportion as he found the lady surpass the idea which he
had formed of her. A suite of rooms furnished with all the
appointments befitting the reception of so great a king, was
placed at his disposal, and after a little rest, breakfast-time being
come, he and the Marchioness took their places at the same
table, while his suite were honourably entertained at other

boards according to their several qualities. Many courses were
served with no lack of excellent and rare wines, whereby the
King was mightily pleased, as also by the extraordinary beauty
of the Marchioness, on whom his eye from time to time rested.
However, as course followed course, the King observed with
some surprise, that, though the dishes were diverse, yet they
were all but variations of one and the same fare, to wit, the
pullet. Besides which he knew that the domain was one
which could not but afford plenty of divers sorts of game, and
by forewarning the lady of his approach, he had allowed time
for hunting ; yet, for all his surprise, he would not broach the
question more directly with her than by a reference to her
hens ; so, turning to her with a smile, he said :—" Madam, do
hens grow in this country without so much as a single cock ? "
The Marchioness, who perfectly apprehended the drift of the
question, saw in it an opportunity, sent her by God, of evincing
her virtuous resolution ; so casting a haughty glance upon the
King she answered thus :—" Sire, no ; but the women, though
they may differ somewhat from others in dress and rank, are
yet of the same nature here as elsewhere." The significance of
the banquet of pullets was made manifest to the King by these
words, as also the virtue which they veiled. He perceived that
on a lady of such a temper words would be wasted, and that
force was out of the question. Wherefore, yielding to the
dictates of prudence and honour, he was now as prompt to
quench, as he had been inconsiderate in conceiving, his unfor-
tunate passion for the lady ; and fearing her answers, he
refrained from further jesting with her, and dismissing his
hopes devoted himself to his breakfast, which done, he disarmed
suspicion of the dishonourable purpose of his visit by an early
departure, and thanking her for the honour she had conferred
upon him, and commending her to God, took the road to
Genoa.

NOVEL VI

*A worthy man by an apt saying puts to shame the wicked hypocrisy
of the religious*

WHEN all had commended the virtue of the Marchioness and
the spirited reproof which she administered to the King of

France, Emilia, who sate next to Fiammetta, obeyed the queen's behest, and with a good courage thus began :—

My story is also of a reproof, but of one administered by a worthy man, who lived the secular life, to a greedy religious, by a jibe as merry as admirable. Know then, dear ladies, that there was in our city, not long ago, a friar minor, an inquisitor in matters of heresy, who, albeit he strove might and main to pass himself off as a holy man and tenderly solicitous for the integrity of the Christian Faith, as they all do, yet he had as keen a scent for a full purse as for a deficiency of faith. Now it so chanced that his zeal was rewarded by the discovery of a good man far better furnished with money than with sense, who in an unguarded moment, not from defect of faith, but rather, perhaps, from excess of hilarity, being heated with wine, had happened to say to his boon companions, that he had a wine good enough for Christ Himself to drink. Which being reported to the inquisitor, he, knowing the man to be possessed of large estates and a well-lined purse, set to work in hot haste, " cum gladiis et fustibus," to bring all the rigour of the law to bear upon him, designing thereby not to lighten the load of his victim's misbelief, but to increase the weight of his own purse by the florins which he might, as he did, receive from him. So he cited him to his presence, and asked him whether what was alleged against him were true. The good man answered in the affirmative, and told him how it had happened. " Then," said our most holy and devout inquisitor of St. John Golden-beard,[1] " then hast thou made Christ a wine-bibber, and a lover of rare vintages, as if He were a sot, a toper and a tavern-haunter even as one of you. And thinkest thou now by a few words of apology to pass this off as a light matter ? It is no such thing as thou supposest. Thou hast deserved the fire ; and we should but do our duty, did we inflict it upon thee." With these and the like words in plenty he upbraided him, bending on him meanwhile a countenance as stern as if Epicurus had stood before him denying the immortality of the soul. In short he so terrified him that the good man was fain to employ certain intermediaries to anoint his palms with a liberal allowance of St. John Goldenmouth's grease, an excellent remedy for the disease of avarice which spreads like a pestilence among the clergy, and notably among the friars minors, who dare not touch a coin, that he might deal gently with him. And great being the virtue of this ointment, albeit no mention is made

---

[1] The fiorino d'oro bore the effigy of St. John.

thereof by Galen in any part of his Medicines, it had so gracious
an effect that the threatened fire gave place to a cross, which
he was to wear as if he were bound for the emprise over seas ;
and to make the ensign more handsome the inquisitor ordered
that it should be yellow upon a black ground. Besides which,
after pocketing the coin, he kept him dangling about him for
some days, bidding him by way of penance hear mass every
morning at Santa Croce, and afterwards wait upon him at the
breakfast-hour, after which he was free to do as he pleased for
the rest of the day. All which he most carefully observed ;
and so it fell out that one of these mornings there were chanted
at the mass at which he assisted the following words of the
Gospel :—You shall receive an hundredfold and shall possess
eternal life. With these words deeply graven in his memory,
he presented himself, as he was bidden, before the inquisitor
where he sate taking his breakfast, and being asked whether
he had heard mass that morning, he promptly answered :—
" Yes, sir." And being further asked :—" Heardest thou
aught therein, as to which thou art in doubt, or hast thou any
question to propound ? " the good man responded :—" Nay
indeed, doubt have I none of aught that I heard ; but rather
assured faith in the verity of all. One thing, however, I heard,
which caused me to commiserate you and the rest of you friars
very heartily, in regard of the evil plight in which you must
find yourselves in the other world." " And what," said the
inquisitor, " was the passage that so moved thee to commiserate
us ? " " Sir," rejoined the good man, " it was that passage in
the Gospel which says :—You shall receive an hundredfold."
" You heard aright," said the inquisitor ; " but why did the
passage so affect you ? " " Sir," replied the good man, " I
will tell you. Since I have been in attendance here, I have
seen a crowd of poor folk receive a daily dole, now of one, now
of two, huge tureens of swill, being the refuse from your table,
and that of the brothers of this convent ; whereof if you are
to receive an hundredfold in the other world, you will have so
much that it will go hard but you are all drowned therein."
This raised a general laugh among those who sat at the inquisi-
tor's table, whereat the inquisitor, feeling that their gluttony
and hypocrisy had received a home-thrust, was very wroth,
and, but that what he had already done had not escaped
censure, would have instituted fresh proceedings against him
in revenge for the pleasantry with which he had rebuked the
baseness of himself and his brother friars ; so in impotent

wrath he bade him go about his business and shew himself
there no more.

NOVEL VII

*Bergamino, with a story of Primasso and the Abbot of Cluny,
finely censures a sudden access of avarice in Messer Cane
della Scala.*

EMILIA'S charming manner and her story drew laughter and
commendation from the queen and all the company, who were
much tickled by her new type of crusader. When the laughter
had subsided, and all were again silent, Filostrato, on whom the
narration now fell, began on this wise :—

A fine thing it is, noble ladies, to hit a fixed mark ; but if,
on the sudden appearance of some strange object, it be forth-
with hit by the bowman, 'tis little short of a miracle. The
corrupt and filthy life of the clergy offers on many sides a fixed
mark of iniquity at which, whoever is so minded, may let fly,
with little doubt that they will reach it, the winged words of
reproof and reprehension. Wherefore, though the worthy man
did well to censure in the person of the inquisitor the pretended
charity of the friars who give to the poor what they ought
rather to give to the pigs or throw away, higher indeed is the
praise which I accord to him, of whom, taking my cue from the
last story, I mean to speak ; seeing that by a clever apologue he
rebuked a sudden and unwonted access of avarice in Messer
Cane della Scala, conveying in a figure what he had at heart to
say touching Messer Cane and himself ; which apologue is to
follow.

Far and wide, almost to the ends of the earth, is borne the
most illustrious renown of Messer Cane della Scala, in many
ways the favoured child of fortune, a lord almost without a peer
among the notables and magnificoes of Italy since the time of
the Emperor Frederic II. Now Messer Cane, being minded to
hold high festival at Verona, whereof fame should speak
marvellous things, and many folk from divers parts, of whom
the greater number were jesters of every order, being already
arrived, Messer Cane did suddenly (for some cause or another)
abandon his design, and dismissed them with a partial recom-
pense. One only, Bergamino by name, a speaker ready and
polished in a degree credible only to such as heard him, remained,

having received no recompense or congé, still cherishing the
hope that this omission might yet turn out to his advantage.
But Messer Cane was possessed with the idea that whatever he
might give Bergamino would be far more completely thrown
away than if he had tossed it into the fire ; so never a word of
the sort said he or sent he to him.   A few days thus passed, and
then Bergamino, seeing that he was in no demand or request
for aught that belonged to his office, and being also at heavy
charges at his inn for the keep of his horses and servants, fell
into a sort of melancholy ; but still he waited a while, not
deeming it expedient to leave.   He had brought with him three
rich and goodly robes, given him by other lords, that he might
make a brave show at the festival, and when his host began
to press for payment he gave him one of the robes ; afterwards,
there being still much outstanding against him, he must needs,
if he would tarry longer at the inn, give the host the second
robe ; after which he began to live on the third, being minded
to remain there, as long as it would hold out, in expectation of
better luck, and then to take his departure.   Now, while he was
thus living on the third robe, it chanced that Messer Cane
encountered him one day as he sate at breakfast with a very
melancholy visage.   Which Messer Cane observing, said, rather
to tease him than expecting to elicit from him any pleasant
retort :—" What ails thee, Bergamino, that thou art still so
melancholy ?   Let me know the reason why."   Whereupon
Bergamino, without a moment's reflection, told the following
story, which could not have fitted his own case more exactly if
it had been long premeditated.

    " My lord, you must know that Primasso was a grammarian
of great eminence, and excellent and quick beyond all others in
versifying ; whereby he waxed so notable and famous that,
albeit he was not everywhere known by sight, yet there were
scarce any that did not at least by name and report know who
Primasso was.   Now it so happened that, being once at Paris
in straitened circumstances, as it was his lot to be most of his
time by reason that virtue is little appreciated by the powerful,
he heard speak of the Abbot of Cluny, who, except the Pope,
is supposed to be the richest prelate, in regard of his vast
revenues, that the Church of God can shew ; and marvellous
and magnificent things were told him of the perpetual court
which the abbot kept, and how, wherever he was, he denied not
to any that came there either meat or drink, so only that he
preferred his request while the abbot was at table.   Which

when Primasso heard, he determined to go and see for himself
what magnificent state this abbot kept, for he was one that took
great delight in observing the ways of powerful and lordly men ;
wherefore he asked how far from Paris was the abbot then so-
journing. He was informed that the abbot was then at one
of his places distant perhaps six miles ; which Primasso con-
cluded he could reach in time for breakfast, if he started early
in the morning. When he had learned the way, he found that
no one else was travelling by it, and fearing lest by mischance
he should lose it, and so find himself where it would not be easy
for him to get food, he determined to obviate so disagreeable a
contingency by taking with him three loaves of bread—as for
drink, water, though not much to his taste, was, he supposed,
to be found everywhere. So, having disposed the loaves in
the fold of his tunic, he took the road and made such progress
that he reached the abbot's place of sojourn before the breakfast-
hour. Having entered, he made the circuit of the entire place,
observing everything, the vast array of tables, and the vast
kitchen well-appointed with all things needful for the prepara-
tion and service of the breakfast, and saying to himself :—' In
very truth this man is even such a magnifico as he is reported
to be.' While his attention was thus occupied, the abbot's
seneschal, it being now breakfast-time, gave order to serve
water for the hands, which being washen, they sat them all
down to breakfast. Now it so happened that Primasso was
placed immediately in front of the door by which the abbot must
pass from his chamber into the hall ; in which, according to
rule of his court, neither wine, nor bread, nor aught else drinkable
or eatable was ever set on the tables before he made his
appearance and was seated. The seneschal, therefore, having
set the tables, sent word to the abbot, that all was now ready,
and they waited only his pleasure. So the abbot gave the
word, the door of his chamber was thrown open, and he took
a step or two forward towards the hall, gazing straight in front
of him as he went. Thus it fell out that the first man on whom
he set eyes was Primasso, who was in very sorry trim. The
abbot, who knew him not by sight, no sooner saw him, than,
surprised by a churlish mood to which he had hitherto been
an entire stranger, he said to himself :—' So it is to such as this
man that I give my hospitality ; ' and going back into the
chamber he bade lock the door, and asked of his attendants
whether the vile fellow that sate at table directly opposite the
door was known to any of them, who, one and all, answered

in the negative. Primasso waited a little, but he was not used to fast, and his journey had whetted his appetite. So, as the abbot did not return, he drew out one of the loaves which he had brought with him, and began to eat. The abbot, after a while, bade one of his servants go see whether Primasso were gone. The servant returned with the answer :—' No, sir, and (what is more) he is eating a loaf of bread, which he seems to have brought with him.' ' Be it so then,' said the abbot, who was vexed that he was not gone of his own accord, but was not disposed to turn him out ; ' let him eat his own bread, if he have any, for he shall have none of ours to-day.' By and by Primasso, having finished his first loaf, began, as the abbot did not make his appearance, to eat the second ; which was likewise reported to the abbot, who had again sent to see if he were gone. Finally, as the abbot still delayed his coming, Primasso, having finished the second loaf, began upon the third ; whereof, once more, word was carried to the abbot, who now began to commune with himself and say :—' Alas ! my soul, what unwonted mood harbourest thou to-day ? What avarice ? what scorn ? and of whom ? I have given my hospitality, now for many a year, to whoso craved it, without looking to see whether he were gentle or churl, poor or rich, merchant or cheat, and mine eyes have seen it squandered on vile fellows without number ; and nought of that which I feel towards this man ever entered my mind. Assuredly it cannot be that he is a man of no consequence, who is the occasion of this access of avarice in me. Though he seem to me a vile fellow, he must be some great man, that my mind is thus obstinately averse to do him honour.' Of which musings the upshot was that he sent to inquire who the vile fellow was, and learning that he was Primasso, come to see if what he had heard of his magnificent state were true, he was stricken with shame, having heard of old Primasso's fame, and knowing him to be a great man. Wherefore, being zealous to make him the amend, he studied to do him honour in many ways ; and after breakfast, that his garb might accord with his native dignity, he caused him to be nobly arrayed, and setting him upon a palfrey and filling his purse, left it to his own choice, whether to go or to stay. So Primasso, with a full heart, thanked him for his courtesy in terms the amplest that he could command, and, having left Paris afoot, returned thither on horseback."

Messer Cane was shrewd enough to apprehend Bergamino's meaning perfectly well without a gloss, and said with a smile :—

" Bergamino, thy parable is apt, and declares to me very plainly thy losses, my avarice, and what thou desirest of me. And in good sooth this access of avarice, of which thou art the occasion, is the first that I have experienced. But I will expel the intruder with the *bâton* which thou thyself hast furnished." So he paid Bergamino's reckoning, habited him nobly in one of his own robes, gave him money and a palfrey, and left it for the time at his discretion, whether to go or to stay.

NOVEL VIII

Guglielmo Borsiere by a neat retort sharply censures avarice in Messer Ermino de' Grimaldi.

Next Filostrato was seated Lauretta, who, when the praises bestowed on Bergamino's address had ceased, knowing that it was now her turn to speak, waited not for the word of command, but with a charming graciousness thus began :—

The last novel, dear gossips, prompts me to relate how a worthy man, likewise a jester, reprehended not without success the greed of a very wealthy merchant ; and though the burden of my story is not unlike the last, yet, perchance, it may not on that account be the less appreciated by you, because it has a happy termination.

Know then that in Genoa there dwelt long ago a gentleman, who was known as Messer Ermino de' Grimaldi, and whose wealth, both in lands and money, was generally supposed to be far in excess of that of any other burgher then in Italy ; and as in wealth he was without a rival in Italy, so in meanness and avarice there was not any in the entire world, however richly endowed with those qualities, whom he did not immeasurably surpass, insomuch that, not only did he keep a tight grip upon his purse when honour was to be done to another, but in his personal expenditure, even upon things meet and proper, contrary to the general custom of the Genoese, whose wont is to array themselves nobly, he was extremely penurious, as also in his outlay upon his table. Wherefore, not without just cause, folk had dropped his surname de' Grimaldi, and called him instead Messer Ermino Avarizia. While thus by thrift his wealth waxed greater and greater, it so chanced that there came to Genoa a jester of good parts, a man debonair and ready of speech, his name Guglielmo Borsiere, whose like is not to

be found to-day, when jesters (to the great reproach be it spoken
of those that claim the name and reputation of gentlemen) are
rather to be called asses, being without courtly breeding, and
formed after the coarse pattern of the basest of churls. And
whereas in the days of which I speak they made it their business,
they spared no pains, to compose quarrels, to allay heart-
burnings, between gentlemen, or arrange marriages, or leagues
of amity, ministering meanwhile relief to jaded minds and
solace to courts by the sprightly sallies of their wit, and with
keen sarcasm, like fathers, censuring churlish manners, being
also satisfied with very trifling guerdons ; nowadays all their
care is to spend their time in scandal-mongering, in sowing
discord, in saying, and (what is worse) in doing in the presence
of company things churlish and flagitious, in bringing accusa-
tions, true or false, of wicked, shameful or flagitious conduct
against one another ; and in drawing gentlemen into base and
nefarious practices by sinister and insidious arts. And by
these wretched and depraved lords he is held most dear and best
rewarded whose words and deeds are the most atrocious, to the
great reproach and scandal of the world of to-day ; whereby it
is abundantly manifest that virtue has departed from the earth,
leaving a degenerate generation to wallow in the lowest depths
of vice.

But reverting to the point at which I started, wherefrom
under stress of just indignation I have deviated somewhat
further than I intended, I say that the said Guglielmo was
had in honour, and was well received by all the gentlemen of
Genoa ; and tarrying some days in the city, heard much of
the meanness and avarice of Messer Ermino, and was curious
to see him. Now Messer Ermino had heard that this Guglielmo
Borsiere was a man of good parts, and, notwithstanding his
avarice, having in him some sparks of good breeding, received
him with words of hearty greeting and a gladsome mien, and
conversed freely with him and of divers matters, and so con-
versing, took him with other Genoese that were of his company
to a new and very beautiful house which he had built, and after
shewing him over the whole of it, said to him :—" Now, Messer
Guglielmo, you have seen and heard many things ; could you
suggest to me something, the like of which has not hitherto
been seen, which I might have painted here in the saloon of this
house ? " To which ill-judged question Guglielmo replied :—
" Sir, it would not, I think, be in my power to suggest anything
the like of which has never been seen, unless it were a sneeze

or something similar ; but if it so please you, I have something
to suggest, which, I think, you have never seen." " Prithee,
what may that be ? " said Messer Ermino, not expecting to
get the answer which he got. For Guglielmo replied forthwith :
—" Paint Courtesy here " ; which Messer Ermino had no
sooner heard, than he was so stricken with shame that his
disposition underwent a complete change, and he said :—
" Messer Guglielmo, I will see to it that Courtesy is here painted
in such wise that neither you nor any one else shall ever again
have reason to tell me that I have not seen or known that
virtue." And henceforward (so enduring was the change
wrought by Guglielmo's words) there was not in Genoa, while
he lived, any gentleman so liberal and so gracious and so lavish
of honour both to strangers and to his fellow-citizens as Messer
Ermino de' Grimaldi.

NOVEL IX

*The censure of a Gascon lady converts the King of Cyprus from
a churlish to an honourable temper.*

EXCEPT Elisa none now remained to answer the call of the
queen, and she without waiting for it, with gladsome alacrity
thus began :—

Bethink, you damsels, how often it has happened that men
who have been obdurate to censures and chastisements have
been reclaimed by some unpremeditated casual word. This
is plainly manifest by the story told by Lauretta ; and by
mine, which will be of the briefest, I mean further to illustrate
it ; seeing that, good stories, being always pleasurable, are
worth listening to with attention, no matter by whom they
may be told.

'Twas, then, in the time of the first king of Cyprus, after the
conquest made of the Holy Land by Godfrey de Bouillon, that
a lady of Gascony made a pilgrimage to the Holy Sepulchre,
and on her way home, having landed at Cyprus, met with brutal
outrage at the hands of certain ruffians. Broken-hearted and
disconsolate she determined to make her complaint to the king ;
but she was told that it would be all in vain, because so spirit-
less and *fainéant* was he that he not only neglected to avenge
affronts put upon others, but endured with a reprehensible
tameness those which were offered to himself insomuch that

whoso had any ill-humour to vent, took occasion to vex or
mortify him. The lady, hearing this report, despaired of
redress, and by way of alleviation of her grief determined to
make the king sensible of his baseness. So in tears she pre-
sented herself before him and said :—" Sire, it is not to seek
redress of the wrong done me that I come here before you :
but only that, so please you, I may learn of you how it is that
you suffer patiently the wrongs which, as I understand, are
done you ; that thus schooled by you in patience I may endure
my own, which, God knows, I would gladly, were it possible,
transfer to you, seeing that you are so well fitted to bear them."
These words aroused the hitherto sluggish and apathetic king
as it were from sleep. He redressed the lady's wrong, and
having thus made a beginning, thenceforth meted out the
most rigorous justice to all that in any wise offended against
the majesty of his crown.

NOVEL X

*Master Alberto da Bologna honourably puts to shame a lady
who sought occasion to put him to shame in that he was in
love with her.*

AFTER Elisa had done, it only remained for the queen to con-
clude the day's story-telling, and thus with manner debonair
did she begin :—

As stars in the serene expanse of heaven, as in spring-time
flowers in the green pastures, so, honourable damsels, in the
hour of rare and excellent converse is wit with its bright sallies.
Which, being brief, are much more proper for ladies than for
men, seeing that prolixity of speech, when brevity is possible,
is much less allowable to them ; albeit (shame be to us all and
all our generation) few ladies or none are left to-day who under-
stand aught that is wittily said, or understanding are able to
answer it. For the place of those graces of the spirit which
distinguished the ladies of the past has now been usurped by
adornments of the person ; and she whose dress is most richly
and variously and curiously dight, accounts herself more worthy
to be had in honour, forgetting, that, were one but so to array
him, an ass would carry a far greater load of finery than any
of them, and for all that be not a whit the more deserving of
honour. I blush to say this, for in censuring others I condemn

myself. Tricked out, bedecked, bedizened thus, we are either
silent and impassive as statues, or, if we answer aught that is
said to us, much better were it we had held our peace. And
we make believe, forsooth, that our failure to acquit ourselves
in converse with our equals of either sex does but proceed from
guilelessness; dignifying stupidity by the name of modesty, as
if no lady could be modest and converse with other folk than
her maid or laundress or bake-house woman; which if Nature
had intended, as we feign she did, she would have set other
limits to our garrulousness. True it is that in this, as in other
matters, time and place and person are to be regarded; because
it sometimes happens that a lady or gentleman thinking by
some sally of wit to put another to shame, has rather been put
to shame by that other, having failed duly to estimate their
relative powers. Wherefore, that you may be on your guard
against such error, and, further, that in you be not exemplified
the common proverb, to wit, that women do ever and on all
occasions choose the worst, I trust that this last of to-day's
stories, which falls to me to tell, may serve you as a lesson;
that, as you are distinguished from others by nobility of nature,
so you may also shew yourselves separate from them by
excellence of manners.

There lived not many years ago, perhaps yet lives, in Bologna,
a very great physician, so great that the fame of his skill was
noised abroad throughout almost the entire world.

Now Master Alberto (such was his name) was of so noble a
temper that, being now nigh upon seventy years of age, and all
but devoid of natural heat of body, he was yet receptive of the
flames of love; and having at an assembly seen a very beautiful
widow lady, Madonna Malgherida de' Ghisolieri, as some say,
and being charmèd with her beyond measure, was, notwith-
standing his age, no less ardently enamoured than a young man,
insomuch that he was not well able to sleep at night, unless
during the day he had seen the fair lady's lovely and delicate
features. Wherefore he began to frequent the vicinity of
her house, passing to and fro in front of it, now on foot now on
horseback, as occasion best served. Which she and many
other ladies perceiving, made merry together more than once,
to see a man of his years and discretion in love, as if they deemed
that this most delightful passion of love were only fit for empty-
headed youths, and could not in men be either harboured or
engendered. Master Alberto thus continuing to haunt the
front of the house, it so happened that one feast-day the lady

with other ladies was seated before her door, and Master
Alberto's approach being thus observed by them for some time
before he arrived, they complotted to receive him and shew
him honour, and then to rally him on his love; and so they
did, rising with one accord to receive him, bidding him welcome,
and ushering him into a cool courtyard, where they regaled
him with the finest wines and comfits; which done, in a tone of
refined and sprightly banter they asked him how it came about
that he was enamoured of this fair lady, seeing that she was
beloved of many a fine gentleman of youth and spirit. Master
Alberto, being thus courteously assailed, put a blithe face on it,
and answered :—" Madame, my love for you need surprise
none that is conversant with such matters, and least of all you
that are worthy of it. And though old men, of course, have lost
the strength which love demands for its full fruition, yet are
they not therefore without the good intent and just appreciation
of what beseems the accepted lover, but indeed understand it
far better than young men, by reason that they have more
experience. My hope in, thus old, aspiring to love you, who
are loved by so many young men, is founded on what I have
frequently observed of ladies' ways at lunch, when they trifle
with the lupin and the leek. In the leek no part is good, but
the head is at any rate not so bad as the rest, and indeed not
unpalatable; you, however, for the most part, following a
depraved taste, hold it in your hand and munch the leaves,
which are not only of no account but actually distasteful.
How am I to know, madam, that in your selection of lovers,
you are not equally eccentric? In which case I should be the
man of your choice, and the rest would be cast aside." Whereto
the gentle lady, somewhat shame-stricken, as were also her
fair friends, thus made answer :—" Master Alberto, our presump-
tion has received from you a most just and no less courteous
reproof; but your love is dear to me, as should ever be that
of a wise and worthy man. And therefore, saving my honour,
I am yours, entirely and devotedly at your pleasure and com-
mand." This speech brought Master Alberto to his feet, and
the others also rising, he thanked the lady for her courtesy,
bade her a gay and smiling adieu, and so left the house. Thus
the lady, not considering on whom she exercised her wit, think-
ing to conquer was conquered herself : against which mishap
you, if you are discreet, will ever be most strictly on your
guard.

As the young ladies and the three young men finished their

story-telling the sun was westering and the heat of the day in
great measure abated. Which their queen observing, debonairly
thus she spoke :—" Now, dear gossips, my day of sovereignty
draws to a close, and nought remains for me to do but to give
you a new queen, by whom on the morrow our common life
may be ordered as she may deem best in a course of seemly
pleasure ; and though there seems to be still some interval
between day and night, yet, as whoso does not in some degree
anticipate the course of time, cannot well provide for the future ;
and in order that what the new queen shall decide to be meet
for the morrow may be made ready beforehand, I decree that
from this time forth the days begin at this hour. And so in
reverent submission to Him, in whom is the life of all beings,
for our comfort and solace we commit the governance of our
realm for the morrow into the hands of Queen Filomena, most
discreet of damsels." So saying she arose, took the laurel
wreath from her brow, and with a gesture of reverence set it
on the brow of Filomena, whom she then, and after her all the
other ladies and the young men, saluted as queen, doing her
due and graceful homage.

Queen Filomena modestly blushed a little to find herself
thus invested with the sovereignty ; but, being put on her
mettle by Pampinea's recent admonitions, she was minded not
to seem awkward, and soon recovered her composure. She
then began by confirming all the appointments made by
Pampinea, and making all needful arrangements for the follow-
ing morning and evening, which they were to pass where they
then were. Whereupon she thus spoke :—" Dearest gossips,
though, thanks rather to Pampinea's courtesy than to merit
of mine, I am made queen of you all ; yet I am not on that
account minded to have respect merely to my own judgment
in the governance of our life, but to unite your wisdom with
mine ; and that you may understand what I think of doing,
and by consequence may be able to amplify or curtail it at
your pleasure, I will in few words make known to you my
purpose. The course observed by Pampinea to-day, if I have
judged aright, seems to be alike commendable and delectable ;
wherefore, until by lapse of time, or for some other cause, it
grow tedious, I purpose not to alter it. So when we have
arranged for what we have already taken in hand, we will go
hence and enjoy a short walk ; at sundown we will sup in the
cool ; and we will then sing a few songs and otherwise divert
ourselves, until it is time to go to sleep. To-morrow we will

rise in the cool of the morning, and after enjoying another
walk, each at his or her sweet will, we will return, as to-day,
and in due time break our fast, dance, sleep, and having risen,
will here resume our story-telling, wherein, methinks, pleasure
and profit unite in superabundant measure. True it is that
Pampinea, by reason of her late election to the sovereignty,
neglected one matter, which I mean to introduce, to wit, the
circumscription of the topic of our story-telling, and its pre-
assignment, that each may be able to premeditate some apt
story bearing upon the theme ; and seeing that from the
beginning of the world Fortune has made men the sport of
divers accidents, and so it will continue until the end, the theme,
so please you, shall in each case be the same ; to wit, the
fortune of such as after divers adventures have at last attained
a goal of unexpected felicity."

The ladies and the young men alike commended the rule thus
laid down, and agreed to follow it. Dioneo, however, when
the rest had done speaking, said :—" Madam, as all the rest
have said, so say I, briefly, that the rule prescribed by you is
commendable and delectable ; but of your especial grace I
crave a favour, which, I trust, may be granted and continued
to me, so long as our company shall endure ; which favour is
this : that I be not bound by the assigned theme if I am not
so minded, but that I have leave to choose such topic as best
shall please me. And lest any suppose that I crave this grace
as one that has not stories ready to hand, I am henceforth
content that mine be always the last." The queen, knowing
him to be a merry and facetious fellow, and feeling sure that
he only craved this favour in order that, if the company were
jaded, he might have an opportunity to recreate them by some
amusing story, gladly, with the consent of the rest, granted
his petition. She then rose, and attended by the rest sauntered
towards a stream, which, issuing clear as crystal from a neigh-
bouring hill, precipitated itself into a valley shaded by trees
close set amid living rock and fresh green herbage. Bare of
foot and arm they entered the stream, and roving hither and
thither amused themselves in divers ways till in due time they
returned to the palace, and gaily supped. Supper ended, the
queen sent for instruments of music, and bade Lauretta lead
a dance, while Emilia was to sing a song accompanied by Dioneo
on the lute.

Accordingly Lauretta led a dance, while Emilia with passion
sang the following song :—

So fain I am of my own loveliness,
    I hope, nor think not e'er
The weight to feel of other amorousness.

When in the mirror I my face behold,
    That see I there which doth my mind content,
    Nor any present hap or memory old
    May me deprive of such sweet ravishment.
    Where else, then, should I find such blandishment
        Of sight and sense that e'er
    My heart should know another amorousness ?

Nor need I fear lest the fair thing retreat,
    When fain I am my solace to renew ;
    Rather, I know, 'twill me advance to meet,
    To pleasure me, and shew so sweet a view
    That speech or thought of none its semblance true
        Paint or conceive may e'er,
    Unless he burn with ev'n such amorousness.

Thereon as more intent I gaze, the fire
    Waxeth within me hourly more and more,
    Myself I yield thereto, myself entire,
    And foretaste have of what it hath in store,
    And hope of greater joyance than before,
        Nay, such as ne'er
    None knew ; for ne'er was felt such amorousness.

This ballade, to which all heartily responded, albeit its words
furnished much matter of thought to some, was followed by
some other dances, and part of the brief night being thus spent,
the queen proclaimed the first day ended, and bade light the
torches, that all might go to rest until the following morning ;
and so, seeking their several chambers, to rest they went.

Endeth here the first day of the Decameron ; beginneth the second, in which, under the rule of Filomena, they discourse of the fortunes of such as after divers misadventures have at last attained a goal of unexpected felicity.

THE sun was already trailing the new day in his wake of light, and the birds, blithely chanting their lays among the green boughs, carried the tidings to the ear, when with one accord all the ladies and the three young men arose, and entered the gardens, where for no little time they found their delight in sauntering about the dewy meads, straying hither and thither, culling flowers, and weaving them into fair garlands. The day passed like its predecessor ; they breakfasted in the shade, and danced and slept until noon, when they rose, and, at their queen's behest, assembled in the cool meadow, and sat them down in a circle about her. Fair and very debonair she shewed, crowned with her laurel wreath, as for a brief space she scanned the company, and then bade Neifile shew others the way with a story. Neifile made no excuse, and gaily thus began.

NOVEL I

Martellino pretends to be a paralytic, and makes it appear as if he were cured by being placed upon the body of St. Arrigo. His trick is detected ; he is beaten and arrested, and is in peril of hanging, but finally escapes.

OFTEN has it happened, dearest ladies, that one who has studied to raise a laugh at others' expense, especially in regard of things worthy to be had in reverence, has found the laugh turn against himself, and sometimes to his loss : as, in obedience to the queen's command, and by way of introducing our theme, I am about to shew you, by the narrative of an adventure which befell one of our own citizens, and after a course of evil fortune had an entirely unexpected and very felicitous issue.

Not long ago there was at Treviso a German, named Arrigo, a poor man who got his living as a common hired porter, but, though of so humble a condition, was respected by all, being

accounted not only an honest but a most holy man ; insomuch
that, whether truly or falsely I know not, the Trevisans affirm,
that on his decease all the bells of the cathedral of Treviso began
to toll of their own accord.   Which being accounted a miracle,
this Arrigo was generally reputed a saint ; and all the people
of the city gathered before the house where his body lay, and
bore it, with a saint's honours, into the cathedral, and brought
thither the halt and paralytic and blind, and others afflicted
with disease or bodily defects, as hoping that by contact with
this holy body they would all be healed.   The people thus
tumultuously thronging the church, it so chanced that there
arrived in Treviso three of our own citizens, of whom one was
named Stecchi, another Martellino, and the third Marchese ;
all three being men whose habit it was to frequent the courts
of the nobles and afford spectators amusement by assuming
disguises and personating other men.   Being entire strangers
to the place, and seeing everybody running to and fro, they
were much astonished, and having learned the why and where-
fore, were curious to go see what was to be seen.   So at the inn,
where they put up, Marchese began :—" We would fain go see
this saint ; but for my part I know not how we are to reach
the spot, for I hear the piazza is full of Germans and other
armed men, posted there by the Lord who rules here to prevent
an uproar, and moreover the church, so far as one may learn,
is so full of folk that scarce another soul may enter it."   Where-
upon Martellino, who was bent on seeing what was to be seen,
said :—" Let not this deter us ; I will assuredly find a way
of getting to the saint's body."   " How ? " rejoined Marchese.
" I will tell you," replied Martellino ;   " I will counterfeit a
paralytic, and thou wilt support me on one side and Stecchi
on the other, as if I were not able to go alone, and so you will
enter the church, making it appear as if you were leading me
up to the body of the saint that he may heal me, and all that
see will make way and give us free passage."   Marchese and
Stecchi approved the plan ; so all three forthwith left the inn
and repaired to a lonely place, where Martellino distorted his
hands, his fingers, his arms, his legs, and also his mouth and
eyes and his entire face in a manner horrible to contemplate ;
so that no stranger that saw him could have doubted that he
was impotent and paralysed in every part of his body.   In
this guise Marchese and Stecchi laid hold of him, and led him
towards the church, assuming a most piteous air, and humbly
beseeching everybody for God's sake to make way for them.

Their request was readily granted ; and, in short, observed by
all, and crying out at almost every step, " make way, make
way," they reached the place where St. Arrigo's body was laid.
Whereupon some gentlemen who stood by hoisted Martellino
on to the saint's body, that thereby he might receive the boon
of health.   There he lay still for a while, the eyes of all in the
church being riveted upon him in expectation of the result ;
then, being a very practised performer, he stretched, first, one
of his fingers, next a hand, afterwards an arm, and so forth,
making as if he gradually recovered the use of all his natural
powers.   Which the people observing raised such a clamour
in honour of St. Arrigo that even thunder would have been
inaudible.   Now it chanced that hard by stood a Florentine,
who knew Martellino well, though he had failed to recognise
him, when, in such strange guise, he was led into the church ;
but now, seeing him resume his natural shape, the Florentine
recognised him, and at once said with a laugh :—" God's curse
upon him.   Who that saw him come but would have believed
that he was really paralysed ? "   These words were overheard
by some of the Trevisans, who began forthwith to question the
Florentine.   " How ? "   said they ;   " was he then not
paralysed ? "   " No, by God ! "   returned the Florentine ;
" he has always been as straight as any of us ; he has merely
shewn you that he knows better than any man alive how to
play this trick of putting on any counterfeit semblance that
he chooses."   Thereupon the Trevisans, without further parley,
made a rush, clearing the way and crying out as they went :—
" Seize this traitor who mocks at God and His saints ; who,
being no paralytic, has come hither in the guise of a paralytic
to deride our patron saint and us."   So saying, they laid hands
on him, dragged him down from where he stood, seized him
by the hair, tore the clothes from his back, and fell to beating
and kicking him, so that it seemed to him as if all the world
were upon him.   He cried out :—" Pity, for God's sake," and
defended himself as best he could : all in vain, however ; the
press became thicker and thicker moment by moment.   Which
Stecchi and Marchese observing began to say one to the other
that 'twas a bad business ; yet, being apprehensive on their
own account, they did not venture to come to his assistance,
but cried out with the rest that he ought to die, at the same
time, however, casting about how they might find the means
to rescue him from the hands of the people, who would certainly
have killed him, but for a diversion which Marchese hastily

effected. The entire posse of the signory being just outside, he ran off at full speed to the Podestà's lieutenant, and said to him :—" Help, for God's sake ; there is a villain here that has cut my purse with full a hundred florins of gold in it; prithee have him arrested that I may have my own again." Whereupon, twelve sergeants or more ran forthwith to the place where hapless Martellino was being carded without a comb, and, forcing their way with the utmost difficulty through the throng, rescued him all bruised and battered from their hands, and led him to the palace ; whither he was followed by many who, resenting what he had done, and hearing that he was arrested as a cutpurse, and lacking better pretext for harassing him, began one and all to charge him with having cut their purses. All which the deputy of the Podestà had no sooner heard, than, being a harsh man, he straightway took Martellino aside and began to examine him. Martellino answered his questions in a bantering tone, making light of the arrest ; whereat the deputy, losing patience, had him bound to the strappado, and caused him to receive a few hints of the cord with intent to extort from him a confession of his guilt, by way of preliminary to hanging him. Taken down from the strappado, and questioned by the deputy if what his accusers said were true, Martellino, as nothing was to be gained by denial, answered :—" My lord, I am ready to confess the truth ; let but my accusers say, each of them, when and where I cut his purse, and I will tell you what I have and what I have not done." " So be it," said the deputy, and caused a few of them to be summoned. Whereupon Martellino, being charged with having cut this, that or the other man's purse eight, six or four days ago, while others averred that he had cut their purses that very day, answered thus :—" My lord, these men lie in the throat, and for token that I speak true, I tell you that, so far from having been here as long as they make out, it is but very lately that I came into these parts, where I never was before ; and no sooner was I come, than, as my ill-luck would have it, I went to see the body of this saint, and so have been carded as you see ; and that what I say is true, his Lord-ship's intendant of arrivals, and his book, and also my host may certify. Wherefore, if you find that even so it is as I say, hearken not to these wicked men, and spare me the torture and death which they would have you inflict." In this posture of affairs Marchese and Stecchi, learning that the Podestà's deputy was dealing rigorously with Martellino, and had already

put him to the strappado, grew mightily alarmed. "We have
made a mess of it," they said to themselves; "we have only
taken him out of the frying-pan to toss him into the fire."
So, hurrying hither and thither with the utmost zeal, they
made diligent search until they found their host, and told
him how matters stood. The host had his laugh over the affair,
and then brought them to one Sandro Agolanti, who dwelt in
Treviso and had great interest with the Lord of the place.
The host laid the whole matter before Sandro, and, backed by
Marchese and Stecchi, besought him to undertake Martellino's
cause. Sandro, after many a hearty laugh, hied him to the
Lord, who at his instance sent for Martellino. The messengers
found Martellino still in his shirt before the deputy, at his wits'
end, and all but beside himself with fear, because the deputy
would hear nothing that he said in his defence. Indeed, the
deputy, having a spite against Florentines, had quite made
up his mind to have him hanged; he was therefore in the last
degree reluctant to surrender him to the Lord, and only did
so upon compulsion. Brought at length before the Lord,
Martellino detailed to him the whole affair, and prayed him as
the greatest of favours to let him depart in peace. The Lord
had a hearty laugh over the adventure, and bestowed a tunic
on each of the three. So, congratulating themselves on their
unexpected deliverance from so great a peril, they returned
home safe and sound.

NOVEL II

*Rinaldo d'Asti is robbed, arrives at Castel Guglielmo, and is
  entertained by a widow lady; his property is restored to
  him, and he returns home safe and sound.*

THE ladies and the young men, especially Filostrato, laughed
inordinately at Neifile's narrative of Martellino's misadventures.
Then Filostrato, who sate next Neifile, received the queen's
command to follow her, and promptly thus began :—
  Fair ladies, 'tis on my mind to tell you a story in which are
mingled things sacred and passages of adverse fortune and love,
which to hear will perchance be not unprofitable, more especially
to travellers in love's treacherous lands; of whom if any fail
to say St. Julian's paternoster, it often happens that, though he
may have a good bed, he is ill lodged.

Know, then, that in the time of the Marquis Azzo da Ferrara,
a merchant, Rinaldo d'Asti by name, having disposed of certain
affairs which had brought him to Bologna, set his face home-
ward, and having left Ferrara behind him was on his way to
Verona, when he fell in with some men that looked like mer-
chants, but were in truth robbers and men of evil life and
condition, whose company he imprudently joined, riding and
conversing with them. They, perceiving that he was a
merchant, and judging that he must have money about him,
complotted to rob him on the first opportunity ; and to obviate
suspicion they played the part of worthy and reputable men,
their discourse of nought but what was seemly and honourable
and leal, their demeanour at once as respectful and as cordial
as they could make it ; so that he deemed himself very lucky
to have met with them, being otherwise alone save for a single
mounted servant. Journeying thus, they conversed, after the
desultory manner of travellers, of divers matters, until at last
they fell a talking of the prayers which men address to God,
and one of the robbers—there were three of them—said to
Rinaldo :—" And you, gentle sir, what is your wonted orison
when you are on your travels ? " Rinaldo answered :—
" Why, to tell the truth, I am a man unskilled, unlearned in
such matters, and few prayers have I at my command, being
one that lives in the good old way and lets two soldi count for
twenty-four deniers ; nevertheless it has always been my
custom in journeying to say of a morning, as I leave the inn,
a paternoster and an avemaria for the souls of the father and
mother of St. Julian, after which I pray God and St. Julian
to provide me with a good inn for the night. And many a time
in the course of my life have I met with great perils by the way,
and evading them all have found comfortable quarters for the
night : whereby my faith is assured, that St. Julian, in whose
honour I say my paternoster, has gotten me this favour of
God ; nor should I look for a prosperous journey and a safe
arrival at night, if I had not said it in the morning." Then
said his interrogator :—" And did you say it this morning ? "
Whereto Rinaldo answered, " Troth, did I," which caused the
other, who by this time knew what course matters would take,
to say to himself :—" 'Twill prove to have been said in the
nick of time ; for if we do not miscarry, I take it thou wilt
have but a sorry lodging." Then turning to Rinaldo he said :
—" I also have travelled much, and never a prayer have I
said, though I have heard them much commended by many ;

nor has it ever been my lot to find other than good quarters for the night ; it may be that this very evening you will be able to determine which of us has the better lodging, you that have said the paternoster, or I that have not said it. True, however, it is that in its stead I am accustomed to say the ' Dirupisti,' or the ' Intemerata,' or the ' De profundis,' which, if what my grandmother used to say is to be believed, are of the greatest efficacy." So, talking of divers matters, and ever on the look-out for time and place suited to their evil purpose, they continued their journey, until towards evening, some distance from Castel Guglielmo, as they were about to ford a stream, these three ruffians, profiting by the lateness of the hour, and the loneliness and straitness of the place, set upon Rinaldo and robbed him, and leaving him afoot and in his shirt, said by way of adieu :—" Go now, and see if thy St. Julian will provide thee with good lodging to-night ; our saint, we doubt not, will do as much by us ; " and so crossing the stream, they went their way. Rinaldo's servant, coward that he was, did nothing to help his master when he saw him attacked, but turned his horse's head, and was off at a smart pace ; nor did he draw rein until he was come to Castel Guglielmo ; where, it being now evening, he put up at an inn and gave himself no further trouble. Rinaldo, left barefoot, and stripped to his shirt, while the night closed in very cold and snowy, was at his wits' end, and shivering so that his teeth chattered in his head, began to peer about, if haply he might find some shelter for the night, that so he might not perish with the cold ; but, seeing none (for during a recent war the whole country had been wasted by fire), he set off for Castel Guglielmo, quickening his pace by reason of the cold. Whether his servant had taken refuge in Castel Guglielmo or elsewhere, he knew not, but he thought that, could he but enter the town, God would surely send him some succour. However, dark night overtook him while he was still about a mile from the castle ; so that on his arrival he found the gates already locked and the bridges raised, and he could not pass in. Sick at heart, disconsolate and bewailing his evil fortune, he looked about for some place where he might ensconce himself, and at any rate find shelter from the snow. And by good luck he espied a house, built with a balcony a little above the castle-wall, under which balcony he purposed to shelter himself until daybreak. Arrived at the spot, he found beneath the balcony a postern, which, however, was locked ; and having gathered some bits of straw that lay about, he placed them in front of the postern, and there in sad and sorrowful plight took up his quarters, with many a piteous appeal to St. Julian, whom he reproached for not better rewarding the faith which he reposed in him. St. Julian, however, had not abandoned him, and in due time provided him with a good lodging.

There was in the castle a widow lady of extraordinary beauty (none fairer) whom Marquis Azzo loved as his own life, and kept there for his pleasure. She lived in the very same house beneath the balcony of which Rinaldo had posted himself. Now it chanced that that very day the Marquis had come to Castel Guglielmo to pass the night with her, and had privily caused a bath to be made ready, and a supper suited to his rank, in the lady's own house. The arrangements were complete ; and only the Marquis was stayed for, when a servant happened to present himself at the castle-gate, bringing tidings for the Marquis which obliged him suddenly to take horse. He therefore sent word to the lady that she must not wait for him, and forthwith took his departure. The lady, somewhat disconsolate, found nothing better to do than to get into the bath which had been intended for the Marquis, sup and go to bed : so into the bath she went. The bath was close to the postern on the other side of which hapless Rinaldo had ensconced himself, and thus the mournful and quavering music which Rinaldo made as he shuddered in the cold, and which seemed rather to proceed from a stork's beak than from the mouth of a human being, was audible to the lady in the bath. She therefore called her maid, and said to her :—" Go up and look out over the wall and down at the postern, and mark who is there, and what he is, and what he does there." The maid obeyed, and, the night being fine, had no difficulty in making out Rinaldo as he sate there, barefoot, as I have said, and in his shirt, and trembling in every limb. So she called out to him, to know who he was. Rinaldo, who could scarcely articulate for shivering, told as briefly as he could, who he was, and how and why he came to be there ; which done, he began piteously to beseech her not, if she could avoid it, to leave him there all night to perish of cold. The maid went back to her mistress full of pity for Rinaldo, and told her all she had seen and heard. The lady felt no less pity for Rinaldo ; and bethinking her that she had the key of the postern by which the Marquis sometimes entered when he paid her a secret visit, she said to the maid :—" Go, and let him in softly ; here is this supper, and there will be

none to eat it ; and we can very well put him up for the night."
Cordially commending her mistress's humanity, the maid
went and let Rinaldo in, and brought him to the lady, who,
seeing that he was all but dead with cold, said to him :—
"Quick, good man, get into that bath, which is still warm."
Gladly he did so, awaiting no second invitation, and was so
much comforted by its warmth that he seemed to have passed
from death to life.   The lady provided him with a suit of clothes,
which had been worn by her husband shortly before his death,
and which, when he had them on, looked as if they had been
made for him.   So he recovered heart, and, while he awaited
the lady's commands, gave thanks to God and St. Julian for
delivering him from a woful night and conducting him, as it
seemed, to comfortable quarters.

The lady meanwhile took a little rest, after which she had a
roaring fire put in one of her large rooms, whither presently she
came, and asked her maid how the good man did.   The maid
replied :—" Madam, he has put on the clothes, in which he shews
to advantage, having a handsome person, and seeming to be
a worthy man, and well-bred."   " Go, call him then, " said the
lady, " tell him to come hither to the fire, and we will sup ; for
I know that he has not supped."   Rinaldo, on entering the room
and seeing the lady, took her to be of no small consequence.
He therefore made her a low bow, and did his utmost to thank
her worthily for the service she had rendered him.   His words
pleased her no less than his person, which accorded with what
the maid had said : so she made him heartily welcome, installed
him at his ease by her side before the fire, and questioned him
of the adventure which had brought him thither.   Rinaldo
detailed all the circumstances, of which the lady had heard
somewhat when Rinaldo's servant made his appearance at
the castle.   She therefore gave entire credence to what he said,
and told him what she knew about his servant, and how he
might easily find him on the morrow.   She then bade set the
table, which done, Rinaldo and she washed their hands and sate
down together to sup.   Tall he was and comely of form and
feature, debonair and gracious of mien and manner, and in his
lusty prime.   The lady had eyed him again and again to her
no small satisfaction, and, her wantonness being already kindled
for the Marquis, who was to have come to lie with her, she had
let Rinaldo take the vacant place in her mind.   So when supper
was done, and they were risen from the table, she conferred
with her maid, whether, after the cruel trick played upon her

by the Marquis, it were not well to take the good gift which
Fortune had sent her. The maid knowing the bent of her
mistress's desire, left no word unsaid that might encourage her
to follow it. Wherefore the lady, turning towards Rinaldo,
who was standing where she had left him by the fire, began
thus :—" So ! Rinaldo, why still so pensive ? Will nothing
console you for the loss of a horse and a few clothes ? Take
heart, put a blithe face on it, you are at home ; nay more, let
me tell you that, seeing you in those clothes which my late
husband used to wear, and taking you for him, I have felt, not
once or twice, but perhaps a hundred times this evening, a
longing to throw my arms round you and kiss you ; and, in
faith, I had so done, but that I feared it might displease you."
Rinaldo, hearing these words, and marking the flame which shot
from the lady's eyes, and being no laggard, came forward with
open arms, and confronted her and said :—" Madam, I am not
unmindful that I must ever acknowledge that to you I owe my
life, in regard of the peril whence you rescued me. If then
there be any way in which I may pleasure you, churlish indeed
were I not to devise it. So you may even embrace and kiss
me to your heart's content, and I will embrace and kiss you
with the best of good wills." There needed no further parley.
The lady, all aflame with amorous desire, forthwith threw
herself into his arms, and straining him to her bosom with a
thousand passionate embraces, gave and received a thousand
kisses before they sought her chamber. There with all speed
they went to bed, nor did day surprise them until again and
again and in full measure they had satisfied their desire. With
the first streaks of dawn they rose, for the lady was minded
that none should surmise aught of the affair. So, having meanly
habited Rinaldo, and replenished his purse, she enjoined him
to keep the secret, shewed him the way to the castle, where
he was to find his servant, and let him out by the same postern
by which he had entered. When it was broad day the gates
were opened, and Rinaldo, passing himself off as a traveller
from distant parts, entered the castle, and found his servant.
Having put on the spare suit which was in his valise, he was
about to mount the servant's horse, when, as if by miracle,
there were brought into the castle the three gentlemen of the
road who had robbed him the evening before, having been taken
a little while after for another offence. Upon their confession
Rinaldo's horse was restored to him, as were also his clothes
and money ; so that he lost nothing except a pair of garters,

of which the robbers knew not where they had bestowed them.
Wherefore Rinaldo, giving thanks to God and St. Julian,
mounted his horse, and returned home safe and sound, and on
the morrow the three robbers kicked heels in the wind.

NOVEL III

Three young men squander their substance and are reduced to
poverty. Their nephew, returning home a desperate man,
falls in with an abbot, in whom he discovers the daughter of
the King of England. She marries him, and he retrieves the
losses and re-establishes the fortune of his uncles.

THE ladies marvelled to hear the adventures of Rinaldo d'Asti,
praised his devotion, and gave thanks to God and St. Julian
for the succour lent him in his extreme need. Nor, though the
verdict was hardly outspoken, was the lady deemed unwise
to take the boon which God had sent her. So they tittered and
talked of her night of delight, while Pampinea, being seated by
Filostrato, and surmising that her turn would, as it did, come
next, was lost in meditation on what she was to say. Roused
from her reverie by the word of the queen, she put on a cheerful
courage, and thus began :—

Noble ladies, discourse as we may of Fortune's handiwork,
much still remains to be said if we but scan events aright, nor
need we marvel thereat, if we but duly consider that all matters,
which we foolishly call our own, are in her hands, and therefore
subject, at her inscrutable will, to every variety of chance and
change without any order therein by us discernible. Which
is indeed signally manifest everywhere and all day long ; yet,
as 'tis our queen's will that we speak thereof, perhaps 'twill
not be unprofitable to you, if, notwithstanding it has been the
theme of some of the foregoing stories, I add to them another,
which, I believe, should give you pleasure.

There was formerly in our city a knight, by name Messer
Tedaldo, of the Lamberti, according to some, or, as others
say, of the Agolanti family, perhaps for no better reason than
that the occupation of his sons was similar to that which always
was and is the occupation of the Agolanti. However, without
professing to determine which of the two houses he belonged
to, I say, that he was in his day a very wealthy knight, and had
three sons, the eldest being by name Lamberto, the second

Tedaldo, and the third Agolante. Fine, spirited young men
were they all, though the eldest was not yet eighteen years old
when their father, Messer Tedaldo, died very rich, leaving to
them as his lawful heirs the whole of his property both movable
and immovable. Finding themselves thus possessed of great
wealth, both in money and in lands and chattels, they fell to
spending without stint or restraint, indulging their every desire,
maintaining a great establishment and a large and well-filled
stable, besides dogs and hawks, keeping ever open house, scatter-
ing largesses, jousting, and, not content with these and the
like pastimes proper to their condition, indulging every appetite
natural to their youth. They had not long followed this
course of life before the cash left them by their father was
exhausted ; and, their rents not sufficing to defray their expendi-
ture, they began to sell and pledge their property, and disposing
of it by degrees, one item to-day and another to-morrow, they
hardly perceived that they were approaching the verge of ruin,
until poverty opened the eyes which wealth had fast sealed.
So one day Lamberto called his brothers to him, reminded
them of the position of wealth and dignity which had been
theirs and their father's before them, and shewed them the
poverty to which their extravagance had reduced them, and
adjured them most earnestly that, before their destitution was
yet further manifest, they should all three sell what little
remained to them and depart thence ; which accordingly they
did. Without leave-taking, or any ceremony, they quitted
Florence ; nor did they rest until they had arrived in England
and established themselves in a small house in London, where,
by living with extreme parsimony and lending at exorbitant
usances, they prospered so well that in the course of a few years
they amassed a fortune ; and so, one by one, they returned to
Florence, purchased not a few of their former estates besides
many others, and married. The management of their affairs
in England where they continued their business of usurers,
they left to a young nephew, Alessandro by name, while,
heedless alike of the teaching of experience and of marital and
parental duty, they all three launched out at Florence into more
extravagant expenditure than before, and contracted debts on
all hands and to large amounts. This expenditure they were
enabled for some years to support by the remittances made by
Alessandro, who, to his great profit, had lent money to the
barons on the security of their castles and rents.
While the three brothers thus continued to spend freely,

and, when short of money, to borrow it, never doubting of help from England, it so happened that, to the surprise of everybody, there broke out in England a war between the King and his son, by which the whole island was divided into two camps ; whereby Alessandro lost all his mortgages of the baronial castles and every other source of income whatsoever. However, in the daily expectation that peace would be concluded between the King and his son, Alessandro, hoping that in that event all would be restored to him, principal and interest, tarried in the island ; and the three brothers at Florence in no degree retrenched their extravagant expenditure, but went on borrowing from day to day. Several years thus passed ; and, their hopes being frustrated, the three brothers not only lost credit, but, being pressed for payment by their creditors, were suddenly arrested, and, their property proving deficient, were kept in prison for the balance, while their wives and little children went into the country parts, or elsewhere, wretchedly equipped, and with no other prospect than to pass the rest of their days in destitution. Alessandro, meanwhile, seeing that the peace, which he had for several years awaited in England, did not come, and deeming that he would hazard his life to no purpose by tarrying longer in the country, made up his mind to return to Italy. He travelled at first altogether alone ; but it so chanced that he left Bruges at the same time with an abbot, habited in white, attended by a numerous retinue, and preceded by a goodly baggage-train. Behind the abbot rode two grey-beard knights, kinsmen of the King, in whom Alessandro recognised acquaintances, and, making himself known to them, was readily received into their company. As thus they journeyed together, Alessandro softly asked them who the monks were that rode in front with so great a train, and whither they were bound. "The foremost rider," replied one of the knights, " is a young kinsman of ours, the newly-elected abbot of one of the greatest abbeys of England ; and as he is not of legal age for such a dignity, we are going with him to Rome to obtain the Holy Father's dispensation and his confirmation in the office ; but this is not a matter for common talk." Now the new abbot, as lords are wont to do when they travel, was sometimes in front, sometimes in rear of his train ; and thus it happened that, as he passed, he set eyes on Alessandro, who was still quite young, and very shapely and well-favoured, and as courteous, gracious and debonair as e'er another. The abbot was marvellously taken with him at first sight, having never seen aught that pleased him so much, called him to his side, addressed him graciously, and asked him who he was, whence he came, and whither he was bound. Alessandro frankly told all about himself, and having thus answered the abbot's questions, placed himself at his service as far as his small ability might extend. The abbot was struck by his easy flow of apt speech, and observing his bearing more closely, he made up his mind that, albeit his occupation was base, he was nevertheless of gentle blood, which added no little to his interest in him ; and being moved to compassion by his misfortunes, he gave him friendly consolation, bidding him be of good hope, that if he lived a worthy life, God would yet set him in a place no less or even more exalted than that whence Fortune had cast him down, and prayed him to be of his company as far as Tuscany, as both were going the same way. Alessandro thanked him for his words of comfort, and professed himself ready to obey his every command.

So fared on the abbot, his mind full of new ideas begotten by the sight of Alessandro, until some days later they came to a town which was none too well provided with inns ; and, as the abbot must needs put up there, Alessandro, who was well acquainted with one of the innkeepers, arranged that the abbot should alight at his house, and procured him the least discomfortable quarters which it could afford. He thus became for the nonce the abbot's seneschal, and being very expert for such office, managed excellently, quartering the retinue in divers parts of the town. So the abbot supped, and, the night being far spent, all went to bed except Alessandro, who then asked the host where he might find quarters for the night. "In good sooth, I know not," replied the host ; "thou seest that every place is occupied, and that I and my household must lie on the benches. However, in the abbot's chamber there are some corn-sacks. I can shew thee the way thither, and lay a bit of a bed upon them, and there, an it like thee, thou mayst pass the night very well." "How sayst thou ?" said Alessandro ; "in the abbot's chamber, which thou knowest is small, so that there was not room for any of the monks to sleep there ? Had I understood this when the curtains were drawn, I would have quartered his monks on the corn-sacks, and slept myself where the monks sleep." "'Tis even so, however," replied the host, "and thou canst, if thou wilt, find excellent quarters there : the abbot sleeps, the curtains are close drawn ; I will go in softly and lay a small bed there, on which thou canst sleep." Alessandro, satisfied that it might be managed without disturbing the abbot, accepted the offer, and made his arrangements for passing the night as quietly as he could.

The abbot was not asleep; his mind being far too overwrought by certain newly-awakened desires. He had heard what had passed between Alessandro and the host, he had marked the place where Alessandro had lain down, and in the great gladness of his heart had begun thus to commune with himself :—" God has sent me the opportunity of gratifying my desire ; if I let it pass, perchance it will be long before another such opportunity occurs." So, being minded by no means to let it slip, when all was quiet in the inn, he softly called Alessandro, and bade him lie down by his side. Alessandro made many excuses, but ended by undressing and obeying ; whereupon the abbot laid a hand on Alessandro's breast, and began to caress him just as amorous girls do their lovers ; whereat Alessandro marvelled greatly, doubting the abbot was prompted to such caresses by a shameful love. Which the abbot speedily divined, or else surmised from some movement on Alessandro's part, and, laughing, threw off a chemise which she had upon her, and taking Alessandro's hand, laid it on her bosom, saying :—" Alessandro, dismiss thy foolish thought, feel here, and learn what I conceal." Alessandro obeyed, laying a hand upon the abbot's bosom, where he encountered two little teats, round, firm and delicate, as they had been of ivory ; whereby he at once knew that 'twas a woman, and without awaiting further encouragement forthwith embraced her, and would have kissed her, when she said :—" Before thou art more familiar with me hearken to what I have to say to thee. As thou mayst perceive, I am no man, but a woman. Virgin I left my home, and was going to the Pope to obtain his sanction for my marriage, when, as Fortune willed, whether for thy gain or my loss, no sooner had I seen thee the other day, than I burned for thee with such a flame of love as never yet had lady for any man. Wherefore I am minded to have thee for my husband rather than any other ; so, if thou wilt not have me to wife, depart at once, and return to thine own place." Albeit he knew not who she was, Alessandro by the retinue which attended her conjectured that she must be noble and wealthy, and he saw that she was very fair ; so it was not long before he answered that, if such were her pleasure, it was very much to his liking. Whereupon she sate up, set a ring on his finger, and espoused him before a tiny

picture of our Lord ; after which they embraced, and to their
no small mutual satisfaction solaced themselves for the rest
of the night.　At daybreak Alessandro rose, and by preconcert
with the lady, left the chamber as he had entered it, so that
none knew where he had passed the night : then, blithe at
heart beyond measure, he rejoined the abbot and his train,
and so, resuming their journey, they after many days arrived
at Rome.　They had not been there more than a few days,
when the abbot, attended by the two knights and Alessandro,
waited on the Pope, whom, after making the due obeisance,
he thus addressed :—" Holy Father, as you must know better
than any other, whoso intends to lead a true and honourable
life ought, as far as may be, to shun all occasion of error ; for
which cause I, having a mind to live honourably, did, the better
to accomplish my purpose, assume the habit in which you see
me, and depart by stealth from the court of my father, the
King of England, who was minded to marry me, young as you
see me to be, to the aged King of Scotland ; and, carrying with
me not a little of his treasure, set my face hitherward that your
Holiness might bestow me in marriage.　Nor was it the age
of the King of Scotland that moved me to flee so much as fear
lest the frailty of my youth should, were I married to him,
betray me to commit some breach of divine law, and sully
the honour of my father's royal blood.　And as in this frame of
mind I journeyed, God, who knows best what is meet for every
one, did, as I believe, of His mercy shew me him whom He is
pleased to appoint me for my husband, even this young man "
(pointing to Alessandro) " whom you see by my side, who for
nobility of nature and bearing is a match for any great lady,
though the strain of his blood, perhaps, be not of royal purity.
Him, therefore, have I chosen, him will I have, and no other,
no matter what my father or any one else may think.　And
albeit the main purpose with which I started is fulfilled, yet I
have thought good to continue my journey, that I may visit
the holy and venerable places which abound in this city, and
your Holiness, and that so in your presence, and by consequence
in the presence of others, I may renew my marriage-vow with
Alessandro, whereof God alone was witness.　Wherefore I
humbly pray you that God's will and mine may be also yours,
and that you pronounce your benison thereon, that therewith,
having the more firm assurance of the favour of Him, whose
vicar you are, we may both live together, and, when the time
comes, die to God's glory and yours."

Alessandro was filled with wonder and secret delight, when he heard that his wife was the daughter of the King of England ; but greater still was the wonder of the two knights, and such their wrath that, had they been anywhere else than in the Pope's presence, they would not have spared to affront Alessandro, and perhaps the lady too. The Pope, on his part, found matter enough for wonder as well in the lady's habit as in her choice ; but, knowing that he could not refuse, he consented to grant her request.

He therefore began by smoothing the ruffled tempers of the knights, and having reconciled them with the lady and Alessandro, proceeded to put matters in train for the marriage. When the day appointed was come, he gave a great reception, at which were assembled all the cardinals and many other great lords ; to whom he presented the lady royally robed, and looking so fair and so gracious that she won, as she deserved, the praise of all, and likewise Alessandro, splendidly arrayed, and bearing himself not a whit like the young usurer but rather as one of royal blood, for which cause he received due honour from the knights. There, before the Pope himself, the marriage-vows were solemnly renewed ; and afterwards the marriage, which was accompanied by every circumstance that could add grace and splendour to the ceremony, received the sanction of his benediction. Alessandro and the lady on leaving Rome saw fit to visit Florence, whither fame had already wafted the news, so that they were received by the citizens with every token of honour. The lady set the three brothers at liberty, paying all their creditors, and reinstated them and their wives in their several properties. So, leaving gracious memories behind them, Alessandro and his lady, accompanied by Agolante, quitted Florence, and arriving at Paris were honourably received by the King. The two knights went before them to England, and by their influence induced the King to restore the lady to his favour, and receive her and his son-in-law with every circumstance of joy and honour. Alessandro he soon afterwards knighted with unwonted ceremony, and bestowed on him the earldom of Cornwall. And such was the Earl's consequence and influence at court that he restored peace between father and son, thereby conferring a great boon on the island and gaining the love and esteem of all the people. Agolante, whom he knighted, recovered all the outstanding debts in full, and returned to Florence immensely rich. The Earl passed the rest of his days with his lady in great renown. Indeed there are those who say, that with the help of his father-in-law he effected by his policy and valour the conquest of Scotland, and was crowned king of that country.

NOVEL IV

Landolfo Ruffolo is reduced to poverty, turns corsair, is captured by Genoese, is shipwrecked, escapes on a chest full of jewels, and, being cast ashore at Corfu, is hospitably entertained by a woman, and returns home wealthy.

WHEN Pampinea had brought her story to this glorious conclusion, Lauretta, who sate next her, delayed not, but thus began :—

Most gracious ladies, the potency of Fortune is never, methinks, more conspicuous than when she raises one, as in Pampinea's story we have seen her raise Alessandro, from abject misery to regal state. And such being the limits which our theme henceforth imposes on our invention, I shall feel no shame to tell a story wherein reverses yet greater are compensated by a sequel somewhat less dazzling. Well I know that my story, being compared with its predecessor, will therefore be followed with the less interest ; but, failing of necessity, I shall be excused.

Scarce any part of Italy is reputed so delectable as the seacoast between Reggio and Gaeta ; and in particular the slope which overlooks the sea by Salerno, and which the dwellers there call the Slope of Amalfi, is studded with little towns, gardens and fountains, and peopled by men as wealthy and enterprising in mercantile affairs as are anywhere to be found ; in one of which towns, to wit, Ravello, rich as its inhabitants are to-day, there was formerly a merchant, who surpassed them all in wealth, Landolfo Ruffolo by name, who yet, not content with his wealth, but desiring to double it, came nigh to lose it all and his own life to boot. Know, then, that this man, having made his calculations, as merchants are wont, bought a great ship, which, entirely at his own expense, he loaded with divers sorts of merchandise, and sailed to Cyprus. There he found several other ships, each laden with just such a cargo as his own, and was therefore fain to dispose of his goods at a very cheap rate, insomuch that he might almost as well have thrown them away, and was brought to the verge of ruin.

Mortified beyond measure to find himself thus reduced in a short space of time from opulence to something like poverty, he was at his wits' end, and rather than go home poor, having left home rich, he was minded to retrieve his losses by piracy or die in the attempt. So he sold his great ship, and with the price and the proceeds of the sale of his merchandise bought a light bark such as corsairs use, and having excellently well equipped her with the armament and all things else meet for such service, took to scouring the seas as a rover, preying upon all folk alike, but more particularly upon the Turk.

In this enterprise he was more favoured by Fortune than in his trading adventures. A year had scarce gone by before he had taken so many ships from the Turk that not only had he recovered the fortune which he had lost in trade, but was well on the way to doubling it. The bitter memory of his late losses taught him sobriety ; he estimated his gains and found them ample ; and lest he should have a second fall, he schooled himself to rest content with them, and made up his mind to return home without attempting to add to them. Shy of adventuring once more in trade, he refrained from investing them in any way, but shaped his course for home, carrying them with him in the very same bark in which he had gotten them. He had already entered the Archipelago when one evening a contrary wind sprang up from the south-east, bringing with it a very heavy sea, in which his bark could not well have lived. He therefore steered her into a bay under the lee of one of the islets, and there determined to await better weather. As he lay there two great carracks of Genoa, homeward-bound from Constantinople, found, not without difficulty, shelter from the tempest in the same bay. The masters of the carracks espied the bark, and found out to whom she belonged : the fame of Landolfo and his vast wealth had already reached them, and had excited their natural cupidity and rapacity. They therefore determined to capture the bark, which lay without means of escape. Part of their men, well armed with cross-bows and other weapons, they accordingly sent ashore, so posting them that no one could leave the bark without being exposed to the bolts ; the rest took to their boats, and rowed up to the side of Landolfo's little craft, which in a little time, with little trouble and no loss or risk, they captured with all aboard her. They then cleared the bark of all she contained, allowing Landolfo, whom they set aboard one of the carracks, only a pitiful doublet, and sunk her. Next day the wind shifted, and the carracks

set sail on a westerly course, which they kept prosperously
enough throughout the day ; but towards evening a tempest
arose, and the sea became very boisterous, so that the two
ships were parted one from the other. And such was the fury
of the gale that the ship, aboard which was poor, hapless
Landolfo, was driven with prodigious force upon a shoal off
the island of Cephalonia, and broke up and went to pieces
like so much glass dashed against a wall. Wherefore the
unfortunate wretches that were aboard her, launched amid the
floating merchandise and chests and planks with which the
sea was strewn, did as men commonly do in such a case ; and
though the night was of the murkiest and the sea rose and fell
in mountainous surges, such as could swim sought to catch hold
of whatever chance brought in their way. Among whom
hapless Landolfo, who only the day before had again and again
prayed for death, rather than he should return home in such
poverty, now, seeing death imminent, was afraid ; and, like
the rest, laid hold of the first plank that came to hand, in the
hope that, if he could but avoid immediate drowning, God
would in some way aid his escape. Gripping the beam with
his legs as best he might, while wind and wave tossed him hither
and thither, he contrived to keep himself afloat until broad day :
when, looking around him, he discerned nothing but clouds
and sea and a chest, which, borne by the wave, from time to
time drew nigh him to his extreme terror, for he apprehended
it might strike against the plank, and do him a mischief ; and
ever, as it came near him, he pushed it off with all the little
force he had in his hand. But, as it happened, a sudden gust
of wind swept down upon the sea, and struck the chest with
such force that it was driven against the plank on which
Landolfo was, and upset it, and Landolfo went under the
waves. Swimming with an energy begotten rather of fear
than of strength, he rose to the surface only to see the plank
so far from him that, doubting he could not reach it, he made
for the chest, which was close at hand ; and resting his breast
upon the lid, he did what he could to keep it straight with his
arms. In this manner, tossed to and fro by the sea, without
tasting food, for not a morsel had he with him, and drinking
more than he cared for, knowing not where he was, and seeing
nothing but the sea, he remained all that day, and the following
night. The next day, as the will of God, or the force of the
wind so ordered, more like a sponge than aught else, but still
with both hands holding fast by the edges of the chest, as we

see those do that clutch aught to save themselves from drowning, he was at length borne to the coast of the island of Corfu, where by chance a poor woman was just then scrubbing her kitchen-ware with sand and salt-water to make it shine. The woman caught sight of him as he drifted shorewards, but making out only a shapeless mass, was at first startled, and shrieked and drew back. Landolfo was scarce able to see, and uttered no sound, for his power of speech was gone. However, when the sea brought him close to the shore, she distinguished the shape of the chest, and gazing more intently, she first made out the arms strained over the chest, and then discerned the face and divined the truth. So, prompted by pity, she went out a little way into the sea, which was then calm, took him by the hair of the head, and drew him to land, chest and all. Then, not without difficulty she disengaged his hands from the chest, which she set on the head of a little girl, her daughter, that was with her, carried him home like a little child, and set him in a bath, where she chafed and laved him with warm water, until, the vital heat and some part of the strength which he had lost being restored, she saw fit to take him out and regale him with some good wine and comfits. Thus for some days she tended him as best she could, until he recovered his strength, and knew where he was. Then, in due time, the good woman, who had kept his chest safe, gave it back to him, and bade him try his fortune.

Landolfo could not recall the chest, but took it when she brought it to him, thinking that, however slight its value, it must suffice for a few days' charges. He found it very light, and quite lost hope ; but when the good woman was out of doors, he opened it to see what was inside, and found there a great number of precious stones, some set, others unset. Having some knowledge of such matters, he saw at a glance that the stones were of great value ; wherefore, feeling that he was still not forsaken by God, he praised His name, and quite recovered heart. But, having in a brief space of time been twice shrewdly hit by the bolts of Fortune, he was apprehensive of a third blow, and deemed it meet to use much circumspection in conveying his treasure home ; so he wrapped it up in rags as best he could, telling the good woman that he had no more use for the chest, but she might keep it if she wished, and give him a sack in exchange. This the good woman readily did ; and he, thanking her as heartily as he could for the service she had rendered him threw his sack over his shoulders, and, taking

ship, crossed to Brindisi. Thence he made his way by the
coast as far as Trani, where he found some of his townsfolk
that were drapers, to whom he narrated all his adventures
except that of the chest. They in charity gave him a suit
of clothes, and lent him a horse and their escort as far as
Ravello, whither, he said, he was minded to return. There,
thanking God for bringing him safe home, he opened his sack,
and examining its contents with more care than before, found
the number and fashion of the stones to be such that the sale
of them at a moderate price, or even less, would leave him
twice as rich as when he left Ravello. So, having disposed of
his stones, he sent a large sum of money to Corfu in recompense
of the service done him by the good woman who had rescued
him from the sea, and also to his friends at Trani who had
furnished him with the clothes; the residue he retained, and,
making no more ventures in trade, lived and died in honourable
estate.

NOVEL V

*Andreuccio da Perugia comes to Naples to buy horses, meets
with three serious adventures in one night, comes safe out
of them all, and returns home with a ruby.*

LANDOLFO'S find of stones, began Fiammetta, on whom the
narration now fell, has brought to my mind a story in which
there are scarce fewer perilous scapes than in Lauretta's story
but with this difference, that, instead of a course of perhaps
several years, a single night, as you shall hear, sufficed for their
occurrence.

In Perugia, by what I once gathered, there lived a young man,
Andreuccio di Pietro by name, a horse-dealer, who, having
learnt that horses were to be had cheap at Naples, put five
hundred florins of gold in his purse, and in company with some
other merchants went thither, never having been away from
home before. On his arrival at Naples, which was on a Sunday
evening, about vespers, he learnt from his host that the fair
would be held on the following morning. Thither accordingly
he then repaired, and looked at many horses which pleased
him much, and cheapening them more and more, and failing
to strike a bargain with any one, he from time to time, being
raw and unwary, drew out his purse of florins in view of all
that came and went, to shew that he meant business.

While he was thus chaffering, and after he had shewn his purse, there chanced to come by a Sicilian girl, fair as fair could be, but ready to pleasure any man for a small considera- tion. He did not see her, but she saw him and his purse, and forthwith said to herself :—" Who would be in better luck than I if all those florins were mine ? " and so she passed on. With the girl was an old woman, also a Sicilian, who, when she saw Andreuccio, dropped behind the girl, and ran towards him, making as if she would tenderly embrace him. The girl observing this said nothing, but stopped and waited a little way off for the old woman to rejoin her. Andreuccio turned as the old woman came up, recognised her, and greeted her very cordially ; but time and place not permitting much converse, she left him, promising to visit him at his inn ; and he resumed his chaffering, but bought nothing that morning.

Her old woman's intimate acquaintance with Andreuccio had no more escaped the girl's notice than the contents of Andreuccio's purse ; and with the view of devising, if possible, some way to make the money, either in whole or in part, her own, she began cautiously to ask the old woman, who and whence he was, what he did there, and how she came to know him. The old woman gave her almost as much and as circumstantial information touching Andreuccio and his affairs as he might have done himself, for she had lived a great while with his father, first in Sicily, and afterwards at Perugia. She likewise told the girl the name of his inn, and the purpose with which he had come to Naples. Thus fully armed with the names and all else that it was needful for her to know touching Andreuccio's kith and kin, the girl founded thereon her hopes of gratifying her cupidity, and forthwith devised a cunning stratagem to effect her purpose. Home she went, and gave the old woman work enough to occupy her all day, that she might not be able to visit Andreuccio ; then, summoning to her aid a little girl whom she had well trained for such services, she sent her about vespers to the inn where Andreuccio lodged. Arrived there, the little girl asked for Andreuccio of Andreuccio himself, who chanced to be just outside the gate. On his answering that he was the man, she took him aside, and said :—" Sir, a lady of this country, so please you, would fain speak with you." Whereto he listened with all his ears, and having a great conceit of his person, made up his mind that the lady was in love with him, as if there were ne'er another handsome fellow in Naples but himself : so forthwith he replied, that he would wait on

the lady, and asked where and when it would be her pleasure
to speak with him. " Sir," replied the little girl, " she expects
you in her own house, if you be pleased to come." " Lead
on then, I follow thee," said Andreuccio promptly, vouchsafing
never a word to any in the inn. So the little girl guided him
to her mistress's house, which was situated in a quarter the
character of which may be inferred from its name, Evil Hole.
Of this, however, he neither knew nor suspected aught, but,
supposing that the quarter was perfectly reputable and that
he was going to see a sweet lady, strode carelessly behind the
little girl into the house of her mistress, whom she summoned
by calling out, " Andreuccio is here " ; and Andreuccio then
saw her advance to the head of the stairs to await his ascent.
She was tall, still in the freshness of her youth, very fair of
face, and very richly and nobly clad. As Andreuccio
approached, she descended three steps to meet him with open
arms, and clasped him round the neck, but for a while stood
silent as if from excess of tenderness ; then, bursting into a
flood of tears, she kissed his brow, and in slightly broken
accents said :—" O Andreuccio, welcome, welcome, my
Andreuccio." Quite lost in wonder to be the recipient of
such caresses, Andreuccio could only answer :—" Madam,
well met." Whereupon she took him by the hand, led him
up into her saloon, and thence without another word into her
chamber, which exhaled throughout the blended fragrance of
roses, orange-blossoms and other perfumes. He observed a
handsome curtained bed, dresses in plenty hanging, as is
customary in that country, on pegs, and other appointments
very fair and sumptuous ; which sights, being strange to him,
confirmed his belief that he was in the house of no other than
a great lady. They sate down side by side on a chest at the
foot of the bed, and thus she began to speak :—" Andreuccio,
I cannot doubt that thou dost marvel both at the caresses
which I bestow upon thee, and at my tears, seeing that thou
knowest me not, and, maybe, hast never so much as heard
my name ; wait but a moment and thou shalt learn what
perhaps will cause thee to marvel still more, to wit, that I am
thy sister ; and I tell thee, that, since of God's especial grace
it is granted me to see one, albeit I would fain see all, of my
brothers before I die, I shall not meet death, when the hour
comes, without consolation ; but thou, perchance, hast never
heard aught of this ; wherefore listen to what I shall say to thee.
Pietro, my father and thine, as I suppose thou mayst have

heard, dwelt a long while at Palermo, where his good heart and
gracious bearing caused him to be (as he still is) much beloved
by all that knew him ; but by none was he loved so much as
by a gentlewoman, afterwards my mother, then a widow, who,
casting aside all respect for her father and brothers, ay, and her
honour, grew so intimate with him that a child was born,
which child am I, thy sister, whom thou seest before thee.
Shortly after my birth it so befell that Pietro must needs leave
Palermo and return to Perugia, and I, his little daughter, was
left behind with my mother at Palermo ; nor, so far as I have
been able to learn, did he ever again bestow a thought upon
either of us.   Wherefore—to say nothing of the love which he
should have borne me, his daughter by no servant or woman
of low degree—I should, were he not my father, gravely censure
the ingratitude which he shewed towards my mother, who,
prompted by a most loyal love, committed her fortune and her-
self to his keeping, without so much as knowing who he was.
But to what end ? The wrongs of long-ago are much more
easily censured than redressed ; enough that so it was.   He
left me a little girl at Palermo, where, when I was grown to
be almost as thou seest me, my mother, who was a rich lady,
gave me in marriage to an honest gentleman of the Girgenti
family, who for love of my mother and myself settled in Palermo,
and there, being a staunch Guelf, entered into correspondence
with our King Charles ;[1] which being discovered by King
Frederic[2] before the time was ripe for action, we had perforce
to flee from Sicily just when I was expecting to become the
greatest lady that ever was in the island.   So, taking with us
such few things as we could, few, I say, in comparison with the
abundance which we possessed, we bade adieu to our estates
and palaces, and found a refuge in this country, and such favour
with King Charles that, in partial compensation for the losses
which we had sustained on his account, he has granted us estates
and houses and an ample pension, which he regularly pays to
my husband and thy brother-in-law, as thou mayst yet see.
In this manner I live here ; but that I am blest with the sight
of thee, I ascribe entirely to the mercy of God ; and no thanks
to thee, my sweet brother."   So saying she embraced him again,
and melting anew into tears kissed his brow.

This story, so congruous, so consistent in every detail, came
trippingly and without the least hesitancy from her tongue.

1 Charles II. of Naples, son of Charles of Anjou.
2 Frederic II. of Sicily, younger son of Peter III. of Arragon.

Andreuccio remembered that his father had indeed lived at
Palermo ; he knew by his own experience the ways of young
folk, how prone they are to love ; he saw her melt into tears,
he felt her embraces and sisterly kisses ; and he took all she
said for gospel. So, when she had done, he answered :—
" Madam, it should not surprise you that I marvel, seeing that,
in sooth, my father, for whatever cause, said never a word
of you and your mother, or, if he did so, it came not to my
knowledge, so that I knew no more of you than if you had not
been ; wherefore, the lonelier I am here, and the less hope I
had of such good luck, the better pleased I am to have found
here my sister. And indeed, I know not any man, however
exalted his station, who ought not to be well pleased to have
such a sister ; much more, then, I, who am but a petty mer-
chant ; but, I pray you, resolve me of one thing : how came
you to know that I was here ? " Then answered she :—
" 'Twas told me this morning by a poor woman who is much
about the house, because, as she tells me, she was long in the
service of our father both at Palermo and at Perugia ; and,
but that it seemed more fitting that thou shouldst come to see
me at home than that I should visit thee at an inn, I had long
ago sought thee out." She then began to inquire particularly
after all his kinsfolk by name, and Andreuccio, becoming ever
more firmly persuaded of that which it was least for his good
to believe, answered all her questions. Their conversation
being thus prolonged and the heat great, she had Greek wine
and sweetmeats brought in, and gave Andreuccio to drink ;
and when towards supper-time he made as if he would leave,
she would in no wise suffer it ; but, feigning to be very much
vexed, she embraced him, saying :—" Alas ! now 'tis plain how
little thou carest for me : to think that thou art with thy
sister, whom thou seest for the first time, and in her own house,
where thou shouldst have alighted on thine arrival, and thou
wouldst fain depart hence to go sup at an inn ! Nay but, for
certain, thou shalt sup with me ; and albeit, to my great regret,
my husband is not here, thou shalt see that I can do a lady's
part in shewing thee honour." Andreuccio, not knowing what
else to say, replied :—" Sister, I care for you with all a brother's
affection ; but if I go not, supper will await me all the evening
at the inn, and I shall justly be taxed with discourtesy."
Then said she :—" Blessed be God, there is even now in the
house one by whom I can send word that they are not to expect
thee at the inn, albeit thou wouldst far better discharge the

debt of courtesy by sending word to thy friends, that they
come here to sup; and then, if go thou must, you might all
go in a body." Andreuccio replied, that he would have none
of his friends that evening, but since she would have him stay,
he would even do her the pleasure. She then made a shew of
sending word to the inn that they should not expect him at
dinner. Much more talk followed; and then they sate down
to a supper of many courses splendidly served, which she
cunningly protracted until nightfall; nor, when they were
risen from table, and Andreuccio was about to take his departure,
would she by any means suffer it, saying, that Naples was no
place to walk about in after dark, least of all for a stranger,
and that, as she had sent word to the inn that they were not
to expect him at supper, so she had done the like in regard of
his bed. Believing what she said, and being (in his false con-
fidence) overjoyed to be with her, he stayed. After supper
there was matter enough for talk both various and prolonged;
and, when the night was in a measure spent, she gave up her
own chamber to Andreuccio, leaving him with a small boy to
shew him aught that he might have need of, while she retired
with her women to another chamber.

It was a very hot night; so, no sooner was Andreuccio alone
than he stripped himself to his doublet, and drew off his stock-
ings and laid them on the bed's head; and nature demanding
a discharge of the surplus weight which he carried within him,
he asked the lad where this might be done, and was shewn a
door in a corner of the room, and told to go in there. Andreuccio,
nothing doubting, did so, but, by ill luck, set his foot on a plank
which was detached from the joist at the further end, whereby
down it went, and he with it. By God's grace he took no hurt
by the fall, though it was from some height, beyond sousing
himself from head to foot in the ordure which filled the whole
place, which, that you may the better understand what has
been said, and that which is to follow, I will describe to you.
A narrow and blind alley, such as we commonly see between
two houses, was spanned by planks supported by joists on either
side, and on the planks was the stool; of which planks that
which fell with Andreuccio was one. Now Andreuccio, finding
himself down there in the alley, fell to calling on the lad, who,
as soon as he heard him fall, had run off, and promptly let the
lady know what had happened. She hied forthwith to her
chamber, and after a hasty search found Andreuccio's clothes
and the money in them, for he foolishly thought to secure

himself against risk by carrying it always on his person, and thus being possessed of the prize for which she had played her ruse, passing herself off as the sister of a man of Perugia, whereas she was really of Palermo, she concerned herself no further with Andreuccio except to close with all speed the door by which he had gone out when he fell. As the lad did not answer, Andreuccio began to shout more loudly; but all to no purpose. Whereby his suspicions were aroused, and he began at last to perceive the trick that had been played upon him; so he climbed over a low wall that divided the alley from the street, and hied him to the door of the house, which he knew very well. There for a long while he stood shouting and battering the door till it shook on its hinges; but all again to no purpose. No doubt of his misadventure now lurking in his mind, he fell to bewailing himself, saying:—"Alas! in how brief a time have I lost five hundred florins and a sister!" with much more of the like sort. Then he recommenced battering the door and shouting, to such a tune that not a few of the neighbours were roused, and finding the nuisance intolerable, got up; and one of the lady's servant-girls presented herself at the window with a very sleepy air, and said angrily:—"Who knocks below there?" "Oh!" said Andreuccio, "dost not know me? I am Andreuccio, Madam Fiordaliso's brother." "Good man," she rejoined, "if thou hast had too much to drink, go, sleep it off, and come back to-morrow. I know not Andreuccio, nor aught of the fantastic stuff thou pratest; prithee begone and be so good as to let us sleep in peace." "How?" said Andreuccio, "dost not understand what I say? For sure thou dost understand; but if Sicilian kinships are of such a sort that folk forget them so soon, at least return me my clothes, which I left within, and right glad shall I be to be off." Half laughing she rejoined:—"Good man, methinks thou dost dream:" and so saying, she withdrew and closed the window. Andreuccio by this time needed no further evidence of his wrongs; his wrath knew no bounds, and mortification well-nigh converted it into frenzy; he was minded to exact by force what he had failed to obtain by entreaties; and so, arming himself with a large stone, he renewed his attack upon the door with fury, dealing much heavier blows than at first. Wherefore, not a few of the neighbours, whom he had already roused from their beds, set him down as an ill-conditioned rogue, and his story as a mere fiction intended to annoy the good woman,[1]

---

[1] *I.e.* the bawd

and resenting the din which he now made, came to their
windows, just as, when a stranger dog makes his appearance,
all the dogs of the quarter will run to bark at him, and called
out in chorus :—" 'Tis a gross affront to come at this time
of night to the house of the good woman with this silly story.
Prithee, good man, let us sleep in peace ; begone in God's
name ; and if thou hast a score to settle with her, come
to-morrow, but a truce to thy pestering to-night."

Emboldened, perhaps, by these words, a man who lurked
within the house, the good woman's bully, whom Andreuccio
had as yet neither seen nor heard, shewed himself at the window,
and said in a gruff voice and savage, menacing tone :—" Who is
below there ? " Andreuccio looked up in the direction of the
voice, and saw standing at the window, yawning and rubbing
his eyes as if he had just been roused from his bed, or at any
rate from deep sleep, a fellow with a black and matted beard,
who, as far as Andreuccio's means of judging went, bade fair
to prove a most redoubtable champion. It was not without
fear, therefore, that he replied :—" I am a brother of the lady
who is within." The bully did not wait for him to finish his
sentence, but, addressing him in a much sterner tone than
before, called out :—" I know not why I come not down and
give thee play with my cudgel, whilst thou givest me sign of
life, ass, tedious driveller that thou must needs be, and drunken
sot, thus to disturb our night's rest." Which said, he withdrew,
and closed the window. Some of the neighbours who best
knew the bully's quality gave Andreuccio fair words. " For
God's sake," said they, " good man, take thyself off, stay not
here to be murdered. 'Twere best for thee to go." These
counsels, which seemed to be dictated by charity, reinforced
the fear which the voice and aspect of the bully had inspired
in Andreuccio, who, thus despairing of recovering his money
and in the deepest of dumps, set his face towards the quarter
whence in the daytime he had blindly followed the little girl,
and began to make his way back to the inn. But so noisome
was the stench which he emitted that he resolved to turn
aside and take a bath in the sea. So he bore leftward up a
street called Ruga Catalana, and was on his way towards the
steep of the city, when by chance he saw two men coming
towards him, bearing a lantern, and fearing that they might
be patrols or other men who might do him a mischief, he stole
away and hid himself in a dismantled house to avoid them. The
house, however, was presently entered by the two men, just as

if they had been guided thither ; and one of them having dis-
burdened himself of some iron tools which he carried on his
shoulder, they both began to examine them, passing meanwhile
divers comments upon them.   While they were thus occupied,
" What," said one, "means this ?   Such a stench as never
before did I smell the like ! "   So saying, he raised the lantern
a little ; whereby they had a view of hapless Andreuccio, and
asked   in   amazement :—" Who   is   there ? "   Whereupon
Andreuccio was at first silent, but when they flashed the light
close upon him, and asked him what he did there in such a
filthy state, he told them all that had befallen him.   Casting
about to fix the place where it occurred, they said one to
another :—" Of a surety 'twas in the house of Scarabone
Buttafuoco."   Then said one, turning to Andreuccio :—" Good
man, albeit thou hast lost thy money, thou hast cause enough
to praise God that thou hadst the luck to fall ; for hadst thou
not fallen, be sure that, no sooner wert thou asleep, than thou
hadst been knocked on the head, and lost not only thy money
but thy life.   But what boots it now to bewail thee ?   Thou
mightest as soon pluck a star from the firmament as recover a
single denier ; nay, 'tis as much as thy life is worth if he do
but hear that thou breathest a word of the affair."

The two men then held a short consultation, at the close of
which they said :—" Lo now ; we are sorry for thee, and so we
make thee a fair offer.   If thou wilt join with us in a little
matter which we have in hand, we doubt not but thy share of
the gain will greatly exceed what thou hast lost."   Andreuccio,
being now desperate, answered that he was ready to join them.
Now Messer Filippo Minutolo, Archbishop of Naples, had that
day been buried with a ruby on his finger, worth over five hun-
dred florins of gold, besides other ornaments of extreme value.
The two men were minded to despoil the Archbishop of his fine
trappings, and imparted their design to Andreuccio, who,
cupidity getting the better of caution, approved it ; and so
they all three set forth.   But as they were on their way to the
cathedral, Andreuccio gave out so rank an odour that one said
to the other :—" Can we not contrive that he somehow wash
himself a little, that he stink not so shrewdly ? "   " Why yes,"
said the other, " we are now close to a well, which is never
without the pulley and a large bucket ; 'tis but a step thither,
and we will wash him out of hand."   Arrived at the well, they
found that the rope was still there, but the bucket had been
removed ; so they determined to attach him to the rope, and

lower him into the well, there to wash himself, which done, he
was to jerk the rope, and they would draw him up. Lowered
accordingly he was ; but just as, now washen, he jerked the
rope, it so happened that a company of patrols, being thirsty
because 'twas a hot night and some rogue had led them a pretty
dance, came to the well to drink. The two men fled, unobserved,
as soon as they caught sight of the newcomers, who, parched
with thirst, laid aside their bucklers, arms and surcoats, and
fell to hauling on the rope, supposing that it bore the bucket,
full of water. When, therefore, they saw Andreuccio, as he
neared the brink of the well, loose the rope and clutch the
brink with his hands, they were stricken with a sudden terror,
and without uttering a word let go the rope, and took to flight
with all the speed they could make. Whereat Andreuccio
marvelled mightily, and had he not kept a tight grip on the
brink of the well, he would certainly have gone back to the
bottom and hardly have escaped grievous hurt, or death. Still
greater was his astonishment, when, fairly landed on *terra firma*,
he found the patrols' arms lying there, which he knew had not
been carried by his comrades. He felt a vague dread, he knew
not why ; he bewailed once more his evil fortune ; and without
venturing to touch the arms, he left the well and wandered he
knew not whither. As he went, however, he fell in with his
two comrades, now returning to draw him out of the well ;
who no sooner saw him than in utter amazement they demanded
who had hauled him up. Andreuccio answered that he knew
not, and then told them in detail how it had come about, and
what he had found beside the well. They laughed as they
apprehended the circumstances, and told him why they had
fled, and who they were that had hauled him up. Then without
further parley, for it was now midnight, they hied them to the
cathedral. They had no difficulty in entering and finding the
tomb, which was a magnificent structure of marble, and with
their iron implements they raised the lid, albeit it was very
heavy, to a height sufficient to allow a man to enter, and propped
it up. This done, a dialogue ensued. " Who shall go in ? "
said one. " Not I," said the other. " Nor I," rejoined his
companion ; " let Andreuccio go in." " That will not I," said
Andreuccio. Whereupon both turned upon him and said :—
" How ? thou wilt not go in ? By God, if thou goest not in,
we will give thee that over the pate with one of these iron
crowbars that thou shalt drop down dead." Terror-stricken,
into the tomb Andreuccio went, saying to himself as he did so :—

" These men will have me go in, that they may play a trick
upon me : when I have handed everything up to them, and
am sweating myself to get out of the tomb, they will be off about
their business, and I shall be left with nothing for my pains."
So he determined to make sure of his own part first ; and
bethinking him of the precious ring of which he had heard them
speak, as soon as he had completed the descent, he drew the
ring off the Archbishop's finger, and put it on his own : he then
handed up one by one the crosier, mitre and gloves, and other
of the Archbishop's trappings, stripping him to his shirt ; which
done, he told his comrades that there was nothing more. They
insisted that the ring must be there, and bade him search every-
where. This he feigned to do, ejaculating from time to time
that he found it not ; and thus he kept them a little while in
suspense. But they, who were in their way as cunning as he,
kept on exhorting him to make a careful search, and, seizing
their opportunity, withdrew the prop that supported the lid of
the tomb, and took to their heels, leaving him there a close
prisoner. You will readily conceive how Andreuccio behaved
when he understood his situation. More than once he applied
his head and shoulders to the lid and sought with might and
main to heave it up ; but all his efforts were fruitless ; so that
at last, overwhelmed with anguish he fell in a swoon on the
corpse of the Archbishop, and whether of the twain were the
more lifeless, Andreuccio or the Archbishop, 'twould have
puzzled an observer to determine.

When he came to himself he burst into a torrent of tears,
seeing now nothing in store for him but either to perish there
of hunger and fetid odours beside the corpse and among the
worms, or, should the tomb be earlier opened, to be taken and
hanged as a thief. These most lugubrious meditations were
interrupted by a sound of persons walking and talking in the
church. They were evidently a numerous company, and their
purpose, as Andreuccio surmised, was the very same with which
he and his comrades had come thither : whereby his terror was
mightily increased. Presently the folk opened the tomb, and
propped up the lid, and then fell to disputing as to who should
go in. None was willing, and the contention was protracted ;
but at length one—'twas a priest—said :—" Of what are ye
afeared ? Think ye to be eaten by him ? Nay, the dead eat
not the living. I will go in myself." So saying he propped
his breast upon the edge of the lid, threw his head back, and
thrust his legs within, that he might go down feet foremost.

On sight whereof Andreuccio started to his feet, and seizing hold of one of the priest's legs, made as if he would drag him down ; which caused the priest to utter a prodigious yell, and bundle himself out of the tomb with no small celerity. The rest took to flight in a panic, as if a hundred thousand devils were at their heels. The tomb being thus left open, Andreuccio, the ring still on his finger, sprang out. The way by which he had entered the church served him for egress, and roaming at random, he arrived towards daybreak at the coast. Diverging thence he came by chance upon his inn, where he found that his host and his comrades had been anxious about him all night. When he told them all that had befallen him, they joined with the host in advising him to leave Naples at once. He accordingly did so, and returned to Perugia, having invested in a ring the money with which he had intended to buy horses.

NOVEL VI

Madam Beritola loses two sons, is found with two kids on an island, goes thence to Lunigiana, where one of her sons takes service with her master, and lies with his daughter, for which he is put in prison. Sicily rebels against King Charles, the son is recognised by the mother, marries the master's daughter, and, his brother being discovered, is reinstated in great honour.

THE ladies and the young men alike had many a hearty laugh over Fiammetta's narrative of Andreuccio's adventures, which ended, Emilia, at the queen's command, thus began :—

Grave and grievous are the vicissitudes with which Fortune makes us acquainted, and as discourse of such matter serves to awaken our minds, which are so readily lulled to sleep by her flatteries, I deem it worthy of attentive hearing by all, whether they enjoy her favour or endure her frown, in that it ministers counsel to the one sort and consolation to the other. Wherefore, albeit great matters have preceded it, I mean to tell you a story, not less true than touching, of adventures whereof the issue was indeed felicitous, but the antecedent bitterness so long drawn out that scarce can I believe that it was ever sweetened by ensuing happiness.

Dearest ladies, you must know that after the death of the Emperor Frederic II. the crown of Sicily passed to Manfred ; whose favour was enjoyed in the highest degree by a gentleman

of Naples, Arrighetto Capece by name, who had to wife Madonna
Beritola Caracciola, a fair and gracious lady, likewise a Neapoli-
tan. Now when Manfred was conquered and slain by King
Charles I. at Benevento, and the whole realm transferred its
allegiance to the conqueror, Arrighetto, who was then governor
of Sicily, no sooner received the tidings than he prepared for
instant flight, knowing that little reliance was to be placed on
the fleeting faith of the Sicilians, and not being minded to
become a subject of his master's enemy. But the Sicilians
having intelligence of his plans, he and many other friends and
servants of King Manfred were surprised, taken prisoners and
delivered over to King Charles, to whom the whole island was
soon afterwards surrendered. In this signal reversal of the
wonted course of things Madam Beritola, knowing not what
was become of Arrighetto, and from the past ever auguring
future evil, lest she should suffer foul dishonour, abandoned all
that she possessed, and with a son of, perhaps, eight years,
Giusfredi by name, being also pregnant, fled in a boat to Lipari,
where she gave birth to another male child, whom she named
Outcast. Then with her sons and a hired nurse she took ship
for Naples, intending there to rejoin her family. Events,
however, fell out otherwise than she expected ; for by stress of
weather the ship was carried out of her course to the desert
island of Ponza,[1] where they put in to a little bay until such
time as they might safely continue their voyage. Madam
Beritola landed with the rest on the island, and, leaving them
all, sought out a lonely and secluded spot, and there abandoned
herself to melancholy brooding on the loss of her dear Arrighetto.
While thus she spent her days in solitary preoccupation with
her grief it chanced that a galley of corsairs swooped down upon
the island, and, before either the mariners or any other folk
were aware of their peril, made an easy capture of them all and
sailed away ; so that, when Madam Beritola, her wailing for
that day ended, returned, as was her wont, to the shore to
solace herself with the sight of her sons, she found none there.
At first she was lost in wonder, then with a sudden suspicion of
the truth she bent her eyes seaward, and there saw the galley
still at no great distance, towing the ship in her wake. Thus
apprehending beyond all manner of doubt that she had lost her
sons as well as her husband, and that, alone, desolate and
destitute, she might not hope that any of her lost ones would
ever be restored to her, she fell down on the shore in a swoon

[1] The largest, now inhabited, of a group of islets in the Gulf of Gaeta.

with the names of her husband and sons upon her lips. None
was there to administer cold water or aught else that might
recall her truant powers ; her animal spirits might even wander
whithersoever they would at their sweet will : strength, however,
did at last return to her poor exhausted frame, and therewith
tears and lamentations, as, plaintively repeating her sons'
names, she roamed in quest of them from cavern to cavern.
Long time she sought them thus ; but when she saw that her
labour was in vain, and that night was closing in, hope, she
knew not why, began to return, and with it some degree of
anxiety on her own account. Wherefore she left the shore and
returned to the cavern where she had been wont to indulge her
plaintive mood. She passed the night in no small fear and
indescribable anguish ; the new day came, and, as she had not
supped, she was fain after tierce to appease her hunger, as best
she could, by a breakfast of herbs : this done, she wept and
began to ruminate on her future way of life. While thus
engaged, she observed a she-goat come by and go into an
adjacent cavern, and after a while come forth again and go
into the wood : thus roused from her reverie she got up, went
into the cavern from which the she-goat had issued, and there
saw two kids, which might have been born that very day, and
seemed to her the sweetest and the most delicious things in the
world : and, having, by reason of her recent delivery, milk still
within her, she took them up tenderly, and set them to her
breast. They, nothing loath, sucked at her teats as if she had
been their own dam ; and thenceforth made no distinction
between her and the dam. Which caused the lady to feel that
she had found company in the desert ; and so, living on herbs
and water, weeping as often as she bethought her of her husband
and sons and her past life, she disposed herself to live and die
there, and became no less familiar with the she-goat than with
her young.

The gentle lady thus leading the life of a wild creature, it
chanced that after some months stress of weather brought a
Pisan ship to the very same bay in which she had landed. The
ship lay there for several days, having on board a gentleman,
Currado de' Malespini by name (of the same family as the
Marquis), who with his noble and most devout lady was return-
ing home from a pilgrimage, having visited all the holy places
in the realm of Apulia. To beguile the tedium of the sojourn
Currado with his lady, some servants and his dogs, set forth
one day upon a tour through the island. As they neared the

place where Madam Beritola dwelt, Currado's dogs on view of
the two kids, which, now of a fair size, were grazing, gave chase.
The kids, pursued by the dogs, made straight for Madam
Beritola's cavern. She, seeing what was toward, started to
her feet, caught up a stick, and drove the dogs back. Currado
and his lady coming up after the dogs, gazed on Madam Beritola,
now tanned and lean and hairy, with wonder, which she more
than reciprocated. At her request Currado called off the dogs ;
and then he and his lady besought her again and again to say
who she was and what she did there. So she told them all about
herself, her rank, her misfortunes, and the savage life which
she was minded to lead. Currado, who had known Arrighetto
Capece very well, was moved to tears by compassion, and
exhausted all his eloquence to induce her to change her mind,
offering to escort her home, or to take her to live with him in
honourable estate as his sister until God should vouchsafe her
kindlier fortune. The lady declining all his offers, Currado left
her with his wife, whom he bade see that food was brought
thither, and let Madam Beritola, who was all in rags, have one
of her own dresses to wear, and do all that she could to persuade
her to go with them. So the gentle lady stayed with Madam
Beritola, and after condoling with her at large on her misfortunes,
had food and clothing brought to her, and with the greatest
difficulty in the world prevailed upon her to eat and dress
herself. At last, after much beseeching, she induced her to
depart from her oft-declared intention never to go where she
might meet any that knew her, and accompany them to Luni-
giana, taking with her the two kids and the dam, which latter
had in the meantime returned, and to the gentle lady's great
surprise had greeted Madam Beritola with the utmost affection.
So with the return of fair weather Madam Beritola, taking with
her the dam and the two kids, embarked with Currado and his
lady on their ship, being called by them—for her true name
was not to be known of all—Cavriuola ; [1] and the wind holding
fair, they speedily reached the mouth of the Magra, [2] and landing
hied them to Currado's castle ; where Madam Beritola abode
with Currado's lady in the quality of her maid, serving her well
and faithfully, wearing widow's weeds and feeding and tending
her kids with assiduous and loving care.

The corsairs, who, not espying Madam Beritola, had left her
at Ponza when they took the ship on which she had come
thither, had made a course to Genoa, taking with them all the

[1] *I.e.* she-goat.   [2] Between Liguria and Tuscany.

other folk. On their arrival the owners of the galley shared
the booty, and so it happened that as part thereof Madam
Beritola's nurse and her two boys fell to the lot of one Messer
Guasparrino d'Oria, who sent all three to his house, being
minded to keep them there as domestic slaves. The nurse,
beside herself with grief at the loss of her mistress and the
woful plight in which she found herself and her two charges,
shed many a bitter tear. But, seeing that they were unavailing,
and that she and the boys were slaves together, she, having,
for all her low estate, her share of wit and good sense, made it
her first care to comfort them ; then, regardful of the condition
to which they were reduced, she bethought her, that, if the lads
were recognised, 'twould very likely be injurious to them. So,
still hoping that some time or another Fortune would change
her mood, and they be able, if living, to regain their lost estate,
she resolved to let none know who they were, until she saw a
fitting occasion ; and accordingly, whenever she was questioned
thereof by any, she gave them out as her own children. The
name of the elder she changed from Giusfredi to Giannotto di
Procida ; the name of the younger she did not think it worth
while to change. She spared no pains to make Giusfredi under-
stand the reason why she had changed his name, and the risk
which he might run if he were recognised. This she impressed
upon him not once only but many times ; and the boy, who
was apt to learn, followed the instructions of the wise nurse with
perfect exactitude.

So the two boys, ill clad and worse shod, continued with the
nurse in Messer Guasparrino's house for two years, patiently
performing all kinds of menial offices. But Giannotto, being
now sixteen years old, and of a spirit that consorted ill with
servitude, brooked not the baseness of his lot, and dismissed
himself from Messer Guasparrino's service by getting aboard a
galley bound for Alexandria, and travelled far and wide, and
fared never the better. In the course of his wanderings he
learned that his father, whom he had supposed to be dead, was
still living, but kept in prison under watch and ward by King
Charles. He was grown a tall handsome young man, when,
perhaps three or four years after he had given Messer Guas-
parrino the slip, weary of roaming and all but despairing of his
fortune, he came to Lunigiana, and by chance took service with
Currado Malespini, who found him handy, and was well-pleased
with him. His mother, who was in attendance on Currado's
lady, he seldom saw, and never recognised her, nor she him ;

so much had time changed both from their former aspect since they last met. While Giannotto was thus in the service of Currado, it fell out by the death of Niccolò da Grignano that his widow, Spina, Currado's daughter, returned to her father's house. Very fair she was and loveable, her age not more than sixteen years, and so it was that she saw Giannotto with favour, and he her, and both fell ardently in love with one another. Their passion was early gratified ; but several months elapsed before any detected its existence. Wherefore, growing overbold, they began to dispense with the precautions which such an affair demanded. So one day, as they walked with others through a wood, where the trees grew fair and close, the girl and Giannotto left the rest of the company some distance behind, and, thinking that they were well in advance, found a fair pleasaunce girt in with trees and carpeted with abundance of grass and flowers, and fell to solacing themselves after the manner of lovers. Long time they thus dallied, though such was their delight that all too brief it seemed to them, and so it befell that they were surprised first by the girl's mother and then by Currado. Pained beyond measure by what he had seen, Currado, without assigning any cause, had them both arrested by three of his servants and taken in chains to one of his castles ; where in a frenzy of passionate wrath he left them, resolved to put them to an ignominious death. The girl's mother was also very angry, and deemed her daughter's fall deserving of the most rigorous chastisement, but, when by one of Currado's chance words she divined the doom which he destined for the guilty pair, she could not reconcile herself to it, and hasted to intercede with her angry husband, beseeching him to refrain the impetuous wrath which would hurry him in his old age to murder his daughter and imbrue his hands in the blood of his servant, and vent it in some other way, as by close confinement and duress, whereby the culprits should be brought to repent them of their fault in tears. Thus, and with much more to the like effect, the devout lady urged her suit, and at length prevailed upon her husband to abandon his murderous design. Wherefore, he commanded that the pair should be confined in separate prisons, and closely guarded, and kept short of food and in sore discomfort, until further order ; which was accordingly done ; and the life which the captives led, their endless tears, their fasts of inordinate duration, may be readily imagined.

Giannotto and Spina had languished in this sorry plight for full a year, entirely ignored by Currado, when in concert with

Messer Gian di Procida, King Peter of Arragon raised a rebellion [1]
in the island of Sicily, and wrested it from King Charles, whereat
Currado, being a Ghibelline, was overjoyed. Hearing the
tidings from one of his warders, Giannotto heaved a great sigh,
and said :—" Alas, fourteen years have I been a wanderer upon
the face of the earth, looking for no other than this very event ;
and now, that my hopes of happiness may be for ever frustrate,
it has come to pass only to find me in prison, whence I may
never think to issue alive." " How ? " said the warder ;
" what signify to thee these doings of these mighty monarchs ?
What part hadst thou in Sicily ? " Giannotto answered :—
" 'Tis as if my heart were breaking when I bethink me of my
father and what part he had in Sicily. I was but a little lad
when I fled the island, but yet I remember him as its governor
in the time of King Manfred." " And who then was thy
father ? " demanded the warder. " His name," rejoined
Giannotto, " I need no longer scruple to disclose, seeing that I
find myself in the very strait which I hoped to avoid by con-
cealing it. He was and still is, if he live, Arrighetto Capece ;
and my name is not Giannotto but Giusfredi ; and I doubt not
but, were I once free, and back in Sicily, I might yet hold a very
honourable position in the island."

The worthy man asked no more questions, but, as soon as he
found opportunity, told what he had learned to Currado ; who,
albeit he made light of it in the warder's presence, repaired to
Madam Beritola, and asked her in a pleasant manner, whether
she had had by Arrighetto a son named Giusfredi. The lady
answered, in tears, that, if the elder of her two sons were living,
such would be his name, and his age twenty-two years. This
inclined Currado to think that Giannotto and Giusfredi were
indeed one and the same ; and it occurred to him, that, if so it
were, he might at once shew himself most merciful and blot
out his daughter's shame and his own by giving her to him in
marriage ; wherefore he sent for Giannotto privily, and ques-
tioned him in detail touching his past life. And finding by
indubitable evidence that he was indeed Giusfredi, son of
Arrighetto Capece, he said to him :—" Giannotto, thou knowest
the wrong which thou hast done me in the person of my daughter,
what and how great it is, seeing that I used thee well and kindly,
and thou shouldst therefore, like a good servant, have shewn
thyself jealous of my honour, and zealous in my interest ; and
many there are who, hadst thou treated them as thou hast

treated me, would have caused thee to die an ignominious death ; which my clemency would not brook. But now, as it is even so as thou sayst, and thou art of gentle blood by both thy parents, I am minded to put an end to thy sufferings as soon as thou wilt, releasing thee from the captivity in which thou languishest, and setting thee in a happy place, and reinstating at once thy honour and my own. Thy intimacy with Spina—albeit shameful to both—was yet prompted by love. Spina, as thou knowest, is a widow, and her dower is ample and secure. What her breeding is, and her father's and her mother's, thou knowest : of thy present condition I say nought. Wherefore, when thou wilt, I am consenting, that, having been with dishonour thy friend, she become with honour thy wife, and that, so long as it seem good to thee, thou tarry here with her and me as my son."

Captivity had wasted Giannotto's flesh, but had in no degree impaired the generosity of spirit which he derived from his ancestry, or the whole-hearted love which he bore his lady. So, albeit he ardently desired that which Currado offered, and knew that he was in Currado's power, yet, even as his magnanimity prompted, so, unswervingly, he made answer :— " Currado, neither ambition nor cupidity nor aught else did ever beguile me to any treacherous machination against either thy person or thy property. Thy daughter I loved, and love and shall ever love, because I deem her worthy of my love ; and, if I dealt with her after a fashion which to the mechanic mind seems hardly honourable, I did but commit that fault which is ever congenial to youth, which can never be eradicated so long as youth continues, and which, if the aged would but remember that they were once young and would measure the delinquencies of others by their own and their own by those of others, would not be deemed so grave as thou and many others depict it ; and what I did, I did as a friend, not as an enemy. That which thou offerest I have ever desired, and should long ago have sought, had I supposed that thou wouldst grant it, and 'twill be the more grateful to me in proportion to the depth of my despair. But if thy intent be not such as thy words import, feed me not with vain hopes, but send me back to prison, there to suffer whatever thou mayst be pleased to inflict ; nor doubt that even as I love Spina, so for love of her shall I ever love thee, though thou do thy worst, and still hold thee in reverent regard."

Currado marvelled to hear him thus speak, and being assured of his magnanimity and the fervour of his love, held him the

more dear ; wherefore he rose, embraced and kissed him, and
without further delay bade privily bring thither Spina, who
left her prison wasted and wan and weak, and so changed that
she seemed almost another woman than of yore, even as Gian-
notto was scarce his former self. Then and there in Currado's
presence they plighted their troth according to our custom of
espousals ; and some days afterwards Currado, having in the
meantime provided all things meet for their convenience and
solace, yet so as that none should surmise what had happened,
deemed it now time to gladden their mothers with the news.
So he sent for his lady and Cavriuola, and thus, addressing first
Cavriuola, he spoke :—" What would you say, madam, were I
to restore you your elder son as the husband of one of my
daughters ? " Cavriuola answered :—" I should say, that,
were it possible for you to strengthen the bond which attaches
me to you, then assuredly you had so done, in that you restored
to me that which I cherish more tenderly than myself, and in
such a guise as in some measure to renew within me the hope
which I had lost : more I could not say." And so, weeping,
she was silent. Then, turning to his lady, Currado said :—
" And thou, madam, what wouldst thou think if I were to
present thee with such a son-in-law ? " " A son-in-law," she
answered, " that was not of gentle blood, but a mere churl, so
he pleased you, would well content me." " So ! " returned
Currado ; " I hope within a few days to gladden the hearts of
both of you."

He waited only until the two young folk had recovered their
wonted mien, and were clad in a manner befitting their rank.
Then, addressing Giusfredi, he said :—" Would it not add
to thy joy to see thy mother here ? " " I dare not hope,"
returned Giusfredi, " that she has survived calamities and
sufferings such as hers ; but were it so, great indeed would
be my joy, and none the less that by her counsel I might be
aided to the recovery (in great measure) of my lost heritage
in Sicily." Whereupon Currado caused both the ladies to come
thither, and presented to them the bride. The gladness with
which they both greeted her was a wonder to behold, and no
less great was their wonder at the benign inspiration that had
prompted Currado to unite her in wedlock with Giannotto,
whom Currado's words caused Madam Beritola to survey with
some attention. A hidden spring of memory was thus touched ;
she recognised in the man the lineaments of her boy, and
awaiting no further evidence she ran with open arms and threw

herself upon his neck.   No word did she utter, for very excess
of maternal tenderness and joy ; but, every avenue of sense
closed, she fell as if bereft of life within her son's embrace.
Giannotto, who had often seen her in the castle and never
recognised her, marvelled not a little, but nevertheless it at
once flashed upon him that 'twas his mother, and blaming
himself for his past inadvertence he took her in his arms and
wept and tenderly kissed her.   With gentle solicitude Currado's
lady and Spina came to her aid, and restored her suspended
animation with cold water and other remedies.   She then with
many tender and endearing words kissed him a thousand times
or more, which tokens of her love he received with a look of
reverential acknowledgment.   Thrice, nay a fourth time were
these glad and gracious greetings exchanged, and joyful
indeed were they that witnessed them, and hearkened while
mother and son compared their past adventures.   Then Currado,
who had already announced his new alliance to his friends,
and received their felicitations, proceeded to give order for the
celebration of the event with all becoming gaiety and splendour.
As he did so, Giusfredi said to him :—" Currado, you have
long given my mother honourable entertainment, and on me
you have conferred many boons ; wherefore, that you may
fill up the measure of your kindness, 'tis now my prayer that
you be pleased to gladden my mother and my marriage feast
and me with the presence of my brother, now in servitude in
the house of Messer Guasparrino d'Oria, who, as I have already
told you, made prize of both him and me ; and that then you
send some one to Sicily, who shall make himself thoroughly
acquainted with the circumstances and condition of the country,
and find out how it has fared with my father Arrighetto,
whether he be alive or dead, and if alive, in what circumstances,
and being thus fully informed, return to us with the tidings."
Currado assented, and forthwith sent most trusty agents both
to Genoa and to Sicily.   So in due time an envoy arrived at
Genoa, and made instant suit to Guasparrino on Currado's
part for the surrender of Outcast and the nurse, setting forth
in detail all that had passed between Currado and Giusfredi
and his mother.   Whereat Messer Guasparrino was mightily
astonished, and said :—" Of a surety there is nought that, being
able, I would not do to pleasure Currado ; and true it is that
I have had in my house for these fourteen years the boy whom
thou dost now demand of me, and his mother, and gladly will
I surrender them ; but tell Currado from me to beware of

excessive credulity, and to put no faith in the idle tales of
Giannotto, or Giusfredi, as thou sayst he calls himself, who
is by no means so guileless as he supposes."

Then, having provided for the honourable entertainment of
the worthy envoy, he sent privily for the nurse, and cautiously
sounded her as to the affair. The nurse had heard of the
revolt of Sicily, and had learned that Arrighetto was still alive.
She therefore banished fear, and told Messer Guasparrino the
whole story, and explained to him the reasons why she had
acted as she had done. Finding that what she said accorded
very well with what he had learned from Currado's envoy, he
inclined to credit the story, and most astutely probing the matter
in divers ways, and always finding fresh grounds for confidence,
he reproached himself for the sorry manner in which he had
treated the boy, and by way of amends gave him one of his
own daughters, a beautiful girl of eleven years, to wife with a
dowry suited to Arrighetto's rank, and celebrated their nuptials
with great festivity. He then brought the boy and girl,
Currado's envoy, and the nurse in a well-armed galliot to
Lerici, being there met by Currado, who had a castle not far
off, where great preparations had been made for their enter-
tainment : and thither accordingly he went with his whole
company. What cheer the mother had of her son, the brothers
of one another, and all the three of the faithful nurse ; what
cheer Messer Guasparrino and his daughter had of all, and all
of them, and what cheer all had of Currado and his lady and
their sons and their friends, words may not describe ; wherefore,
my ladies, I leave it to your imagination. And that their
joy might be full, God, who, when He gives, gives most
abundantly, added the glad tidings that Arrighetto Capece
was alive and prosperous. For, when in the best of spirits the
ladies and gentlemen had sat them down to feast, and they
were yet at the first course, the envoy from Sicily arrived, and
among other matters reported that, no sooner had the insurrec-
tion broken out in the island than the people hied them in hot
haste to the prison where Arrighetto was kept in confinement
by King Charles, and despatching the guards, brought him
forth, and knowing him to be a capital enemy to King Charles
made him their captain, and under his command fell upon and
massacred the French. Whereby he had won the highest place
in the favour of King Peter, who had granted him restitution
of all his estates and honours, so that he was now both prosperous
and mighty. The envoy added that Arrighetto had received

him with every token of honour, had manifested the utmost delight on hearing of his lady and son, of whom no tidings had reached him since his arrest, and had sent, to bring them home, a brigantine with some gentlemen aboard, whose arrival might hourly be expected.

The envoy, and the good news which he brought, were heartily welcome ; and presently Currado, with some of his friends, encountered the gentlemen who came for Madam Beritola and Giusfredi, and saluting them cordially invited them to his feast, which was not yet half done. Joy unheard-of was depicted on the faces of the lady, of Giusfredi, and of all the rest as they greeted them ; nor did they on their part take their places at the table before, as best they might, they had conveyed to Currado and his lady Arrighetto's greetings and grateful acknowledgments of the honour which they had conferred upon his lady and his son, and had placed Arrighetto, to the uttermost of his power, entirely at their service. Then, turning to Messer Guasparrino, of whose kindness Arrighetto surmised nothing, they said that they were very sure that, when he learned the boon which Outcast had received at his hands, he would pay him the like and an even greater tribute of gratitude. This speech ended, they feasted most joyously with the brides and bridegrooms. So passed the day, the first of many which Currado devoted to honouring his son in law and his other intimates, both kinsfolk and friends. The time of festivity ended, Madam Beritola and Giusfredi and the rest felt that they must leave : so, taking Spina with them, they parted, not without many tears, from Currado and his lady and Guasparrino, and went aboard the brigantine, which, wafted by a prosperous wind, soon brought them to Sicily. At Palermo they were met by Arrighetto, who received them all, ladies and sons alike, with such cheer as it were vain to attempt to describe. There it is believed that they all lived long and happily and in amity with God, being not unmindful of the blessings which He had conferred upon them.

NOVEL VII

The Soldan of Babylon sends one of his daughters overseas, design-
ing to marry her to the King of Algarve. By divers adventures
she comes in the space of four years into the hands of nine
men in divers places. At last she is restored to her father,
whom she quits again in the guise of a virgin, and, as was at
first intended, is married to the King of Algarve.

HAD Emilia's story but lasted a little longer, the young ladies
would perhaps have been moved to tears, so great was the sym-
pathy which they felt for Madam Beritola in her various fortunes.
But now that it was ended, the Queen bade Pamfilo follow suit ;
and he, than whom none was more obedient, thus began :—

Hardly, gracious ladies, is it given to us to know that which
makes for our good ; insomuch that, as has been observable
in a multitude of instances, many, deeming that the acquisition
of great riches would ensure them an easy and tranquil existence,
have not only besought them of God in prayer, but have sought
them with such ardour that they have spared no pains and
shrunk from no danger in the quest, and have attained their
end only to lose, at the hands of some one covetous of their
vast inheritance, a life with which before the days of their
prosperity they were well content. Others, whose course,
perilous with a thousand battles, stained with the blood of
their brothers and their friends, has raised them from base
to regal estate, have found in place of the felicity they expected
an infinity of cares and fears, and have proved by experience
that a chalice may be poisoned, though it be of gold, and set
on the table of a king. Many have most ardently desired beauty
and strength and other advantages of person, and have only
been taught their error by the death or dolorous life which
these very advantages entailed upon them. And so, not to
instance each particular human desire, I say, in sum, that
there is none of them that men may indulge in full confidence
as exempt from the chances and changes of fortune ; wherefore,
if we would act rightly, we ought to school ourselves to take
and be content with that which He gives us, who alone knows
and can afford us that of which we have need. But, divers
as are the aberrations of desire to which men are prone, so,
gracious ladies, there is one to which you are especially liable,
in that you are unduly solicitous of beauty, insomuch, that,
not content with the charms which nature has allotted you,

you endeavour to enhance them with wondrous ingenuity of art ; wherefore I am minded to make you acquainted with the coil of misadventures in which her beauty involved a fair Saracen, who in the course of, perhaps, four years was wedded nine several times.

There was of yore a Soldan of Babylon,[1] by name of Beminedab, who in his day had cause enough to be well content with his luck. Many children male and female had he, and among them a daughter, Alatiel by name, who by common consent of all that saw her was the most beautiful woman then to be found in the world. Now the Soldan, having been signally aided by the King of Algarve[2] in inflicting a great defeat upon a host of Arabs that had attacked him, had at his instance and by way of special favour given Alatiel to the King to wife ; wherefore, with an honourable escort of gentlemen and ladies most nobly and richly equipped, he placed her aboard a well-armed, well-furnished ship, and, commending her to God, sped her on her journey. The mariners, as soon as the weather was favourable, hoisted sail, and for some days after their departure from Alexandria had a prosperous voyage ; but when they had passed Sardinia, and were beginning to think that they were nearing their journey's end, they were caught one day between divers cross winds, each blowing with extreme fury, whereby the ship laboured so sorely that not only the lady but the seamen from time to time gave themselves up for lost. But still, most manfully and skilfully they struggled might and main with the tempest, which, ever waxing rather than waning, buffeted them for two days with immense unintermittent surges ; and being not far from the island of Majorca, as the third night began to close in, wrapt in clouds and mist and thick darkness, so that they saw neither the sky nor aught else, nor by any nautical skill might conjecture where they were, they felt the ship's timbers part. Wherefore, seeing no way to save the ship, each thought only how best to save himself, and, a boat being thrown out, the masters first, and then the men, one by one, though the first-comers sought with knives in their hands to bar the passage of the rest, all, rather than remain in the leaky ship, crowded into it, and there found the death which they hoped to escape. For the boat, being in such stress of weather and with such a burden quite unmanageable, went under, and all aboard her perished ;

[1] *I.e.* according to medieval usage, Egypt.
[2] *I.e.* Garbo, the coast of Africa opposite Andalusia and Granada.

whereas the ship, leaky though she was, and all but full of
water, yet, driven by the fury of the tempest, was hurled with
prodigious velocity upon the shore of the island of Majorca,
and struck it with such force as to embed herself in the sand,
perhaps a stone's throw from *terra firma*, where she remained
all night beaten and washed by the sea, but no more to be
moved by the utmost violence of the gale. None had remained
aboard her but the lady and her women, whom the malice of
the elements and their fears had brought to the verge of death.
When it was broad day and the storm was somewhat abated,
the lady, half dead, raised her head, and in faltering accents
began to call first one and then another of her servants. She
called in vain, however ; for those whom she called were too
far off to hear. Great indeed was her wonder and fear to
find herself thus without sight of human face or sound of other
voice than her own ; but, struggling to her feet as best she
might, she looked about her, and saw the ladies that were of
her escort, and the other women, all prostrate on the deck ;
so, after calling them one by one, she began at length to touch
them, and finding few that shewed sign of life, for indeed,
between grievous sea-sickness and fear, they had little life left,
she grew more terrified than before. However, being in sore
need of counsel, all alone as she was, and without knowledge
or means of learning where she was, she at last induced such
as had life in them to get upon their feet, with whom, as none
knew where the men were gone, and the ship was now full of
water and visibly breaking up, she abandoned herself to piteous
lamentations.

It was already none before they descried any one on the
shore or elsewhere to whom they could make appeal for help ;
but shortly after none it so chanced that a gentleman, Pericone
da Visalgo by name, being on his return from one of his estates,
passed that way with some mounted servants. Catching sight
of the ship, he apprehended the circumstances at a glance,
and bade one of his servants try to get aboard her, and let
him know the result. The servant with some difficulty
succeeded in boarding the vessel, and found the gentle lady
with her few companions ensconced under shelter of the prow,
and shrinking timidly from observation. At the first sight of
him they wept, and again and again implored him to have
pity on them ; but finding that he did not understand them,
nor they him, they sought by gestures to make him apprehend
their forlorn condition.

With these tidings the servant, after making such survey of
the ship as he could, returned to Pericone, who forthwith
caused the ladies, and all articles of value which were in the
ship and could be removed, to be brought off her, and took
them with him to one of his castles. The ladies' powers were
soon in a measure restored by food and rest, and by the honour
which was paid to Alatiel, and Alatiel alone by all the rest,
as well as by the richness of her dress, Pericone perceived that
she must be some great lady. Nor, though she was still pale,
and her person bore evident marks of the sea's rough usage,
did he fail to note that it was cast in a mould of extraordinary
beauty. Wherefore his mind was soon made up that, if she
lacked a husband, he would take her to wife, and that, if he
could not have her to wife, then he would make her his mistress.
So this ardent lover, who was a man of powerful frame and
haughty mien, devoted himself for several days to the service
of the lady with excellent effect, for the lady completely
recovered her strength and spirits, so that her beauty far
exceeded Pericone's most sanguine conjectures. Great there-
fore beyond measure was his sorrow that he understood not
her speech, nor she his, so that neither could know who the
other was ; but being inordinately enamoured of her beauty,
he sought by such mute blandishments as he could devise to
declare his love, and bring her of her own accord to gratify his
desire. All in vain, however ; she repulsed his advances point
blank ; whereby his passion only grew the stronger. So some
days passed ; and the lady perceiving Pericone's constancy,
and bethinking her that sooner or later she must yield either
to force or to love, and gratify his passion, and judging by what
she observed of the customs of the people that she was amongst
Christians, and in a part where, were she able to speak their
language, she would gain little, by making herself known,
determined with a lofty courage to stand firm and immovable
in this extremity of her misfortunes. Wherefore she bade the
three women, who were all that were left to her, on no account
to let any know who they were, unless they were so circum-
stanced that they might safely count on assistance in effecting
their escape : she also exhorted them most earnestly to preserve
their chastity, averring that she was firmly resolved that none
but her husband should enjoy her. The women heartily
assented, and promised that her injunctions should be obeyed
to the utmost of their power.

Day by day Pericone's passion waxed more ardent, being

fomented by the proximity and contrariety of its object.
Wherefore seeing that blandishment availed nothing, he was
minded to have recourse to wiles and stratagems, and in the
last resort to force. The lady, debarred by her law from the
use of wine, found it, perhaps, on that account all the more
palatable; which Pericone observing determined to enlist
Bacchus in the service of Venus. So, ignoring her coyness,
he provided one evening a supper, which was ordered with
all possible pomp and beauty, and graced by the presence of
the lady. No lack was there of incentives to hilarity; and
Pericone directed the servant who waited on Alatiel to ply
her with divers sorts of blended wines; which command the
man faithfully executed. She, suspecting nothing, and seduced
by the delicious flavour of the liquor, drank somewhat more
freely than was seemly, and forgetting her past woes, became
frolicsome, and incited by some women who trod some measures
in the Majorcan style, she shewed the company how they footed
it in Alexandria. This novel demeanour was by no means
lost on Pericone, who saw in it a good omen of his speedy
success; so, with profuse relays of food and wine he prolonged
the supper far into the night.

When the guests were at length gone, he attended the lady
alone to her chamber, where, the heat of the wine overpowering
the cold counsels of modesty, she made no more account of
Pericone's presence than if he had been one of her women, and
forthwith undressed and went to bed. Pericone was not slow
to follow her, and as soon as the light was out lay down by her
side, and taking her in his arms, without the least demur on
her part, began to solace himself with her after the manner
of lovers; which experience—she knew not till then with
what horn men butt—caused her to repent that she had not
yielded to his blandishments; nor did she thereafter wait to
be invited to such nights of delight, but many a time declared
her readiness, not by words, for she had none to convey her
meaning, but by gestures.

But this great felicity which she now shared with Pericone
was not to last: for not content with making her, instead of
the consort of a king, the mistress of a castellan, Fortune had
now in store for her a harsher experience, though of an amorous
character. Pericone had a brother, twenty-five years of age,
fair and fresh as a rose, his name Marato. On sight of Alatiel
Marato had been mightily taken with her; he inferred from
her bearing that he stood high in her good graces; he believed

that nothing stood between him and the gratification of his passion but the jealous vigilance with which Pericone guarded her. So musing, he hit upon a ruthless expedient, which had effect in action as hasty as heinous.

It so chanced that there then lay in the port of the city a ship, commanded by two Genoese, bound with a cargo of merchandise for Klarenza in the Morea : her sails were already hoist ; and she tarried only for a favourable breeze. Marato approached the masters and arranged with them to take himself and the lady aboard on the following night. This done he concerted further action with some of his most trusty friends, who readily lent him their aid to carry his design into execution. So on the following evening towards nightfall, the conspirators stole unobserved into Pericone's house, which was entirely unguarded, and there hid themselves, as pre-arranged. Then, as the night wore on, Marato shewed them where Pericone and the lady slept, and they entered the room, and slew Pericone. The lady thus rudely roused wept ; but silencing her by menaces of death they carried her off with the best part of Pericone's treasure, and hied them unobserved to the coast, where Marato parted from his companions, and forthwith took the lady aboard the ship. The wind was now fair and fresh, the mariners spread the canvas, and the vessel sped on her course.

This new misadventure, following so hard upon the former, caused the lady no small chagrin ; but Marato, with the aid of the good St. Crescent-in-hand that God has given us, found means to afford her such consolation that she was already grown so familiar with him as entirely to forget Pericone, when Fortune, not content with her former caprices, added a new dispensation of woe ; for what with the beauty of her person, which, as we have often said, was extraordinary, and the exquisite charm of her manners, the two young men, who commanded the ship, fell so desperately in love with her that they thought of nothing but how they might best serve and please her, so only that Marato should not discover the reason of their assiduous attentions. And neither being ignorant of the other's love, they held secret counsel together, and resolved to make conquest of the lady on joint account : as if love admitted of being held in partnership like merchandise or money. Which design being thwarted by the jealousy with which Alatiel was guarded by Marato, they chose a day and hour, when the ship was speeding amain under canvas, and Marato was on the poop looking out over the sea and quite off his guard ; and going stealthily up behind him, they suddenly laid hands on him, and threw him into the sea, and were already more than a mile on their course before any perceived that Marato was overboard. Which when the lady learned, and knew that he was irretrievably lost, she relapsed into her former plaintive mood. But the twain were forthwith by her side with soft speeches and profuse promises, which, however ill she understood them, were not altogether inapt to allay a grief which had in it more of concern for her own hapless self than of sorrow for her lost lover. So, in course of time, the lady beginning visibly to recover heart, they began privily to debate which of them should first take her to bed with him ; and neither being willing to give way to the other, and no compromise being discoverable, high words passed between them, and the dispute grew so hot, that they both waxed very wroth, drew their knives, and rushed madly at one another, and before they could be parted by their men, several stabs had been given and received on either side, whereby the one fell dead on the spot, and the other was severely wounded in divers parts of the body. The lady was much disconcerted to find herself thus alone with none to afford her either succour or counsel, and was mightily afraid lest the wrath of the kinsfolk and friends of the twain should vent itself upon her. From this mortal peril she was, however, delivered by the intercessions of the wounded man and their speedy arrival at Klarenza.

As there she tarried at the same inn with her wounded lover, the fame of her great beauty was speedily bruited abroad, and reached the ears of the Prince of the Morea, who was then staying there. The Prince was curious to see her, and having so done, pronounced her even more beautiful than rumour had reported her ; nay, he fell in love with her in such a degree that he could think of nought else ; and having heard in what guise she had come thither, he deemed that he might have her. While he was casting about how to compass his end, the kinsfolk of the wounded man, being apprised of the fact, forthwith sent her to him to the boundless delight, as well of the lady, who saw therein her deliverance from a great peril, as of the Prince. The royal bearing, which enhanced the lady's charms, did not escape the Prince, who, being unable to discover her true rank, set her down as at any rate of noble lineage ; wherefore he loved her as much again as before, and shewed her no small honour, treating her not as his mistress but as his wife. So the lady, contrasting her present happy

estate with her past woes, was comforted ; and, as her gaiety
revived, her beauty waxed in such a degree that all the Morea
talked of it and of little else : insomuch that the Prince's
friend and kinsman, the young, handsome and gallant Duke of
Athens, was smitten with a desire to see her, and taking occasion
to pay the Prince a visit, as he was now and again wont to do,
came to Klarenza with a goodly company of honourable gentle-
men. The Prince received him with all distinction and made
him heartily welcome, but did not at first shew him the lady.
By and by, however, their conversation began to turn upon
her and her charms, and the Duke asked if she were really so
marvellous a creature as folk said. The Prince replied :—
" Nay, but even more so ; and thereof thou shalt have better
assurance than my words, to wit, the witness of thine own
eyes." So, without delay, for the Duke was now all impatience,
they waited on the lady, who was prepared for their visit, and
received them very courteously and graciously. They seated
her between them, and being debarred from the pleasure of
conversing with her, for of their speech she understood little
or nothing, they both, and especially the Duke, who was scarce
able to believe that she was of mortal mould, gazed upon her
in mute admiration ; whereby the Duke, cheating himself with
the idea that he was but gratifying his curiosity, drank with
his eyes, unawares, deep draughts of the poisoned chalice of
love, and, to his own lamentable hurt, fell a prey to a most
ardent passion. His first thought, when they had left her, and
he had time for reflection, was that the Prince was the luckiest
man in the world to have a creature so fair to solace him ;
and swayed by his passion, his mind soon inclined to divers
other and less honourable meditations, whereof the issue was
that, come what might, he would despoil the Prince of his
felicity, and, if possible, make it his own. This resolution was
no sooner taken than, being of a hasty temperament, he cast
to the winds all considerations of honour and justice, and studied
only how to compass his end by craft. So, one day, as the first
step towards the accomplishment of his evil purpose, he arranged
with the Prince's most trusted chamberlain, one Ciuriaci, that
his horses and all his other personal effects should, with the
utmost secrecy, be got ready against a possible sudden
departure : and then at nightfall, attended by a single comrade
(both carrying arms), he was privily admitted by Ciuriaci into
the Prince's chamber. It was a hot night, and the Prince had
risen without disturbing the lady, and was standing bare to the

skin at an open window fronting the sea, to enjoy a light
breeze that blew thence. So, by preconcert with his comrade,
the Duke stole up to the window, and in a trice ran the Prince
through the body, and caught him up, and threw him out of
the window. The palace was close by the sea, but at a consider-
able altitude above it, and the window, through which the
Prince's body was thrown, looked over some houses, which,
being sapped by the sea, had become ruinous, and were rarely
or never visited by a soul ; whereby, as the Duke had foreseen,
the fall of the Prince's body passed, as indeed it could not but
pass, unobserved. Thereupon the Duke's accomplice whipped
out a halter, which he had brought with him for the purpose,
and, making as if he were but in play, threw it round Ciuriaci's
neck, drew it so tight that he could not utter a sound, and then,
with the Duke's aid, strangled him, and sent him after his
master. All this was accomplished, as the Duke knew full
well, without awakening any in the palace, not even the lady,
whom he now approached with a light, and holding it over
the bed gently uncovered her person, as she lay fast asleep, and
surveyed her from head to foot to his no small satisfaction ;
for fair as she had seemed to him dressed, he found her unadorned
charms incomparably greater. As he gazed, his passion waxed
beyond measure, and, reckless of his recent crime, and of the
blood which still stained his hands, he got forthwith into the
bed ; and she, being too sound asleep to distinguish between
him and the Prince, suffered him to lie with her.

But, boundless as was his delight, it brooked no long con-
tinuance ; so, rising, he called to him some of his comrades,
by whom he had the lady secured in such manner that she could
utter no sound, and borne out of the palace by the same secret
door by which he had gained entrance ; he then set her on horse-
back and in dead silence put his troop in motion, taking the
road to Athens. He did not, however, venture to take the
lady to Athens, where she would have encountered his Duchess
—for he was married—but lodged her in a very beautiful villa
which he had hard by the city overlooking the sea, where,
most forlorn of ladies, she lived secluded, but with no lack of
meet and respectful service.

On the following morning the Prince's courtiers awaited his
rising until none, but perceiving no sign of it, opened the doors,
which had not been secured, and entered his bedroom. Finding
it vacant, they supposed that the Prince was gone off privily
somewhere to have a few days of unbroken delight with his

fair lady ; and so they gave themselves no further trouble. But the next day it so chanced that an idiot, roaming about the ruins where lay the corpses of the Prince and Ciuriaci, drew the latter out by the halter and went off dragging it after him. The corpse was soon recognised by not a few, who, at first struck dumb with amazement, soon recovered sense enough to cajole the idiot into retracing his steps and shewing them the spot where he had found it ; and having thus, to the immeasurable grief of all the citizens, discovered the Prince's body, they buried it with all honour. Needless to say that no pains were spared to trace the perpetrators of so heinous a crime, and that the absence and evidently furtive departure of the Duke of Athens caused him to be suspected both of the murder and of the abduction of the lady. So the citizens were instant with one accord that the Prince's brother, whom they chose as his successor, should exact the debt of vengeance ; and he, having satisfied himself by further investigation that their suspicion was well founded, summoned to his aid his kinsfolk, friends and divers vassals, and speedily gathered a large, powerful and well-equipped army, with intent to make war upon the Duke of Athens. The Duke, being informed of his movements, made ready likewise to defend himself with all his power ; nor had he any lack of allies, among whom the Emperor of Constantinople sent his son, Constantine, and his nephew, Manuel, with a great and goodly force. The two young men were honourably received by the Duke, and still more so by the Duchess, who was Constantine's sister.

Day by day war grew more imminent ; and at last the Duchess took occasion to call Constantine and Manuel into her private chamber, and with many tears told them the whole story at large, explaining the *casus belli*, dilating on the indignity which she suffered at the hands of the Duke, if, as was believed, he really kept a mistress in secret, and beseeching them in most piteous accents to do the best they could to devise some expedient whereby the Duke's honour might be cleared, and her own peace of mind assured. The young men knew exactly how matters stood ; and so, without wearying the Duchess with many questions, they did their best to console her, and succeeded in raising her hopes. Before taking their leave they learned from her where the lady was, whose marvellous beauty they had heard lauded so often ; and being eager to see her, they besought the Duke to afford them an opportunity. Forgetful of what a like complaisance had cost the Prince, he

consented, and next morning brought them to the villa where
the lady lived, and with her and a few of his boon companions
regaled them with a lordly breakfast, which was served in a
most lovely garden. Constantine had no sooner seated
himself and surveyed the lady, than he was lost in admiration,
inly affirming that he had never seen so beautiful a creature,
and that for such a prize the Duke, or any other man, might
well be pardoned treachery or any other crime : he scanned
her again and again, and ever with more and more admiration ;
whereby it fared with him even as it had fared with the Duke.
He went away hotly in love with her, and dismissing all thought
of the war, cast about for some method by which, without
betraying his passion to any, he might devise some means of
wresting the lady from the Duke.

As he thus burned and brooded, the Prince drew dangerously
near the Duke's dominions ; wherefore order was given for an
advance, and the Duke, with Constantine and the rest,
marshalled his forces and led them forth from Athens to bar
the Prince's passage of the frontier at certain points. Some
days thus passed, during which Constantine, whose mind and
soul were entirely absorbed by his passion for the lady, be-
thought him, that, as the Duke was no longer in her neighbour-
hood, he might readily compass his end. He therefore feigned
to be seriously unwell, and, having by this pretext obtained
the Duke's leave, he ceded his command to Manuel, and returned
to his sister at Athens. He had not been there many days
before the Duchess recurred to the dishonour which the Duke
did her by keeping the lady ; whereupon he said that of that,
if she approved, he would certainly relieve her by seeing that
the lady was removed from the villa to some distant place.
The Duchess, supposing that Constantine was prompted not
by jealousy of the Duke but by jealousy for her honour, gave
her hearty consent to his plan, provided he so contrived that
the Duke should never know that she had been privy to it ;
on which point Constantine gave her ample assurance. So,
being authorised by the Duchess to act as he might deem best,
he secretly equipped a light bark and manned her with some
of his men, to whom he confided his plan, bidding them lie to
off the garden of the lady's villa ; and so, having sent the bark
forward, he hied him with other of his men to the villa. He
gained ready admission of the servants, and was made heartily
welcome by the lady, who, at his desire, attended by some of
her servants, walked with him and some of his comrades in

the garden. By and by, feigning that he had a message for
her from the Duke, he drew her aside towards a gate that led
down to the sea, and which one of his confederates had already
opened. A concerted signal brought the bark alongside, and
to seize the lady and set her aboard the bark was but the work
of an instant. Her retinue hung back as they heard Constantine
menace with death whoso but stirred or spoke, and suffered
him, protesting that what he did was done not to wrong the
Duke but solely to vindicate his sister's honour, to embark with
his men. The lady wept, of course, but Constantine was at
her side, the rowers gave way, and the bark, speeding like a
thing of life over the waves, made Egina shortly after dawn.
There Constantine and the lady landed, she still lamenting her
fatal beauty, and took a little rest and pleasure. Then, re-
embarking, they continued their voyage, and in the course of
a few days reached Chios, which Constantine, fearing paternal
censure, and that he might be deprived of his fair booty, deemed
a safe place of sojourn. So, after some days of repose the lady
ceased to bewail her harsh destiny, and suffering Constantine
to console her as his predecessors had done, began once more
to enjoy the good gifts which Fortune sent her.

Now while they thus dallied, Osbech, King of the Turks,
who was perennially at war with the Emperor, came by chance
to Smyrna ; and there learning that Constantine was wantoning
in careless ease at Chios with a lady of whom he had made prize,
he made a descent by night upon the island with an armed
flotilla. Landing his men in dead silence, he made captives
of not a few of the Chians whom he surprised in their beds ;
others, who took the alarm and rushed to arms, he slew ; and
having wasted the whole island with fire, he shipped the booty
and the prisoners, and sailed back to Smyrna. As there he
overhauled the booty, he lit upon the fair lady, and knew her
for the same that had been taken in bed and fast asleep with
Constantine : whereat, being a young man, he was delighted
beyond measure, and made her his wife out of hand with all
due form and ceremony. And so for several months he enjoyed
her.

Now there had been for some time and still was a treaty
pending between the Emperor and Basano, King of Cappadocia,
whereby Basano with his forces was to fall on Osbech on one
side while the Emperor attacked him on the other. Some
demands made by Basano, which the Emperor deemed un-
reasonable, had so far retarded the conclusion of the treaty ;

but no sooner had the Emperor learned the fate of his son than,
distraught with grief, he forthwith conceded the King of
Cappadocia's demands, and was instant with him to fall at
once upon Osbech while he made ready to attack him on the
other side. Getting wind of the Emperor's design, Osbech
collected his forces, and, lest he should be caught and crushed
between the convergent armies of two most mighty potentates,
advanced against the King of Cappadocia. The fair lady he
left at Smyrna in the care of a faithful dependant and friend,
and after a while joined battle with the King of Cappadocia,
in which battle he was slain, and his army defeated and dis-
persed. Wherefore Basano with his victorious host advanced,
carrying everything before him, upon Smyrna, and receiving
everywhere the submission due to a conqueror.

Meanwhile Osbech's dependant, by name Antioco, who had
charge of the fair lady, was so smitten with her charms that,
albeit he was somewhat advanced in years, he broke faith with
his friend and lord, and allowed himself to become enamoured
of her. He had the advantage of knowing her language, which
counted for much with one who for some years had been, as
it were, compelled to live the life of a deaf mute, finding none
whom she could understand or by whom she might be under-
stood ; and goaded by passion, he in the course of a few days
established such a degree of intimacy with her that in no long
time it passed from friendship into love, so that their lord,
far away amid the clash of arms and the tumult of the battle,
was forgotten, and marvellous pleasure had they of one another
between the sheets.

However, news came at last of Osbech's defeat and death,
and the victorious and unchecked advance of Basano, whose
advent they were by no means minded to await. Wherefore,
taking with them the best part of the treasure that Osbech had
left there, they hied them with all possible secrecy to Rhodes.
There they had not long abode before Antioco fell ill of a mortal
disease. He had then with him a Cypriote merchant, an
intimate and very dear friend, to whom, as he felt his end
approach, he resolved to leave all that he possessed, including
his dear lady. So, when he felt death imminent, he called them
to him and said :—" 'Tis now quite evident to me that my life
is fast ebbing away ; and sorely do I regret it, for never had
I so much pleasure of life as now. Well content indeed I am
in one respect, in that, as die I must, I at least die in the arms
of the two persons whom I love more than any other in the

world, to wit, in thine arms, dearest friend, and those of this
lady, whom, since I have known her, I have loved more than
myself. But yet 'tis grievous to me to know that I must leave
her here in a strange land with none to afford her either pro-
tection or counsel; and but that I leave her with thee, who,
I doubt not, wilt have for my sake no less care of her than thou
wouldst have had of me, 'twould grieve me still more; wherefore
with all my heart and soul I pray thee, that, if I die, thou
take her with all else that belongs to me into thy charge, and so
acquit thyself of thy trust as thou mayst deem conducive to
the peace of my soul. And of thee, dearest lady, I entreat one
favour, that I be not forgotten of thee, after my death, so that
there whither I go it may still be my boast to be beloved here
of the most beautiful lady that nature ever formed. Let me
but die with these two hopes assured, and without doubt I
shall depart in peace."

Both the merchant and the lady wept to hear him thus speak,
and, when he had done, comforted him, and promised faithfully,
in the event of his death, to do even as he besought them. He
died almost immediately afterwards, and was honourably
buried by them. A few days sufficed the merchant to wind up
all his affairs in Rhodes; and being minded to return to Cyprus
aboard a Catalan boat that was there, he asked the fair lady
what she purposed to do if he went back to Cyprus. The
lady answered, that, if it were agreeable to him, she would
gladly accompany him, hoping that for love of Antioco he
would treat and regard her as his sister. The merchant replied
that it would afford him all the pleasure in the world; and, to
protect her from insult until their arrival in Cyprus, he gave
her out as his wife, and, suiting action to word, slept with her
on the boat in an alcove in a little cabin in the poop. Whereby
that happened which on neither side was intended when they
left Rhodes, to wit, that the darkness and the comfort and the
warmth of the bed, forces of no mean efficacy, did so prevail
with them that dead Antioco was forgotten alike as lover and
as friend, and by a common impulse they began to wanton
together, insomuch that before they were arrived at Baffa,
where the Cypriote resided, they were indeed man and wife.
At Baffa the lady tarried with the merchant a good while,
during which it so befell that a gentleman, Antigono by name,
a man of ripe age and riper wisdom but no great wealth, being
one that had had vast and various experience of affairs in the
service of the King of Cyprus but had found fortune adverse

to him, came to Baffa on business; and passing one day by
the house where the fair lady was then living by herself, for
the Cypriote merchant was gone to Armenia with some of his
wares, he chanced to catch sight of the lady at one of the
windows, and, being struck by her extraordinary beauty,
regarded her attentively, and began to have some vague recollec-
tion of having seen her before, but could by no means remember
where. The fair lady, however, so long the sport of Fortune,
but now nearing the term of her woes, no sooner saw Antigono
than she remembered to have seen him in her father's service,
and in no mean capacity, at Alexandria. Wherefore she
forthwith sent for him, hoping that by his counsel she might
elude her merchant and be reinstated in her true character and
dignity of princess. When he presented himself, she asked him
with some embarrassment whether he were, as she took him to
be, Antigono of Famagosta. He answered in the affirmative,
adding :—" And of you, madam, I have a sort of recollection,
though I cannot say where I have seen you; wherefore, so
it irk you not, bring, I pray you, yourself to my remembrance."
Satisfied that it was Antigono himself, the lady in a flood of
tears threw herself upon him to his no small amazement, and
embraced his neck : then, after a little while, she asked him
whether he had never seen her in Alexandria. The question
awakened Antigono's memory; he at once recognised Alatiel,
the Soldan's daughter, whom he had thought to have been
drowned at sea, and would have paid her due homage; but
she would not suffer it, and bade him be seated with her for a
while. Being seated, he respectfully asked her, how, and when
and whence she had come thither, seeing that all Egypt believed
for certain that she had been drowned at sea some years before.
" And would that so it had been," said the lady, " rather than
I should have led the life that I have led; and so doubtless
will my father say, if he shall ever come to know of it." And
so saying, she burst into such a flood of tears that 'twas a
wonder to see. Wherefore Antigono said to her :—" Nay
but, madam, be not distressed before the occasion arises. I
pray you, tell me the story of your adventures, and what has
been the tenor of your life; perchance 'twill prove to be no
such matter but, God helping us, we may set it all straight."
" Antigono," said the fair lady, " when I saw thee, 'twas as
if I saw my father, and 'twas the tender love by which I am
holden to him that prompted me to make myself known to
thee, though I might have kept my secret; and few indeed

there are, whom to have met would have afforded me such
pleasure as this which I have in meeting and recognising thee
before all others ; wherefore I will now make known to thee as
to a father that which in my evil fortune I have ever kept
close. If, when thou hast heard my story, thou seest any
means whereby I may be reinstated in my former honour, I
pray thee use it. If not, disclose to none that thou hast seen
me or heard aught of me."

Then, weeping between every word, she told him her whole
story from the day of the shipwreck at Majorca to that hour.
Antigono wept in sympathy, and then said :—" Madam, as
throughout this train of misfortunes you have happily escaped
recognition, I undertake to restore you to your father in such
sort that you shall be dearer to him than ever before, and be
afterwards married to the King of Algarve." " How ? " she
asked. Whereupon he explained to her in detail how he meant
to proceed ; and, lest delay should give occasion to another
to interfere, he went back at once to Famagosta, and having
obtained audience of the King, thus he spoke :—" Sire, so
please you, you have it in your power at little cost to yourself
to do a thing, which will at once redound most signally to your
honour and confer a great boon on me, who have grown poor
in your service." " How ? " asked the King. Then said
Antigono :—" At Baffa is of late arrived a fair damsel, daughter
of the Soldan, long thought to be drowned, who to preserve
her chastity has suffered long and severe hardship. She is
now reduced to poverty, and is desirous of returning to her
father. If you should be pleased to send her back to him under
my escort, your honour and my interest would be served in
high and equal measure ; nor do I think that such a service
would ever be forgotten by the Soldan."

With true royal generosity the King forthwith signified his
approval, and had Alatiel brought under honourable escort to
Famagosta, where, attended by his Queen, he received her
with every circumstance of festal pomp and courtly magnificence.
Schooled by Antigono, she gave the King and Queen such a
version of her adventures as satisfied their inquiries in every
particular. So, after a few days, the King sent her back to
the Soldan under escort of Antigono, attended by a goodly
company of honourable men and women ; and of the cheer
which the Soldan made her, and not her only but Antigono
and all his company, it boots not to ask. When she was some-
what rested, the Soldan inquired how it was that she was yet

alive, and where she had been so long without letting him know
how it fared with her. Whereupon the lady, who had got
Antigono's lesson by heart, answered thus :—" My father,
'twas perhaps the twentieth night after my departure from you
when our ship parted her timbers in a terrible storm and went
ashore nigh a place called Aguamorta, away there in the West :
what was the fate of the men that were aboard our ship I know
not, nor knew I ever ; I remember only, that, when day came,
and I returned, as it were, from death to life, the wreck, having
been sighted, was boarded by folk from all the country-side,
intent on plunder ; and I and two of my women were taken
ashore, where the women were forthwith parted from me by
the young men, nor did I ever learn their fate. Now hear my
own. Struggling might and main, I was seized by two young
men, who dragged me, weeping bitterly, by the hair of the
head, towards a great forest ; but, on sight of four men who
were then passing that way on horseback, they forthwith
loosed me and took to flight. Whereupon the four men, who
struck me as persons of great authority, ran up to me ; and
much they questioned me, and much I said to them ; but neither
did they understand me, nor I them. So, after long time
conferring together, they set me on one of their horses and
brought me to a house, where dwelt a community of ladies,
religious according to their law ; and what the men may have
said I know not, but there I was kindly received and ever
honourably entreated by all ; and with them I did afterwards
most reverentially pay my devotions to St. Crescent-in-Hollow,
who is held in great honour by the women of that country.
When I had been some time with them, and had learned some-
thing of their language, they asked me who and whence I was :
whereto I, knowing that I was in a convent, and fearing to be
cast out as a foe to their law if I told the truth, answered that
I was the daughter of a great gentleman of Cyprus, who had
intended to marry me to a gentleman of Crete ; but that on
the voyage we had been driven out of our course and wrecked
at Aguamorta. And so I continued, as occasion required,
observing their usages with much assiduity, lest worse should
befall me ; but being one day asked by their superior, whom
they call abbess, whether I was minded to go back to Cyprus,
I answered that there was nought that I desired so much.
However, so solicitous for my honour was the abbess, that
there was none going to Cyprus to whom she would entrust
me, until, two months or so ago, there arrived some worthy

men from France, of whom one was a kinsman of the abbess,
with their wives. They were on their way to visit the sepulchre
where He whom they hold to be God was buried after He
had suffered death at the hands of the Jews ; and the abbess,
learning their destination, prayed them to take charge of me,
and restore me to my father in Cyprus. With what cheer,
with what honour, these gentlemen and their wives entertained
me, 'twere long to tell. But, in brief, we embarked, and in the
course of a few days arrived at Baffa, where it was so ordered
by the providence of God, who perchance took pity on me, that
in the very hour of our disembarkation I, not knowing a soul
and being at a loss how to answer the gentlemen, who would
fain have discharged the trust laid upon them by the reverend
abbess and restored me to my father, fell in, on the shore,
with Antigono, whom I forthwith called, and in our language,
that I might be understood neither of the gentlemen nor of their
wives, bade him acknowledge me as his daughter. He under-
stood my case at once, made much of me, and to the utmost of
his slender power honourably requited the gentlemen. He
then brought me to the King of Cyprus, who accorded me
welcome there and conduct hither so honourable as words of
mine can never describe. If aught remains to tell, you may best
learn it from the lips of Antigono, who has often heard my
story."

Then Antigono, addressing the Soldan, said :—" Sire, what
she has told you accords with what she has often told me, and
with what I have learned from the gentlemen and ladies who
accompanied her. One thing, however, she has omitted,
because, I suppose, it hardly becomes her to tell it ; to wit,
all that the gentlemen and ladies, who accompanied her, said
of the virtuous and gracious and noble life which she led with
the devout ladies, and of the tears and wailings of both the
ladies and the gentlemen, when they parted with her to me.
But were I to essay to repeat all that they said to me, the day
that now is, and the night that is to follow, were all too short :
suffice it to say so much as this, that, by what I gathered from
their words and have been able to see for myself, you may make
it your boast, that among all the daughters of all your peers
that wear the crown none can be matched with yours for virtue
and true worth."

By all which the Soldan was so overjoyed that 'twas a wonder
to see. Again and again he made supplication to God, that of
His grace power might be vouchsafed him adequately to recom-

pense all who had done honour to his daughter, and most
especially the King of Cyprus, for the honourable escort under
which he had sent her thither ; for Antigono he provided a
magnificent guerdon, and some days later gave him his *congé*
to return to Cyprus, at the same time by a special ambassage
conveying to the King his grateful acknowledgments of the
manner in which he had treated his daughter. Then, being
minded that his first intent, to wit, that his daughter should be
the bride of the King of Algarve, should not be frustrate,
he wrote to the King, telling him all, and adding that, if he
were still minded to have her, he might send for her. The
King was overjoyed by these tidings, and having sent for her
with great pomp, gave her on her arrival a hearty welcome.
So she, who had lain with eight men, in all, perhaps, ten
thousand times, was bedded with him as a virgin, and made
him believe that a virgin she was, and lived long and happily
with him as his queen : wherefore 'twas said :—" Mouth, for
kisses, was never the worse : like as the moon reneweth her
course."

NOVEL VIII

*The Count of Antwerp, labouring under a false accusation, goes
into exile. He leaves his two children in different places in
England, and takes service in Ireland. Returning to
England an unknown man, he finds his children prosperous.
He serves as a groom in the army of the King of France ;
his innocence is established, and he is restored to his former
honours.*

THE ladies heaved many sighs over the various fortunes of the
fair lady : but what prompted those sighs who shall say ?
With some, perchance, 'twas as much envy as pity of one to
whose lot fell so many nights of delight. But, however this
may be, when Pamfilo's story was ended, and the laughter
which greeted his last words had subsided, the queen turned
to Elisa, and bade her follow suit with one of her stories. So
Elisa with a cheerful courage thus began :—

Vast indeed is the field that lies before us, wherein to roam
at large ; 'twould readily afford each of us not one course but
ten, so richly has Fortune diversified it with episodes both
strange and sombre ; wherefore selecting one such from this
infinite store, I say :—That, after the transference of the

Roman Empire from the Franks to the Germans, the greatest
enmity prevailed between the two nations, with warfare per-
petual and relentless : wherefore, deeming that the offensive
would be their best defence, the King of France and his son
mustered all the forces they could raise from their own dominions
and those of their kinsmen and allies, and arrayed a grand army
for the subjugation of their enemies. Before they took the
field, as they could not leave the realm without a governor,
they chose for that office Gautier, Count of Antwerp, a true
knight and sage counsellor, and their very loyal ally and vassal,
choosing him the rather, because, albeit he was a thorough
master of the art of war, yet they deemed him less apt to support
its hardships than for the conduct of affairs of a delicate nature.
Him, therefore, they set in their place as their vicar-general
and regent of the whole realm of France, and having so done,
they took the field.

Count Gautier ordered his administration wisely and in a
regular course, discussing all matters with the queen and her
daughter-in-law ; whom, albeit they were left under his charge
and jurisdiction, he nevertheless treated as his ladies para-
mount. The Count was about forty years of age, and the
very mould of manly beauty ; in bearing as courteous and
chivalrous as ever a gentleman might be, and withal so debonair
and dainty, so feat and trim of person that he had not his
peer among the gallants of that day. His wife was dead, leaving
him two children and no more, to wit, a boy and a girl, still
quite young. Now the King and his son being thus away at
the war, and the Count frequenting the court of the two said
ladies, and consulting with them upon affairs of state, it so
befell that the Prince's lady regarded him with no small favour,
being very sensible alike of the advantages of his person and
the nobility of his bearing ; whereby she conceived for him a
passion which was all the more ardent because it was secret.
And, as he was without a wife, and she was still in the freshness
of her youth, she saw not why she should not readily be grati-
fied ; but supposing that nothing stood in the way but her own
shamefastness, she resolved to be rid of that, and disclose her
mind to him without any reserve. So one day, when she was
alone, she seized her opportunity, and sent for him, as if she
were desirous to converse with him on indifferent topics. The
Count, his mind entirely aloof from the lady's purpose, pre-
sented himself forthwith, and at her invitation sate down by
her side on a settee. They were quite alone in the room ;

but the Count had twice asked her the reason why she had so
honoured him, before, overcome by passion, she broke silence,
and crimson from brow to neck with shame, half sobbing,
trembling in every limb, and faltering at every word, she thus
spoke :—" Dearest friend and sweet my lord, sagacity such
as yours cannot but be apt to perceive how great is the frailty
of men and women, and how, for divers reasons, it varies in
different persons in such a degree that no just judge would mete
out the same measure to each indifferently, though the fault
were apparently the same. Who would not acknowledge that
a poor man or woman, fain to earn daily bread by the sweat of
the brow, is far more reprehensible in yielding to the solicita-
tions of love, than a rich lady, whose life is lapped in ease and
unrestricted luxury ? Not a soul, I am persuaded, but would
so acknowledge ! Wherefore I deem that the possession of
these boons of fortune should go far indeed to acquit the
possessor, if she, perchance, indulge an errant love ; and, for
the rest, that, if she have chosen a wise and worthy lover,
she should be entirely exonerated. And as I think I may
fairly claim the benefit of both these pleas, and of others beside,
to wit, my youth and my husband's absence, which naturally
incline me to love, 'tis meet that I now urge them in your
presence in defence of my passion ; and if they have the weight
with you which they should have with the wise, I pray you to
afford me your help and counsel in the matter wherein I shall
demand it. I avow that in the absence of my husband I have
been unable to withstand the promptings of the flesh and the
power of love, forces of such potency that even the strongest
men—not to speak of delicate women—have not seldom been,
nay daily are, overcome by them ; and so, living thus, as you
see me, in ease and luxury, I have allowed the allurements of
love to draw me on until at last I find myself a prey to passion.
Wherein were I discovered, I were, I confess, dishonoured ;
but discovery being avoided, I count the dishonour all but
nought. Moreover, love has been so gracious to me that not
only has he spared to blind me in the choice of my lover, but
he has even lent me his most effective aid, pointing me to one
well worthy of the love of a lady such as I, even to yourself ;
whom, if I misread not my mind, I deem the most handsome
and courteous and debonair, and therewithal the sagest cavalier
that the realm of France may shew. And as you are without
a wife, so may I say that I find myself without a husband.
Wherefore in return for this great love I bear you, deny me

not, I pray you, yours ; but have pity on my youth, which
wastes away for you like ice before the fire."

These words were followed by such a flood of tears, that,
albeit she had intended yet further to press her suit, speech
failed her ; her eyes drooped, and, almost swooning with
emotion, she let her head fall upon the Count's breast. The
Count, who was the most loyal of knights, began with all
severity to chide her mad passion and to thrust her from him
—for she was now making as if she would throw her arms around
his neck—and to asseverate with oaths that he would rather
be hewn in pieces than either commit, or abet another in com-
mitting such an offence against the honour of his lord ; when
the lady, catching his drift, and forgetting all her love in a
sudden frenzy of rage, cried out :—"So ! unknightly knight,
is it thus you flout my love ? Now Heaven forbid, but, as
you would be the death of me, I either do you to death or drive
you from the world ! " So saying, she dishevelled and tore
her hair and rent her garments to shreds about her bosom.
Which done, she began shrieking at the top of her voice :—
"Help ! help ! The Count of Antwerp threatens to violate
me ! " Whereupon the Count, who knew that a clear con-
science was no protection against the envy of courtiers, and
doubted that his innocence would prove scarce a match for the
cunning of the lady, started to his feet, and hied him with all
speed out of the room, out of the palace, and back to his own
house. Counsel of none he sought ; but forthwith set his
children on horseback, and taking horse himself, departed
post haste for Calais. The lady's cries brought not a few to
her aid, who, observing her plight, not only gave entire credence
to her story, but improved upon it, alleging that the debonair
and accomplished Count had long employed all the arts of
seduction to compass his end. So they rushed in hot haste
to the Count's house, with intent to arrest him, and not finding
him, sacked it and razed it to the ground. The news, as glosed
and garbled, being carried to the King and Prince in the field,
they were mightily incensed, and offered a great reward for
the Count, dead or alive, and condemned him and his posterity
to perpetual banishment.

Meanwhile the Count, sorely troubled that by his flight his
innocence shewed as guilt, pursued his journey, and concealing
his identity, and being recognised by none, arrived with his
two children at Calais. Thence he forthwith crossed to England,
and, meanly clad, fared on for London, taking care as he went

to school his children in all that belonged to their new way of life, and especially in two main articles : to wit, that they should bear with resignation the poverty to which, by no fault of theirs, but solely by one of Fortune's caprices, they and he were reduced, and that they should be most sedulously on their guard to betray to none, as they valued their lives, whence they were, or who their father was. The son, Louis by name, was perhaps nine, and the daughter, Violante, perhaps seven years of age. For years so tender they proved apt pupils, and afterwards shewed by their conduct that they had well learned their father's lesson. He deemed it expedient to change their names, and accordingly called the boy Perrot and the girl Jeannette. So, meanly clad, the Count and his two children arrived at London, and there made shift to get a living by going about soliciting alms in the guise of French mendicants.

Now, as for this purpose they waited one morning outside a church, it so befell that a great lady, the wife of one of the marshals of the King of England, observed them, as she left the church, asking alms, and demanded of the Count whence he was, and whether the children were his. He answered that he was from Picardy, that the children were his, and that he had been fain to leave Picardy by reason of the misconduct of their reprobate elder brother. The lady looked at the girl, who being fair, and of gentle and winning mien and manners, found much favour in her eyes. So the kind-hearted lady said to the Count :—" My good man, if thou art willing to leave thy little daughter with me, I like her looks so well that I will gladly take her ; and if she grow up a good woman, I will see that she is suitably married when the right time comes." The Count was much gratified by the proposal, which he forthwith accepted, and parted with the girl, charging the lady with tears to take every care of her.

Having thus placed the girl with one in whom he felt sure that he might trust, he determined to tarry no longer in London ; wherefore, taking Perrot with him and begging as he went, he made his way to Wales, not without great suffering, being unused to go afoot. Now in Wales another of the King's marshals had his court, maintaining great state and a large number of retainers ; to which court the Count and his son frequently repaired, there to get food ; and there Perrot, finding the marshal's son and other gentlemen's sons vying with one another in boyish exercises, as running and leaping, little by little joined their company, and shewed himself a

match or more for them all in all their contests. The marshal's
attention being thus drawn to him, he was well pleased with
the boy's mien and bearing, and asked who he was. He was
told that he was the son of a poor man who sometimes came
there to solicit alms. Whereupon he asked the Count to let
him have the boy, and the Count, to whom God could have
granted no greater boon, readily consented, albeit he was very
loath to part with Perrot.

Having thus provided for his son and daughter, the Count
resolved to quit the island ; and did so, making his way as best
he could to Stamford, in Ireland, where he obtained a menial's
place in the service of a knight, retainer to one of the earls of
that country, and so abode there a long while, doing all the
irksome and wearisome drudgery of a lackey or groom.

Meanwhile under the care of the gentle lady at London
Violante or Jeannette increased, as in years and stature so
also in beauty, and in such favour with the lady and her
husband and every other member of the household and all who
knew her that 'twas a wonder to see ; nor was there any that,
observing her bearing and manners, would not have said that
estate or dignity there was none so high or honourable but she
was worthy of it. So the lady, who, since she had received her
from her father, had been unable to learn aught else about
him than what he had himself told, was minded to marry her
honourably according to what she deemed to be her rank. But
God, who justly apportions reward according to merit, having
regard to her noble birth, her innocence, and the load of suffer-
ing which the sin of another had laid upon her, ordered other-
wise ; and in His good providence, lest the young gentlewoman
should be mated with a churl, permitted, we must believe, events
to take the course they did.

The gentle lady with whom Jeannette lived had an only son,
whom she and her husband loved most dearly, as well because
he was a son as for his rare and noble qualities, for in truth
there were few that could compare with him in courtesy and
courage and personal beauty. Now the young man marked
the extraordinary beauty and grace of Jeannette, who was
about six years his junior, and fell so desperately in love with
her that he had no eyes for any other maiden ; but, deeming
her to be of low degree, he not only hesitated to ask her of his
parents in marriage, but, fearing to incur reproof for indulging
a passion for an inferior, he did his utmost to conceal his love.
Whereby it gave him far more disquietude than if he had avowed

it; insomuch that—so extreme waxed his suffering—he fell
ill, and that seriously. Divers physicians were called in, but,
for all their scrutiny of his symptoms, they could not determine
the nature of his malady, and one and all gave him up for lost.
Nothing could exceed the sorrow and dejection of his father
and mother, who again and again piteously implored him to
discover to them the cause of his malady, and received no other
answer than sighs or complaints that he seemed to be wasting
away. Now it so happened that one day, Jeannette, who from
regard for his mother was sedulous in waiting upon him, for
some reason or another came into the room where he lay, while
a very young but very skilful physician sate by him and held his
pulse. The young man gave her not a word or other sign of
recognition; but his passion waxed, his heart smote him, and
the acceleration of his pulse at once betrayed his inward com-
motion to the physician, who, albeit surprised, remained quietly
attentive to see how long it would last, and observing that it
ceased when Jeannette left the room, conjectured that he was
on the way to explain the young man's malady. So, after a
while, still holding the young man's pulse, he sent for Jeannette,
as if he had something to ask of her. She returned forthwith;
the young man's pulse mounted as soon as she entered the
room, and fell again as soon as she left it. Wherefore the
physician no longer hesitated, but rose, and taking the young
man's father and mother aside, said to them :—" The restora-
tion of your son's health rests not with medical skill, but solely
with Jeannette, whom, as by unmistakable signs I have
discovered, he ardently loves, though, so far I can see, she is
not aware of it. So you know what you have to do, if you
value his life." The prospect thus afforded of their son's
deliverance from death reassured the gentleman and his lady,
albeit they were troubled, misdoubting it must be by his
marriage with Jeannette. So, when the physician was gone,
they went to the sick lad, and the lady thus spoke :—" My
son, never would I have believed that thou wouldst have con-
cealed from me any desire of thine, least of all if such it were that
privation should cause thee to languish; for well assured thou
shouldst have been and shouldst be, that I hold thee dear as
my very self, and that whatever may be for thy contentment,
even though it were scarce seemly, I would do it for thee;
but, for all thou hast so done, God has shewn Himself more
merciful to theeward than thyself, and, lest thou die of this
malady, has given me to know its cause, which is nothing else

than the excessive love which thou bearest to a young woman, be she who she may. Which love in good sooth thou needest not have been ashamed to declare ; for it is but natural at thy age ; and hadst thou not loved, I should have deemed thee of very little worth. So, my son, be not shy of me, but frankly discover to me thy whole heart ; and away with this gloom and melancholy whereof thy sickness is engendered, and be comforted, and assure thyself that there is nought that thou mayst require of me which I will not do to give thee ease, so far as my powers may reach, seeing that thou art dearer to me than my own life. Away with thy shamefastness and fears, and tell me if there is aught wherein I may be helpful to thee in the matter of thy love ; and if I bestir not myself and bring it to pass, account me the most harsh mother that ever bore son."

The young man was at first somewhat shamefast to hear his mother thus speak, but, reflecting that none could do more for his happiness than she, he took courage, and thus spoke :—
" Madam, my sole reason for concealing my love from you was that I have observed that old people for the most part forget that they once were young ; but, as I see that no such unreasonableness is to be apprehended in you, I not only acknowledge the truth of what you say that you have discerned, but I will also disclose to you the object of my passion, on the understanding that your promise shall to the best of your power be performed, as it must be, if I am to be restored to you in sound health." Whereupon the lady, making too sure of that which was destined to fall out otherwise than she expected, gave him every encouragement to discover all his heart, and promised to lose no time and spare no pains in endeavouring to compass his gratification. " Madam," said then the young man, " the rare beauty and exquisite manners of our Jeannette, my powerlessness to make her understand— I do not say commiserate—my love, and my reluctance to disclose it to any, have brought me to the condition in which you see me ; and if your promise be not in one way or another performed, be sure that my life will be brief." The lady, deeming that the occasion called rather for comfort than for admonition, replied with a smile :—" Ah ! my son, was this then of all things the secret of thy suffering ? Be of good cheer, and leave me to arrange the affair, when you are recovered." So, animated by a cheerful hope, the young man speedily gave sign of a most marked improvement, which the lady observed with great satisfaction, and then began to

cast about how she might keep her promise. So one day
she sent for Jeannette, and in a tone of gentle raillery asked her
if she had a lover.   Jeannette turned very red as she answered :
—" Madam, 'twould scarce, nay, 'twould ill become a damsel
such as I, poor, outcast from home, and in the service of another,
to occupy herself with thoughts of love."   Whereto the lady
answered :—" So you have none, we will give you one, who will
brighten all your life and give you more joy of your beauty ;
for it is not right that so fair a damsel as you remain without a
lover."   " Madam," rejoined Jeannette, " you found me living
in poverty with my father, you adopted me, you have brought
me up as your daughter ; wherefore I should, if possible,
comply with your every wish ; but in this matter I will render
you no compliance, nor do I doubt that I do well. So you
will give me a husband, I will love him, but no other will I
love ; for, as patrimony I now have none save my honour,
that I am minded to guard and preserve while my life shall
last."   Serious though the obstacle was which these words
opposed to the plan by which the lady had intended to keep
her promise to her son, her sound judgment could not but
secretly acknowledge that the spirit which they evinced was
much to be commended in the damsel. Wherefore she said :
—" Nay but, Jeannette ; suppose that our Lord the King, who
is a young knight as thou art a most fair damsel, craved some
indulgence of thy love, wouldst thou deny him ? "   " The
King," returned Jeannette without the least hesitation,
" might constrain me, but with my consent he should never
have aught of me that was not honourable."   Whereto the
lady made no answer, for she now understood the girl's temper ;
but, being minded to put her to the proof, she told her son
that, as soon as he was recovered, she would arrange that he
should be closeted with her in the same room, and be thus able
to use all his arts to bring her to his will, saying that it ill
became her to play the part of procuress and urge her son's
suit upon her own maid. But as the young man, by no means
approving this idea, suddenly grew worse, the lady at length
opened her mind to Jeannette, whom she found in the same
frame as before, and indeed even more resolute. Wherefore
she told her husband all that she had done ; and as both
preferred that their son should marry beneath him, and live,
than that he should remain single and die, they resolved,
albeit much disconcerted, to give Jeannette to him to wife ;
and so after long debate they did. Whereat Jeannette was

overjoyed, and with devout heart gave thanks to God that He had not forgotten her; nevertheless she still gave no other account of herself than that she was the daughter of a Picard. So the young man recovered, and blithe at heart as ne'er another, was married, and began to speed the time gaily with his bride.

Meanwhile Perrot, left in Wales with the marshal of the King of England, had likewise with increase of years increase of favour with his master, and grew up most shapely and well-favoured, and of such prowess that in all the island at tourney or joust or any other passage of arms he had not his peer; being everywhere known and renowned as Perrot the Picard. And as God had not forgotten Jeannette, so likewise He made manifest by what follows that He had not forgotten Perrot. Well-nigh half the population of those parts being swept off by a sudden visitation of deadly pestilence, most of the survivors fled therefrom in a panic, so that the country was, to all appearance, entirely deserted. Among those that died of the pest were the marshal, his lady, and his son, besides brothers and nephews and kinsfolk in great number; whereby of his entire household there were left only one of his daughters, now marriageable, and a few servants, among them Perrot. Now Perrot being a man of such notable prowess, the damsel, soon after the pestilence had spent itself, took him, with the approval and by the advice of the few folk that survived, to be her husband, and made him lord of all that fell to her by inheritance. Nor was it long before the King of England, learning that the marshal was dead, made Perrot the Picard, to whose merit he was no stranger, marshal in the dead man's room. Such, in brief, was the history of the two innocent children, with whom the Count of Antwerp had parted, never expecting to see them again.

'Twas now the eighteenth year since the Count of Antwerp had taken flight from Paris, when, being still in Ireland, where he had led a very sorry and suffering sort of life, and feeling that age was now come upon him, he felt a longing to learn, if possible, what was become of his children. The fashion of his outward man was now completely changed; for long hardship had (as he well knew) given to his age a vigour which his youth, lapped in ease, had lacked. So he hesitated not to take his leave of the knight with whom he had so long resided, and poor and in sorry trim he crossed to England, and made his way to the place where he had left Perrot —to find him a great lord

and marshal of the King, and in good health, and withal a
hardy man and very handsome. All which was very grateful
to the old man ; but yet he would not make himself known to
his son, until he had learned the fate of Jeannette. So forth
he fared again, nor did he halt until he was come to London,
where, cautiously questing about for news of the lady with
whom he had left his daughter, and how it fared with her, he
learned that Jeannette was married to the lady's son. Whereat,
in the great gladness of his heart, he counted all his past adver-
sity but a light matter, since he had found his children alive
and prosperous. But sore he yearned to see Jeannette. Where-
fore he took to loitering, as poor folk are wont, in the neighbour-
hood of the house. And so one day Jacques Lamiens—such
was the name of Jeannette's husband—saw him and had pity on
him, observing that he was poor and aged, and bade one of his
servants take him indoors, and for God's sake give him some-
thing to eat ; and nothing loath the servant did so. Now
Jeannette had borne Jacques several children, the finest and
the most winsome children in the world, the eldest no more
than eight years old ; who gathered about the Count as he ate,
and, as if by instinct divining that he was their grandfather,
began to make friends with him. He, knowing them for his
grandchildren, could not conceal his love, and repaid them
with caresses ; insomuch that they would not hearken to their
governor when he called them, but remained with the Count.
Which being reported to Jeannette, she came out of her room,
crossed to where the Count was sitting with the children, and
bade them do as their master told them, or she would certainly
have them whipped. The children began to cry, and to say
that they would rather stay with the worthy man, whom
they liked much better than their master ; whereat both the
lady and the Count laughed in sympathy. The Count had
risen, with no other intention—for he was not minded to disclose
his paternity—than to pay his daughter the respect due from
his poverty to her rank, and the sight of her had thrilled his
soul with a wondrous delight. By her he was and remained
unrecognised ; utterly changed as he was from his former self ;
aged, grey-haired, bearded, lean and tanned—in short to all
appearance another man than the Count.

However, seeing that the children were unwilling to leave
him, but wept when she made as if she would constrain them,
she bade the master let them be for a time. So the children
remained with the worthy man, until by chance Jacques' father

came home, and learned from the master what had happened.
Whereupon, having a grudge against Jeannette, he said:—
"Let them be; and God give them the ill luck which He owes
them: whence they sprang, thither they must needs return;
they descend from a vagabond on the mother's side, and so 'tis
no wonder that they consort readily with vagabonds." The
Count caught these words and was sorely pained, but, shrugging
his shoulders, bore the affront silently as he had borne many
another. Jacques, who had noted his children's fondness for
the worthy man, to wit, the Count, was displeased; but never-
theless, such was the love he bore them, that, rather than see
them weep, he gave order that, if the worthy man cared to stay
there in his service, he should be received. The Count answered
that he would gladly do so, but that he was fit for nothing except
to look after horses, to which he had been used all his life. So
a horse was assigned him, and when he had groomed him, he
occupied himself in playing with the children.

While Fortune thus shaped the destinies of the Count of
Antwerp and his children, it so befell that after a long series of
truces made with the Germans the King of France died, and
his crown passed to his son, whose wife had been the occasion
of the Count's banishment. The new king, as soon as the last
truce with the Germans was run out, renewed hostilities with
extraordinary vigour, being aided by his brother of England
with a large army under the command of his marshal, Perrot,
and his other marshal's son, Jacques Lamiens. With them went
the worthy man, that is to say, the Count, who, unrecognised
by any, served for a long while in the army in the capacity of
groom, and acquitted himself both in counsel and in arms with
a wisdom and valour unwonted in one of his supposed rank.
The war was still raging when the Queen of France fell seriously
ill, and, as she felt her end approach, made a humble and
contrite confession of all her sins to the Archbishop of Rouen,
who was universally reputed a good and most holy man.
Among her other sins she confessed the great wrong that she
had done to the Count of Antwerp; nor was she satisfied to
confide it to the Archbishop, but recounted the whole affair,
as it had passed, to not a few other worthy men, whom she
besought to use their influence with the King to procure the
restitution of the Count, if he were still alive, and if not, of his
children, to honour and estate. And so, dying shortly after-
wards, she was honourably buried. The Queen's confession
wrung from the King a sigh or two of compunction for a brave

man cruelly wronged ; after which he caused proclamation to
be made throughout the army and in many other parts, that
whoso should bring him tidings of the Count of Antwerp, or his
children, should receive from him such a guerdon for each of
them as should justly be matter of marvel ; seeing that he held
him acquitted, by confession of the Queen, of the crime for
which he had been banished, and was therefore now minded to
grant him not only restitution but increase of honour and estate.

Now the Count, being still with the army in his character of
groom, heard the proclamation, which he did not doubt was
made in good faith. Wherefore he hied him forthwith to
Jacques, and begged a private interview with him and Perrot,
that he might discover to them that whereof the King was in
quest. So the meeting was had ; and Perrot was on the point
of declaring himself, when the Count anticipated him :—
" Perrot," he said, " Jacques here has thy sister to wife, but
never a dowry had he with her. Wherefore that thy sister be
not dowerless, 'tis my will that he, and no other, have this
great reward which the King offers for thee, son, as he shall
certify, of the Count of Antwerp, and for his wife and thy sister,
Violante, and for me, Count of Antwerp, thy father." So
hearing, Perrot scanned the Count closely, and forthwith
recognising him, burst into tears, and throwing himself at his
feet embraced him, saying :—" My father, welcome, welcome
indeed art thou." Whereupon, between what he had heard
from the Count and what he had witnessed on the part of
Perrot, Jacques was so overcome with wonder and delight, that
at first he was at a loss to know how to act. However, giving
entire credence to what he had heard, and recalling insulting
language which he had used towards the quondam groom, the
Count, he was sore stricken with shame, and wept, and fell at
the Count's feet, and humbly craved his pardon for all past
offences ; which the Count, raising him to his feet, most graci-
ously granted him. So with many a tear and many a hearty
laugh the three men compared their several fortunes ; which
done, Perrot and Jacques would have arrayed the Count in
manner befitting his rank, but he would by no means suffer it,
being minded that Jacques, so soon as he was well assured that
the guerdon was forthcoming, should present him to the King
in his garb of groom, that thereby the King might be the more
shamed. So Jacques, with the Count and Perrot, went presently
to the King and offered to present to him the Count and his
children, provided the guerdon were forthcoming according to

the proclamation.   Jacques wondered not a little as forthwith at a word from the King a guerdon was produced ample for all three, and he was bidden take it away with him, so only that he should in very truth produce, as he had promised, the Count and his children in the royal presence.   Then, withdrawing a little and causing his quondam groom, now Count, to come forward with Perrot, he said :—" Sire, father and son are before you ; the daughter, my wife, is not here, but, God willing, you shall soon see her."   So hearing, the King surveyed the Count, whom, notwithstanding his greatly changed appearance, he at length recognised, and well-nigh moved to tears, he raised him from his knees to his feet, and kissed and embraced him.   He also gave a kindly welcome to Perrot, and bade forthwith furnish the Count with apparel, servants and horses, suited to his rank ; all which was no sooner said than done.   Moreover the King shewed Jacques no little honour, and particularly questioned him of all his past adventures.

As Jacques was about to take the noble guerdons assigned him for the discovery of the Count and his children, the Count said to him :—" Take these tokens of the magnificence of our Lord the King, and forget not to tell thy father that 'tis from no vagabond that thy children, his and my grandchildren, descend on the mother's side."   So Jacques took the guerdons, and sent for his wife and mother to join him at Paris.   Thither also came Perrot's wife : and there with all magnificence they were entertained by the Count, to whom the King had not only restored all his former estates and honours, but added thereto others, whereby he was now become a greater man than he had ever been before.   Then with the Count's leave they all returned to their several houses.   The Count himself spent the rest of his days at Paris in greater glory than ever.

NOVEL IX

Bernabò of Genoa, deceived by Ambrogiuolo, loses his money and commands his innocent wife to be put to death. She escapes, habits herself as a man, and serves the Soldan. She discovers the deceiver, and brings Bernabò to Alexandria, where the deceiver is punished. She then resumes the garb of a woman, and with her husband returns wealthy to Genoa.

WHEN Elisa had performed her part, and brought her touching story to a close, Queen Filomena, a damsel no less stately than

fair of person, and of a surpassingly sweet and smiling mien,
having composed herself to speak, thus began :—

Our engagements with Dioneo shall be faithfully observed ;
wherefore, as he and I alone remain to complete the day's
narration, I will tell my story first, and he shall have the grace
he craved, and be the last to speak. After which prelude she
thus began her story :—'Tis a proverb current among the vulgar
that the deceived has the better of the deceiver ; a proverb
which, were it not exemplified by events, might hardly in any
manner be justified. Wherefore, while adhering to our theme,
I am minded at the same time, dearest ladies, to shew you that
there is truth in this proverb ; the proof whereof should be
none the less welcome to you that it may put you on your
guard against deceivers.

Know then that certain very great merchants of Italy, being
met, as merchants use, for divers reasons proper to each, at
a hostelry in Paris, and having one evening jovially supped
together, fell a talking of divers matters, and so, passing from
one topic to another, they came at last to discuss the ladies
whom they had left at home, and one jocosely said :—" I cannot
answer for my wife ; but for myself I own, that, whenever a
girl that is to my mind comes in my way, I give the go-by to
the love that I bear my wife, and take my pleasure of the new-
comer to the best of my power." " And so do I," said another,
" because I know that, whether I suspect her or no, my wife
tries her fortune, and so 'tis do as you are done by ; the ass and
the wall are quits." A third added his testimony to the same
effect ; and in short all seemed to concur in the opinion that
the ladies they had left behind them were not likely to neglect
their opportunities, when one, a Genoese, Bernabò Lomellin
by name, dissociated himself from the rest, affirming that by
especial grace of God he was blessed with a wife who was,
perhaps, the most perfect paragon to be found in Italy of all
the virtues proper to a lady, ay, and in great measure, to a
knight or squire ; inasmuch as she was fair, still quite young,
handy, hardy, and clever beyond all other women in embroidery
work and all other forms of lady's handicraft. Moreover so
well-mannered, discreet and sensible was she that she was as
fit to wait at a lord's table as any squire or manservant or such
like, the best and most adroit that could be found. To which
encomium he added that she knew how to manage a horse, fly
a hawk, read, write and cast up accounts better than as if she
were a merchant ; and after much more in the same strain of

commendation he came at length to the topic of their conversation, asseverating with an oath that 'twas not possible to find a woman more honest, more chaste than she : nay, he verily believed that, if he remained from home for ten years, or indeed for the rest of his days, she would never think of any of these casual amours with any other man.

Among the merchants who thus gossiped was a young man, Ambrogiuolo da Piacenza by name, who, when Bernabò thus concluded his eulogy of his wife, broke out into a mighty laugh, and asked him with a leer, whether he of all men had this privilege by special patent of the Emperor. Bernabò replied, somewhat angrily, that 'twas a boon conferred upon him by God, who was rather more powerful than the Emperor. To which Ambrogiuolo rejoined :—" I make no doubt, Bernabò, that thou believest that what thou sayst is true ; but, methinks, thou hast been but a careless observer of the nature of things ; otherwise, I do not take thee to be of so gross understanding but that thou must have discerned therein reasons for speaking more judiciously of this matter. And that thou mayst not think that we, who have spoken with much freedom about our wives, deem them to be of another nature and mould than thine, but mayst know that we have but uttered what common sense dictates, I am minded to go a little further into this matter with thee. I have always understood, that of all mortal beings created by God man is the most noble, and next after him woman : man, then, being, as is universally believed, and is indeed apparent by his works, more perfect than woman, must without doubt be endowed with more firmness and constancy, women being one and all more mobile, for reasons not a few and founded in nature, which I might adduce, but mean for the present to pass over. And yet, for all his greater firmness, man cannot withstand—I do not say a woman's supplications, but— the mere lust of the eye which she unwittingly excites, and that in such sort that he will do all that is in his power to induce her to pleasure him, not once, perhaps, in the course of a month, but a thousand times a day. How, then, shouldst thou expect a woman, mobile by nature, to resist the supplications, the flatteries, the gifts, and all the other modes of attack that an accomplished seducer will employ ? Thou thinkest that she may hold out ! Nay verily, affirm it as thou mayst, I doubt thou dost not really so think. Thou dost not deny that thy wife is a woman, a creature of flesh and blood like the rest ; and if so, she must have the same cravings, the same natural propensities as they, and no more force to withstand them ; wherefore 'tis at least possible, that, however honest she be, she will do as others do ; and nought that is possible admits such peremptory denial or affirmation of its contrary as this of thine."

Whereto Bernabò returned :—" I am a merchant and no philosopher, and I will give thee a merchant's answer. I acknowledge that what thou sayst is true of vain and foolish women who have no modesty, but such as are discreet are so sensitive in regard of their honour that they become better able to preserve it than men, who have no such solicitude ; and my wife is one of this sort." " Doubtless," observed Ambrogiuolo, " few would be found to indulge in these casual amours, if every time they did so a horn grew out on the brow to attest the fact ; but not only does no horn make its appearance but not so much as a trace or vestige of a horn, so only they be but prudent ; and the shame and dishonour consist only in the discovery : wherefore, if they can do it secretly, they do it, or are fools to refrain.   Hold it for certain that she alone is chaste who either had never suit made to her, or, suing herself, was repulsed.   And albeit I know that for reasons true and founded in nature this must needs be, yet I should not speak so positively thereof as I do, had I not many a time with many a woman verified it by experience.   And I assure thee that, had I but access to this most saintly wife of thine, I should confidently expect very soon to have the same success with her as with others."   Then Bernabò angrily :—" 'Twere long and tedious to continue this discussion.   I should have my say, and thou thine, and in the end 'twould come to nothing.   But, as thou sayst that they are all so compliant, and that thou art so accomplished a seducer, I give thee this pledge of the honour of my wife : I consent to forfeit my head, if thou shouldst succeed in bringing her to pleasure thee in such a sort ; and shouldst thou fail, thou shalt forfeit to me no more than one thousand florins of gold."

Elated by this unexpected offer, Ambrogiuolo replied :—" I know not what I should do with thy blood, Bernabò, if I won the wager ; but, if thou wouldst have proof of what I have told thee, lay five thousand florins of gold, which must be worth less to thee than thy head, against a thousand of mine, and, whereas thou makest no stipulation as to time, I will bind myself to go to Genoa, and within three months from my departure hence to have had my pleasure of thy wife, and in witness thereof to bring back with me, of the things which she prizes most dearly, evidence of her compliance so weighty and conclusive that thou thyself shalt admit the fact ; nor do I require ought of thee but that thou pledge thy faith neither to come to Genoa nor to write word to her of this matter during the said three months." Bernabò professed himself well content ; and though the rest of the company, seeing that the compact might well have very evil consequences, did all that they could to frustrate it, yet the two men were now so heated that, against the will of the others, they set it down fairly in writing, and signed it each with his own hand. This done, Ambrogiuolo, leaving Bernabò at Paris, posted with all speed for Genoa. Arrived there, he set to work with great caution ; and having found out the quarter in which the lady resided, he learned in the course of a few days enough about her habits of life and her character to know that what Bernabò had told him was rather less than the truth. So, recognising that his enterprise was hopeless, he cast about for some device whereby he might cover his defeat ; and having got speech of a poor woman, who was much in the lady's house, as also in her favour, he bribed her (other means failing) to convey him in a chest, which he had had made for the purpose, not only into the house but into the bedroom of the lady, whom the good woman, following Bernabò's instructions, induced to take charge of it for some days, during which, she said, she would be away.

So the lady suffered the chest to remain in the room ; and when the night was so far spent that Bernabò thought she must be asleep, he opened it with some tools with which he had provided himself, and stole softly out. There was a light in the room, so that he was able to form an idea of its situation, to take note of the pictures and everything else of consequence that it contained, and to commit the whole to memory. This done, he approached the bed ; and observing that the lady, and a little girl that was with her, were fast asleep, he gently uncovered her, and saw that nude she was not a whit less lovely than when dressed : he looked about for some mark that might serve him as evidence that he had seen her in this state, but found nothing except a mole, which she had under the left breast, and which was fringed with a few fair hairs that shone like gold. So beautiful was she that he was tempted at the hazard of his life to take his place by her side in the bed ; but, remembering what he had heard of her inflexible obduracy in such affairs, he did not venture ; but quietly replaced the

bedclothes ; and having passed the best part of the night very
much at his ease in her room, he took from one of the lady's
boxes a purse, a gown, a ring and a girdle, and with these
tokens returned to the chest, and locked himself in as before.
In this manner he passed two nights, nor did the lady in the
least suspect his presence. On the third day the good woman
came by preconcert to fetch her chest, and took it back to the
place whence she had brought it. So Ambrogiuolo got out,
paid her the stipulated sum, and hied him back with all speed
to Paris, where he arrived within the appointed time. Then,
in presence of the merchants who were witnesses of his alterca-
tion with Bernabò, and the wager to which it had given occasion,
he told Bernabò that he had won the bet, having done what he
had boasted that he would do ; and in proof thereof he first of
all described the appearance of the room and the pictures, and
then displayed the articles belonging to the lady which he had
brought away with him, averring that she had given them to
him. Bernabò acknowledged the accuracy of his description
of the room, and that the articles did really belong to his wife,
but objected that Ambrogiuolo might have learned characteristic
features of the room from one of the servants, and have come
by the things in a similar way, and therefore, unless he had
something more to say, he could not justly claim to have won
the bet. "Verily," rejoined Ambrogiuolo, "this should
suffice ; but, as thou requirest that I say somewhat further, I
will satisfy thee. I say, then, that Madam Zinevra, thy wife,
has under her left breast a mole of some size, around which are,
perhaps, six hairs of a golden hue." As Bernabò heard this, it
was as if a knife pierced his heart, so poignant was his suffering ;
and, though no word escaped him, the complete alteration of
his mien bore unmistakable witness to the truth of Ambrogiuolo's
words. After a while he said :—"Gentlemen, 'tis even as
Ambrogiuolo says ; he has won the bet ; he has but to come
when he will, and he shall be paid." And so the very next day
Ambrogiuolo was paid in full, and Bernabò, intent on wreaking
vengeance on his wife, left Paris and set his face towards Genoa.
He had no mind, however, to go home, and accordingly halted
at an estate which he had some twenty miles from the city,
whither he sent forward a servant, in whom he reposed much
trust, with two horses and a letter advising the lady of his
return, and bidding her come out to meet him. At the same
time he gave the servant secret instructions to choose some
convenient place, and ruthlessly put the lady to death, and so

return to him. On his arrival at Genoa the servant delivered his message and the letter to the lady, who received him with great cheer, and next morning got on horseback and set forth with him for her husband's estate. So they rode on, talking of divers matters, until they came to a deep gorge, very lonely, and shut in by high rocks and trees. The servant, deeming this just the place in which he might without risk of discovery fulfil his lord's behest, whipped out a knife, and seizing the lady by the arm, said :—" Madam, commend your soul to God, for here must end at once your journey and your life." Terror-stricken by what she saw and heard, the lady cried out :—" Mercy for God's sake ; before thou slay me, tell me at least wherein I have wronged thee, that thou art thus minded to put me to death." " Madam," said the servant, " me you have in no wise wronged ; but your husband—how you may have wronged him I know not—charged me shew you no mercy, but to slay you on this journey, and threatened to have me hanged by the neck, should I not do so. You know well how bound I am to him, and that I may not disobey any of his commands : God knows I pity you, but yet I can no otherwise." Whereat the lady burst into tears, saying :—" Mercy for God's sake ; make not thyself the murderer of one that has done thee no wrong, at the behest of another. The all-seeing God knows that I never did aught to merit such requital at my husband's hands. But enough of this for the present : there is a way in which thou canst serve at once God and thy master and myself, if thou wilt do as I bid thee : take, then, these clothes of mine and give me in exchange just thy doublet and a hood ; and carry the clothes with thee to my lord and thine, and tell him that thou hast slain me ; and I swear to thee by the life which I shall have received at thy hands, that I will get me gone, and there abide whence news of me shall never reach either him or thee or these parts." The servant, being loath to put her to death, soon yielded to pity ; and so he took her clothes, allowing her to retain a little money that she had, and gave her one of his worser doublets and a hood ; then, praying her to depart the country, he left her afoot in the gorge, and returned to his master, whom he gave to understand that he had not only carried out his orders but had left the lady's body a prey to wolves. Bernabò after a while returned to Genoa, where, the supposed murder being bruited abroad, he was severely censured.

Alone and disconsolate, the lady, as night fell, disguised her-self as best she could, and hied her to a neighbouring village, where, having procured what was needful from an old woman, she shortened the doublet and fitted it to her figure, converted her chemise into a pair of breeches, cut her hair close, and, in short, completely disguised herself as a sailor. She then made her way to the coast, where by chance she encountered a Catalan gentleman, by name Segner Encararch, who had landed from one of his ships, which lay in the offing, to recreate himself at Alba, where there was a fountain. So she made overture to him of her services, was engaged and taken aboard the ship, assuming the name Sicurano da Finale. The gentleman put her in better trim as to clothes, and found her so apt and handy at service that he was exceeding well pleased with her.

Not long afterwards the Catalan sailed one of his carracks to Alexandria. He took with him some peregrine falcons, which he presented to the Soldan, who feasted him once or twice ; and noting with approbation the behaviour of Sicurano, who always attended his master, he craved him of the Catalan, which request the Catalan reluctantly granted. Sicurano proved so apt for his new service that he was soon as high in grace and favour with the Soldan as he had been with the Catalan. Wherefore, when the time of year came at which there was wont to be held at Acre, then under the Soldan's sway, a great fair, much fre-quented by merchants, Christian and Saracen alike, and to which, for the security of the merchants and their goods, the Soldan always sent one of his great officers of state with other officers and a guard to attend upon them, he determined to send Sicurano, who by this time knew the language very well. So Sicurano was sent to Acre as governor and captain of the guard for the protection of the merchants and merchandise. Arrived there, he bestirred himself with great zeal in all matters apper-taining to his office ; and as he went his rounds of inspection, he espied among the merchants not a few from Italy, Sicilians, Pisans, Genoese, Venetians, and so forth, with whom he con-sorted the more readily because they reminded him of his native land. And so it befell that, alighting once at a shop belonging to some Venetian merchants, he saw there among other trinkets a purse and a girdle, which he forthwith recognised as having once been his own. Concealing his surprise, he blandly asked whose they were, and if they were for sale. He was answered by Ambrogiuolo da Piacenza, who had come thither with much merchandise aboard a Venetian ship, and hearing that the captain of the guard was asking about the ownership of the purse and girdle, came forward, and said with a smile :—

" The things are mine, Sir, and I am not disposed to sell them, but, if they take your fancy, I will gladly give them to you." Observing the smile, Sicurano misdoubted that something had escaped him by which Ambrogiuolo had recognised him ; but he answered with a composed air :—" Thou dost smile, perchance, to see me, a soldier, come asking about this woman's gear ? "   " Not so, Sir," returned Ambrogiuolo ;   " I smile to think of the manner in which I came by it."   " And pray," said Sicurano, " if thou hast no reason to conceal it, tell me, in God's name, how thou didst come by the things."   " Why, Sir," said Ambrogiuolo, " they were given me by a Genoese lady, with whom I once spent a night, Madam Zinevra by name, wife of Bernabò Lomellin, who prayed me to keep them as a token of her love.   I smiled just now to think of the folly of Bernabò, who was so mad as to stake five thousand florins of gold against my thousand that I could not bring his wife to surrender to me ; which I did.   I won the bet ; and he, who should rather have been punished for his insensate folly, than she for doing what all women do, had her put to death, as I afterwards gathered, on his way back from Paris to Genoa."

Ambrogiuolo had not done speaking before Sicurano had discerned in him the evident cause of her husband's animosity against her, and all her woe, and had made up her mind that he should not escape with impunity.   She therefore feigned to be much interested by this story, consorted frequently and very familiarly with Ambrogiuolo, and insidiously captured his confidence, insomuch that at her suggestion, when the fair was done, he, taking with him all his wares, accompanied her to Alexandria, where she provided him with a shop, and put no little of her own money in his hands ; so that he, finding it very profitable, was glad enough to stay.   Anxious to make her innocence manifest to Bernabò, Sicurano did not rest until, with the help of some great Genoese merchants that were in Alexandria, she had devised an expedient to draw him thither. Her plan succeeded ; Bernabò arrived ; and, as he was now very poor, she privily arranged that he should be entertained by one of her friends until occasion should serve to carry out her design.   She had already induced Ambrogiuolo to tell his story to the Soldan, and the Soldan to interest himself in the matter.   So Bernabò being come, and further delay inexpedient, she seized her opportunity, and persuaded the Soldan to cite Ambrogiuolo and Bernabò before him, that in Bernabò's presence Ambrogiuolo might be examined of his boast touching

Bernabò's wife, and the truth thereof, if not to be had from him
by gentle means, be elicited by torture. So the Soldan, having
Ambrogiuolo and Bernabò before him, amid a great concourse
of his people questioned Ambrogiuolo of the five thousand
florins of gold that he had won from Bernabò, and sternly bade
him tell the truth. Still more harsh was the aspect of Sicurano,
in whom Ambrogiuolo had placed his chief reliance, but who
now threatened him with the direst torments if the truth were
not forthcoming. Thus hard bested on this side and on that,
and in a manner coerced, Ambrogiuolo, thinking he had but to
refund, in presence of Bernabò and many others accurately
recounted the affair as it had happened. When he had done,
Sicurano, as minister of the Soldan for the time being, turned
to Bernabò and said :—" And thy wife, thus falsely accused,
what treatment did she meet with at thy hands ? "
" Mortified," said Bernabò, " by the loss of my money, and the
dishonour which I deemed to have been done me by my wife,
I was so overcome by wrath that I had her put to death by one
of my servants, who brought me word that her corpse had been
instantly devoured by a pack of wolves."

Albeit the Soldan had heard and understood all that had
passed, yet he did not as yet apprehend the object for which
Sicurano had pursued the investigation. Wherefore Sicurano
thus addressed him :—" My lord, what cause this good lady
has to boast of her lover and her husband you have now abund-
ant means of judging ; seeing that the lover at one and the same
time despoils her of her honour, blasting her fair fame with
slanderous accusations, and ruins her husband ; who, more
prompt to trust the falsehood of another than the verity of
which his own long experience should have assured him, devotes
her to death and the devouring wolves ; and, moreover, such
is the regard, such the love which both bear her that, though
both tarry a long time with her, neither recognises her. How-
ever, that you may know full well what chastisements they
have severally deserved, I will now cause her to appear in your
presence and theirs, provided you, of your especial grace, be
pleased to punish the deceiver and pardon the deceived." The
Soldan, being minded in this matter to defer entirely to Sicurano,
answered that he was well content, and bade produce the lady.
Bernabò, who had firmly believed that she was dead, was lost
in wonder ; likewise Ambrogiuolo, who now divined his evil
plight, and dreading something worse than the disbursement
of money, knew not whether to expect the lady's advent with

fear or with hope. His suspense was not of long duration ;
for, as soon as the Soldan signified his assent, Sicurano, weeping,
threw herself on her knees at his feet, and discarding the tones,
as she would fain have divested herself of the outward semblance,
of a man, said :—" My lord, that forlorn, hapless Zinevra am I,
falsely and foully slandered by this traitor Ambrogiuolo, and
by my cruel and unjust husband delivered over to his servant
to slaughter and cast out as a prey to the wolves ; for which
cause I have now for six years been a wanderer on the face of
the earth in the guise of a man."   Then rending her robes in
front and baring her breast, she made it manifest to the Soldan
and all others who were present, that she was indeed a woman ;
then turning to Ambrogiuolo she haughtily challenged him to
say when she had ever lain with him, as he had boasted.
Ambrogiuolo said never a word, for he now recognised her,
and it was as if shame had reft from him the power of speech.
The Soldan, who had never doubted that Sicurano was a man,
was so wonder-struck by what he saw and heard that at times
he thought it must be all a dream.   But, as wonder gave place
to conviction of the truth he extolled in the amplest terms the
constancy and virtue and seemliness with which Zinevra, erst-
while Sicurano, had ordered her life.   He then directed that
she should be most nobly arrayed in the garb of her sex and
surrounded by a bevy of ladies.   Mindful of her intercession,
he granted to Bernabò the life which he had forfeited ; and she,
when Bernabò threw himself at her feet and wept and craved
her pardon, raised him, unworthy though he was, to his feet
and generously forgave him, and tenderly embraced him as
her husband.   Ambrogiuolo the Soldan commanded to be
bound to a stake, that his bare flesh, anointed with honey,
might be exposed to the sun on one of the heights of the city,
there to remain until it should fall to pieces of its own accord :
and so 'twas done.   He then decreed that the lady should have
the traitor's estate, which was worth not less but rather more
than ten thousand doubloons ; whereto he added, in jewels
and vessels of gold and silver and in money, the equivalent of
upwards of other ten thousand doubloons, having first enter-
tained her and her husband with most magnificent and cere-
monious cheer, accordant with the lady's worth.   Which done,
he placed a ship at their disposal, and gave them leave to return
to Genoa at their pleasure.   So to Genoa they returned very
rich and happy, and were received with all honour, especially
Madam Zinevra, whom all the citizens had believed to be dead,

and whom thenceforth, so long as she lived, they held of great
consequence and excellency. As for Ambrogiuolo, the very
same day that he was bound to the stake, the honey with which
his body was anointed attracted such swarms of flies, wasps
and gadflies, wherewith that country abounds, that not only
was his life sucked from him but his very bones were completely
denuded of flesh ; in which state, hanging by the sinews, they
remained a long time undisturbed, for a sign and a testimony
of his baseness to all that passed by. And so the deceived had
the better of the deceiver.

NOVEL X

*Paganino da Monaco carries off the wife of Messer Ricciardo di
Chinzica, who, having learned where she is, goes to Paganino
and in a friendly manner asks him to restore her. He
consents, provided she be willing. She refuses to go back
with her husband. Messer Ricciardo dies, and she marries
Paganino.*

THEIR queen's story, by its beauty, elicited hearty commenda-
tion from all the honourable company, and most especially
from Dioneo, with whom it now rested to conclude the day's
narration. Again and again he renewed his eulogy of the
queen's story ; and then began on this wise :—

Fair ladies, there is that in the queen's story which has caused
me to change my purpose, and substitute another story for
that which I had meant to tell : I refer to the insensate folly of
Bernabò (well though it was with him in the end) and of all
others, who delude themselves, as he seemed to do, with the
vain imagination that, while they go about the world, taking
their pleasure now of this, now of the other woman, their wives,
left at home, suffer not their hands to stray from their girdles ;
as if we, who are born of them and bred among them, could be
ignorant of the bent of their desires. Wherefore, by my story
I purpose at one and the same time to shew you how great is
the folly of all such, and how much greater is the folly of those
who, deeming themselves mightier than nature, think by
sophistical arguments to bring that to pass which is beyond their
power, and strive might and main to conform others to their
own pattern, however little the nature of the latter may brook
such treatment. Know then that there was in Pisa a judge,

better endowed with mental than with physical vigour, by
name Messer Ricciardo di Chinzica, who, being minded to take
a wife, and thinking, perhaps, to satisfy her by the same re-
sources which served him for his studies, was to be suited with
none that had not both youth and beauty, qualities which he
would rather have eschewed, if he had known how to give
himself as good counsel as he gave to others.   However, being
very rich, he had his desire.   Messer Lotto Gualandi gave him
in marriage one of his daughters, Bartolomea by name, a maid
as fair and fit for amorous dalliance as any in Pisa, though few
maids be there that do not shew as spotted lizards.   The judge
brought her home with all pomp and ceremony, and had a brave
and lordly wedding ; but in the essay which he made the very
first night to serve her so as to consummate the marriage he
made a false move, and drew the game much to his own dis-
advantage ; for next morning his lean, withered and scarce
animate frame was only to be re-quickened by draughts of
vernaccia,[1] artificial restoratives and the like remedies.   So,
taking a more sober estimate of his powers than he had been
wont, the worthy judge began to give his wife lessons from a
calendar, which might have served as a horn-book, and perhaps
had been put together at Ravenna :[2] inasmuch as, according
to his shewing, there was not a day in the year but was sacred,
not to one saint only, but to many ; in honour of whom for
divers reasons it behoved men and women to abstain from carnal
intercourse ; whereto he added fast-days, Ember-days, vigils
of Apostles and other saints, Friday, Saturday, Sunday, the
whole of Lent, certain lunar mansions, and many other excep-
tions, arguing perchance, that the practice of men with women
abed should have its times of vacation no less than the adminis-
tration of the law.   In this method, which caused the lady
grievous dumps, he long persisted, hardly touching her once a
month, and observing her closely, lest another should give her
to know working-days, as he had taught her holidays.

Now it so befell that, one hot season, Messer Ricciardo thought
he would like to visit a very beautiful estate which he had near
Monte Nero, there to take the air and recreate himself for some
days, and thither accordingly he went with his fair lady.   While
there, to amuse her, he arranged for a day's fishing ; and so,
he in one boat with the fishermen, and she in another with other

---

[1] A strong white wine.
[2] The saying went, that owing to the multitude of churches at Ravenna
every day was there a saint's day.

I—*F 845

ladies, they put out to watch the sport, which they found so
delightsome, that almost before they knew where they were
they were some miles out to sea. And while they were thus
engrossed with the sport, a galliot of Paganino da Mare, a very
famous corsair of those days, hove in sight and bore down upon
the boats, and, for all the speed they made, came up with that in
which were the ladies ; and on sight of the fair lady Paganino,
regardless of all else, bore her off to his galliot before the very
eyes of Messer Ricciardo, who was by this time ashore, and
forthwith was gone. The chagrin of the judge, who was jealous
of the very air, may readily be imagined. But 'twas to no
purpose that, both at Pisa and elsewhere, he moaned and
groaned over the wickedness of the corsairs, for he knew neither
by whom his wife had been abducted, nor whither she had been
taken. Paganino, meanwhile, deemed himself lucky to have
gotten so beautiful a prize ; and being unmarried, he was
minded never to part with her, and addressed himself by soft
words to soothe the sorrow which kept her in a flood of tears.
Finding words of little avail, he at night passed—the more
readily that the calendar had slipped from his girdle, and all
feasts and holidays from his mind—to acts of love, and on this
wise administered consolation so effective that before they were
come to Monaco she had completely forgotten the judge and
his canons, and had begun to live with Paganino as merrily as
might be. So he brought her to Monaco, where, besides the
daily and nightly solace which he gave her, he honourably
entreated her as his wife.

Not long afterwards Messer Ricciardo coming to know where
his wife was, and being most ardently desirous to have her
back, and thinking none but he would understand exactly what
to do in the circumstances, determined to go and fetch her
himself, being prepared to spend any sum of money that might
be demanded by way of ransom. So he took ship, and being
come to Monaco, he both saw her and was seen by her ; which
news she communicated to Paganino in the evening, and told
him how she was minded to behave. Next morning Messer
Ricciardo, encountering Paganino, made up to him ; and soon
assumed a very familiar and friendly air, while Paganino pre-
tended not to know him, being on his guard to see what he
would be at. So Messer Ricciardo, as soon as he deemed the
time ripe, as best and most delicately he was able, disclosed to
Paganino the business on which he had come, praying him to
take whatever in the way of ransom he chose and restore him

the lady. Paganino replied cheerily :—" Right glad I am to
see you here, Sir ; and briefly thus I answer you :—True it is
that I have here a young woman ; whether she be your wife or
another man's, I know not, for you are none of my acquaintance,
nor is she, except for the short time that she has been with me.
If, as you say, you are her husband, why, as you seem to me to
be a pleasant gentleman, I will even take you to her, and I
doubt not she will know you well ; if she says that it is even
as you say, and is minded to go with you, you shall give me just
what you like by way of ransom, so pleasant have I found you ;
otherwise 'twill be churlish in you to think of taking her from
me, who am a young man, and as fit to keep a woman as another,
and moreover never knew any woman so agreeable." " My
wife," said Ricciardo, " she is beyond all manner of doubt, as
thou shalt see ; for so soon as thou bringest me to her, she will
throw her arms about my neck ; wherefore as thou art minded,
even so be it ; I ask no more." " Go we then," said Paganino ;
and forthwith they went into the house, and Paganino sent for
the lady while they waited in one of the halls. By and by she
entered from one of the adjoining rooms all trim and tricked
out, and advanced to the place where Paganino and Messer
Ricciardo were standing, but never a word did she vouchsafe to
her husband, any more than if he had been some stranger whom
Paganino had brought into the house. Whereat the judge was
mightily amazed, having expected to be greeted by her with
the heartiest of cheer, and began to ruminate thus :—Perhaps
I am so changed by the melancholy and prolonged heartache,
to which I have been a prey since I lost her, that she does not
recognise me. Wherefore he said :—" Madam, cause enough
have I to rue it that I took thee a-fishing, for never yet was
known such grief as has been mine since I lost thee ; and now
it seems as if thou dost not recognise me, so scant of courtesy
is thy greeting. Seest thou not that I am thy Messer Ricciardo,
come hither prepared to pay whatever this gentleman, in whose
house we are, may demand, that I may have thee back and take
thee away with me : and he is so good as to surrender thee on
my own terms ? " The lady turned to him with a slight smile,
and said :—" Is it to me you speak, Sir ? Bethink you that
you may have mistaken me for another, for I, for my part, do
not remember ever to have seen you." " Nay," said Messer
Ricciardo, " but bethink thee what thou sayst ; scan me closely ;
and if thou wilt but search thy memory, thou wilt find that I
am thy Ricciardo di Chinzica." " Your pardon, Sir," answered

the lady, " 'tis not, perhaps, as seemly for me, as you imagine,
to gaze long upon you ; but I have gazed long enough to know
that I never saw you before." Messer Ricciardo supposed that
she so spoke for fear of Paganino, in whose presence she durst
not acknowledge that she knew him : so, after a while, he
craved as a favour of Paganino that he might speak with her in
a room alone. Which request Paganino granted, so only that
he did not kiss her against her will. He then bade the lady
go with Messer Ricciardo into a room apart, and hear what he
had to say, and give him such answer as she deemed meet. So
the lady and Messer Ricciardo went together into a room alone,
and sate down, and Messer Ricciardo began on this wise :—
" Ah ! dear heart of me, sweet soul of me, hope of me, dost not
recognise thy Ricciardo that loves thee better than himself ?
how comes it thus to pass ? am I then so changed ? Ah !
goodly eye of me, do but look on me a little." Whereat the
lady burst into a laugh, and interrupting him, said :—" Rest
assured that my memory is not so short but that I know you
for what you are, my husband, Messer Ricciardo di Chinzica ;
but far enough you shewed yourself to be, while I was with you,
from knowing me for what I was, young, lusty, lively ; which,
had you been the wise man you would fain be reputed, you
would not have ignored, nor by consequence that which, besides
food and clothing, it behoves men to give young ladies, albeit
for shame they demand it not ; which in what sort you gave,
you know. You should not have taken a wife if she was to be
less to you than the study of the law, albeit 'twas never as a
judge that I regarded you, but rather as a bellman of encænia
and saints' days, so well you knew them all, and fasts and vigils.
And I tell you that, had you imposed the observance of as many
saints' days on the labourers that till your lands as on yourself
who had but my little plot to till, you would never have harvested
a single grain of corn. God in His mercy, having regard unto
my youth, has caused me to fall in with this gentleman, with
whom I am much closeted in this room, where nought is known
of feasts, such feasts, I mean, as you, more devoted to the
service of God than to the service of ladies, were wont to observe
in such profusion ; nor was this threshold ever crossed by
Saturday or Friday or vigil or Ember-days or Lent, that is so
long ; rather here we are at work day and night, threshing the
wool, and well I know how featly it went when the matin bell
last sounded. Wherefore with him I mean to stay, and to work
while I am young, and postpone the observance of feasts and

times of indulgence and fasts until I am old : so get you hence, and good luck go with you, but depart with what speed you may, and observe as many feasts as you like, so I be not with you."

The pain with which Messer Ricciardo followed this outburst was more than he could bear, and when she had done, he exclaimed :—" Ah ! sweet soul of me, what words are these that thou utterest ? Hast thou no care for thy parents' honour and thine own ? Wilt thou remain here to be this man's harlot, and to live in mortal sin, rather than live with me at Pisa as my wife ? Why, when he is tired of thee, he will cast thee out to thy most grievous dishonour. I will ever cherish thee, and ever, will I nill I, thou wilt be the mistress of my house. Wouldst thou, to gratify this unbridled and unseemly passion, part at once with thy honour and with me, who love thee more dearly than my very life ? Ah ! cherished hope of me, say not so again : make up thy mind to come with me. As I now know thy bent, I will henceforth constrain myself to pleasure thee : wherefore, sweet my treasure, think better of it, and come with me, who have never known a happy hour since thou wert reft from me." The lady answered :—" I expect not, nor is it possible, that another should be more tender of my honour than I am myself. Were my parents so, when they gave me to you ? I trow not ; nor mean I to be more tender of their honour now than they were then of mine. And if now I live in mortal sin, I will ever abide there until it be pestle sin :[1] concern yourself no further on my account. Moreover, let me tell you, that, whereas at Pisa 'twas as if I were your harlot, seeing that the planets in conjunction according to lunar mansion and geometric square intervened between you and me, here with Paganino I deem myself a wife, for he holds me in his arms all night long and hugs and bites me, and how he serves me, God be my witness. Ah ! but you say you will constrain yourself to serve me : to what end ? to do it on the third essay, and raise it by stroke of bâton ? I doubt not you are become a perfect knight since last I saw you. Begone, and constrain yourself to live ; for here, methinks, your tenure is but precarious, so hectic and wasted is your appearance. Nay more ; I tell you this, that, should Paganino desert me (which he does not seem disposed to do so long as I am willing to stay with him), never will I return to your house, where for one while I staid to my most grievous loss and prejudice, but

1 A poor jeu de mots, mortaio, mortar, being substituted for mortale.

will seek my commodity elsewhere, than with one from whose whole body I could not wring a single cupful of sap. So, again, I tell you that here is neither feast nor vigil ; wherefore here I mean to abide ; and you, get you gone, in God's name with what speed you may, lest I raise the cry that you threaten to violate me."

Messer Ricciardo felt himself hard bested, but he could not but recognise that, worn out as he was, he had been foolish to take a young wife ; so sad and woebegone he quitted the room, and, after expending on Paganino a wealth of words which signified nothing, he at last gave up his bootless enterprise, and leaving the lady to her own devices, returned to Pisa ; where for very grief he lapsed into such utter imbecility that, when he was met by any with greeting or question in the street, he made no other answer than " the evil hole brooks no holiday," and soon afterwards died. Which when Paganino learned, being well assured of the love the lady bore him, he made her his lawful wife ; and so, keeping neither feast nor vigil nor Lent, they worked as hard as their legs permitted, and had a good time. Wherefore, dear my ladies, I am of opinion that Messer Bernabò in his altercation with Ambrogiuolo rode the goat downhill.[1]

This story provoked so much laughter that the jaws of every one in the company ached ; and all the ladies by common consent acknowledged that Dioneo was right, and pronounced Bernabò a blockhead. But when the story was ended and the laughter had subsided, the queen, observing that the hour was now late, and that with the completion of the day's story-telling the end of her sovereignty was come, followed the example of her predecessor, and took off her wreath and set it on Neifile's brow, saying with gladsome mien, " Now, dear gossip, thine be the sovereignty of this little people ; " and so she resumed her seat. Neifile coloured somewhat to receive such honour, shewing of aspect even as the fresh-blown rose of April or May in the radiance of the dawn, her eyes rather downcast, and glowing with love's fire like the morning-star. But when the respectful murmur, by which the rest of the company gave blithe token of the favour in which they held their queen, was hushed, and her courage revived, she raised herself somewhat more in her seat than she was wont, and thus spoke :—" As so it is that I am your queen, I purpose not to

[1] *I.e.* argued preposterously, the goat being the last animal to carry a rider comfortably downhill.

depart from the usage observed by my predecessors, whose rule has commanded not only your obedience but your approbation. I will therefore in few words explain to you the course which, if it commend itself to your wisdom, we will follow. To-morrow, you know, is Friday, and the next day Saturday, days which most folk find somewhat wearisome by reason of the viands which are then customary, to say nothing of the reverence in which Friday is meet to be held, seeing that 'twas on that day that He who died for us bore His passion ; wherefore 'twould be in my judgment both right and very seemly, if, in honour of God, we then bade story-telling give place to prayer. On Saturday ladies are wont to wash the head, and rid their persons of whatever of dust or other soilure they may have gathered by the labours of the past week ; not a few, likewise, are wont to practise abstinence for devotion to the Virgin Mother of the Son of God, and to honour the approaching Sunday by an entire surcease from work. Wherefore, as we cannot then completely carry out our plan of life, we shall, I think, do well to intermit our story-telling on that day also. We shall then have been here four days ; and lest we should be surprised by new-comers, I deem it expedient that we shift our quarters, and I have already taken thought for our next place of sojourn. Where, being arrived on Sunday, we will assemble after our sleep ; and, whereas to-day our discourse has had an ample field to range in, I propose, both because you will thereby have more time for thought, and it will be best to set some limits to the license of our story-telling, that of the many diversities of Fortune's handiwork we make one our theme, whereof I have also made choice, to wit, the luck of such as have painfully acquired some much-coveted thing, or having lost, have recovered it. Wherein let each meditate some matter, which to tell may be profitable or at least delectable to the company, saving always Dioneo's privilege."

All applauded the queen's speech and plan, to which, there-fore, it was decided to give effect. Thereupon the queen called her seneschal, told him where to place the tables that evening, and then explained to him all that he had to do during the time of her sovereignty. This done, she rose with her train, and gave leave to all to take their pleasure as to each might seem best. So the ladies and the men hied them away to a little garden, where they diverted themselves a while ; then supper-time being come, they supped with all gay and festal cheer. When they were risen from the table, Emilia, at the queen's command, led the dance, while Pampinea, the other ladies responding, sang the ensuing song.

> Shall any lady sing, if I not sing,
> I to whom Love did full contentment bring?
>
> Come hither, Love, thou cause of all my joy,
> Of all my hope, and all its sequel blest,
>   And with me tune the lay,
> No more to sighs and bitter past annoy,
> That now but serve to lend thy bliss more zest;
>   But to that fire's clear ray,
> Wherewith enwrapt I blithely live and gay,
> Thee as my God for ever worshipping.
>
> 'Twas thou, O Love, didst set before mine eyes,
> When first thy fire my soul did penetrate,
>   A youth to be my fere,
> So fair, so fit for deeds of high emprise,
> That ne'er another shall be found more great,
>   Nay, nor, I ween, his peer:
> Such flame he kindled that my heart's full cheer
> I now pour out in chant with thee, my King.
>
> And that wherein I most delight is this,
> That as I love him, so he loveth me:
>   So thank thee, Love, I must.
> For whatsoe'er this world can yield of bliss
> Is mine, and in the next at peace to be
>   I hope through that full trust
> I place in him. And thou, O God, that dost
> It see, wilt grant of joy thy plenishing.

Some other songs and dances followed, to the accompaniment of divers sorts of music; after which, the queen deeming it time to go to rest, all, following in the wake of the torches, sought their several chambers. The next two days they devoted to the duties to which the queen had adverted, looking forward to the Sunday with eager expectancy.

Endeth here the second day of the Decameron, beginneth the third in which, under the rule of Neifile, discourse is had of the fortune of such as have painfully acquired some much-coveted thing, or, having lost, have recovered it.

THE dawn of Sunday was already changing from vermilion to orange, as the sun hasted to the horizon, when the queen rose and roused all the company. The seneschal had early sent forward to their next place of sojourn ample store of things meet with folk to make all things ready, and now seeing the queen on the road, and the decampment, as it were, begun, he hastily completed the equipment of the baggage-train, and set off therewith, attended by the rest of the servants, in rear of the ladies and gentlemen. So, to the chant of, perhaps, a score of nightingales and other birds, the queen, her ladies and the three young men trooping beside or after her, paced leisurely westward by a path little frequented and overgrown with herbage and flowers, which, as they caught the sunlight, began one and all to unfold their petals. So fared she on with her train, while the quirk and the jest and the laugh passed from mouth to mouth ; nor had they completed more than two thousand paces when, well before half tierce,[1] they arrived at a palace most fair and sumptuous, which stood out somewhat from the plain, being situate upon a low eminence. On entering, they first traversed its great halls and dainty chambers furnished throughout with all brave and meet appointments ; and finding all most commendable, they reputed its lord a magnifico. Then descending, they surveyed its spacious and cheerful court, its vaults of excellent wines and copious springs of most cool water, and found it still more commendable. After which, being fain of rest, they sat them down in a gallery which commanded the court, and was close imbosked with leafage and such flowers as the season afforded, and thither the discreet seneschal brought comfits and wines most choice and excellent, wherewith they were refreshed. Whereupon they hied them to a walled garden adjoining the palace ; which, the gate being opened, they entered, and wonder-struck by the beauty of the whole passed

[1] *I.e.* midway between prime and tierce, about 7.30 a.m.

on to examine more attentively the several parts. It was
bordered and traversed in many parts by alleys, each very
wide and straight as an arrow and roofed in with trellis of
vines, which gave good promise of bearing clusters that year,
and, being all in flower, dispersed such fragrance throughout
the garden as blended with that exhaled by many another
plant that grew therein made the garden seem redolent of all
the spices that ever grew in the East. The sides of the alleys
were all, as it were, walled in with roses white and red and
jasmine ; insomuch that there was no part of the garden but
one might walk there not merely in the morning but at high
noon in grateful shade and fragrance, completely screened from
the sun. As for the plants that were in the garden, 'twere long
to enumerate them, to specify their sorts, to describe the order
of their arrangement ; enough, in brief, that there was abund-
ance of every rarer species that our climate allows. In the
middle of the garden, a thing not less but much more to be
commended than aught else, was a lawn of the finest turf, and
so green that it seemed almost black, pranked with flowers of,
perhaps, a thousand sorts, and girt about with the richest
living verdure of orange-trees and cedars, which shewed not
only flowers but fruits both new and old, and were no less grateful
to the smell by their fragrance than to the eye by their shade.
In the middle of the lawn was a basin of whitest marble, graven
with marvellous art ; in the centre whereof—whether the
spring were natural or artificial I know not—rose a column
supporting a figure which sent forth a jet of water of such
volume and to such an altitude that it fell, not without a
delicious plash, into the basin in quantity amply sufficient to
turn a mill-wheel. The overflow was carried away from the
lawn by a hidden conduit, and then, re-emerging, was distributed
through tiny channels, very fair and cunningly contrived, in
such sort as to flow round the entire lawn, and by similar deriva-
tive channels to penetrate almost every part of the fair garden,
until, re-uniting at a certain point, it issued thence, and, clear
as crystal, slid down towards the plain, turning by the way
two mill-wheels with extreme velocity to the no small profit of
the lord. The aspect of this garden, its fair order, the plants
and the fountain and the rivulets that flowed from it, so charmed
the ladies and the three young men that with one accord they
affirmed that they knew not how it could receive any accession
of beauty, or what other form could be given to Paradise, if it
were to be planted on earth. So, excellently well pleased, they

roved about it, plucking sprays from the trees, and weaving them into the fairest of garlands, while songsters of, perhaps, a score of different sorts warbled as if in mutual emulation, when suddenly a sight as fair and delightsome as novel, which, engrossed by the other beauties of the place, they had hitherto overlooked, met their eyes. For the garden, they now saw, was peopled with a host of living creatures, fair and of, perhaps, a hundred sorts; and they pointed out to one another how here emerged a cony, or there scampered a hare, or couched a goat, or grazed a fawn, or many another harmless, all but domesticated, creature roved carelessly seeking his pleasure at his own sweet will. All which served immensely to reinforce their already abundant delight. At length, however, they had enough of wandering about the garden and observing this thing and that: wherefore they repaired to the beautiful fountain, around which were ranged the tables, and there, after they had sung half-a-dozen songs and trod some measures, they sat them down, at the queen's command, to breakfast, which was served with all celerity and in fair and orderly manner, the viands being both good and delicate; whereby their spirits rose, and up they got, and betook themselves again to music and song and dance, and so sped the hours, until, as the heat increased, the queen deemed it time that whoso was so minded should go to sleep. Some there were that did so; others were too charmed by the beauty of the place to think of leaving it; but tarried there, and, while the rest slept, amused themselves with reading romances or playing at chess or dice. However, after none, there was a general *levée*; and, with faces laved and refreshed with cold water, they gathered by the queen's command upon the lawn, and, having sat them down in their wonted order by the fountain, waited for the story-telling to begin upon the theme assigned by the queen. With this duty the queen first charged Filostrato, who began in this wise.

NOVEL I

Masetto da Lamporecchio feigns to be dumb, and obtains a gardener's place at a convent of women, who with one accord make haste to lie with him.

FAIREST ladies, not a few there are both of men and of women, who are so foolish as blindly to believe that, so soon as a young woman has been veiled in white and cowled in black, she ceases to be a woman, and is no more subject to the cravings proper to her sex, than if, in assuming the garb and profession of a nun, she had put on the nature of a stone : and if, perchance, they hear of aught that is counter to this their faith, they are no less vehement in their censure than if some most heinous and unnatural crime had been committed ; neither bethinking them of themselves, whom unrestricted liberty avails not to satisfy, nor making due allowance for the prepotent forces of idleness and solitude. And likewise not a few there are that blindly believe that, what with the hoe and the spade and coarse fare and hardship, the carnal propensities are utterly eradicated from the tillers of the soil, and therewith all nimbleness of wit and understanding. But how gross is the error of such as so suppose, I, on whom the queen has laid her commands, am minded, without deviating from the theme prescribed by her, to make manifest to you by a little story.

In this very country-side of ours there was and yet is a convent of women of great repute for sanctity—name it I will not, lest I should in some measure diminish its repute—the nuns being at the time of which I speak but nine in number, including the abbess, and all young women. Their very beautiful garden was in charge of a foolish fellow, who, not being content with his wage, squared accounts with their steward, and hied him back to Lamporecchio, whence he came. Among others who welcomed him home was a young husbandman, Masetto by name, a stout and hardy fellow, and handsome for a contadino, who asked him where he had been so long. Nuto, as our good friend was called, told him. Masetto then asked how he had been employed at the convent, and Nuto answered :—" I kept their large and beautiful garden in good trim, and, besides, I sometimes went to the wood to fetch the faggots, I drew water, and did some other trifling services ; but the ladies gave so little wage that it scarce kept me in shoes. And moreover they are all young, and, I think, they are one and all possessed of the devil, for 'tis impossible to do anything to their mind ; indeed, when I would be at work in the kitchen-garden, ' put this here,' would say one, ' put that here,' would say another, and a third would snatch the hoe from my hand, and say, ' that is not as it should be ' ; and so they would worry me until I would give up working and go out of the garden ; so that, what with this thing and that, I was minded to stay there no more, and so I am come hither. The steward asked me before I left to send him any one whom on my return I might find fit for the work, and I promised ; but God bless his loins, I shall be at no pains to find out and send him any one."

As Nuto thus ran on, Masetto was seized by such a desire to be with these nuns that he quite pined, as he gathered from what Nuto said that his desire might be gratified. And as that could not be, if he said nothing to Nuto, he remarked :—" Ah ! 'twas well done of thee to come hither. A man to live with women ! he might as well live with so many devils : six times out of seven they know not themselves what they want." There the conversation ended ; but Masetto began to cast about how he should proceed to get permission to live with them. He knew that he was quite competent for the services of which Nuto spoke, and had therefore no fear of failing on that score ; but he doubted he should not be received, because he was too young and well-favoured. So, after much pondering, he fell into the following train of thought :—The place is a long way off, and no one there knows me ; if I make believe that I am dumb, doubtless I shall be admitted. Whereupon he made his mind up, laid a hatchet across his shoulder, and saying not a word to any of his destination, set forth, intending to present himself at the convent in the character of a destitute man. Arrived there, he had no sooner entered than he chanced to encounter the steward in the courtyard, and making signs to him as dumb folk do, he let him know that of his charity he craved something to eat, and that, if need were, he would split firewood. The steward promptly gave him to eat, and then set before him some logs which Nuto had not been able to split, all which Masetto, who was very strong, split in a very short time. The steward, having occasion to go to the wood, took him with him, and there set him at work on the lopping ; which done he placed the ass in front of him, and by signs made him understand that he was to take the loppings back to the convent. This he did so well that the steward kept him for some days to do one or two odd jobs. Whereby it so befell that one day the abbess saw him, and asked the steward who he was. " Madam," replied the steward, " 'tis a poor deaf mute that came here a day or two ago craving alms, so I have treated him kindly, and have let him make himself useful in many ways. If he knew how to do the work of the kitchen-garden and would stay with us, I doubt not we should be well served ; for we have need of him, and he is strong, and would be able for whatever he might turn his hand to ; besides which you would have no cause to be apprehensive lest he should be cracking his jokes with your young women." "As I trust in God," said the abbess, "thou sayst sooth; find out if he can do the garden work, and if he can, do all thou canst to keep him with us; give him a pair of shoes, an old hood, and speak him well, make much of him, and let him be well fed." All which the steward promised to do.

Masetto, meanwhile, was close at hand, making as if he were sweeping the courtyard, and heard all that passed between the abbess and the steward, whereat he gleefully communed with himself on this wise :—Put me once within there, and you will see that I will do the work of the kitchen-garden as it never was done before. So the steward set him to work in the kitchen-garden, and finding that he knew his business excellently well, made signs to him to know whether he would stay, and he made answer by signs that he was ready to do whatever the steward wished. The steward then signified that he was engaged, told him to take charge of the kitchen-garden, and shewed him what he had to do there. Then, having other matters to attend to, he went away, and left him there. Now, as Masetto worked there day by day, the nuns began to tease him, and make him their butt (as it commonly happens that folk serve the dumb) and used bad language to him, the worst they could think of, supposing that he could not understand them : all which passed scarce heeded by the abbess, who perhaps deemed him as destitute of virility as of speech. Now it so befell that after a hard day's work he was taking a little rest, when two young nuns, who were walking in the garden, approached the spot where he lay, and stopped to look at him, while he pretended to be asleep. And so the bolder of the two said to the other :—" If I thought thou wouldst keep the secret, I would tell thee what I have sometimes meditated, and which thou perhaps mightest also find agreeable." The other replied :—" Speak thy mind freely and be sure that I will never tell a soul." Whereupon the bold one began :—" I know not if thou hast ever considered how close we are kept here, and that within these precincts dare never enter any man, unless it be the old steward or this mute : and I have often heard from ladies that have come hither, that all the other sweets that the world has to offer signify not a jot in comparison of the pleasure that a woman has in connexion with a man. Whereof I have more than once been minded to make experiment with this mute, no other man being available. Nor, indeed, could one find any man in the whole world so meet therefor ; seeing that

he could not blab if he would ; thou seest that he is but a dull
clownish lad, whose size has increased out of all proportion to
his sense ; wherefore I would fain hear what thou hast to say
to it." "Alas !" said the other, "what is 't thou sayst ?
Knowest thou not that we have vowed our virginity to God ? "
"Oh," rejoined the first, "think but how many vows are
made to Him all day long, and never a one performed : and
so, for our vow, let Him find another or others to perform it."
"But," said her companion, "suppose that we conceived, how
then ? " "Nay but," protested the first, "thou goest about
to imagine evil before it befalls thee : time enough to think of
that when it comes to pass ; there will be a thousand ways to
prevent its ever being known, so only we do not publish it our-
selves." Thus reassured, the other was now the more eager of
the two to test the quality of the male human animal. "Well
then," she said, "how shall we go about it ? " and was an-
swered :—"Thou seest 'tis past none ; I make no doubt but
all the sisters are asleep, except ourselves ; search we through
the kitchen-garden, to see if there be any there, and if there be
none, we have but to take him by the hand and lead him hither
to the hut where he takes shelter from the rain ; and then one
shall mount guard while the other has him with her inside.
He is such a simpleton that he will do just whatever we bid
him." No word of this conversation escaped Masetto, who,
being disposed to obey, hoped for nothing so much as that one
of them should take him by the hand. They, meanwhile,
looked carefully all about them, and satisfied themselves that
they were secure from observation : then she that had broached
the subject came close up to Masetto, and shook him ; where-
upon he started to his feet. So she took him by the hand with
a blandishing air, to which he replied with some clownish grins.
And then she led him into the hut, where he needed no pressing
to do what she desired of him. Which done, she changed places
with the other, as loyal comradeship required ; and Masetto,
still keeping up the pretence of simplicity, did their pleasure.
Wherefore before they left, each must needs make another
assay of the mute's powers of riding ; and afterwards, talking
the matter over many times, they agreed that it was in truth
not less but even more delightful than they had been given to
understand ; and so, as they found convenient opportunity,
they continued to go and disport themselves with the mute.

Now it so chanced that one of their gossips, looking out of
the window of her cell, saw what they did, and imparted it to

two others. The three held counsel together whether they should not denounce the offenders to the abbess, but soon changed their mind, and came to an understanding with them, whereby they became partners in Masetto. And in course of time by divers chances the remaining three nuns also entered the partnership. Last of all the abbess, still witting nought of these doings, happened one very hot day, as she walked by herself through the garden, to find Masetto, who now rode so much by night that he could stand very little fatigue by day, stretched at full length asleep under the shade of an almond-tree, his person quite exposed in front by reason that the wind had disarranged his clothes. Which the lady observing, and knowing that she was alone, fell a prey to the same appetite to which her nuns had yielded : she aroused Masetto, and took him with her to her chamber, where, for some days, though the nuns loudly complained that the gardener no longer came to work in the kitchen-garden, she kept him, tasting and re-tasting the sweetness of that indulgence which she was wont to be the first to censure in others. And when at last she had sent him back from her chamber to his room, she must needs send for him again and again, and made such exorbitant demands upon him, that Masetto, not being able to satisfy so many women, bethought him that his part of mute, should he persist in it, might entail disastrous consequences. So one night, when he was with the abbess, he cut the tongue-string, and thus broke silence :—" Madam, I have understood that a cock may very well serve ten hens, but that ten men are sorely tasked to satisfy a single woman ; and here am I expected to serve nine, a burden quite beyond my power to bear ; nay, by what I have already undergone I am now so reduced that my strength is quite spent ; wherefore either bid me Godspeed, or find some means to make matters tolerable." Wonder-struck to hear the supposed mute thus speak, the lady exclaimed :—" What means this ? I took thee to be dumb." " And in sooth, Madam, so was I," said Masetto, " not indeed from my birth, but through an illness which took from me the power of speech, which only this very night have I recovered ; and so I praise God with all my heart." The lady believed him ; and asked him what he meant by saying that he had nine to serve. Masetto told her how things stood ; whereby she perceived that of all her nuns there was not any but was much wiser than she ; and lest, if Masetto were sent away, he should give the convent a bad name, she discreetly determined to arrange matters with the nuns in such sort that he might remain there. So, the steward having died within the last few days, she assembled all the nuns; and their and her own past errors being fully avowed, they by common consent, and with Masetto's concurrence, resolved that the neighbours should be given to understand that by their prayers and the merits of their patron saint, Masetto, long mute, had recovered the power of speech; after which they made him steward, and so ordered matters among themselves that he was able to endure the burden of their service. In the course of which, though he procreated not a few little monastics, yet 'twas all managed so discreetly that no breath of scandal stirred, until after the abbess's death, by which time Masetto was advanced in years and minded to return home with the wealth that he had gotten; which he was suffered to do as soon as he made his desire known. And so Masetto, who had left Lamporecchio with a hatchet on his shoulder, returned thither in his old age rich and a father, having by the wisdom with which he employed his youth, spared himself the pains and expense of rearing children, and averring that such was the measure that Christ meted out to the man that set horns on his cap.

NOVEL II

A groom lies with the wife of King Agilulf, who learns the fact, keeps his own counsel, finds out the groom and shears him. The shorn shears all his fellows, and so comes safe out of the scrape.

FILOSTRATO'S story, which the ladies had received now with blushes now with laughter, being ended, the queen bade Pampinea follow suit. Which behest Pampinea smilingly obeyed, and thus began:—

Some there are whose indiscretion is such that they must needs evince that they are fully cognizant of that which it were best they should not know, and censuring the covert misdeeds of others, augment beyond measure the disgrace which they would fain diminish. The truth whereof, fair ladies, I mean to shew you in the contrary case, wherein appears the astuteness of one that held, perhaps, an even lower place than would have been Masetto's in the esteem of a doughty king.

Agilulf, King of the Lombards, who like his predecessors
made the city of Pavia in Lombardy the seat of his government,
took to wife Theodelinde, the widow of Authari, likewise King
of the Lombards, a lady very fair, wise and virtuous, but who
was unfortunate in her lover. For while the Lombards pros-
pered in peace under the wise and firm rule of King Agilulf, it
so befell that one of the Queen's grooms, a man born to very
low estate, but in native worth far above his mean office, and
moreover not a whit less tall and goodly of person than the
King, became inordinately enamoured of her. And as, for all
his base condition, he had sense enough to recognize that his
love was in the last degree presumptuous, he disclosed it to
none, nay, he did not even venture to tell her the tale by the
mute eloquence of his eyes. And albeit he lived without hope
that he should ever be able to win her favour, yet he inwardly
gloried that he had fixed his affections in so high a place ; and
being all aflame with passion, he shewed himself zealous beyond
any of his comrades to do whatever he thought was likely to
please the Queen. Whereby it came about, that, when the
Queen had to take horse, she would mount the palfrey that he
groomed rather than any other ; and when she did so, he
deemed himself most highly favoured, and never quitted her
stirrup, esteeming himself happy if he might but touch her
clothes. But as 'tis frequently observed that love waxes as
hope wanes, so was it with this poor groom, insomuch that the
burden of this great hidden passion, alleviated by no hope, was
most grievous to bear, and from time to time, not being able to
shake it off, he purposed to die. And meditating on the mode,
he was minded that it should be of a kind to make it manifest
that he died for the love which he had borne and bore to the
Queen, and also to afford him an opportunity of trying his
fortune whether his desire might in whole or in part be gratified.
He had no thought of speaking to the Queen, nor yet of declaring
his love to her by letter, for he knew that 'twould be vain either
to speak or to write ; but he resolved to try to devise some
means whereby he might lie with the Queen ; which end might
in no other way be compassed than by contriving to get access
to her in her bedroom ; which could only be by passing himself
off as the King, who, as he knew, did not always lie with her.
Wherefore, that he might observe the carriage and dress of the
King as he passed to her room, he contrived to conceal himself
for several nights in a great hall of the King's palace which
separated the King's room from that of the Queen : and on one

of these nights he saw the King issue from his room, wrapped
in a great mantle, with a lighted torch in one hand and a wand
in the other, and cross the hall, and, saying nothing, tap the
door of the Queen's room with the wand once or twice ; where-
upon the door was at once opened and the torch taken from his
hand. Having observed the King thus go and return, and
being bent on doing likewise, he found means to come by a
mantle like that which he had seen the King wear, and also
a torch and a wand : he then took a warm bath, and having
thoroughly cleansed himself, that the smell of the foul straw
might not offend the lady, or discover to her the deceit, he in
this guise concealed himself as he was wont in the great hall.
He waited only until all were asleep, and then, deeming the
time come to accomplish his purpose, or by his presumption
clear a way to the death which he coveted, he struck a light
with the flint and steel which he had brought with him ; and
having kindled his torch and wrapped himself close in his mantle,
he went to the door of the Queen's room and tapped on it
twice with his wand. The door was opened by a very drowsy
chambermaid, who took the torch and put it out of sight ;
whereupon without a word he passed within the curtain, laid
aside the mantle, and got into the bed where the Queen lay
asleep. Then, taking her in his arms and straining her to him
with ardour, making as if he were moody, because he knew that,
when the King was in such a frame, he would never hear aught,
in such wise, without word said either on his part or on hers,
he had more than once carnal cognizance of the Queen. Loath
indeed was he to leave her, but, fearing lest by too long tarrying
his achieved delight might be converted into woe, he rose, re-
sumed the mantle and the light, and leaving the room without
a word, returned with all speed to his bed. He was hardly
there when the King got up and entered the Queen's room ;
whereat she wondered not a little ; but, reassured by the glad-
some greeting which he gave her as he got into bed, she said :—
" My lord, what a surprise is this to-night ! 'Twas but now you
left me after an unwonted measure of enjoyment, and do you
not return so soon ? consider what you do." From these words
the King at once inferred that the Queen had been deceived by
some one that had counterfeited his person and carriage ; but,
at the same time, bethinking himself that, as neither the Queen
nor any other had detected the cheat, 'twas best to leave her in
ignorance, he wisely kept silence. Which many a fool would
not have done, but would have said :—" Nay, 'twas not I that

was here. Who was it that was here? How came it to pass?
Who came hither?" Whereby in the sequel he might have
caused the lady needless chagrin, and given her occasion to
desire another such experience as she had had; and so have
brought disgrace upon himself by uttering that, from which,
unuttered, no shame could have resulted. Wherefore, betraying
little, either by his mien or by his words, of the disquietude
which he felt, the King replied :—" Madam, seem I such to you
that you cannot suppose that I should have been with you once,
and returned to you immediately afterwards?" "Nay, not
so, my lord," returned the lady, " but none the less I pray you
to look to your health." Then said the King :—" And I am
minded to take your advice; wherefore, without giving you
further trouble I will leave you." So, angered and incensed
beyond measure by the trick which, he saw, had been played
upon him, he resumed his mantle and quitted the room with
the intention of privily detecting the offender, deeming that
he must belong to the palace, and that, whoever he might be.
he could not have quitted it. So, taking with him a small
lantern which shewed only a glimmer of light, he went into the
dormitory which was over the palace-stables and was of great
length, insomuch that well-nigh all the men-servants slept there
in divers beds, and arguing that, by whomsoever that of which
the Queen spoke was done, his heart and pulse could not after
such a strain as yet have ceased to throb, he began cautiously
with one of the head-grooms, and so went from bed to bed
feeling at the heart of each man to see if it was thumping. All
were asleep, save only he that had been with the Queen, who,
seeing the King come, and guessing what he sought to discover,
began to be mightily afraid, insomuch that to the agitation
which his late exertion had communicated to his heart, terror
now added one yet more violent; nor did he doubt that, should
the King perceive it, he would kill him. Divers alternatives of
action thronged his mind; but at last, observing that the
King was unarmed, he resolved to make as if he were asleep,
and wait to see what the King would do. So, having tried
many and found none that he deemed the culprit, the King
came at last to the culprit himself, and marking the thumping
of his heart, said to himself :—This is he. But being minded
to afford no clue to his ulterior purpose, he did no more than
with a pair of scissors which he had brought with him shear
away on one side of the man's head a portion of his locks, which,
as was then the fashion, he wore very long, that by this token

he might recognize him on the morrow ; and having so done, he departed and returned to his room. The groom, who was fully sensible of what the King had done, and being a shrewd fellow understood very well to what end he was so marked, got up without a moment's delay ; and, having found a pair of scissors—for, as it chanced, there were several pairs there belonging to the stables for use in grooming the horses—he went quietly through the dormitory and in like manner sheared the locks of each of the sleepers just above the ear ; which done without disturbing any, he went back to bed.

On the morrow, as soon as the King was risen, and before the gates of the palace were opened, he summoned all his men-servants to his presence, and, as they stood bareheaded before him, scanned them closely to see whether the one whom he had sheared was there ; and observing with surprise that the more part of them were all sheared in the same manner, said to himself :—Of a surety this fellow, whom I go about to detect, evinces, for all his base condition, a high degree of sense. Then, recognizing that he could not compass his end without causing a bruit, and not being minded to brave so great a dishonour in order to be avenged upon so petty an offender, he was content by a single word of admonition to shew him that his offence had not escaped notice. Wherefore turning to them all, he said :—" He that did it, let him do it no more, and get you hence in God's peace." Another would have put them to the strappado, the question, the torture, and thereby have brought to light that which one should rather be sedulous to cloak ; and having so brought it to light, would, however complete the retribution which he exacted, have not lessened but vastly augmented his disgrace, and sullied the fair fame of his lady. Those who heard the King's parting admonition wondered, and made much question with one another, what the King might have meant to convey by it : but 'twas understood by none but him to whom it referred : who was discreet enough never to reveal the secret as long as the King lived, or again to stake his life on such a venture.

NOVEL III

Under cloak of confession and a most spotless conscience, a lady,
enamoured of a young man, induces a booby friar unwittingly
to provide a means to the entire gratification of her passion.

WHEN Pampinea had done, and several of the company had
commended the hardihood and wariness of the groom, as also
the wisdom of the King, the queen, turning to Filomena, bade
her follow suit : wherefore with manner debonair Filomena
thus began :—

The story which I shall tell you is of a trick which was actually
played by a fair lady upon a booby religious, and which every
layman should find the more diverting that these religious,
being, for the most part, great blockheads and men of odd
manners and habits, do nevertheless credit themselves with
more ability and knowledge in all kinds than fall to the lot of
the rest of the world ; whereas, in truth, they are far inferior,
and so, not being able, like others, to provide their own susten-
ance, are prompted by sheer baseness to fly thither for refuge
where they may find provender, like pigs. Which story, sweet
my ladies, I shall tell you, not merely that thereby I may
continue the sequence in obedience to the queen's behest, but
also to the end that I may let you see that even the religious, in
whom we in our boundless credulity repose exorbitant faith,
may be, and sometimes are, made—not to say by men—even
by some of us women the sport of their sly wit.

In our city, where wiles do more abound than either love or
faith, there dwelt, not many years ago, a gentlewoman richly
endowed (none more so) by nature with physical charms, as also
with gracious manners, high spirit and fine discernment. Her
name I know, but will not disclose it, nor yet that of any other
who figures in this story, because there yet live those who might
take offence thereat, though after all it might well be passed off
with a laugh. High-born and married to an artificer of woollen
fabrics, she could not rid her mind of the disdain with which,
by reason of his occupation, she regarded her husband ; for
no man, however wealthy, so he were of low condition, seemed
to her worthy to have a gentlewoman to wife ; and seeing that
for all his wealth he was fit for nothing better than to devise a
blend, set up a warp, or higgle about yarn with a spinster, she
determined to dispense with his embraces, save so far as she

might find it impossible to refuse them ; and to find her satis-
faction elsewhere with one that seemed to her more meet to
afford it than her artificer of woollens.   In this frame of mind
she became enamoured of a man well worthy of her love and
not yet past middle age, insomuch that, if she saw him not in
the day, she must needs pass an unquiet night.   The gallant,
meanwhile, remained fancy-free, for he knew nought of the
lady's case ; and she, being apprehensive of possible perils to
ensue, was far too circumspect to make it known to him either
by writing or by word of mouth of any of her female friends.
Then she learned that he had much to do with a religious, a
simple, clownish fellow, but nevertheless, as being a man of
most holy life, reputed by almost everybody a most worthy
friar, and decided that she could not find a better intermediary
between herself and her lover than this same friar.   So, having
matured her plan, she hied her at a convenient time to the
convent where the friar abode, and sent for him, saying, that,
if he so pleased, she would be confessed by him.   The friar, who
saw at a glance that she was a gentlewoman, gladly heard her
confession ; which done, she said :— " My father, I have yet a
matter to confide to you, in which I must crave your aid and
counsel.   Who my kinsfolk and husband are, I wot you know,
for I have myself told you.   My husband loves me more dearly
than his life, and being very wealthy, he can well and does
forthwith afford me whatever I desire.   Wherefore, as he loves
me, even so I love him more dearly than myself ; nor was there
ever yet wicked woman that deserved the fire so richly as should
I, were I guilty—I speak not of acts, but of so much as a single
thought of crossing his will or tarnishing his honour.   Now a
man there is— his name, indeed, I know not, but he seems to
me to be a gentleman, and, if I mistake not, he is much with
you—a fine man and tall, his garb dun and very decent, who,
the bent of my mind being, belike, quite unknown to him,
would seem to have laid siege to me, insomuch that I cannot
shew myself at door or casement, or quit the house, but forth-
with he presents himself before me ; indeed I find it passing
strange that he is not here now ; whereat I am sorely troubled,
because, when men so act, unmerited reproach will often thereby
be cast upon honest women.   At times I have been minded to
inform my brothers of the matter ; but then I have bethought
me that men sometimes frame messages in such a way as to
evoke untoward answers, whence follow high words ; and so
they proceed to rash acts : wherefore, to obviate trouble and

scandal, I have kept silence, and by preference have made you my confidant, both because you are the gentleman's friend, and because it befits your office to censure such behaviour not only in friends but in strangers. And so I beseech you for the love of our only Lord God to make him sensible of his fault, and pray him to offend no more in such sort. Other ladies there are in plenty, who may, perchance, be disposed to welcome such advances, and be flattered to attract his fond and assiduous regard, which to me, who am in no wise inclined to encourage it, is but a most grievous molestation."

Having thus spoken, the lady bowed her head as if she were ready to weep. The holy friar was at no loss to apprehend who it was of whom she spoke ; he commended her virtuous frame, firmly believing that what she said was true, and promised to take such action that she should not again suffer the like annoyance : nor, knowing that she was very wealthy, did he omit to extol works of charity and almsgiving, at the same time opening to her his own needs. " I make my suit to you," said she, " for the love of God ; and if your friend should deny what I have told you, tell him roundly that 'twas from me you had it, and that I made complaint to you thereof." So, her confession ended and penance imposed, bethinking her of the hints which the friar had dropped touching almsgiving, she slipped into his hand as many coins as it would hold, praying him to say masses for the souls of her dead. She then rose and went home.

Not long afterwards the gallant paid one of his wonted visits to the holy friar. They conversed for a while of divers topics, and then the friar took him aside, and very courteously reproved him for so haunting and pursuing the lady with his gaze, as from what she had given him to understand, he supposed was his wont. The gallant, who had never regarded her with any attention, and very rarely passed her house, was amazed, and was about to clear himself, when the friar closed his mouth, saying :—" Now away with this pretence of amazement, and waste not words in denial, for 'twill not avail thee. I have it not from the neighbours ; she herself, bitterly complaining of thy conduct, told it me. I say not how ill this levity beseems thee ; but of her I tell thee so much as this, that, if I ever knew woman averse to such idle philandering, she is so ; and therefore for thy honour's sake, and that she be no more vexed, I pray thee refrain therefrom, and let her be in peace." The gallant, having rather more insight than the holy friar, was not slow to penetrate the lady's finesse ; he therefore made as if he were rather shame-stricken, promised to go no further with the matter, and hied him straight from the friar to the lady's house, where she was always posted at a little casement to see if he were passing by. As she saw him come, she shewed him so gay and gracious a mien that he could no longer harbour any doubt that he had put the true construction upon what he had heard from the friar ; and thenceforth, to his own satisfaction and the immense delight and solace of the lady, he omitted not daily to pass that way, being careful to make it appear as if he came upon other business. 'Twas thus not long before the lady understood that she met with no less favour in his eyes than he in hers ; and being desirous to add fuel to his flame, and to assure him of the love she bore him, as soon as time and occasion served, she returned to the holy friar, and having sat herself down at his feet in the church, fell a-weeping. The friar asked her in a soothing tone what her new trouble might be. Whereto the lady answered :—" My father, 'tis still that accursed friend of thine, of whom I made complaint to you some days ago, and who would now seem to have been born for my most grievous torment, and to cause me to do that by reason whereof I shall never be glad again, nor venture to place myself at your feet." " How ? " said the friar ; " has he not forborne to annoy thee ? " " Not he, indeed," said the lady ; " on the contrary, 'tis my belief that, since I complained to you of him, he has, as if in despite, being offended, belike, that I did so, passed my house seven times for once that he did so before. Nay, would to God he were content to pass and fix me with his eyes ; but he is waxed so bold and unabashed that only yesterday he sent a woman to me at home with his compliments and cajoleries, and, as if I had not purses and girdles enough, he sent me a purse and a girdle ; whereat I was, as I still am, so wroth, that, had not conscience first, and then regard for you, weighed with me, I had flown into a frenzy of rage. However, I restrained myself, and resolved neither to do nor to say aught without first letting you know it. Nor only so ; but, lest the woman who brought the purse and girdle, and to whom I at first returned them, shortly bidding her begone and take them back to the sender, should keep them and tell him that I had accepted them, as I believe they sometimes do, I recalled her and had them back, albeit 'twas in no friendly spirit that I received them from her hand ; and I have brought them to you, that you may return them to him and tell him that I stand in no need of such gifts from him, because, thanks be to God and my husband, I have purses and girdles enough to smother him in. And if after this he leave me not alone, I pray you as my father to hold me excused if, come what may, I tell it to my husband and brothers ; for much liefer had I that he suffer indignity, if so it must be, than that my fair fame should be sullied on his account : that holds good, friar." Weeping bitterly as she thus ended, she drew from under her robe a purse of very fine and ornate workmanship and a dainty and costly little girdle, and threw them into the lap of the friar, who, fully believing what she said, manifested the utmost indignation as he took them, and said :—" Daughter, that by these advances thou shouldst be moved to anger, I deem neither strange nor censurable ; but I am instant with thee to follow my advice in the matter. I chid him some days ago, and ill has he kept the promise that he made me ; for which cause and this last feat of his I will surely make his ears so tingle that he will give thee no more trouble ; wherefore, for God's sake, let not thyself be so over-come by wrath as to tell it to any of thy kinsfolk ; which might bring upon him a retribution greater than he deserves. Nor fear lest thereby thy fair fame should suffer ; for I shall ever be thy most sure witness before God and men that thou art innocent." The lady made a shew of being somewhat com-forted : then, after a pause—for well she knew the greed of him and his likes—she said :—" Of late, Sir, by night, the spirits of divers of my kinsfolk have appeared to me in my sleep, and methinks they are in most grievous torment ; alms, alms, they crave, nought else, especially my mother, who seems to be in so woful and abject a plight that 'tis pitiful to see. Methinks 'tis a most grievous torment to her to see the tribulation which this enemy of God has brought upon me. I would therefore have you say for their souls the forty masses of St. Gregory and some of your prayers, that God may deliver them from this purging fire." So saying she slipped a florin into the hand of the holy friar, who took it gleefully, and having with edifying words and many examples fortified her in her devotion, gave her his benediction, and suffered her to depart.

The lady gone, the friar, who had still no idea of the trick that had been played upon him, sent for his friend ; who was no sooner come than he gathered from the friar's troubled air that he had news of the lady, and waited to hear what he would say. The friar repeated what he had said before, and then broke out into violent and heated objurgation on the score of the lady's latest imputation. The gallant, who did not as yet apprehend the friar's drift, gave but a very faint denial to the charge of sending the purse and girdle, in order that he might not discredit the lady with the friar, if, perchance, she had given him the purse and girdle. Whereupon the friar exclaimed with great heat :—" How canst thou deny it, thou wicked man ? Why, here they are ; she brought them to me in tears with her own hand. Look at them, and say if thou knowest them not." The gallant now feigned to be much ashamed, and said :— " Why, yes, indeed, I do know them ; I confess that I did wrong ; and I swear to you that, now I know her character, you shall never hear word more of this matter." Many words followed ; and then the blockheadly friar gave the purse and girdle to his friend, after which he read him a long lecture, besought him to meddle no more with such matters, and on his promising obedience dismissed him.

Elated beyond measure by the assurance which he now had of the lady's love, and the beautiful present, the gallant, on leaving the friar, hied him straight to a spot whence he stealthily gave the lady to see that he had both her gifts : whereat the lady was well content, the more so as her intrigue seemed ever to prosper more and more. She waited now only for her husband's departure from home to crown her enterprise with success. Nor was it long before occasion required that her husband should go to Genoa. The very morning that he took horse and rode away she hied her to the holy friar, and after many a lamentation she said to him betwixt her sobs :—" My father, now at last I tell you out and out that I can bear my suffering no longer. I promised you some days ago to do nought in this matter without first letting you know it : I am now come to crave release from that promise ; and that you may believe that my lamentations and complaints are not groundless, I will tell you how this friend of yours, who should rather be called a devil let loose from hell, treated me only this very morning, a little before matins. As ill-luck would have it, he learned, I know not how, that yesterday morning my husband went to Genoa, and so this morning at the said hour he came into my garden, and got up by a tree to the window of my bedroom, which looks out over the garden, and had already opened the casement, and was about to enter the room, when I suddenly awoke, and got up and uttered a cry, and should have continued to cry out, had not he, who was still outside, implored my mercy for God's sake and yours, telling me who he was. So, for love of you I was silent, and naked as I was born, ran

and shut the window in his face, and he—bad luck to him—
made off, I suppose, for I saw him no more. Consider now if
such behaviour be seemly and tolerable : I for my part am
minded to put up with no more of it ; indeed I have endured
too much already for love of you."

Wroth beyond measure was the friar, as he heard her thus
speak, nor knew he what to say, except that he several times
asked her if she were quite certain that it was no other than he.
" Holy name of God ! " replied the lady, " as if I did not yet
know him from another ! He it was, I tell you ; and do you
give no credence to his denial." " Daughter," said then the
friar, " there is here nought else to say but that this is a mon-
strous presumption and a most heinous offence ; and thou didst
well to send him away as thou didst. But seeing that God has
preserved thee from shame, I would implore thee that, as thou
hast twice followed my advice, thou do so likewise on this
occasion, and making no complaint to any of thy kinsfolk, leave
it to me to try if I can control this devil that has slipt his chain,
whom I supposed to be a saint ; and if I succeed in weaning
him from this insensate folly, well and good ; and if I fail,
thenceforth I give thee leave, with my blessing, to do whatsoever
may commend itself to thy own judgment." " Lo now,"
answered the lady, " once again I will not vex or disobey you ;
but be sure that you so order matters that he refrain from
further annoyance, as I give you my word that never will I
have recourse to you again touching this matter." Then,
without another word, and with a troubled air, she took leave
of him. Scarcely was she out of the church when the gallant
came up. The friar called him, took him aside, and gave him
the affront in such sort as 'twas never before given to any man,
reviling him as a disloyal and perjured traitor. The gallant,
who by his two previous lessons had been taught how to value
the friar's censures, listened attentively, and sought to draw
him out by ambiguous answers. " Wherefore this wrath, Sir ? "
he began. " Have I crucified Christ ? " " Ay, mark the fel-
low's effrontery ! " retorted the friar : " list to what he says !
He talks, forsooth, as if 'twere a year or so since, and his villanies
and lewdnesses were clean gone from his memory for lapse of
time. Between matins and now hast thou forgotten this
morning's outrage ? Where wast thou this morning shortly
before daybreak ? " " Where was I ? " rejoined the gallant ;
" that know not I. 'Tis indeed betimes that the news has
reached you." " True indeed it is," said the friar, " that the

news has reached me : I suppose that, because the husband was not there, thou never doubtedst that thou wouldst forthwith be received by the lady with open arms. Ah ! the gay gallant ! the honourable gentleman ! he is now turned prowler by night, and breaks into gardens, and climbs trees ! Dost thou think by sheer importunity to vanquish the virtue of this lady, that thou escaladest her windows at night by the trees ? She dislikes thee of all things in the world, and yet thou must still persist. Well indeed hast thou laid my admonitions to heart, to say nothing of the many proofs which she has given thee of her disdain ! But I have yet a word for thee : hitherto, not that she bears thee any love, but that she has yielded to my urgent prayers, she has kept silence as to thy misdeeds : she will do so no more : I have given her leave to act as she may think fit, if thou givest her any further annoyance. And what wilt thou do if she informs her brothers ? " The gallant, now fully apprised of what it imported him to know, was profuse in promises, whereby as best he might he reassured the friar, and so left him. The very next night, as soon as the matin hour was come, he entered the garden, climbed up the tree, found the window open, entered the chamber, and in a trice was in the embrace of his fair lady. Anxiously had she expected him, and blithely did she now greet him, saying :—" All thanks to master friar that he so well taught thee the way hither." Then, with many a jest and laugh at the simplicity of the asinine friar, and many a flout at distaff-fuls and combs and cards, they solaced themselves with one another to their no small delight. Nor did they omit so to arrange matters that they were well able to dispense with master friar, and yet pass many another night together with no less satisfaction : to which goal I pray that I, and all other Christian souls that are so minded, may be speedily guided of God in His holy mercy.

NOVEL IV

Dom Felice instructs Fra Puccio how to attain blessedness by doing a penance. Fra Puccio does the penance, and meanwhile Dom Felice has a good time with Fra Puccio's wife.

WHEN Filomena, having concluded her story, was silent, and Dioneo had added a few honeyed phrases in praise of the lady's wit and Filomena's closing prayer, the queen glanced with a smile to Pamfilo, and said :—" Now, Pamfilo, give us some pleasant trifle to speed our delight." " That gladly will I," returned forthwith Pamfilo, and then :—Madam, he began, not a few there are that, while they use their best endeavours to get themselves places in Paradise, do, by inadvertence, send others thither : as did, not long ago, betide a fair neighbour of ours, as you shall hear.

Hard by San Pancrazio there used to live, as I have heard tell, a worthy man and wealthy, Puccio di Rinieri by name, who in later life, under an overpowering sense of religion, became a tertiary of the order of St. Francis, and was thus known as Fra Puccio. In which spiritual life he was the better able to persevere that his household consisted but of a wife and a maid, and having no need to occupy himself with any craft, he spent no small part of his time at church ; where, being a simple soul and slow of wit, he said his paternosters, heard sermons, assisted at the mass, never missed lauds (*i.e.* when chanted by the seculars), fasted and mortified his flesh ; nay—so 'twas whispered—he was of the Flagellants. His wife, Monna Isabetta by name, a woman of from twenty-eight to thirty summers, still young for her age, lusty, comely and plump as a casolan[1] apple, had not unfrequently, by reason of her husband's devoutness, if not also of his age, more than she cared for, of abstinence ; and when she was sleepy, or, maybe, riggish, he would repeat to her the life of Christ, and the sermons of Fra Nastagio, or the lament of the Magdalen, or the like. Now, while such was the tenor of her life, there returned from Paris a young monk, by name Dom Felice, of the convent of San Pancrazio, a well-favoured man and keen-witted, and profoundly learned, with whom Fra Puccio became very intimate ; and as there was no question which he could put to him but Dom Felice could answer it, and moreover he made great shew of holiness, for well he knew Fra Puccio's bent, Fra Puccio took to bringing him home and entertaining him at breakfast and supper, as occasion served ; and for love of her husband the lady also grew familiar with Dom Felice, and was zealous to do him honour. So the monk, being a constant visitor at Fra Puccio's house, and seeing the lady so lusty and plump, surmised that of which she must have most lack, and made up his mind to afford, if he could, at once relief to Fra Puccio and contentment to the lady. So cautiously, now and

---

[1] Perhaps from Casoli, near Naples.

again, he cast an admiring glance in her direction with such effect that he kindled in her the same desire with which he burned, and marking his success, took the first opportunity to declare his passion to her. He found her fully disposed to gratify it ; but how this might be, he was at a loss to discover, for she would not trust herself with him in any place whatever except her own house, and there it could not be, because Fra Puccio never travelled ; whereby the monk was greatly dejected. Long he pondered the matter, and at length thought of an expedient, whereby he might be with the lady in her own house without incurring suspicion, notwithstanding that Fra Puccio was there. So, being with Fra Puccio one day, he said to him :— " Reasons many have I to know, Fra Puccio, that all thy desire is to become a saint ; but it seems to me that thou farest by a circuitous route, whereas there is one very direct, which the Pope and the greater prelates that are about him know and use, but will have it remain a secret, because otherwise the clergy, who for the most part live by alms, and could not then expect alms or aught else from the laity, would be speedily ruined. However, as thou art my friend, and hast shewn me much honour, I would teach thee that way, if I were assured that thou wouldst follow it without letting another soul in the world hear of it." Fra Puccio was now all agog to hear more of the matter, and began most earnestly entreating Dom Felice to teach him the way, swearing that without Dom Felice's leave none should ever hear of it from him, and averring that, if he found it practicable, he would certainly follow it. " I am satisfied with thy promises," said the monk, " and I will shew thee the way. Know then that the holy doctors hold that whoso would achieve blessedness must do the penance of which I shall tell thee ; but see thou take me judiciously. I do not say that after the penance thou wilt not be a sinner, as thou art ; but the effect will be that the sins which thou hast committed up to the very hour of the penance will all be purged away and thereby remitted to thee, and the sins which thou shalt commit thereafter will not be written against thee to thy damnation, but will be quit by holy water, like venial sins. First of all then the penitent must with great exactitude confess his sins when he comes to begin the penance. Then follows a period of fasting and very strict abstinence which must last for forty days, during which time he is to touch no woman whomsoever, not even his wife. Moreover, thou must have in thy house some place whence thou mayst see the sky by night, whither thou must resort at compline; and there thou must have a beam, very broad, and placed in such a way, that, standing, thou canst rest thy nether part upon it, and so, not raising thy feet from the ground, thou must extend thy arms, so as to make a sort of crucifix, and if thou wouldst have pegs to rest them on thou mayst; and on this manner, thy gaze fixed on the sky, and never moving a jot, thou must stand until matins.   And wert thou lettered, it were proper for thee to say meanwhile certain prayers that I would give thee; but as thou art not so, thou must say three hundred paternosters and as many avemarias in honour of the Trinity; and thus contemplating the sky, be ever mindful that God was the creator of the heaven and the earth, and being set even as Christ was upon the cross, meditate on His passion.   Then, when the matin-bell sounds, thou mayst, if thou please, go to bed—but see that thou undress not—and sleep; but in the morning thou must go to church, and hear at least three masses, and say fifty paternosters and as many avemarias; after which thou mayst with a pure heart do aught that thou hast to do, and breakfast; but at vespers thou must be again at church, and say there certain prayers, which I shall give thee in writing and which are indispensable, and after compline thou must repeat thy former exercise.   Do this, and I, who have done it before thee, have good hope that even before thou shalt have reached the end of the penance, thou wilt, if thou shalt do it in a devout spirit, have already a marvellous foretaste of the eternal blessedness."   "This," said Fra Puccio, "is neither a very severe nor a very long penance, and can be very easily managed: wherefore in God's name I will begin on Sunday."   And so he took his leave of Dom Felice, and went home, and, by Dom Felice's permission, informed his wife of every particular of his intended penance.

The lady understood very well what the monk meant by enjoining him not to stir from his post until matins; and deeming it an excellent device, she said that she was well content that he should do this or aught else that he thought good for his soul; and to the end that his penance might be blest of God, she would herself fast with him, though she would go no further. So they did as they had agreed: when Sunday came Fra Puccio began his penance, and master monk, by understanding with the lady, came most evenings, at the hour when he was secure from discovery, to sup with her, always bringing with him abundance both of meat and of drink, and after slept with her till the matin hour, when he got up and left her, and Fra

Puccio went to bed. The place which Fra Puccio had chosen
for his penance was close to the room in which the lady slept,
and only separated from it by the thinnest of partitions ; so
that, the monk and the lady disporting themselves with one
another without stint or restraint, Fra Puccio thought he felt
the floor of the house shake a little, and pausing at his hundredth
paternoster, but without leaving his post, called out to the lady
to know what she was about. The lady, who dearly loved a
jest, and was just then riding the horse of St. Benedict or St.
John Gualbert, answered :—" I'faith, husband, I am as restless
as may be." " Restless," said Fra Puccio, " how so ? What
means this restlessness ? " Whereto with a hearty laugh, for
which she doubtless had good occasion, the bonny lady
replied :—" What means it ? How should you ask such a
question ? Why, I have heard you say a thousand times :—
' Who fasting goes to bed, uneasy lies his head.' " Fra Puccio,
supposing that her wakefulness and restlessness abed was due
to want of food, said in good faith :—" Wife, I told thee I would
have thee not fast ; but as thou hast chosen to fast, think not
of it, but think how thou mayst compose thyself to sleep ; thou
tossest about the bed in such sort that the shaking is felt here."
" That need cause thee no alarm," rejoined the lady. " I
know what I am about ; I will manage as well as I can, and do
thou likewise." So Fra Puccio said no more to her, but resumed
his paternosters ; and thenceforth every night, while Fra
Puccio's penance lasted, the lady and master monk, having had
a bed made up for them in another part of the house, did there
wanton it most gamesomely, the monk departing and the lady
going back to her bed at one and the same time, being shortly
before Fra Puccio's return from his nightly vigil. The friar
thus persisting in his penance while the lady took her fill of
pleasure with the monk, she would from time to time say jest-
ingly to him :—" Thou layest a penance upon Fra Puccio
whereby we are rewarded with Paradise." So well indeed did
she relish the dainties with which the monk regaled her, the
more so by contrast with the abstemious life to which her
husband had long accustomed her, that, when Fra Puccio's
penance was done, she found means to enjoy them elsewhere,
and ordered her indulgence with such discretion as to ensure
its long continuance. Whereby (that my story may end as it
began) it came to pass that Fra Puccio, hoping by his penance
to win a place for himself in Paradise, did in fact translate
thither the monk who had shewn him the way, and the wife

who lived with him in great dearth of that of which the monk
in his charity gave her superabundant largess.

NOVEL V

*Zima gives a palfrey to Messer Francesco Vergellesi, who in
return suffers him to speak with his wife. She keeping
silence, he answers in her stead, and the sequel is in accordance
with his answer.*

WHEN Pamfilo had brought the story of Fra Puccio to a close
amid the laughter of the ladies, the queen debonairly bade Elisa
follow suit ; and she, whose manner had in it a slight touch of
severity, which betokened not despite, but was habitual to her,
thus began :—

Many there are that, being very knowing, think that others
are quite the reverse ; and so, many a time, thinking to beguile
others, are themselves beguiled ; wherefore I deem it the height
of folly for any one wantonly to challenge another to a contest
of wit.   But, as, perchance, all may not be of the same opinion,
I am minded, without deviating from the prescribed order, to
acquaint you with that which thereby befell a certain knight
of Pistoia.   Know then that at Pistoia there lived a knight,
Messer Francesco by name, of the Vergellesi family, a man of
much wealth and good parts, being both wise and clever, but
withal niggardly beyond measure.   Which Messer Francesco,
having to go to Milan in the capacity of podestà, had provided
himself with all that was meet for the honourable support of
such a dignity, save only a palfrey handsome enough for him ;
and not being able to come by any such, he felt himself at a
loss.   Now there was then in Pistoia a young man, Ricciardo
by name, of low origin but great wealth, who went always so
trim and fine and foppish of person, that folk had bestowed
upon him the name of Zima,[1] by which he was generally known.
Zima had long and to no purpose burned and yearned for love
of Messer Francesco's very fair and no less virtuous wife.   His
passion was matter of common notoriety ; and so it befell that
some one told Messer Francesco that he had but to ask Zima,

[1] From the Low Latin aczima, explained by Du Cange as " tonture de
draps," the process of dressing cloth so as to give it an even nap.   Zima
is thus equivalent to " nitidus."   Cf. Vocab. degli Accademici della Crusca,
" Azzimare."

who was the possessor of one of the handsomest palfreys in
Tuscany, which on that account he greatly prized, and he
would not hesitate to give him the horse for the love which he
bore his wife. So our niggardly knight sent for Zima, and
offered to buy the horse of him, hoping thereby to get him
from Zima as a gift. Zima heard the knight gladly, and thus
made answer :—" Sell you my horse, Sir, I would not, though
you gave me all that you have in the world ; but I shall be
happy to give him to you, when you will, on this condition,
that, before he pass into your hands, I may by your leave and
in your presence say a few words to your wife so privately that
I may be heard by her alone." Thinking at once to gratify his
cupidity and to outwit Zima, the knight answered that he was
content that it should be even as Zima wished. Then, leaving
him in the hall of the palace, he went to his lady's chamber,
and told her the easy terms on which he might acquire the
palfrey, bidding her give Zima his audience, but on no account
to vouchsafe him a word of reply. This the lady found by no
means to her mind, but, as she must needs obey her husband's
commands, she promised compliance, and followed him into
the hall to hear what Zima might have to say. Zima then
renewed his contract with the knight in due form ; whereupon,
the lady being seated in a part of the hall where she was quite
by herself, he sate down by her side, and thus began :—" Noble
lady, I have too much respect for your understanding to doubt
that you have long been well aware of the extremity of passion
whereto I have been brought by your beauty, which certainly
exceeds that of any other lady that I have ever seen, to say
nothing of your exquisite manners and incomparable virtues,
which might well serve to captivate every soaring spirit that is
in the world ; wherefore there need no words of mine to assure
you that I love you with a love greater and more ardent than
any that man yet bore to woman, and so without doubt I shall
do, as long as my woful life shall hold this frame together ;
nay, longer yet, for, if love there be in the next world as in this,
I shall love you evermore. And so you may make your mind
secure that there is nothing that is yours, be it precious or be it
common, which you may count as in such and so sure a sort
your own as me, for all that I am and have. And that thereof
you may not lack evidence of infallible cogency, I tell you, that
I should deem myself more highly favoured, if I might at your
command do somewhat to pleasure you, than if at my command
the whole world were forthwith to yield me obedience. And

as 'tis even in such sort that I am yours, 'tis not unworthily
that I make bold to offer my petitions to Your Highness, as
being to me the sole, exclusive source of all peace, of all bliss,
of all health.   Wherefore, as your most lowly vassal, I pray
you, dear my bliss, my soul's one hope, wherein she nourishes
herself in love's devouring flame, that in your great benignity
you deign so far to mitigate the harshness which in the past you
have shewn towards me, yours though I am, that, consoled by
your compassion, I may say, that, as 'twas by your beauty
that I was smitten with love, so 'tis to your pity that I owe my
life, which, if in your haughtiness you lend not ear unto my
prayers, will assuredly fail, so that I shall die, and, it may be,
'twill be said that you slew me.   'Twould not redound to your
honour that I died for love of you ; but let that pass ; I cannot
but think, however, that you would sometimes feel a touch of
remorse, and would grieve that 'twas your doing, and that
now and again, relenting, you would say to yourself :—' Ah !
how wrong it was of me that I had not pity on my Zima ; ' by
which too late repentance you would but enhance your grief.
Wherefore, that this come not to pass, repent you while it is in
your power to give me ease, and shew pity on me before I die,
seeing that with you it rests to make me either the gladdest or
the saddest man that lives.   My trust is in your generosity, that
'twill not brook that a love so great and of such a sort as mine
should receive death for guerdon, and that by a gladsome and
gracious answer you will repair my shattered spirits, which are
all a-tremble in your presence for very fear."   When he had
done, he heaved several very deep sighs, and a few tears started
from his eyes, while he awaited the lady's answer.

Long time he had wooed her with his eyes, had tilted in her
honour, had greeted her rising with music ; and against these
and all like modes of attack she had been proof ; but the heart-
felt words of her most ardent lover were not without their
effect, and she now began to understand what she had never
till then understood, to wit, what love really means.   So,
albeit she obeyed her lord's behest, and kept silence, yet she
could not but betray by a slight sigh that which, if she might
have given Zima his answer, she would readily have avowed.
After waiting a while, Zima found it strange that no answer
was forthcoming ; and he then began to perceive the trick
which the knight had played him.   However, he kept his eyes
fixed on the lady, and observing that her eyes glowed now and
again, as they met his, and noting the partially suppressed

sighs which escaped her, he gathered a little hope, which gave
him courage to try a novel plan of attack. So, while the
lady listened, he began to make answer for her to himself
on this wise :—" Zima mine, true indeed it is that long since
I discerned that thou didst love me with a love exceeding great
and whole-hearted, whereof I have now yet ampler assurance
by thine own words, and well content I am therewith, as indeed
I ought to be.   And however harsh and cruel I may have seemed
to thee, I would by no means have thee believe, that I have
been such at heart as I have seemed in aspect ; rather, be
assured that I have ever loved thee and held thee dear above
all other men ; the mien which I have worn was but prescribed
by fear of another and solicitude for my fair fame.   But a
time will soon come when I shall be able to give thee plain
proof of my love, and to accord the love which thou hast
borne and dost bear me its due guerdon.   Wherefore be com-
forted and of good hope ; for, Messer Francesco is to go in a
few days' time to Milan as podestà, as thou well knowest,
seeing that for love of me thou hast given him thy fine palfrey ;
and I vow to thee upon my faith, upon the true love which
I bear thee, that without fail, within a few days thereafter
thou shalt be with me, and we will give our love complete and
gladsome consummation.   And that I may have no more
occasion to speak to thee of this matter, be it understood
between us that henceforth when thou shalt observe two
towels disposed at the window of my room which overlooks
the garden, thou shalt come to me after nightfall of that
same day by the garden door (and look well to it that thou
be not seen), and thou shalt find me waiting for thee, and
we will have our fill of mutual cheer and solace all night
long."

Having thus answered for the lady, Zima resumed his own
person and thus replied to the lady :—" Dearest madam, your
boon response so overpowers my every faculty that scarce
can I frame words to render you due thanks ; and, were I able to
utter all I feel, time, however long, would fail me fully to thank
you as I would fain and as I ought : wherefore I must even leave
it to your sage judgment to divine that which I yearn in vain
to put in words.   Let this one word suffice, that as you bid me,
so I shall not fail to do ; and then, having, perchance, firmer
assurance of the great boon which you have granted me, I
will do my best endeavour to thank you in terms the amplest
that I may command.   For the present there is no more to

say; and so, dearest my lady, I commend you to God; and
may He grant you your heart's content of joy and bliss." To
all which the lady returned never a word: wherefore Zima
rose and turned to rejoin the knight, who, seeing him on his
feet, came towards him, and said with a laugh:—" How sayst
thou? Have I faithfully kept my promise to thee?" "Not
so, Sir," replied Zima; "for by thy word I was to have spoken
with thy wife, and by thy deed I have spoken to a statue of
marble." Which remark was much relished by the knight,
who, well as he had thought of his wife, thought now even
better of her, and said:—" So thy palfrey, that was, is now mine
out and out." "'Tis even so, Sir," replied Zima; "but had
I thought to have gotten such fruit as I have from this favour
of yours, I would not have craved it, but would have let you
have the palfrey as a free gift: and would to God I had done
so, for, as it is, you have bought the palfrey and I have not
sold him." This drew a laugh from the knight, who within
a few days thereafter mounted the palfrey which he had gotten,
and took the road for Milan, there to enter on his podestate.
The lady, now mistress of herself, bethought her of Zima's
words, and the love which he bore her, and for which he had
parted with his palfrey; and observing that he frequently
passed her house, said to herself:—" What am I about? Why
throw I my youth away? My husband is gone to Milan, and
will not return for six months, and when can he ever restore
them to me? When I am old! And besides, shall I ever
find another such lover as Zima? I am quite by myself.
There is none to fear. I know not why I take not my good
time while I may: I shall not always have the like oppor-
tunity as at present: no one will ever know; and if it should
get known, 'tis better to do and repent than to forbear and
repent." Of which meditations the issue was that one day she
set two towels in the window overlooking the garden, according
to Zima's word; and Zima having marked them with much
exultation, stole at nightfall alone to the door of the lady's
garden, and finding it open, crossed to another door that led
into the house, where he found the lady awaiting him. On
sight of him she rose to meet him, and gave him the heartiest
of welcomes. A hundred thousand times he embraced and
kissed her, as he followed her upstairs: then without delay
they hied them to bed, and knew love's furthest bourne. And
so far was the first time from being in this case the last, that,
while the knight was at Milan, and indeed after his return,

there were seasons not a few at which Zima resorted thither
to the immense delight of both parties.

NOVEL VI

*Ricciardo Minutolo loves the wife of Filippello Fighinolfi, and
knowing her to be jealous, makes her believe that his own
wife is to meet Filippello at a bagnio on the ensuing day ;
whereby she is induced to go thither, where, thinking to have
been with her husband, she discovers that she has tarried with
Ricciardo.*

WHEN Elisa had quite done, the queen, after some commenda-
tion of Zima's sagacity, bade Fiammetta follow with a story.
Whereto Fiammetta, all smiles, responded :—" Madam, with
all my heart ; " and thus began :—

Richly though our city abounds, as in all things else, so also
in instances to suit every topic, yet I am minded to journey
some distance thence, and, like Elisa, to tell you something
of what goes on in other parts of the world : wherefore pass we
to Naples, where you shall hear how one of these sanctified
that shew themselves so shy of love, was by the subtlety of
her lover brought to taste of the fruit before she had known
the flowers of love ; whereby at one and the same time you
may derive from the past counsel of prudence for the future,
and present delectation.

In the very ancient city of Naples, which for loveliness has
not its superior or perhaps its equal in Italy, there once lived
a young man, renowned alike for noble blood and the splendour
of his vast wealth, his name Ricciardo Minutolo. He was
mated with a very fair and loving wife ; but nevertheless he
became enamoured of a lady who in the general opinion vastly
surpassed in beauty every other lady in Naples.   Catella—
such was the lady's name—was married to a young man, like-
wise of gentle blood, Filippello Fighinolfi by name, whom she,
most virtuous of ladies, loved and held dear above all else
in the world.   Being thus enamoured of Catella, Ricciardo
Minutolo left none of those means untried whereby a lady's
favour and love are wont to be gained, but for all that he made
no way towards the attainment of his heart's desire : whereby
he fell into a sort of despair, and witless and powerless to loose
himself from his love, found life scarce tolerable, and yet knew

not how to die. While in this frame he languished, it befell
one day that some ladies that were of kin to him counselled
him earnestly to be quit of such a love, whereby he could but
fret himself to no purpose, seeing that Catella cared for nought
in the world save Filippello, and lived in such a state of jealousy
on his account that never a bird flew but she feared lest it
should snatch him from her. So soon as Ricciardo heard of
Catella's jealousy, he forthwith began to ponder how he might
make it subserve his end. He feigned to have given up his
love for Catella as hopeless, and to have transferred it to
another lady, in whose honour he accordingly began to tilt
and joust and do all that he had wont to do in honour of
Catella. Nor was it long before well-nigh all the Neapolitans,
including Catella herself, began to think that he had forgotten
Catella, and was to the last degree enamoured of the other
lady. In this course he persisted, until the opinion was so
firmly rooted in the minds of all that even Catella laid aside
a certain reserve which she had used towards him while she
deemed him her lover, and, coming and going, greeted him in
friendly, neighbourly fashion, like the rest. Now it so befell
that during the hot season, when, according to the custom of
the Neapolitans, many companies of ladies and gentlemen
went down to the sea-coast to recreate themselves and break-
fast and sup, Ricciardo, knowing that Catella was gone thither
with her company, went likewise with his, but, making as if
he were not minded to stay there, he received several invitations
from the ladies of Catella's company before he accepted any.
When the ladies received him, they all with one accord,
including Catella, began to rally him on his new love, and he
furnished them with more matter for talk by feigning a most
ardent passion. At length most of the ladies being gone off,
one hither, another thither, as they do in such places, leaving
Catella and a few others with Ricciardo, he tossed at Catella
a light allusion to a certain love of her husband Filippello,
which threw her at once into such a fit of jealousy, that she
inly burned with a vehement desire to know what Ricciardo
meant. For a while she kept her own counsel ; then, brooking
no more suspense, she adjured Ricciardo, by the love he bore
the lady whom most he loved, to expound to her what he had
said touching Filippello. He answered thus :—" You have
adjured me by her to whom I dare not deny aught that you
may ask of me ; my riddle therefore I will presently read you,
provided you promise me that neither to him nor to any one

else will you impart aught of what I shall relate to you, until you shall have ocular evidence of its truth ; which, so you desire it, I will teach you how you may obtain." The lady accepted his terms, which rather confirmed her belief in his veracity, and swore that she would not tell a soul. They then drew a little apart, that they might not be overheard by the rest, and Ricciardo thus began :—" Madam, did I love you, as I once did, I should not dare to tell you aught that I thought might cause you pain ; but, now that that love is past, I shall have the less hesitation in telling you the truth. Whether Filippello ever resented the love which I bore you, or deemed that it was returned by you, I know not : whether it were so or no, he certainly never shewed any such feeling to me ; but so it is that now, having waited, perhaps, until, as he supposes, I am less likely to be on my guard, he shews a disposition to serve me as I doubt he suspects that I served him ; that is to say, he would fain have his pleasure of my wife, whom for some time past he has, as I discover, plied with messages through most secret channels. She has told me all, and has answered him according to my instructions : but only this morning, just before I came hither, I found a woman in close parley with her in the house, whose true character and purpose I forthwith divined ; so I called my wife, and asked what the woman wanted. Whereto she answered :—' 'Tis this persecution by Filippello which thou hast brought upon me by the encouraging answers that thou wouldst have me give him : he now tells me that he is most earnestly desirous to know my intentions, and that, should I be so minded, he would contrive that I should have secret access to a bagnio in this city, and he is most urgent and instant that I should consent. And hadst thou not, wherefore I know not, bidden me keep the affair afoot, I would have dismissed him in such a sort that my movements would have been exempt from his prying observation for ever.' Upon this I saw that the affair was going too far ; I determined to have no more of it, and to let you know it, that you may understand how he requites your whole-hearted faith, which brought me of late to the verge of death. And that you may not suppose that these are but empty words and idle tales, but may be able, should you so desire, to verify them by sight and touch, I caused my wife to tell the woman who still waited her answer, that she would be at the bagnio to-morrow about none, during the siesta : with which answer the woman went away well content. Now

you do not, I suppose, imagine that I would send her thither ;
but if I were in your place, he should find me there instead of
her whom he thinks to find there ; and when I had been some
little time with him, I would give him to understand with
whom he had been, and he should have of me such honour as
he deserved.   Whereby, I doubt not, he would be put to such
shame as would at one and the same time avenge both the
wrong which he has done to you and that which he plots
against me."

Catella, as is the wont of the jealous, hearkened to Ricciardo's
words without so much as giving a thought to the speaker or
his wiles, inclined at once to credit his story, and began to
twist certain antecedent matters into accord with it ; then,
suddenly kindling with wrath, she answered, that to the
bagnio she would certainly go ; 'twould cause her no great
inconvenience, and if he should come, she would so shame
him that he should never again set eyes on woman but his ears
would tingle.   Satisfied by what he heard, that his stratagem
was well conceived, and success sure, Ricciardo added much
in corroboration of his story, and having thus confirmed her
belief in it, besought her to keep it always close, whereto she
pledged her faith.

Next morning Ricciardo hied him to the good woman that
kept the bagnio to which he had directed Catella, told her the
enterprise which he had in hand, and prayed her to aid him
therein so far as she might be able.   The good woman, who was
much beholden to him, assured him that she would gladly do
so, and concerted with him all that was to be said and done.
She had in the bagnio a room which was very dark, being with-
out any window to admit the light.   This room, by Ricciardo's
direction, she set in order, and made up a bed there as well as
she could, into which bed Ricciardo got, as soon as he had
breakfasted, and there awaited Catella's coming.

Now Catella, still giving more credence to Ricciardo's story
than it merited, had gone home in the evening in a most resent-
ful mood, and Filippello, returning home the same evening
with a mind greatly preoccupied, was scarce as familiar with
her as he was wont to be.   Which she marking, grew yet more
suspicious than before, and said to herself :—" Doubtless he
is thinking of the lady of whom he expects to take his pleasure
to-morrow, as most assuredly he shall not ; " and so, musing
and meditating what she should say to him after their encounter
at the bagnio, she spent the best part of the night.   But

—to shorten my story—upon the stroke of none Catella, taking
with her a single attendant, but otherwise adhering to her
original intention, hied her to the bagnio which Ricciardo had
indicated ; and finding the good woman there, asked her
whether Filippello had been there that day. Primed by
Ricciardo, the good woman asked her, whether she were the
lady that was to come to speak with him ; to which she
answered in the affirmative. " Go to him, then," said the good
woman. And so Catella, in quest of that which she would
gladly not have found, was shewn to the chamber where
Ricciardo was, and having entered without uncovering her
head, closed the door behind her. Overjoyed to see her,
Ricciardo sprang out of bed, took her in his arms, and said
caressingly :—" Welcome, my soul." Catella, dissembling, for
she was minded at first to counterfeit another woman, returned
his embrace, kissed him, and lavished endearments upon him ;
saying, the while, not a word, lest her speech should betray her.
The darkness of the room, which was profound, was equally
welcome to both ; nor were they there long enough for their
eyes to recover power. Ricciardo helped Catella on to the bed,
where, with no word said on either side in a voice that might
be recognized, they lay a long while, much more to the solace
and satisfaction of the one than of the other party. Then,
Catella, deeming it high time to vent her harboured resentment,
burst forth in a blaze of wrath on this wise :—" Alas ! how
wretched is the lot of women, how misplaced of not a few the
love they bear their husbands ! Ah, woe is me ! for eight years
have I loved thee more dearly than my life ; and now I find
that thou, base miscreant that thou art, dost nought but burn
and languish for love of another woman ! Here thou hast
been—with whom, thinkest thou ? Even with her whom thou
hast too long deluded with thy false blandishments, making
pretence to love her while thou art enamoured of another.
'Tis I, Catella, not the wife of Ricciardo, false traitor that thou
art ; list if thou knowest my voice ; 'tis I indeed ! Ah !
would we were but in the light !—it seems to me a thousand
years till then—that I might shame thee as thou deservest,
vile, pestilent dog that thou art ! Alas ! woe is me ! such love
as I have borne so many years—to whom ? To this faithless
dog, that, thinking to have a strange woman in his embrace,
has in the brief while that I have been with him here lavished
upon me more caresses and endearments than during all the
forepast time that I have been his ! A lively spark indeed

art thou to-day, renegade dog, that shewest thyself so limp
and enervate and impotent at home! But, God be praised,
thou hast tilled thine own plot, and not another's, as thou
didst believe. No wonder that last night thou heldest aloof
from me ; thou wast thinking of scattering thy seed elsewhere,
and wast minded to shew thyself a lusty knight when thou
shouldst join battle. But praise be to God and my sagacity,
the water has nevertheless taken its proper course. Where
is thy answer, culprit ? Hast thou nought to say ? Have
my words struck thee dumb ? God's faith ! I know not why
I forbear to pluck thine eyes out with my fingers ! Thou
thoughtest to perpetrate this treason with no small secrecy ;
but, by God, one is as knowing as another ; thy plot has failed ;
I had better hounds on thy trail than thou didst think for."
Ricciardo, inly delighted by her words, made no answer, but
embraced and kissed her more than ever, and overwhelmed her
with his endearments. So she continued her reproaches,
saying :—" Ay, thou thinkest to cajole me with thy feigned
caresses, wearisome dog that thou art, and so to pacify and
mollify me ; but thou art mistaken. I shall never be mollified,
until I have covered thee with infamy in the presence of all
our kinsfolk and friends and neighbours. Am I not, miscreant,
as fair as the wife of Ricciardo Minutolo ? Am I not as good
a lady as she ? Why dost not answer, vile dog ? Wherein
has she the advantage of me ? Away with thee ! touch me
not ; thou hast done feats of arms more than enough for
to-day. Well I know that, now that thou knowest who I am,
thou wilt wreak thy will on me by force : but by God's grace
I will yet disappoint thee. I know not why I forbear to send
for Ricciardo, who loved me more than himself and yet was never
able to boast that he had a single glance from me ; nor know I
why 'twere wrong to do so. Thou thoughtest to have his
wife here, and 'tis no fault of thine that thou hadst her not :
so, if I had him, thou couldst not justly blame me."

Enough had now been said : the lady's mortification was
extreme ; and, as she ended, Ricciardo bethought him that,
if he suffered her, thus deluded, to depart, much evil might
ensue. He therefore resolved to make himself known, and
disabuse her of her error. So, taking her in his arms, and clip-
ping her so close that she could not get loose, he said :—" Sweet
my soul, be not wroth : that which, while artlessly I loved, I
might not have, Love has taught me to compass by guile :
know that I am thy Ricciardo."

At these words and the voice, which she recognized, Catella started, and would have sprung out of the bed ; which being impossible, she essayed a cry ; but Ricciardo laid a hand upon her mouth, and closed it, saying :—" Madam, that which is done can never be undone, though you should cry out for the rest of your days, and should you in such or any other wise publish this matter to any, two consequences will ensue. In the first place (and this is a point which touches you very nearly) your honour and fair fame will be blasted ; for, however you may say that I lured you hither by guile, I shall deny it, and affirm, on the contrary, that I induced you to come hither by promises of money and gifts, and that 'tis but because you are vexed that what I gave you did not altogether come up to your expectations, that you make such a cry and clamour ; and you know that folk are more prone to believe evil than good, and therefore I am no less likely to be believed than you. The further consequence will be mortal enmity between your husband and me, and the event were as like to be that I killed him as that he killed me : which if I did, you would never more know joy or peace. Wherefore, heart of my body, do not at one and the same time bring dishonour upon yourself and set your husband and me at strife and in jeopardy of our lives. You are not the first, nor will you be the last to be beguiled ; nor have I beguiled you to rob you of aught, but for excess of love that I bear, and shall ever bear, you, being your most lowly vassal. And though it is now a great while that I, and what I have and can and am worth, are yours, yet I am minded that so it shall be henceforth more than ever before. Your discretion in other matters is not unknown to me, and I doubt not 'twill be equally manifest in this."

Ricciardo's admonitions were received by Catella with many a bitter tear ; but though she was very wroth and very sad at heart, yet Ricciardo's true words so far commanded the assent of her reason, that she acknowledged that 'twas possible they might be verified by the event. Wherefore she made answer :—" Ricciardo, I know not how God will grant me patience to bear the villainy and knavery which thou hast practised upon me ; and though in this place, to which simplicity and excess of jealousy guided my steps, I raise no cry, rest assured that I shall never be happy, until in one way or another I know myself avenged of that which thou hast done to me. Wherefore unhand me, let me go : thou hast had thy desire of me, and hast tormented me to thy heart's content :

tis time to release me ; let me go, I pray thee." But Ricciardo,
seeing that she was still much ruffled in spirit, was resolved not
to let her go, until he had made his peace with her. So he
addressed himself to soothe her ; and by dint of most dulcet
phrases and entreaties and adjurations he did at last prevail
with her to give him her pardon ; nay, by joint consent, they
tarried there a great while to the exceeding great delight of
both. Indeed the lady, finding her lover's kisses smack much
better than those of her husband, converted her asperity into
sweetness, and from that day forth cherished a most tender
love for Ricciardo ; whereof, using all circumspection, they
many a time had solace. God grant us solace of ours.

NOVEL VII

Tedaldo, being in disfavour with his lady, departs from Florence.
He returns thither after a while in the guise of a pilgrim, has
speech of his lady, and makes her sensible of her fault. Her
husband, convicted of slaying him, he delivers from peril
of death, reconciles him with his brothers, and thereafter
discreetly enjoys his lady.

So ceased Fiammetta ; and, when all had bestowed on her
their meed of praise, the queen—to lose no time—forthwith
bade Emilia resume the narration. So thus Emilia began :—
   I am minded to return to our city, whence my two last pre-
decessors saw fit to depart, and to shew you how one of our
citizens recovered the lady he had lost. Know then that
there was in Florence a young noble, his name Tedaldo Elisei,
who being beyond measure enamoured of a lady hight Monna
Ermellina, wife of one Aldobrandino Palermini, and by reason
of his admirable qualities richly deserving to have his desire,
found Fortune nevertheless adverse, as she is wont to be to the
prosperous. Inasmuch as, for some reason or another, the
lady, having shewn herself gracious towards Tedaldo for a
while, completely altered her mien, and not only shewed him
no further favour, but would not so much as receive a message
from him or suffer him to see her face ; whereby he fell a prey
to a grievous and distressful melancholy ; but so well had he
concealed his love that the cause of his melancholy was surmised
by none. He tried hard in divers ways to recover the love
which he deemed himself to have lost for no fault of his, and

finding all his efforts unavailing, he resolved to bid the world
adieu, that he might not afford her who was the cause of his
distress the satisfaction of seeing him languish. So he got
together as much money as he might, and secretly, no word
said to friend or kinsman except only a familiar gossip, who
knew all, he took his departure for Ancona. Arrived there,
he assumed the name of Filippo Santodeccio, and having
forgathered with a rich merchant, entered his service. The
merchant took him with him to Cyprus aboard one of his ships,
and was so well pleased with his bearing and behaviour that
he not only gave him a handsome salary but made him in a
sort his companion, and entrusted him with the management
of no small part of his affairs : wherein he proved himself so
apt and assiduous, that in the course of a few years he was
himself established in credit and wealth and great repute as a
merchant. Seven years thus passed, during which, albeit
his thoughts frequently reverted to his cruel mistress, and sorely
love smote him, and much he yearned to see her again, yet such
was his firmness that he came off conqueror, until one day in
Cyprus it so befell that there was sung in his hearing a song
that he had himself composed, and of which the theme was the
mutual love that was between his lady and him, and the delight
that he had of her ; which as he heard, he found it incredible
that she should have forgotten him, and burned with such a
desire to see her once more, that, being able to hold out no
longer, he made up his mind to return to Florence. So, having
set all his affairs in order, he betook him, attended only by a
single servant, to Ancona ; whence he sent all his effects, as
they arrived, forward to Florence, consigning them to a friend
of his Anconitan partner, and followed with his servant in the
disguise of a pilgrim returned from the Holy Sepulchre. Arrived
at Florence, he put up at a little hostelry kept by two brothers
hard by his lady's house, whither he forthwith hied him, hoping
that, perchance, he might have sight of her from the street ;
but, finding all barred and bolted, doors, windows and all else,
he doubted much, she must be dead, or have removed thence.
So, with a very heavy heart, he returned to the house of the
two brothers, and to his great surprise found his own four
brothers standing in front of it, all in black. He knew that
he was so changed from his former semblance, both in dress
and in person, that he might not readily be recognized, and he
had therefore no hesitation in going up to a shoemaker and
asking him why these men were all dressed in black. The

shoemaker answered :—" 'Tis because 'tis not fifteen days since
a brother of theirs, Tedaldo by name, that had been long
abroad, was slain ; and I understand that they have proved
in court that one Aldobrandino Palermini, who is under arrest,
did the deed, because Tedaldo, who loved his wife, was come
back to Florence incognito to forgather with her." Tedaldo
found it passing strange that there should be any one so like
him as to be mistaken for him, and deplored Aldobrandino's
evil plight. He had learned, however, that the lady was alive
and well. So, as 'twas now night, he hied him, much perplexed
in mind, into the inn, and supped with his servant. The bed-
room assigned him was almost at the top of the house, and the
bed was none of the best. Thoughts many and disquieting
haunted his mind, and his supper had been but light. Whereby
it befell that midnight came and went, and Tedaldo was still
awake. As thus he watched, he heard shortly after midnight,
a noise as of persons descending from the roof into the house,
and then through the chinks of the door of his room he caught
the flicker of an ascending light. Wherefore he stole softly
to the door, and peeping through a chink to make out what
was afoot, he saw a very fine young woman bearing a light, and
three men making towards her, being evidently those that had
descended from the roof. The men exchanged friendly greetings
with the young woman, and then one said to her :—" Now,
God be praised, we may make our minds easy, for we are well
assured that judgment for the death of Tedaldo Elisei is gotten
by his brothers against Aldobrandino Palermini, and he has
confessed, and the sentence is already drawn up ; but still it
behoves us to hold our peace ; for, should it ever get abroad
that we were guilty, we shall stand in the like jeopardy as
Aldobrandino." So saying, they took leave of the woman,
who seemed much cheered, and went to bed. What he had
heard set Tedaldo musing on the number and variety of the
errors to which men are liable : as, first, how his brothers had
mourned and interred a stranger in his stead, and then charged
an innocent man upon false suspicion, and by false witness
brought him into imminent peril of death : from which he
passed to ponder the blind severity of laws and magistrates,
who from misguided zeal to elicit the truth not unfrequently
become ruthless, and, adjudging that which is false, forfeit
the title which they claim of ministers of God and justice,
and do but execute the mandates of iniquity and the Evil
One. And so he came at last to consider the possibility of

saving Aldobrandino, and formed a plan for the purpose.
Accordingly, on the morrow, when he was risen, he left his
servant at the inn, and hied him alone, at what he deemed a
convenient time, to his lady's house, where, finding, by chance,
the door open, he entered, and saw his lady sitting, all tears
and lamentations, in a little parlour on the ground-floor.
Whereat he all but wept for sympathy; and drawing near her,
he said :—" Madam, be not troubled in spirit : your peace is
nigh you." Whereupon the lady raised her head, and said
between her sobs :—" Good man, what dost thou, a pilgrim, if
I mistake not, from distant parts, know either of my peace
or of my affliction ? " " Madam," returned the pilgrim, " I
am of Constantinople, and am but now come hither, at God's
behest, that I may give you laughter for tears, and deliver your
husband from death." " But," said the lady, " if thou art
of Constantinople, and but now arrived, how is 't that thou
knowest either who my husband is, or who I am ? " Where-
upon the pilgrim gave her the whole narrative, from the very
beginning, of Aldobrandino's sufferings ; he also told her,
who she was, how long she had been married, and much besides
that was known to him of her affairs : whereat the lady was
lost in wonder, and, taking him to be a prophet, threw herself
on her knees at his feet, and besought him for God's sake, if
he were come to save Aldobrandino, to lose no time, for the
matter brooked no delay. Thus adjured, the pilgrim assumed
an air of great sanctity, as he said :—" Arise, Madam, weep
not, but hearken diligently to what I shall say to you, and look
to it that you impart it to none. I have it by revelation of
God that the tribulation wherein you stand is come upon you
in requital of a sin which you did once commit, of which
God is minded that this suffering be a partial purgation, and
that you make reparation in full, if you would not find your-
self in a far more grievous plight." " Sir," replied the lady,
" many sins have I committed, nor know I how among them
all to single out that whereof, more than another, God requires
reparation at my hands : wherefore, if you know it, tell it
me, and what by way of reparation I may do, that will I do."
" Madam," returned the pilgrim, " well wot I what it is, nor
shall I question you thereof for my better instruction, but that
the rehearsal may give you increase of remorse therefor. But
pass we now to fact. Tell me, mind you ever to have had a
lover ? " Whereat the lady heaved a deep sigh ; then,
marvelling not a little, for she had thought 'twas known to

none, albeit on the day when the man was slain, who was after-
wards buried as Tedaldo, there had been some buzz about it,
occasioned by some indiscreet words dropped by Tedaldo's
gossip and confidant, she made answer :—" I see that there
is nought that men keep secret but God reveals it to you ;
wherefore I shall not endeavour to hide my secrets from you.
True it is that in my youth I was beyond measure enamoured
of the unfortunate young man whose death is imputed to my
husband ; whom I mourned with grief unfeigned, for, albeit I
shewed myself harsh and cruel towards him before his departure,
yet neither thereby, nor by his long absence, nor yet by his
calamitous death was my heart estranged from him." Then
said the pilgrim :—" 'Twas not the unfortunate young man
now dead that you did love, but Tedaldo Elisei. But let that
pass ; now tell me : wherefore lost he your good graces ?
Did he ever offend you ? " " Nay verily," answered the lady,
" he never offended me at all. My harshness was prompted
by an accursed friar, to whom I once confessed, and who,
when I told him of the love I bore Tedaldo, and my intimacy
with him, made my ears so tingle and sing that I still shudder
to think of it, warning me that, if I gave it not up, I should fall
into the jaws of the Devil in the abyss of hell, and be cast
into the avenging fire. Whereby I was so terrified that I
quite made my mind up to discontinue my intimacy with him,
and, to trench the matter, I would thenceforth have none of
his letters or messages ; and so, I suppose, he went away in
despair, though I doubt not, had he persevered a while longer,
I should not have seen him wasting away like snow in sunshine
without relenting of my harsh resolve ; for in sooth there was
nothing in the world I would so gladly have done." Then
said the pilgrim :—" Madam, 'tis this sin, and this only, that
has brought upon you your present tribulation. I know
positively that Tedaldo did never put force upon you : 'twas
of your own free will, and for that he pleased you, that you
became enamoured of him : your constant visitor, your intimate
friend he became, because you yourself would have it so ;
and in the course of your intimacy you shewed him such favour
by word and deed that, if he loved you first, you multiplied his
love full a thousandfold. And if so it was, and well I know
it was so, what justification had you for thus harshly severing
yourself from him ? You should have considered the whole
matter before the die was cast, and not have entered upon it,
if you deemed you might have cause to repent you of it as a sin.

As soon as he became yours, you became his. Had he not been yours, you might have acted as you had thought fit, at your own unfettered discretion ; but, as you were his, 'twas robbery, 'twas conduct most disgraceful, to sever yourself from him against his will. Now you must know that I am a friar ; and therefore all the ways of friars are familiar to me ; nor does it misbecome me, as it might another, to speak for your behoof somewhat freely of them ; as I am minded to do that you may have better understanding of them in the future than you would seem to have had in the past. Time was when the friars were most holy and worthy men, but those who to-day take the name and claim the reputation of friars have nought of the friar save only the habit : nay, they have not even that : for, whereas their founders ordained that their habits should be strait, of a sorry sort, and of coarse stuff, apt symbols of a soul that in arraying the body in so mean a garb did despite to all things temporal, our modern friars will have them full, and double, and resplendent, and of the finest stuff, and of a fashion goodly and pontifical, wherein without shame they flaunt it like peacocks in the church, in the piazza, even as do the laity in their robes. And as the fisherman casts his net into the stream with intent to take many fish at one throw : so 'tis the main solicitude and study, art and craft of these friars to embrace and entangle within the ample folds of their vast swelling skirts beguines, widows and other foolish women, ay, and men likewise in great number. Wherefore, to speak with more exactitude, the friars of to-day have nought of the habit of the friar save only the colour thereof. And, whereas the friars of old time sought to win men to their salvation, those of to-day seek to win their women and their wealth ; wherefore they have made it and make it their sole concern by declamation and imagery to strike terror into the souls of fools, and to make believe that sins are purged by alms and masses ; to the end that they, base wretches that have fled to friarage not to ensue holiness but to escape hardship, may receive from this man bread, from that man wine, and from the other man a donation for masses for the souls of his dead. True indeed it is that sins are purged by almsgiving and prayer ; but, did they who give the alms know, did they but understand to whom they give them, they would be more apt to keep them to themselves, or throw them to so many pigs. And, knowing that the fewer be they that share great riches, the greater their ease, 'tis the study of each how best by declamation and intimi-

dation to oust others from that whereof he would fain be the
sole owner They censure lust in men, that, they turning
therefrom, the sole use of their women may remain to the
censors : they condemn usury and unlawful gains, that, being
entrusted with the restitution thereof, they may be able to
enlarge their habits, and to purchase bishoprics and other
great preferments with the very money which they have made
believe must bring its possessor to perdition. And when they
are taxed with these and many other discreditable practices,
they deem that there is no censure, however grave, of which
they may not be quit by their glib formula :—' Follow our
precepts, not our practice : ' as if 'twere possible that the sheep
should be of a more austere and rigid virtue than the shepherds.
And how many of these, whom they put off with this formula,
understand it not in the way in which they enunciate it, not
a few of them know. The friars of to-day would have you
follow their precepts, that is to say, they would have you fill
their purses with coin, confide to them your secrets, practise
continence, be long-suffering, forgive those that trespass against
you, keep yourselves from evil speaking ; all which things are
good, seemly, holy. But to what end ? To the end that
they may be able to do that which, if the laity do it, they will
not be able to do. Who knows not that idleness cannot subsist
without money ? Spend thy money on thy pleasures, and the
friar will not be able to live in sloth in his order. Go after
women, and there will be no place for the friar. Be not long-
suffering, pardon not the wrong-doer, and the friar will not
dare to cross thy threshold to corrupt thy family. But where-
fore pursue I the topic through every detail ? They accuse
themselves as often as they so excuse themselves in the hearing
of all that have understanding. Why seclude they not them-
selves, if they misdoubt their power to lead continent and holy
lives ? Or if they must needs not live as recluses, why follow
they not that other holy text of the Gospel :—Christ began to
do and to teach ? [1] Let them practise first, and school us with
their precepts afterwards. A thousand such have I seen in
my day, admirers, lovers, philanderers, not of ladies of the
world alone, but of nuns ; ay, and they too such as made the
most noise in the pulpits. Is it such as they that we are to

---

[1] As pointed out by Mr. Payne, these words are not from any of the
Gospels, but from the first verse of the Acts of the Apostles. Boccaccio
doubtless used " Evangelio " in a large sense for the whole of the New
Testament.

follow? He that does so, pleases himself; but God knows if he do wisely. But assume that herein we must allow that your censor, the friar, spoke truth, to wit, that none may break the marriage-vow without very grave sin. What then? to rob a man, to slay him, to make of him an exile and a wanderer on the face of the earth, are not these yet greater sins? None will deny that so they are. A woman that indulges herself in the intimate use with a man commits but a sin of nature; but if she rob him, or slay him, or drive him out into exile, her sin proceeds from depravity of spirit. That you did rob Tedaldo, I have already shewn you, in that, having of your own free will become his, you reft you from him. I now go further and say that, so far as in you lay, you slew him, seeing that, shewing yourself ever more and more cruel, you did your utmost to drive him to take his own life; and in the law's intent he that is the cause that wrong is done is as culpable as he that does it. Nor is it deniable that you were the cause that for seven years he has been an exile and a wanderer upon the face of the earth. Wherefore upon each of the said three articles you are found guilty of a greater crime than you committed by your intimacy with him. But consider we the matter more closely: perchance Tedaldo merited such treatment: nay, but assuredly 'twas not so. You have yourself so confessed: besides which I know that he loves you more dearly than himself. He would laud, he would extol, he would magnify you above all other ladies so as never was heard the like, wheresoever 'twas seemly for him to speak of you, and it might be done without exciting suspicion. All his bliss, all his honour, all his liberty he avowed was entirely in your disposal. Was he not of noble birth? And for beauty might he not compare with the rest of his townsfolk? Did he not excel in all the exercises and accomplishments proper to youth? Was he not beloved, held dear, well seen of all men? You will not deny it. How then could you at the behest of a paltry friar, silly, brutish and envious, bring yourself to deal with him in any harsh sort? I cannot estimate the error of those ladies who look askance on men and hold them cheap; whereas, bethinking them of what they are themselves, and what and how great is the nobility with which God has endowed man above all the other animals, they ought rather to glory in the love which men give them, and hold them most dear, and with all zeal study to please them, that so their love may never fail. In what sort you did so, instigated by the chatter of a friar, some

broth-guzzling, pastry-gorging knave without a doubt, you
know; and peradventure his purpose was but to instal him-
self in the place whence he sought to oust another. This
then is the sin which the Divine justice, which, ever operative,
suffers no perturbation of its even balance, or arrest of judgment,
has decreed not to leave unpunished: wherefore, as without
due cause you devised how you might despoil Tedaldo of
yourself, so without due cause your husband has been placed
and is in jeopardy of his life on Tedaldo's account, and to your
sore affliction. Wherefrom if you would be delivered, there
is that which you must promise, ay, and (much more) which
you must perform: to wit, that, should it ever betide that
Tedaldo return hither from his long exile, you will restore to
him your favour, your love, your tender regard, your intimacy,
and reinstate him in the position which he held before you
foolishly hearkened to the half-witted friar."

Thus ended the pilgrim; and the lady, who had followed him
with the closest attention, deeming all that he advanced very
sound, and doubting not that her tribulation was, as he said,
in requital of her sin, spoke thus:—"Friend of God, well I
wot that the matters which you discourse are true, and, thanks
to your delineation, I now in great measure know what manner
of men are the friars, whom I have hitherto regarded as all
alike holy; nor doubt I that great was my fault in the course
which I pursued towards Tedaldo; and gladly, were it in my
power, would I make reparation in the manner which you have
indicated. But how is this feasible? Tedaldo can never
return to us. He is dead. Wherefore I know not why I
must needs give you a promise which cannot be performed."
"Madam," returned the pilgrim, "'tis revealed to me by God
that Tedaldo is by no means dead, but alive and well and happy,
so only he enjoyed your favour." "Nay, but," said the lady,
"speak advisedly; I saw his body done to death by more than
one knife-wound; I folded it in these arms, and drenched the
dead face with many a tear; whereby, perchance, I gave
occasion for the bruit that has been made to my disadvantage."
"Say what you may, Madam," rejoined the pilgrim, "I assure
you that Tedaldo lives, and if you will but give the promise,
then, for its fulfilment, I have good hope that you will soon
see him." Whereupon: "I give the promise," said the lady,
"and right gladly will I make it good; nor is there aught that
might happen that would yield me such delight as to see
my husband free and scatheless, and Tedaldo alive." Tedaldo

now deemed it wise to make himself known, and establish the lady in a more sure hope of her husband's safety. Wherefore he said :—" Madam, to set your mind at ease in regard of your husband, I must first impart to you a secret, which be mindful to disclose to none so long as you live." Then—for such was the confidence which the lady reposed in the pilgrim's apparent sanctity that they were by themselves in a place remote from observation—Tedaldo drew forth a ring which he had guarded with the most jealous care, since it had been given him by the lady on the last night when they were together, and said, as he shewed it to her :—" Madam, know you this ? " The lady recognized it forthwith, and answered :—" I do, Sir ; I gave it long ago to Tedaldo." Then the pilgrim, rising and throwing off his sclavine [1] and hat, said with the Florentine accent :— " And know you me ? " The lady, recognizing forthwith the form and semblance of Tedaldo, was struck dumb with wonder and fear as of a corpse that is seen to go about as if alive, and was much rather disposed to turn and flee from Tedaldo returned from the tomb than to come forward and welcome Tedaldo arrived from Cyprus. But when Tedaldo said to her :—" Fear not, Madam, your Tedaldo am I, alive and well, nor was I ever dead, whatever you and my brothers may think," the lady, partly awed, partly reassured by his voice, regarded him with rather more attention, and inly affirming that 'twas in very truth Tedaldo, threw herself upon his neck, and wept, and kissed him, saying :—" Sweet my Tedaldo, welcome home." " Madam," replied Tedaldo after he had kissed and embraced her, " time serves not now for greetings more intimate. 'Tis for me to be up and doing, that Aldobrandino may be restored to you safe and sound ; touching which matter you will, I trust, before to-morrow at even hear tidings that will gladden your heart ; indeed I expect to have good news to-night, and, if so, will come and tell it you, when I shall be less straitened than I am at present." He then resumed his sclavine and hat, and having kissed the lady again, and bade her be of good cheer, took his leave, and hied him to the prison, where Aldobrandino lay more occupied with apprehension of imminent death than hope of deliverance to come. As ministrant of consolation, he gained ready admittance of the warders, and, seating himself by Aldobrandino's side, he said :—" Aldobrandino, in me thou seest a friend sent thee by God, who is touched with pity of

---

[1] Schiavina, Low Lat. sclavina, the long coarse frock worn, among others, by palmers.

thee by reason of thy innocence ; wherefore, if in reverent
submission to Him thou wilt grant me a slight favour that I
shall ask of thee, without fail, before to-morrow at even, thou
shalt, in lieu of the doom of death that thou awaitest, hear thy
acquittal pronounced." "Worthy man," replied Aldobrandino,
" I know thee not, nor mind I ever to have seen thee ; where-
fore, as thou shewest thyself solicitous for my safety, my friend
indeed thou must needs be, even as thou sayst. And in sooth
the crime, for which they say I ought to be doomed to death,
I never committed, though others enough I have committed,
which perchance have brought me to this extremity. However,
if so be that God has now pity on me, this I tell thee in reverent
submission to Him, that, whereas 'tis but a little thing that
thou cravest of me, there is nought, however great, but I would
not only promise but gladly do it ; wherefore, even ask what
thou wilt, and, if so be that I escape, I will without fail keep
my word to the letter." "Nay," returned the pilgrim, " I
ask but this of thee, that thou pardon Tedaldo's four brothers,
that in the belief that thou wast guilty of their brother's death
they brought thee to this strait, and, so they ask thy forgiveness,
account them as thy brothers and friends." "How sweet,"
replied Aldobrandino, " is the savour, how ardent the desire,
of vengeance, none knows but he that is wronged ; but yet, so
God may take thought for my deliverance, I will gladly pardon,
nay, I do now pardon them, and if I go hence alive and free,
I will thenceforth have them in such regard as shall content
thee." Satisfied with this answer, the pilgrim, without further
parley, heartily exhorted Aldobrandino to be of good cheer ;
assuring him that, before the next day was done, he should be
certified beyond all manner of doubt of his deliverance ; and
so he left him.

On quitting the prison the pilgrim hied him forthwith to the
signory, and being closeted with a knight that was in charge,
thus spoke :—" My lord, 'tis the duty of all, and most especially
of those who hold your place, zealously to bestir themselves
that the truth be brought to light, in order as well that those
bear not the penalty who have not committed the crime, as
that the guilty be punished. And that this may come to pass
to your honour and the undoing of the delinquent, I am come
hither to you. You wot that you have dealt rigorously with
Aldobrandino Palermini, and have found, as you think, that
'twas he that slew Tedaldo Elisei, and you are about to condemn
him ; wherein you are most certainly in error, as I doubt not

before midnight to prove to you, delivering the murderers
into your hands." The worthy knight, who was not without
pity for Aldobrandino, readily gave ear to the pilgrim's words.
He conversed at large with him, and availing himself of his
guidance, made an easy capture of the two brothers that kept
the inn and their servant in their first sleep. He was about
to put them to the torture to elicit the true state of the case,
when, their courage failing, they confessed without the least
reserve, severally at first, and then jointly, that 'twas they that
had slain Tedaldo Elisei, not knowing who he was. Asked for
why, they answered that 'twas because he had sorely harassed
the wife of one of them, and would have constrained her to do
his pleasure, while they were out of doors. Whereof the pilgrim
was no sooner apprised, than by leave of the knight he with-
drew, and hied him privily to the house of Madonna Ermellina,
whom (the rest of the household being gone to bed) he found
awaiting him alone, and equally anxious for good news of her
husband and a complete reconciliation with her Tedaldo.
On entering, he blithely exclaimed :—" Rejoice, dearest my
lady, for thou mayst rest assured that to-morrow thou shalt
have thy Aldobrandino back here safe and sound ; " and to
confirm her faith in his words, he told her all that he had done.
Greater joy was never woman's than hers of two such glad sur-
prises ; to wit, to have Tedaldo with her alive again, whom
she had wailed for verily dead, and to know Aldobrandino,
whom she had thought in no long time to wail for dead, now out
of jeopardy. Wherefore, when she had affectionately embraced
and kissed her Tedaldo, they hied them to bed together, and
with hearty good-will made gracious and gladsome consumma-
tion of their peace by interchange of sweet solace.

With the approach of day Tedaldo rose, and having first
apprised the lady of his purpose and enjoined her, as before,
to keep it most secret, resumed his pilgrim's habit, and sallied
forth of her house, to be ready, as occasion should serve, to act
in Aldobrandino's interest. As soon as 'twas day, the signory,
deeming themselves amply conversant with the affair, set
Aldobrandino at large ; and a few days later they caused the
malefactors to be beheaded in the place where they had done
the murder.

Great was Aldobrandino's joy to find himself free, nor less
great was that of his lady and all his friends and kinsfolk ;
and as 'twas through the pilgrim that it had come about, they
brought him to their house, there to reside as long as he cared to

tarry in the city ; nor could they do him honour and cheer
enough, and most of all the lady, who knew her man. But after a
while, seeing that his brothers were not only become a common
laughing-stock by reason of Aldobrandino's acquittal, but had
armed themselves for very fear, he felt that their reconciliation
with him brooked no delay, and accordingly craved of him per-
formance of his promise. Aldobrandino replied handsomely
that it should be had at once. The pilgrim then bade him
arrange for the following day a grand banquet, at which he
and his kinsfolk and their ladies were to entertain the four
brothers and their ladies, adding that he would himself go
forthwith as Aldobrandino's envoy, and bid them welcome to
his peace and banquet. All which being approved by Aldo-
brandino, the pilgrim hied him with all speed to the four
brothers, whom by ample, apt and unanswerable argument
he readily induced to reinstate themselves in Aldobrandino's
friendship by suing for his forgiveness : which done, he bade
them and their ladies to breakfast with Aldobrandino on the
morrow, and they, being assured of his good faith, were con-
senting to come. So, on the morrow, at the breakfast hour,
Tedaldo's four brothers, still wearing their black, came with
certain of their friends to Aldobrandino's house, where he
awaited them ; and, in presence of the company that had been
bidden to meet them, laid down their arms, and made surrender
to Aldobrandino, asking his pardon of that which they had done
against him. Aldobrandino received them compassionately,
wept, kissed each on the mouth, and let few words suffice to
remit each offence. After them came their sisters and their
wives, all habited sadly, and were graciously received by
Madonna Ermellina and the other ladies. The guests, men and
women alike, found all things ordered at the banquet with
magnificence, nor aught unmeet for commendation save the
restraint which the yet recent grief, betokened by the sombre
garb of Tedaldo's kinsfolk, laid upon speech (wherein some had
found matter to except against the banquet and the pilgrim
for devising it, as he well knew), but, as he had premeditated,
in due time, he stood up, the others being occupied with their
dessert, and spoke thus :—" Nothing is wanting to complete
the gaiety of this banquet except the presence of Tedaldo ;
whom, as you have been long time with him and have not known
him, I will point out to you." So, having divested himself
of his sclavine and whatever else in his garb denoted the pilgrim,
he remained habited in a tunic of green taffeta, in which guise,

so great was the wonder with which all regarded him that,
though they recognized him, 'twas long before any dared to
believe that 'twas actually Tedaldo. Marking their surprise,
Tedaldo told them not a little about themselves, their family
connexions, their recent history, and his own adventures.
Whereat his brothers and the rest of the men, all weeping for
joy, hasted to embrace him, followed by the women, as well
those that were not, as those that were, of kin to him, save only
Madonna Ermellina. Which Aldobrandino observing, said :—
" What is this, Ermellina ? How comes it that, unlike the
other ladies, thou alone dost Tedaldo no cheer ? " " Cheer,"
replied the lady in the hearing of all, " would I gladly do him
such as no other woman has done or could do, seeing that I
am more beholden to him than any other woman, in that to
him I owe it that I have thee with me again ; 'tis but the words
spoken to my disadvantage, while we mourned him that we
deemed Tedaldo, that give me pause."   " Now out upon thee,"
said Aldobrandino, " thinkest thou that I heed the yelping of
these curs ? His zeal for my deliverance has abundantly dis-
proved it, besides which I never believed it. Quick, get thee
up, and go and embrace him." The lady, who desired nothing
better, was in this not slow to obey her husband ; she rose
forthwith, and embraced Tedaldo as the other ladies had done,
and did him gladsome cheer. Tedaldo's brothers and all the
company, men and women alike, heartily approved Aldo-
brandino's handsomeness ; and so whatever of despite the
rumour had engendered in the minds of any was done away.
And, now that all had done him cheer, Tedaldo with his own
hands rent his brothers' suits of black upon their backs, as
also the sad-hued garments which his sisters and sisters-in-law
wore, and bade bring other apparel. Which when they had
donned, there was no lack of singing, dancing and other sorts
of merry-making ; whereby the banquet, for all its subdued
beginning, had a sonorous close. Then, just as they were, in
the blithest of spirits, they hied them all to Tedaldo's house,
where in the evening they supped : and in this manner they
held festival for several days.

'Twas some time before the Florentines ceased to look on
Tedaldo as a portent, as if he were risen from the dead ; and
a shadow of doubt whether he were really Tedaldo or no con-
tinued to lurk in the minds of not a few, including even his
brothers : they had no assured belief ; and in that frame had
perchance long continued, but for a casual occurrence that

shewed them who the murdered man was. It so befell that one day some men-at-arms from Lunigiana passed by their house, and seeing Tedaldo accosted him, saying :—" Good-morrow to thee, Faziuolo." To whom Tedaldo, in the presence of his brothers, answered :—" You take me for another." Whereat they were abashed, and asked his pardon, saying :—" Sooth to tell, you are liker than we ever knew any man like to another to a comrade of ours, Faziuolo da Pontremoli by name, who came hither a fortnight ago, or perhaps a little more, since when we have not been able to learn what became of him. Most true it is that your dress surprised us, because he, like ourselves, was a soldier." Whereupon Tedaldo's eldest brother came forward, and asked how their comrade had been accoutred. They told him, and 'twas found to have been exactly as they said : by which and other evidence 'twas established that 'twas Faziuolo that had been murdered, and not Tedaldo ; of whom thenceforth no suspicion lurked in the minds of his brothers or any one else.

So, then, Tedaldo returned home very rich, and remained constant in his love ; nor did the lady again treat him harshly ; but, using discretion, they long had mutual solace of their love.   God grant us solace of ours.

NOVEL VIII

Ferondo, having taken a certain powder, is interred for dead ; is disinterred by the abbot, who enjoys his wife ; is put in prison and taught to believe that he is in purgatory ; is then resuscitated, and rears as his own a boy begotten by the abbot upon his wife.

ENDED Emilia's long story, which to none was the less pleasing for its length, but was deemed of all the ladies brief in regard to the number and variety of the events therein recounted, a gesture of the queen sufficed to convey her behest to Lauretta, and cause her thus to begin :—" Dearest ladies, I have it in mind to tell you a true story, which wears far more of the aspect of a lie than of that which it really was : 'tis brought to my recollection by that which we have heard of one being bewailed and buried in lieu of another. My story then is of one that, living, was buried for dead, and after believed with many others that he came out of the tomb not as one that had not died but

as one risen from the dead; whereby he was venerated as a
saint who ought rather to have been condemned as a criminal.

Know then that there was and still is in Tuscany an abbey,
situate, as we see not a few, in a somewhat solitary spot, wherein
the office of abbot was held by a monk, who in all other matters
ordered his life with great sanctity, save only in the commerce
with women, and therein knew so well how to cloak his indul-
gence, that scarce any there were that so much as suspected—
not to say detected it—so holy and just was he reputed in all
matters.   Now the abbot consorted much with a very wealthy
contadino, Ferondo by name, a man coarse and gross beyond
measure, whose friendship the abbot only cared for because
of the opportunities which it afforded of deriving amusement
from his simplicity; and during their intercourse the abbot
discovered that Ferondo had a most beautiful wife; of whom
he became so hotly enamoured that he could think of nought
else either by day or by night.   But learning that, however
simple and inept in all other matters, Ferondo shewed excellent
good sense in cherishing and watching over this wife of his, he
almost despaired.   However, being very astute, he prevailed
so far with Ferondo, that he would sometimes bring his wife
with him to take a little recreation in the abbey-garden, where
he discoursed to them with all lowliness of the blessedness of
life eternal, and the most pious works of many men and women
of times past, insomuch that the lady conceived a desire to
confess to him, and craved and had Ferondo's leave therefor.
So, to the abbot's boundless delight, the lady came and seated
herself at his feet to make her confession, whereto she prefixed
the following exordium :—" If God, Sir, had given me a husband,
or had not permitted me to have one, perchance 'twould be
easy for me, under your guidance, to enter the way, of which
you have spoken, that leads to life eternal.   But, considering
what manner of man Ferondo is, and his stupidity, I may call
myself a widow while yet I am married in that, so long as he
lives, I may have no other husband; and he, fool that he is,
is without the least cause so inordinately jealous of me that 'tis
not possible but that my life with him be one of perpetual
tribulation and woe.   Wherefore, before I address myself to
make further confession, I in all humility beseech you to be
pleased to give me some counsel of this matter, for here or
nowhere is to be found the source of the amelioration of my
life, and if it be not found, neither confession nor any other good
work will be of any avail."   The abbot was overjoyed to hear

her thus speak, deeming that Fortune had opened a way to the
fulfilment of his heart's desire. Wherefore he said :—" My
daughter, I doubt not that 'tis a great affliction to a lady, fair
and delicate as you are, to have a fool for a husband, and still
more so that he should be jealous : and as your husband is both
the one and the other, I readily credit what you say of your
tribulation. But, to come to the point, I see no resource or
remedy in this case, save this only, that Ferondo be cured of his
jealousy. The medicine that shall cure him I know very well
how to devise, but it behoves you to keep secret what I am about
to tell you." " Doubt not of it, my father," said the lady ;
" for I had rather suffer death than tell aught that you for-
bade me to tell. But the medicine, how is it to be devised ? "
" If we would have him cured," replied the abbot, " it can only
be by his going to purgatory." " And how may that be ? "
returned the lady ; " can he go thither while he yet lives ? "
" He must die," answered the abbot ; " and so he will go
thither ; and when he has suffered pain enough to be cured of
his jealousy, we have certain prayers with which we will
supplicate God to restore him to life, and He will do so."
" Then," said the lady ; " am I to remain a widow ? " " Yes,"
replied the abbot, " for a certain time, during which you must
be very careful not to let yourself be married to another,
because 'twould offend God, and when Ferondo was restored to
life, you would have to go back to him, and he would be more
jealous than ever." " Be it so then," said the lady ; " if he
be but cured of his jealousy, and so I be not doomed to pass
the rest of my days in prison, I shall be content : do as you
think best." " And so will I," said the abbot ; " but what
reward shall I have for such a service ? " " My father," said
the lady, " what you please ; so only it be in my power. But
what may the like of me do that may be acceptable to a man
such as you ? " " Madam," replied the abbot, " 'tis in your
power to do no less for me than I am about to do for you :
as that which I am minded to do will ensure your comfort
and consolation, so there is that which you may do which will
be the deliverance and salvation of my life." " If so it be,"
said the lady, " I shall not be found wanting." " In that
case," said the abbot, " you will give me your love, and gratify
my passion for you, with which I am all afire and wasting away."
Whereto the lady, all consternation, replied :—" Alas ! my
father, what is this you crave ? I took you for a holy man ;
now does it beseem holy men to make such overtures to ladies

that come to them for counsel ? "   " Marvel not, fair my
soul," returned the abbot ; " hereby is my holiness in no
wise diminished, for holiness resides in the soul, and this which
I ask of you is but a sin of the flesh.   But, however it may be,
such is the might of your bewitching beauty, that love con-
strains me thus to act.   And, let me tell you, good cause have
you to vaunt you of your beauty more than other women, in
that it delights the saints, who are used to contemplate celestial
beauties ; whereto I may add that, albeit I am an abbot, yet
I am a man even as others, and, as you see, not yet old.   Nor
need this matter seem formidable to you, but rather to be
anticipated with pleasure, for, while Ferondo is in purgatory,
I shall be your nightly companion, and will give you such solace
as he should have given you ; nor will it ever be discovered
by any, for all think of me even as you did a while ago, or even
more so.   Reject not the grace that God accords you ; for
'tis in your power to have, and, if you are wise and follow my
advice, you shall have that which women not a few desire in
vain to have.   And moreover I have jewels fair and rare, which
I am minded shall be yours and none other's.   Wherefore,
sweet my hope, deny me not due guerdon of the service which
I gladly render you."

The lady, her eyes still downcast, knew not how to deny
him, and yet scrupled to gratify him : wherefore the abbot,
seeing that she had hearkened and hesitated to answer, deemed
that she was already half won, and following up what he had
said with much more to the like effect, did not rest until he had
persuaded her that she would do well to comply : and so with
some confusion she told him that she was ready to obey his
every behest ; but it might not be until Ferondo was in pur-
gatory.   The abbot, well content, replied :—" And we will
send him thither forthwith : do but arrange that he come
hither to stay with me to-morrow or the day after."   Which
said, he slipped a most beautiful ring on her finger, and dismissed
her.   Pleased with the gift, and expecting more to come, the
lady rejoined her attendants, with whom she forthwith fell a-
talking marvellous things of the abbot's sanctity, and so went
home with them.

Some few days after, Ferondo being come to the abbey, the
abbot no sooner saw him than he resolved to send him to
purgatory.   So he selected from among his drugs a powder
of marvellous virtue, which he had gotten in the Levant from
a great prince, who averred that 'twas wont to be used by the

Old Man of the Mountain, when he would send any one to or bring him from his paradise, and that, without doing the recipient any harm, 'twould induce in him, according to the quantity of the dose, a sleep of such duration and quality that, while the efficacy of the powder lasted, none would deem him to be alive.[1] Whereof he took enough to cause a three days' sleep, and gave it to Ferondo in his cell in a beaker that had still some wine in it, so that he drank it unwittingly : after which he took Ferondo to the cloister, and there with some of his monks fell to making merry with him and his ineptitudes. In no long time, however, the powder so wrought, that Ferondo was seized in the head with a fit of somnolence so sudden and violent that he slept as he stood, and sleeping fell to the ground. The abbot put on an agitated air, caused him to be untrussed, sent for cold water, and had it sprinkled on his face, and applied such other remedies as if he would fain call back life and sense banished by vapours of the stomach, or some other intrusive force ; but, as, for all that he and his monks did, Ferondo did not revive, they, after feeling his pulse and finding there no sign of life, one and all pronounced him certainly dead. Wherefore they sent word to his wife and kinsfolk, who came forthwith, and mourned a while ; after which Ferondo in his clothes was by the abbot's order laid in a tomb. The lady went home, saying that nothing should ever part her from a little son that she had borne Ferondo ; and so she occupied herself with the care of her son and Ferondo's estate. At night the abbot rose noiselessly, and with the help of a Bolognese monk, in whom he reposed much trust, and who was that very day arrived from Bologna, got Ferondo out of the tomb, and bore him to a vault, which admitted no light, having been made to serve as a prison for delinquent monks ; and having stripped him of his clothes, and habited him as a monk, they laid him on a truss of straw, and left him there until he should revive. Expecting which event, and instructed by the abbot how he was then to act, the Bolognese monk (none else knowing aught of what was afoot) kept watch by the tomb.

The day after, the abbot with some of his monks paid a pastoral visit to the lady's house, where he found her in mourning weeds and sad at heart ; and, after administering a little consolation, he gently asked her to redeem her promise. Free

[1] By the Old Man of the Mountain is meant the head of the confraternity of hashish-eaters (Assassins), whose chief stronghold was at Alamut in Persia (1090–1256). Cf. Marco Polo, ed. Yule, I. cap. xxiii.

as she now felt herself, and hampered neither by Ferondo nor by any other, the lady, who had noticed another beautiful ring on the abbot's finger, promised immediate compliance, and arranged with the abbot that he should visit her the very next night. So, at nightfall, the abbot donned Ferondo's clothes, and, attended by his monk, paid his visit, and lay with her until matins to his immense delight and solace, and so returned to the abbey ; and many visits he paid her on the same errand ; whereby some that met him, coming or going that way, supposed that 'twas Ferondo perambulating those parts by way of penance ; and fables not a few passed from mouth to mouth of the foolish rustics, and sometimes reached the ears of the lady, who was at no loss to account for them.

As for Ferondo, when he revived, 'twas only to find himself he knew not where, while the Bolognese monk entered the tomb, gibbering horribly, and armed with a rod, wherewith, having laid hold of Ferondo, he gave him a severe thrashing. Blubbering and bellowing for pain, Ferondo could only ejaculate :— " Where am I ? " " In purgatory," replied the monk. " How ? " returned Ferondo, " am I dead then ? " and the monk assuring him that 'twas even so, he fell a bewailing his own and his lady's and his son's fate, after the most ridiculous fashion in the world. The monk brought him somewhat to eat and drink. Of which when Ferondo caught sight, " Oh ! " said he, " dead folk eat then, do they ? " " They do," replied the monk ; " and this, which I bring thee, is what the lady that was thy wife sent this morning to the church by way of alms for masses for thy soul ; and God is minded that it be assigned to thee." " Now God grant her a happy year," said Ferondo ; " dearly I loved her while I yet lived, and would hold her all night long in my arms, and cease not to kiss her, ay, and would do yet more to her, when I was so minded." Whereupon he fell to eating and drinking with great avidity, and finding the wine not much to his taste, he said :—" Now God do her a mischief ! Why gave she not the priest of the wine that is in the cask by the wall ? " When he had done eating, the monk laid hold of him again, and gave him another sound thrashing with the rod. Ferondo bellowed mightily, and then cried out : —" Alas ! why servest thou me so ? " " God," answered the monk, " has decreed that thou be so served twice a day." " For why ? " said Ferondo. " Because," returned the monk, " thou wast jealous, notwithstanding thou hadst to wife a woman that has not her peer in thy countryside." " Alas,"

said Ferondo, " she was indeed all that thou sayst, ay, and
the sweetest creature too,—no comfit so honeyed—but I knew
not that God took it amiss that a man should be jealous, or
I had not been so." " Of that," replied the monk, " thou
shouldst have bethought thee while thou wast there, and have
amended thy ways ; and should it fall to thy lot ever to return
thither, be sure that thou so lay to heart the lesson that I
now give thee, that thou be no more jealous." " Oh ! " said
Ferondo ; " dead folk sometimes return to earth, do they ? "
" They do," replied the monk ; " if God so will." " Oh ! "
said Ferondo ; " if I ever return, I will be the best husband in
the world ; never will I beat her or scold her, save for the wine
that she has sent me this morning, and also for sending me
never a candle, so that I have had perforce to eat in the dark."
" Nay," said the monk, " she sent them, but they were burned
at the masses." " Oh ! " said Ferondo, " I doubt not you
say true ; and, of a surety, if I ever return, I will let her do
just as she likes. But tell me, who art thou that entreatest me
thus ? " " Late of Sardinia I," answered the monk, " dead
too ; and, for that I gave my lord much countenance in his
jealousy, doomed by God for my proper penance to entreat
thee thus with food and drink and thrashings, until such time
as He may ordain otherwise touching thee and me." " And
are we two the only folk here ? " inquired Ferondo. " Nay,
there are thousands beside," answered the monk ; " but thou
canst neither see nor hear them, nor they thee." " And how
far," said Ferondo, " may we be from our country ? " " Oh !
ho ! " returned the monk, " why, 'tis some miles clean out of
shit-range." " I'faith," said Ferondo, " that is far indeed :
methinks we must be out of the world."

In such a course, alternately beaten, fed and amused with
idle tales, was Ferondo kept for ten months, while the abbot,
to his great felicity, paid many a visit to the fair lady, and had
the jolliest time in the world with her. But, as misfortunes
will happen, the lady conceived, which fact, as soon as she was
aware of it, she imparted to the abbot ; whereupon both agreed
that Ferondo must without delay be brought back from pur-
gatory to earth and her, and be given to understand that she
was with child of him. So the very next night the abbot went
to the prison, and in a disguised voice pronounced Ferondo's
name, and said to him :—" Ferondo, be of good cheer, for God
is minded that thou return to earth ; and on thy return thou
shalt have a son by thy lady, and thou shalt call him Benedetto ;

because 'tis in answer to the prayers of thy holy abbot and
thy lady, and for love of St. Benedict, that God accords thee
this grace." Whereafter Ferondo was overjoyed, and said :—
" It likes me well. God give a good year to Master Lord God,
and the abbot, and St. Benedict, and my cheese-powdered,
honey-sweet wife." Then, in the wine that he sent him, the
abbot administered enough of the powder to cause him to
sleep for four hours ; and so, with the aid of the monk, having
first habited him in his proper clothes, he privily conveyed
him back to the tomb in which he had been buried. On the
morrow at daybreak Ferondo revived, and perceiving through
a chink in the tomb a glimmer of light, to which he had been
a stranger for full ten months, he knew that he was alive, and
began to bellow :—" Let me out, let me out : " then, setting
his head to the lid of the tomb, he heaved amain ; whereby
the lid, being insecure, started ; and he was already thrusting
it aside, when the monks, matins being now ended, ran to the
spot and recognized Ferondo's voice, and saw him issue from
the tomb ; by which unwonted event they were all so affrighted
that they took to flight, and hied them to the abbot : who,
rising as if from prayer, said :—" Sons, be not afraid ; take
the cross and the holy water, and follow me, and let us see what
sign of His might God will vouchsafe us." And so he led
the way to the tomb ; beside which they found Ferondo stand-
ing, deathly pale by reason of his long estrangement from the
light. On sight of the abbot he ran and threw himself at his
feet, saying :—" My father, it has been revealed to me that
'tis to your prayers and those of St. Benedict and my lady that
I owe my release from purgatorial pain, and restoration to life ;
wherefore 'tis my prayer that God give you a good year and
good calends, to-day and all days." " Laud we the power of
God ! " said the abbot. " Go then, son, as God has restored
thee to earth, comfort thy wife, who, since thou didst depart
this life, has been ever in tears, and mayst thou live henceforth
in the love and service of God." " Sir," answered Ferondo,
" 'tis well said ; and, for the doing, trust me that, as soon as
I find her, I shall kiss her, such is the love I bear her." So
saying, he went his way ; and the abbot, left alone with his
monks, made as if he marvelled greatly at the affair, and
caused devoutly chant the Miserere. So Ferondo returned to
his hamlet, where all that saw him fleeing, as folk are wont to
flee from spectacles of horror, he called them back, asseverating
that he was risen from the tomb. His wife at first was no less

timorous : but, as folk began to take heart of grace, perceiving
that he was alive, they plied him with many questions, all
which he answered as one that had returned with ripe experience,
and gave them tidings of the souls of their kinsfolk, and told
of his own invention the prettiest fables of the purgatorial
state, and in full folkmoot recounted the revelation vouchsafed
him by the mouth of Ragnolo Braghiello [1] before his
resuscitation.

Thus was Ferondo reinstated in his property and reunited
to his wife, who, being pregnant, as he thought, by himself,
chanced by the time of her delivery to countenance the vulgar
error that the woman must bear the infant in the womb for
exactly nine months, and gave birth to a male child, who was
named Benedetto Ferondi. Ferondo's return from purgatory,
and the report he brought thence, immeasurably enhanced the
fame of the abbot's holiness. So Ferondo, cured of his jealousy
by the thrashings which he had gotten for it, verified the abbot's
prediction, and never offended the lady again in that sort.
Wherefore she lived with him, as before, in all outward seem-
liness ; albeit she failed not, as occasion served, to forgather
with the holy abbot, who had so well and sedulously served
her in her especial need.

NOVEL IX

*Gillette of Narbonne cures the King of France of a fistula, craves
for spouse Bertrand de Roussillon, who marries her against
his will, and hies him in despite to Florence, where, as he
courts a young woman, Gillette lies with him in her stead,
and has two sons by him ; for which cause he afterwards
takes her into favour and entreats her as his wife.*

LAURETTA's story being ended, and the queen being minded
not to break her engagement with Dioneo, 'twas now her turn
to speak. Wherefore without awaiting the call of her subjects,
thus with mien most gracious she began :—Now that we have
heard Lauretta's story, who shall tell any to compare with it
for beauty ? Lucky indeed was it that she was not the first ;
for few that followed would have pleased ; and so, I misdoubt

---

[1] Derisively for Agnolo Gabriello (the *h* having merely the effect of
preserving the hardness of the g before *i*), *i.e.* Angel Gabriel.

me, 'twill fare ill with those that remain to complete the day's narration. However, for what it may be worth, I will tell you a story which seems to me germane to our theme.

Know, then, that in the realm of France there was a gentleman, Isnard, Comte de Roussillon, by name, who, being in ill-health, kept ever in attendance on him a physician, one Master Gerard of Narbonne. The said Count had an only son named Bertrand, a very fine and winsome little lad ; with whom were brought up other children of his own age, among them the said physician's little daughter Gillette ; who with a love boundless and ardent out of all keeping with her tender years became enamoured of this Bertrand. And so, when the Count died, and his son, being left a ward of the King, must needs go to Paris, the girl remained beside herself with grief, and, her father dying soon after, would gladly have gone to Paris to see Bertrand, might she but have found a fair excuse ; but no decent pretext could she come by, being left a great and sole heiress and very closely guarded. So being come of marriageable age, still cherishing Bertrand's memory, she rejected not a few suitors, to whom her kinsfolk would fain have married her, without assigning any reason.

Now her passion waxing ever more ardent for Bertrand, as she learned that he was grown a most goodly gallant, tidings reached her that the King of France, in consequence of a tumour which he had had in the breast and which had been ill tended, was now troubled with a fistula, which occasioned him extreme distress and suffering ; nor had he as yet come by a physician that was able, though many had essayed, to cure him, but had rather grown worse under their hands ; wherefore in despair he was minded no more to have recourse to any for counsel or aid. Whereat the damsel was overjoyed, deeming not only that she might find therein lawful occasion to go to Paris, but, that, if the disease was what she took it to be, it might well betide that she should be wedded to Bertrand. So— for not a little knowledge had she gotten from her father—she prepared a powder from certain herbs serviceable in the treatment of the supposed disease, and straightway took horse, and hied her to Paris. Arrived there she made it her first concern to have sight of Bertrand ; and then, having obtained access to the King, she besought him of his grace to shew her his disease. The King knew not how to refuse so young, fair and winsome a damsel, and let her see the place. Whereupon, no longer doubting that she should cure him, she said :—" Sire, so please

you, I hope in God to cure you of this malady within eight
days without causing you the least distress or discomfort."
The King inly scoffed at her words, saying to himself :—" How
should a damsel have come by a knowledge and skill that the
greatest physicians in the world do not possess ? " He there-
fore graciously acknowledged her good intention, and answered
that he had resolved no more to follow advice of physician.
" Sire," said the damsel, " you disdain my art, because I am
young and a woman ; but I bid you bear in mind that I rely
not on my own skill, but on the help of God, and the skill of
Master Gerard of Narbonne, my father, and a famous physician
in his day." Whereupon the King said to himself :—" Per-
chance she is sent me by God ; why put I not her skill to the
proof, seeing that she says that she can cure me in a short time,
and cause me no distress ? " And being minded to make the
experiment, he said :—" Damsel, and if, having caused me to
cancel my resolve, you should fail to cure me, what are you
content should ensue ? " " Sire," answered the damsel, " set
a guard upon me ; and if within eight days I cure you not, have
me burned ; but if I cure you, what shall be my guerdon ? "
" You seem," said the King, " to be yet unmarried ; if you shall
effect the cure, we will marry you well and in high place."
" Sire," returned the damsel, " well content indeed am I that
you should marry me, so it be to such a husband as I shall ask
of you, save that I may not ask any of your sons or any other
member of the royal house." Whereto the King forthwith
consented, and the damsel, thereupon applying her treatment,
restored him to health before the period assigned. Wherefore,
as soon as the King knew that he was cured :—" Damsel," said
he, " well have you won your husband." She answered :—
" In that case, Sire, I have won Bertrand de Roussillon, of
whom, while yet a child, I was enamoured, and whom I have
ever since most ardently loved." To give her Bertrand seemed
to the King no small matter ; but, having pledged his word,
he would not break it : so he sent for Bertrand, and said to
him :—" Bertrand, you are now come to man's estate, and fully
equipped to enter on it ; 'tis therefore our will that you go back
and assume the governance of your county, and that you take
with you a damsel, whom we have given you to wife." " And
who is the damsel, Sire ? " said Bertrand. " She it is," answered
the King, " that has restored us to health by her physic."
Now Bertrand, knowing Gillette, and that her lineage was not
such as matched his nobility, albeit, seeing her, he had found

her very fair, was overcome with disdain, and answered :—
" So, Sire, you would fain give me a she-doctor to wife. Now
God forbid that I should ever marry any such woman."
" Then," said the King, " you would have us fail of the faith
which we pledged to the damsel, who asked you in marriage by
way of guerdon for our restoration to health." " Sire," said
Bertrand, " you may take from me all that I possess, and give
me as your man to whomsoever you may be minded ; but rest
assured that I shall never be satisfied with such a match."
" Nay, but you will," replied the King ; " for the damsel is
fair and discreet, and loves you well ; wherefore we anticipate
that you will live far more happily with her than with a dame
of much higher lineage." Bertrand was silent ; and the King
made great preparations for the celebration of the nuptials.
The appointed day came, and Bertrand, albeit reluctantly,
nevertheless complied, and in the presence of the King was
wedded to the damsel, who loved him more dearly than herself.
Which done, Bertrand, who had already taken his resolution,
said that he was minded to go down to his county, there to
consummate the marriage ; and so, having craved and had
leave of absence of the King, he took horse, but instead of
returning to his county he hied him to Tuscany ; where, finding
the Florentines at war with the Sienese, he determined to take
service with the Florentines, and being made heartily and
honourably welcome, was appointed to the command of part
of their forces, at a liberal stipend, and so remained in their
service for a long while. Distressed by this turn of fortune,
and hoping by her wise management to bring Bertrand back to
his county, the bride hied her to Roussillon, where she was
received by all the tenants as their liege lady. She found that
during the long absence of the lord, everything had fallen into
decay and disorder ; which, being a capable woman, she rectified
with great and sedulous care, to the great joy of the tenants,
who held her in great esteem and love, and severely censured the
Count, that he was not satisfied with her. When the lady had
duly ordered all things in the county, she despatched two
knights to the Count with the intelligence, praying him, that,
if 'twas on her account that he came not home, he would so
inform her ; in which case she would gratify him by departing.
To whom with all harshness he replied :—" She may even please
herself in the matter. For my part I will go home and live
with her, when she has this ring on her finger and a son gotten
of me upon her arm." The ring was one which he greatly

prized, and never removed from his finger, by reason of a virtue
which he had been given to understand that it possessed. The
knights appreciated the harshness of a condition which con-
tained two articles, both of which were all but impossible ; and,
seeing that by no words of theirs could they alter his resolve,
they returned to the lady, and delivered his message. Sorely
distressed, the lady after long pondering determined to try
how and where the two conditions might be satisfied, that so
her husband might be hers again. Having formed her plan,
she assembled certain of the more considerable and notable men
of the county, to whom she gave a consecutive and most touching
narrative of all that she had done for love of the Count, with
the result ; concluding by saying that she was not minded to
tarry there to the Count's perpetual exile, but to pass the rest
of her days in pilgrimages and pious works for the good of her
soul : wherefore she prayed them to undertake the defence and
governance of the county, and to inform the Count that she had
made entire and absolute cession of it to him, and was gone
away with the intention of never more returning to Roussillon.
As she spoke, tears not a few coursed down the cheeks of the
honest men, and again and again they besought her to change
her mind, and stay. All in vain, however ; she commended
them to God, and, accompanied only by one of her male cousins
and a chambermaid (all three habited as pilgrims and amply
provided with money and precious jewels), she took the road,
nor tarried until she was arrived at Florence. There she lodged
in a little inn kept by a good woman that was a widow, bearing
herself lowly as a poor pilgrim, and eagerly expectant of news
of her lord.

  Now it so befell that the very next day she saw Bertrand pass
in front of the inn on horseback at the head of his company ;
and though she knew him very well, nevertheless she asked the
good woman of the inn who he was. The hostess replied :—
" 'Tis a foreign gentleman—Count Bertrand they call him—a
very pleasant gentleman, and courteous, and much beloved in
this city ; and he is in the last degree enamoured of one of our
neighbours here, who is a gentlewoman, but in poor circum-
stances. A very virtuous damsel she is too, and, being as yet
unmarried by reason of her poverty, she lives with her mother,
who is an excellent and most discreet lady, but for whom,
perchance, she would before now have yielded and gratified the
Count's desire." No word of this was lost on the lady ; she
pondered and meditated every detail with the closest attention,

and having laid it all to heart, took her resolution : she ascertained the names and abode of the lady and her daughter that the Count loved, and hied her one day privily, wearing her pilgrim's weeds, to their house, where she found the lady and her daughter in very evident poverty, and after greeting them, told the lady that, if it were agreeable to her, she would speak with her. The gentlewoman rose and signified her willingness to listen to what she had to say ; so they went into a room by themselves and sate down, and then the Countess began thus :— "Madam, methinks you are, as I am, under Fortune's frown ; but perchance you have it in your power, if you are so minded, to afford solace to both of us." The lady answered that, so she might honourably find it, solace indeed was what she craved most of all things in the world. Whereupon the Countess continued :—" I must first be assured of your faith, wherein if I confide and am deceived, the interests of both of us will suffer." "Have no fear," said the gentlewoman, "speak your whole mind without reserve, for you will find that there is no deceit in me." So the Countess told who she was, and the whole course of her love affair, from its commencement to that hour, on such wise that the gentlewoman, believing her story the more readily that she had already heard it in part from others, was touched with compassion for her. The narrative of her woes complete, the Countess added : "Now that you have heard my misfortunes, you know the two conditions that I must fulfil, if I would come by my husband ; nor know I any other person than you, that may enable me to fulfil them ; but so you may, if this which I hear is true, to wit, that my husband is in the last degree enamoured of your daughter." "Madam," replied the gentlewoman, "I know not if the Count loves my daughter, but true it is that he makes great shew of loving her ; but how may this enable me to do aught for you in the matter that you have at heart ?" "The how, madam," returned the Countess, "I will shortly explain to you ; but you shall first hear what I intend shall ensue, if you serve me. Your daughter, I see, is fair and of marriageable age, and, by what I have learned and may well understand, 'tis because you have not the wherewith to marry her that you keep her at home. Now, in recompense of the service that you shall do me, I mean to provide her forthwith from my own moneys with such a dowry as you yourself shall deem adequate for her marriage." The lady was too needy not to be gratified by the proposal ; but, nevertheless, with the true spirit of the gentlewoman, she answered :—" Nay

but, madam, tell me that which I may do for you, and if it
shall be such as I may honourably do, gladly will I do it, and
then you shall do as you may be minded." Said then the
Countess :—" I require of you, that through some one in whom
you trust you send word to the Count, my husband, that your
daughter is ready to yield herself entirely to his will, so she may
be sure that he loves her even as he professes ; whereof she will
never be convinced, until he send her the ring which he wears
on his finger, and which, she understands, he prizes so much :
which, being sent, you shall give to me, and shall then send him
word that your daughter is ready to do his pleasure, and, having
brought him hither secretly, you shall contrive that I lie by his
side instead of your daughter. Perchance, by God's grace I
shall conceive, and so, having his ring on my finger, and a son
gotten of him on my arm, shall have him for my own again,
and live with him even as a wife should live with her husband,
and owe it all to you."

The lady felt that 'twas not a little that the Countess craved
of her, for she feared lest it should bring reproach upon her
daughter : but she reflected that to aid the good lady to recover
her husband was an honourable enterprise, and that in under-
taking it she would be subserving a like end ; and so, trusting
in the good and virtuous disposition of the Countess, she not
only promised to do as she was required, but in no long time,
proceeding with caution and secrecy, as she had been bidden,
she both had the ring from the Count, loath though he was to
part with it, and cunningly contrived that the Countess should
lie with him in place of her daughter. In which first com-
mingling, so ardently sought by the Count, it so pleased God
that the lady was gotten, as in due time her delivery made
manifest, with two sons. Nor once only, but many times did
the lady gratify the Countess with the embraces of her husband,
using such secrecy that no word thereof ever got wind, the Count
all the while supposing that he lay, not with his wife, but with
her that he loved, and being wont to give her, as he left her in
the morning, some fair and rare jewel, which she jealously
guarded.

When she perceived that she was with child, the Countess,
being minded no more to burden the lady with such service,
said to her :—" Madam, thanks be to God and to you, I now
have that which I desired, and therefore 'tis time that I make
you grateful requital, and take my leave of you." The lady
answered that she was glad if the Countess had gotten aught

that gave her joy ; but that 'twas not as hoping to have guerdon thereof that she had done her part, but simply because she deemed it meet and her duty so to do. " Well said, madam," returned the Countess, " and in like manner that which you shall ask of me I shall not give you by way of guerdon, but because I deem it meet and my duty to give it." Whereupon the lady, yielding to necessity, and abashed beyond measure, asked of her a hundred pounds wherewith to marry her daughter. The Countess, marking her embarrassment, and the modesty of her request, gave her five hundred pounds besides jewels fair and rare, worth, perhaps, no less ; and having thus much more than contented her, and received her superabundant thanks, she took leave of her and returned to the inn. The lady, to render purposeless further visits or messages on Bertrand's part, withdrew with her daughter to the house of her kinsfolk in the country ; nor was it long before Bertrand, on the urgent entreaty of his vassals and intelligence of the departure of his wife, quitted Florence and returned home. Greatly elated by this intelligence, the Countess tarried awhile in Florence, and was there delivered of two sons as like as possible to their father, whom she nurtured with sedulous care. But by and by she saw fit to take the road, and being come, unrecognized by any, to Montpellier, rested there a few days ; and being on the alert for news of the Count and where he was, she learned that on All Saints' day he was to hold a great reception of ladies and gentlemen at Roussillon. Whither, retaining her now wonted pilgrim's weeds, she hied her, and finding that the ladies and gentlemen were all gathered in the Count's palace and on the point of going to table, she tarried not to change her dress, but went up into the hall, bearing her little ones in her arms, and threading her way through the throng to the place where she saw the Count stand, she threw herself at his feet, and sobbing, said to him :—" My lord, thy hapless bride am I, who to ensure thy homecoming and abidance in peace have long time been a wanderer, and now demand of thee observance of the condition whereof word was brought me by the two knights whom I sent to thee. Lo in my arms not one son only but twain, gotten of thee, and on my finger thy ring. 'Tis time, then, that I be received of thee as thy wife according to thy word." Whereat the Count was all dumfounded, recognizing the ring and his own lineaments in the children, so like were they to him ; but saying to himself nevertheless :—" How can it have come about ? " So the Countess, while the Count and all that were

present marvelled exceedingly, told what had happened, and
the manner of it, in precise detail. Wherefore the Count,
perceiving that she spoke truth, and having regard to her
perseverance and address and her two fine boys, and the wishes
of all his vassals and the ladies, who with one accord besought
him to own and honour her thenceforth as his lawful bride,
laid aside his harsh obduracy, and raised the Countess to her
feet, and embraced and kissed her, and acknowledged her for
his lawful wife, and the children for his own. Then, having
caused her to be rearrayed in garments befitting her rank, he,
to the boundless delight of as many as were there, and of all
other his vassals, gave up that day and some that followed to
feasting and merrymaking; and did ever thenceforth honour,
love and most tenderly cherish her as his bride and wife.

NOVEL X

*Alibech turns hermit, and is taught by Rustico, a monk, how the
Devil is put in hell. She is afterwards conveyed thence, and
becomes the wife of Neerbale.*

DIONEO, observing that the queen's story, which he had followed
with the closest attention, was now ended, and that it only
remained for him to speak, waited not to be bidden, but smilingly
thus began:

Gracious ladies, perchance you have not yet heard how the
Devil is put in hell; wherefore, without deviating far from the
topic of which you have discoursed throughout the day, I will
tell you how 'tis done; it may be the lesson will prove inspiring;
besides which, you may learn therefrom that, albeit Love pre-
fers the gay palace and the dainty chamber to the rude cabin,
yet, for all that, he may at times manifest his might in wilds
matted with forests, rugged with alps, and desolate with caverns:
whereby it may be understood that all things are subject to his
sway. But—to come to my story—I say that in the city of
Capsa ¹ in Barbary there was once a very rich man, who with

---

¹ Now Gafsa, in Tunis.

other children had a fair and dainty little daughter, Alibech by
name.   Now Alibech, not being a Christian, and hearing many
Christians, that were in the city, speak much in praise of the
Christian Faith and the service of God, did one day inquire of
one of them after what fashion it were possible to serve God
with as few impediments as might be, and was informed that
they served God best who most completely renounced the world
and its affairs, like those who had fixed their abode in the wilds
of the Thebaid desert.   Whereupon, actuated by no sober pre-
dilection, but by childish impulse, the girl, who was very simple
and about fourteen years of age, said never a word more of the
matter, but stole away on the morrow, and quite alone set out
to walk to the Thebaid desert; and, by force of resolution,
albeit with no small suffering, she after some days reached those
wilds; where espying a cabin a great way off, she hied her
thither, and found a holy man by the door, who, marvelling to
see her there asked, what she came there to seek.   She answered
that, guided by the spirit of God, she was come thither seeking,
if haply she might serve Him, and also find some one that might
teach her how He ought to be served.   Marking her youth and
great beauty, the worthy man, fearing lest, if he suffered her to
remain with him, he should be ensnared by the Devil, com-
mended her good intention, set before her a frugal repast of
roots of herbs, crab-apples, and dates, with a little water to
wash them down, and said to her: 'My daughter, there is a holy
man not far from here, who is much better able to teach thee
that of which thou art in quest than I am; go to him, therefore';
and he shewed her the way.   But when she was come whither
she was directed, she met with the same answer as before, and
so, setting forth again, she came at length to the cell of a young
hermit, a worthy man and very devout—his name Rustico—
whom she interrogated as she had the others.   Rustico, being
minded to make severe trial of his constancy, did not send her
away, as the others had done, but kept her with him in his cell,
and when night came, made her a little bed of palm-leaves;
whereon he bade her compose herself to sleep.   Hardly had she
done so before the solicitations of the flesh joined battle with the
powers of Rustico's spirit, and he, finding himself left in the
lurch by the latter, endured not many assaults before he beat a
retreat, and surrendered at discretion: wherefore he bade adieu
to holy meditation and prayer and discipline, and fell a musing
on the youth and beauty of his companion, and also how he
might so order his conversation with her, that without seeming

to her to be a libertine he might yet compass that which he
craved of her. So, probing her by certain questions, he dis-
covered that she was as yet entirely without cognizance of man,
and as simple as she seemed: wherefore he excogitated a plan
for bringing her to pleasure him under colour of serving God.
He began by giving her a long lecture on the great enmity that
subsists between God and the Devil; after which he gave her
to understand that, God having condemned the Devil to hell,
to put him there was of all services the most acceptable to God.
The girl asking him how it might be done, Rustico answered:
'Thou shalt know it in a trice; thou hast but to do that which
thou seest me do.' Then, having divested himself of his scanty
clothing, he threw himself stark naked on his knees, as if he
would pray; whereby he caused the girl, who followed his
example, to confront him in the same posture.

[1] E così stando, essendo Rustico più che mai nel suo disi-
derio acceso per lo vederla così bella venne la resurrezione
della carne, la quale riguardando Alibech e maravigliatasi,
disse:

— Rustico, quella cosa che è che io ti veggio che così si pigne
in fuori, e non l' ho io?

— O figliuola mia, disse Rustico, questo è il diavolo di che io
t' ho parlato: e vedi tu? Ora egli mi dà grandissima molestia,
tanta che io appena la posso sofferire. —

Allora disse la giovane:

— Oh lodato sia Iddio, chè io veggio che io sto meglio che
non stai tu, chè io non cotesto diabolo io. —

Disse Rustico:

— Tu di' vero, ma tu hai un altra cosa che non la ho io, e
hàila in iscambio di questo. —

Disse Alibech:

— O che? —

A cui Rustico disse:

— Hai il ninferno; e dicoti che io mi credo che Iddio t' abbia
qui mandata per la salute della anima mia, per ciò che se questo
diavolo pur mi darà questa noia, ove tu vogli aver di me tanta
pietà, e sofferire che io in inferno il rimetta, tu mi darai
grandissima consolazione, e a Dio farai grandissimo piacere
e servigio, se tu per quello fare in queste parti venuta se',
che tu di'. —

La giovane di buona fede rispose:

[1] No apology is needed for leaving, in accordance with precedent, the
subsequent detail untranslated.

— O padre mio, poscia che io ho il ninferno, sia pure quando vi piacerà. —

Disse allora Rustico:

— Figliuola mia, benedetta sia tu; andiamo dunque, e rimettiamlovi sì che egli poscia mi lasci stare. —

E così detto, menata la giovane sopra uno de' loro letticelli, le 'nsegnò come star si dovesse a dovere incarcerare quel maladetto da Dio.

La giovane, che mai più non aveva in inferno messo diavolo alcuno, per la prima volta sentì un poco di noia, per che ella disse a Rustico:

— Per certo, padre mio, mala cosa dee essere questo diavolo, e veramente nimico di Dio, chè ancora al ninferno, non che altrui, duole quando egli v' è dentro rimesso. —

Disse Rustico:

— Figliuola, egli non avverrà sempre così. —

E per fare che questo non avvenisse, da sei volte, anzi che di su il letticel si movessero, ve 'l rimisero, tanto che per quella volta gli trasser sì la superbia del capo, che egli si stette volentieri in pace.

Ma, ritornatagli poi nel seguente tempo più volte, e la giovane ubbidiente sempre a trargliele si disponesse, avvenne che il giuoco le cominciò a piacere, e cominciò a dire a Rustico:

— Ben veggio che il ver dicevano que' valentuomini in Capsa, che il servire a Dio era così dolce cosa: e per certo io non mi ricordo che mai alcuna altra ne facessi, che di tanto diletto e piacer mi fosse, quanto è il rimettere il diavolo in inferno; e per ciò io giudico ogn' altra persona, che ad altro che a servire a Dio attende, essere una bestia. —

Per la qual cosa essa spesse volte andava a Rustico, e gli dicea:

— Padre mio, io son qui venuta per servire a Dio e non per istare oziosa; andiamo a rimettere il diavolo in inferno. —

La qual cosa faccendo, diceva ella alcuna volta:

— Rustico, io non so perchè il diavolo si fugga di ninferno; chè, s' egli vi stesse così volentieri, come il ninferno il riceve e tiene, egli non se ne uscirebbe mai. —

Così adunque invitando spesso la giovane Rustico, e al servigio di Dio confortandolo, sì la bambagia del farsetto tratta gli avea, che egli a tal ora sentiva freddo, che un altro sarebbe sudato; e per ciò egli incominciò a dire alla giovane, che il diavolo non era da gastigare nè da rimettere in inferno, se non quando egli per superbia levasse il capo: e noi per la

grazia di Dio l'abbiamo sì sgannato, che egli priega Iddo
di starsi ini pace: e così alquanto impose di silenzio alla
giovane.

La qual, poi che vide che Rustico non la richiedeva a dovere
il diavolo rimettere in inferno, gli disse un giorno:

— Rustico, se il diavolo tuo è gastigato e più non ti dà noia,
me il mio ninferno non lascia stare: per che tu farai bene che
tu col tuo diavolo aiuti attutare la rabbia al mio ninferno,
com' io col mio ninferno ho aiutato a trarre la superbia al tuo
diavolo. —

Rustico, che di radici d'erba e d'acqua vivea, poteva male
rispondere alle poste; e dissele che troppi diavoli vorrebbono
essere a potere il ninferno attutare, ma che egli ne farebbe ciò
che per lui si potesse; e così alcuna volta le sodisfaceva, ma sì
era di rado, che altro non era che gittare una fava in bocca al
leone: di che la giovane, non parendole tanto servire a Dio
quanto voleva, mormorava anzi che no.

However, the case standing thus (deficiency of power against
superfluity of desire) between Rustico's Devil and Alibech's
hell, it chanced that fire broke out in Capsa, whereby the house
of Alibech's father was burned, and he and all his sons and the
rest of his household perished; so that Alibech was left sole
heiress of all his estate. And a young gallant, Neerbale by
name, who by reckless munificence had wasted all his substance,
having discovered that she was alive, addressed himself to the
pursuit of her, and, having found her in time to prevent the
confiscation of her father's estate as an escheat for failure of
heirs, took her, much to Rustico's relief and against her own
will, back to Capsa, and made her his wife, and shared with
her her vast patrimony. But before he had lain with her, she
was questioned by the ladies of the manner in which she had
served God in the desert; whereto she answered, that she had
been wont to serve Him by putting the Devil in hell, and that
Neerbale had committed a great sin when he took her out of
such service. The ladies being curious to know how the Devil
was put in hell, the girl satisfied them, partly by words, partly
by signs. Whereat they laughed exorbitantly (and still laugh)
and said to her: 'Be not downhearted, daughter; 'tis done here
too; Neerbale will know well how to serve God with you in
that way.' And so the story passing from mouth to mouth
throughout the city, it came at last to be a common proverb,
that the most acceptable service that can be rendered to God
is to put the Devil in hell; which proverb having travelled

hither across the sea, is still current. Wherefore, young ladies, you that have need of the grace of God, see to it that you learn how to put the Devil in hell, because 'tis mightily pleasing to God, and of great solace to both the parties, and much good may thereby be engendered and ensue.

A thousand times or more had Dioneo's story brought the laugh to the lips of the honourable ladies, so quaint and curiously entertaining found they the fashion of it. And now at its close the queen, seeing the term of her sovereignty come, took the laurel wreath from her head, and with mien most debonair, set it on the brow of Filostrato, saying: 'We shall soon see whether the wolf will know better how to guide the sheep than the sheep have yet succeeded in guiding the wolves.' Whereat Filostrato said with a laugh: 'Had I been hearkened to, the wolves would have taught the sheep to put the Devil in hell even as Rustico taught Alibech. Wherefore call us not wolves, seeing that you have not shewn yourselves sheep: however, as best I may be able, I will govern the kingdom committed to my charge.' Whereupon Neifile took him up: 'Hark ye, Filostrato,' she said, 'while you thought to teach us, you might have learnt a lesson from us, as did Masetto da Lamporecchio from the nuns, and have recovered your speech when the bones had learned to whistle without a master.' [1] Filostrato, perceiving that there was a scythe for each of his arrows, gave up jesting, and addressed himself to the governance of his kingdom. He called the seneschal, and held him strictly to account in every particular; he then judiciously ordered all matters as he deemed would be best and most to the satisfaction of the company, while his sovereignty should last; and having done so, he turned to the ladies, and said: 'Loving ladies, as my ill luck would have it, since I have had wit to tell good from evil, the charms of one or other of you have kept me ever a slave to Love: and for all I shewed myself humble and obedient and conformable, so far as I knew how, to all his ways, my fate has been still the same, to be discarded for another, and go ever from bad to worse; and so, I suppose, 'twill be with me to the hour of my death. Wherefore I am minded that to-morrow our discourse be of no other topic than that which is most germane to my condition, to wit, of those whose loves had a disastrous close: because mine, I expect, will in the long run be most disastrous; nor for other cause was the name, by which you address me, given me

---

[1] i.e. when you were so emaciated that your bones made music like a skeleton in the wind.

by one that well knew its signification.' Which said, he arose, and dismissed them all until supper-time.

So fair and delightsome was the garden that none saw fit to quit it, and seek diversion elsewhere. Rather—for the sun now shone with a tempered radiance that caused no discomfort —some of the ladies gave chase to the kids and conies and other creatures that haunted it, and, scampering to and fro among them as they sate, had caused them a hundred times, or so, slight embarrassment. Bioneo and Fiammetta fell a singing of Messer Guglielmo and the lady of Vergiù.[1] Filomena and Pamfilo sat them down to a game of chess; and, as thus they pursued each their several diversions, time sped so swiftly that the supper-hour stole upon them almost unawares: whereupon they ranged the tables round the beautiful fountain, and supped with all glad and festal cheer. When the tables were removed, Filostrato, being minded to follow in the footsteps of his fair predecessors in sway, bade Lauretta lead a dance and sing a song. She answered: 'My Lord, songs of others know I none, nor does my memory furnish me with any of mine own that seems meet for so gay a company; but, if you will be content with what I have, gladly will I give you thereof.' 'Nought of thine,' returned the king, 'could be other than goodly and delectable. Wherefore give us even what thou hast.' So encouraged, Lauretta, with dulcet voice, but manner somewhat languishing, raised the ensuing strain, to which the other ladies responded:

"What dame disconsolate
     May so lament as I,
     That vainly sigh, to Love still dedicate?

He that the heaven and every orb doth move
     Formed me for His delight
Fair, debonair and gracious, apt for love;
     That here on earth each soaring spirit might
     Have foretaste how, above,
That beauty shews that standeth in His sight.
     Ah! but dull wit and slight,
     For that it judgeth ill,
Liketh me not, nay, doth me vilely rate.

[1] Evidently some version of the tragical *conte* 'de la Chastelaine de Vergi, qui mori por laialment amer son ami.' See *Fabliaux et Contes*, ed. Barbazan, iv. 296; and cf. Bandello, Pt. IV, Nov. v, and Heptameron, Journée vii, Nouvelle lxx.

There was who loved me, and my maiden grace
   Did fondly clip and strain,
   As in his arms, so in his soul's embrace,
   And from mine eyes Love's fire did drink amain,
   And time that glides apace
   In nought but courting me to spend was fain;
   Whom courteous I did deign
   Ev'n as my peer to entreat;
   But am of him bereft!   Ah! dolorous fate!

Came to me next a gallant swol'n with pride,
   Brave, in his own conceit,
   And no less noble eke.   Whom woe betide
   That he me took, and holds in all unmeet
   Suspicion, jealous-eyed!
   And I, who wot that me the world should greet
   As the predestined sweet
   Of many men, well-nigh
   Despair, to be to one thus subjugate.

Ah! woe is me! cursed be the luckless day,
   When, a new gown to wear,
   I said the fatal ay; for blithe and gay
   In that plain gown I lived, no whit less fair;
   While in this rich array
   A sad and far less honoured life I bear!
   Would I had died, or e'er
   Sounded those notes of joy
   (Ah! dolorous cheer!) my woe to celebrate!

So list my supplication, lover dear,
   Of whom such joyance I,
   As ne'er another, had.   Thou that in clear
   Light of the Maker's presence art, deny
   Not pity to thy fere,
   Who thee may ne'er forget; but let one sigh
   Breathe tidings that on high
   Thou burnest still for me;
   And sue of God that He me there translate."

So ended Lauretta her song, to which all hearkened atten-
tively, though not all interpreted it alike.   Some were inclined
to give it a moral after the Milanese fashion, to wit, that a good

porker was better than a pretty quean.   Others construed it in
a higher, better and truer sense, which 'tis not to the present
purpose to unfold.   Some more songs followed by command of
the king, who caused torches not a few to be lighted and ranged
about the flowery mead; and so the night was prolonged until
the last star that had risen had begun to set.   Then, bethinking
him that 'twas time for slumber, the king bade all good night,
and dismissed them to their several chambers.

Endeth here the third day of the Decameron, beginneth the fourth, in which, under the rule of Filostrato, discourse is had of those whose loves had a disastrous close.

DEAREST ladies, as well from what I heard in converse with the wise, as from matters that not seldom fell within my own observation and reading, I formed the opinion that the vehement and scorching blast of envy was apt to vent itself only upon lofty towers or the highest tree-tops : but therein I find that I misjudged ; for, whereas I ever sought and studied how best to elude the buffetings of that furious hurricane, and to that end kept a course not merely on the plain, but, by preference, in the depth of the valley ; as should be abundantly clear to whoso looks at these little stories, written as they are not only in the vulgar Florentine, and in prose, and without dedicatory flourish, but also in as homely and simple a style as may be ; nevertheless all this has not stood me in such stead but that I have been shrewdly shaken, nay, all but uprooted by the blast, and altogether lacerated by the bite of this same envy. Whereby I may very well understand that 'tis true, what the sages aver, that only misery is exempt from envy in the present life. Know then, discreet my ladies, that some there are, who, reading these little stories, have alleged that I am too fond of you, and that 'tis not a seemly thing that I should take so much pleasure in ministering to your gratification and solace ; and some have found more fault with me for praising you as I do. Others, affecting to deliver a more considered judgment, have said that it ill befits my time of life to ensue such matters, to wit, the discoursing of women, or endeavouring to pleasure them. And not a few, feigning a mighty tender regard to my fame, aver that I should do more wisely to keep ever with the Muses on Parnassus, than to forgather with you in such vain dalliance. Those again there are, who, evincing less wisdom than despite, have told me that I should shew sounder sense if I bethought me how to get my daily bread, than, going after these idle toys, to nourish myself upon the wind ; while certain others, in disparagement of my work, strive might and main to make it appear that the matters which I relate fell out otherwise than as I set them forth. Such then, noble ladies, are the blasts, such the sharp and cruel fangs, by which, while I champion your cause, I am assailed, harassed and well-nigh pierced through and through. Which censures I hear and mark, God knows, with equal mind : and, though to you belongs all my defence, yet I mean not to be niggard of my own powers, but rather, without dealing out to them the castigation they deserve, to give them such slight answer as may secure my ears some respite of their clamour ; and that without delay ; seeing that, if already, though I have not completed the third part of my work, they are not a few and very presumptuous, I deem it possible, that before I have reached the end, should they receive no check, they may have grown so numerous, that 'twould scarce tax their powers to sink me ; and that your forces, great though they be, would not suffice to withstand them. However I am minded to answer none of them, until I have related in my behoof, not indeed an entire story, for I would not seem to foist my stories in among those of so honourable a company as that with which I have made you acquainted, but a part of one, that its very incompleteness may shew that it is not one of them : wherefore, addressing my assailants, I say :—That in our city there was in old time a citizen named Filippo Balducci, a man of quite low origin, but of good substance and well versed and expert in matters belonging to his condition, who had a wife that he most dearly loved, as did she him, so that their life passed in peace and concord, nor was there aught they studied so much as how to please each other perfectly. Now it came to pass, as it does to every one, that the good lady departed this life, leaving Filippo nought of hers but an only son, that she had had by him, and who was then about two years old. His wife's death left Filippo as disconsolate as ever was any man for the loss of a loved one : and sorely missing the companionship that was most dear to him, he resolved to have done with the world, and devote himself and his little son to the service of God. Wherefore, having dedicated all his goods to charitable uses, he forthwith betook him to the summit of Monte Asinaio, where he installed himself with his son in a little cell, and living on alms, passed his days in fasting and prayer, being careful above all things to say nothing to the boy of any temporal matters, nor to let him see aught of the kind, lest they should distract his mind from his religious exercises, but discoursing with him continually of the glory of the life eternal and of God and the saints, and teaching him nought else but holy orisons : in which way of life he kept him not a few years, never suffering him to quit the cell or see aught but himself.   From time to time the worthy man would go to Florence, where divers of the faithful would afford him relief according to his needs, and so he would return to his cell. And thus it fell out that one day Filippo, now an aged man, being asked by the boy, who was about eighteen years old, whither he went, told him.   Whereupon :—" Father," said the boy, " you are now old, and scarce able to support fatigue ; why take you me not with you for once to Florence, and give me to know devout friends of God and you, so that I, who am young and fitter for such exertion than you, may thereafter go to Florence for our supplies at your pleasure, and you remain here ? "

The worthy man, bethinking him that his son was now grown up, and so habituated to the service of God as hardly to be seduced by the things of the world, said to himself :—" He says well."   And so, as he must needs go to Florence, he took the boy with him.   Where, seeing the palaces, the houses, the churches, and all matters else with which the city abounds, and of which he had no more recollection than if he had never seen them, the boy found all passing strange, and questioned his father of not a few of them, what they were and how they were named ; his curiosity being no sooner satisfied in one particular than he plied his father with a further question.   And so it befell that, while son and father were thus occupied in asking and answering questions, they encountered a bevy of damsels, fair and richly arrayed, being on their return from a wedding ; whom the young man no sooner saw, than he asked his father what they might be.   " My son," answered the father, " fix thy gaze on the ground, regard them not at all, for naughty things are they."   " Oh ! " said the son, " and what is their name ? "   The father, fearing to awaken some mischievous craving of concupiscence in the young man, would not denote them truly, to wit, as women, but said :—" They are called goslings."   Whereupon, wonderful to tell ! the lad who had never before set eyes on any woman, thought no more of the palaces, the oxen, the horses, the asses, the money, or aught else that he had seen, but exclaimed :—" Prithee, father, let me have one of those goslings."   " Alas, my son," replied the father, " speak not of them ; they are naughty things."   " Oh ! " questioned the son ; " but are naughty things made like that ? " " Ay," returned the father.   Whereupon the son :—" I know

not," he said, " what you say, nor why they should be naughty
things : for my part I have as yet seen nought that seemed to
me so fair and delectable. They are fairer than the painted
angels that you have so often shewn me. Oh ! if you love me,
do but let us take one of these goslings up there, and I will see
that she have whereon to bill." " Nay," said the father, " that
will not I. Thou knowest not whereon they bill ; " and straight-
way, being ware that nature was more potent than his art, he
repented him that he had brought the boy to Florence.

But enough of this story : 'tis time for me to cut it short, and
return to those, for whose instruction 'tis told. They say then,
some of these my censors, that I am too fond of you, young
ladies, and am at too great pains to pleasure you. Now that
I am fond of you, and am at pains to pleasure you, I do most
frankly and fully confess ; and I ask them whether, considering
only all that it means to have had, and to have continually,
before one's eyes your debonair demeanour, your bewitching
beauty and exquisite grace, and therewithal your modest
womanliness, not to speak of having known the amorous kisses,
the caressing embraces, the voluptuous comminglings, whereof
our intercourse with you, ladies most sweet, not seldom is
productive, they do verily marvel that I am fond of you, seeing
that one who was nurtured, reared, and brought up on a savage
and solitary mountain, within the narrow circuit of a cell,
without other companion than his father, had no sooner seen
you than 'twas you alone that he desired, that he demanded,
that he sought with ardour ? Will they tear, will they lacerate
me with their censures, if I, whose body Heaven fashioned all
apt for love, whose soul from very boyhood was dedicate to you,
am not insensible to the power of the light of your eyes, to the
sweetness of your honeyed words, to the flame that is kindled
by your gentle sighs, but am fond of you and sedulous to
pleasure you ; you, again I bid them remember, in whom a
hermit, a rude, witless lad, liker to an animal than to a human
being, found more to delight him than in aught else that he
saw ? Of a truth whoso taxes me thus must be one that, feeling,
knowing nought of the pleasure and power of natural affection,
loves you not, nor craves your love ; and such an one I hold in
light esteem. And as for those that go about to find ground of
exception in my age, they do but shew that they ill understand
that the leek, albeit its head is white, has a green tail. But
jesting apart, thus I answer them, that never to the end of my
life shall I deem it shameful to me to pleasure those to whom

Guido Cavalcanti and Dante Alighieri in their old age, and
Messer Cino da Pistoia in extreme old age, accounted it an
honour and found it a delight to minister gratification. And
but that 'twere a deviation from the use and wont of discourse,
I would call history to my aid, and shew it to abound with
stories of noble men of old time, who in their ripest age studied
above all things else to pleasure the ladies ; whereof if they be
ignorant, go they and get them to school. To keep with the
Muses on Parnassus is counsel I approve ; but tarry with them
always we cannot, nor they with us, nor is a man blameworthy,
if, when he happen to part from them, he find his delight in
those that resemble them. The Muses are ladies, and albeit
ladies are not the peers of the Muses, yet they have their outward
semblance ; for which cause, if for no other, 'tis reasonable that
I should be fond of them. Besides which, ladies have been to
me the occasion of composing some thousand verses, but of
never a verse that I made were the Muses the occasion. How-
beit 'twas with their aid, 'twas under their influence that I
composed those thousand verses, and perchance they have
sometimes visited me to encourage me in my present task,
humble indeed though it be, doing honour and paying, as it
were, tribute, to the likeness which the ladies have to them ;
wherefore, while I weave these stories, I stray not so far from
Mount Parnassus and the Muses as not a few perchance suppose.
But what shall we say to those, in whom my hunger excites
such commiseration that they bid me get me bread ? Verily
I know not, save this :—Suppose that in my need I were to beg
bread of them, what would be their answer ? I doubt not they
would say :—" Go seek it among the fables." And in sooth
the poets have found more bread among their fables than many
rich men among their treasures. And many that have gone
after fables have crowned their days with splendour, while, on
the other hand, not a few, in the endeavour to get them more
bread than they needed, have perished miserably. But why
waste more words on them ? Let them send me packing, when
I ask bread of them ; not that, thank God, I have yet need of
it, and should I ever come to be in need of it, I know, like the
Apostle, how to abound and to be in want, and so am minded
to be beholden to none but myself. As for those who say
that these matters fell out otherwise than as I relate them, I
should account it no small favour, if they would produce the
originals, and should what I write not accord with them, I would
acknowledge the justice of their censure, and study to amend

my ways ; but, until better evidence is forthcoming than their words, I shall adhere to my own opinion without seeking to deprive them of theirs, and give them tit for tat. And being minded that for this while this answer suffice, I say that with God and you, in whom I trust, most gentle ladies, to aid and protect me, and patience for my stay, I shall go forward with my work, turning my back on this tempest, however it may rage ; for I see not that I can fare worse than the fine dust, which the blast of the whirlwind either leaves where it lies, or bears aloft, not seldom over the heads of men, over the crowns of kings, of emperors, and sometimes suffers to settle on the roofs of lofty palaces, and the summits of the tallest towers, whence if it fall, it cannot sink lower than the level from which it was raised. And if I ever devoted myself and all my powers to minister in any wise to your gratification, I am now minded more than ever so to do, because I know that there is nought that any can justly say in regard thereof, but that I, and others who love you, follow the promptings of nature, whose laws whoso would withstand, has need of powers pre-eminent, and, even so, will oft-times labour not merely in vain but to his own most grievous disadvantage. Such powers I own that I neither have, nor, to such end, desire to have ; and had I them, I would rather leave them to another than use them myself. Wherefore let my detractors hold their peace, and if they cannot get heat, why, let them shiver their life away ; and, while they remain addicted to their delights, or rather corrupt tastes, let them leave me to follow my own bent during the brief life that is accorded us. But this has been a long digression, fair ladies, and 'tis time to retrace our steps to the point where we deviated, and continue in the course on which we started.

The sun had chased every star from the sky, and lifted the dank murk of night from the earth, when, Filostrato being risen, and having roused all his company, they hied them to the fair garden, and there fell to disporting themselves : the time for breakfast being come, they took it where they had supped on the preceding evening, and after they had slept they rose, when the sun was in his zenith, and seated themselves in their wonted manner by the beautiful fountain ; where Fiammetta, being bidden by Filostrato to lead off the story-telling, awaited no second command, but debonairly thus began.

NOVEL I

*Tancred, Prince of Salerno, slays his daughter's lover, and sends
her his heart in a golden cup : she pours upon it a poisonous
distillation, which she drinks and dies.*

A DIREFUL theme has our king allotted us for to-day's discourse ;
seeing that, whereas we are here met for our common delectation,
needs must we now tell of others' tears, whereby, whether telling
or hearing, we cannot but be moved to pity. Perchance 'twas
to temper in some degree the gaiety of the past days that he so
ordained, but, whatever may have been his intent, his will
must be to me immutable law ; wherefore I will narrate to you
a matter that befell piteously, nay woefully, and so as you may
well weep thereat.

Tancred, Prince of Salerno, a lord most humane and kind of
heart, but that in his old age he imbrued his hands in the blood
of a lover, had in the whole course of his life but one daughter ;
and had he not had her, he had been more fortunate.

Never was daughter more tenderly beloved of father than
she of the Prince, who, for that cause not knowing how to part
with her, kept her unmarried for many a year after she had
come of marriageable age : then at last he gave her to a son of
the Duke of Capua, with whom she had lived but a short while,
when he died and she returned to her father. Most lovely was
she of form and feature (never woman more so), and young and
light of heart, and more knowing, perchance, than beseemed a
woman. Dwelling thus with her loving father, as a great lady,
in no small luxury, nor failing to see that the Prince, for the
great love he bore her, was at no pains to provide her with
another husband, and deeming it unseemly on her part to ask
one of him, she cast about how she might come by a gallant to
be her secret lover. And seeing at her father's court not a
few men, both gentle and simple, that resorted thither, as we
know men use to frequent courts, and closely scanning their
mien and manners, she preferred before all others the Prince's
page, Guiscardo by name, a man of very humble origin, but
pre-eminent for native worth and noble bearing ; of whom,
seeing him frequently, she became hotly enamoured, hourly
extolling his qualities more and more highly. The young man,
who for all his youth by no means lacked shrewdness, read her
heart, and gave her his own on such wise that his love for her

engrossed his mind to the exclusion of almost everything else. While thus they burned in secret for one another, the lady, desiring of all things a meeting with Guiscardo, but being shy of making any her confidant, hit upon a novel expedient to concert the affair with him. She wrote him a letter containing her commands for the ensuing day, and thrust it into a cane in the space between two of the knots, which cane she gave to Guiscardo, saying :—" Thou canst let thy servant have it for a bellows to blow thy fire up to night." Guiscardo took it, and feeling sure that 'twas not unadvisedly that she made him such a present, accompanied with such words, hied him straight home, where, carefully examining the cane, he observed that it was cleft, and, opening it, found the letter ; which he had no sooner read, and learned what he was to do, than, pleased as ne'er another, he fell to devising how to set all in order that he might not fail to meet the lady on the following day, after the manner she had prescribed.

Now hard by the Prince's palace was a grotto, hewn in days of old in the solid rock, and now long disused, so that an artificial orifice, by which it received a little light, was all but choked with brambles and plants that grew about and overspread it. From one of the ground-floor rooms of the palace, which room was part of the lady's suite, a secret stair led to the grotto, though the entrance was barred by a very strong door. This stair, having been from time immemorial disused, had passed out of mind so completely that there was scarce any that remembered that it was there : but Love, whose eyes nothing, however secret, may escape, had brought it to the mind of the enamoured lady. For many a day, using all secrecy, that none should discover her, she had wrought with her tools, until she had succeeded in opening the door ; which done, she had gone down into the grotto alone, and having observed the orifice, had by her letter apprised Guiscardo of its apparent height above the floor of the grotto, and bidden him contrive some means of descending thereby. Eager to carry the affair through, Guiscardo lost no time in rigging up a ladder of ropes, whereby he might ascend and descend ; and having put on a suit of leather to protect him from the brambles, he hied him the following night (keeping the affair close from all) to the orifice, made the ladder fast by one of its ends to a massive trunk that was rooted in the mouth of the orifice, climbed down the ladder, and awaited the lady. On the morrow, making as if she would fain sleep, the lady dismissed her damsels, and locked herself

into her room : she then opened the door of the grotto, hied
her down, and met Guiscardo, to their marvellous mutual
satisfaction. The lovers then repaired to her room, where in
exceeding great joyance they spent no small part of the day.
Nor were they neglectful of the precautions needful to prevent
discovery of their amour ; but in due time Guiscardo returned
to the grotto ; whereupon the lady locked the door and rejoined
her damsels. At nightfall Guiscardo reascended his ladder, and,
issuing forth of the orifice, hied him home ; nor, knowing now
the way, did he fail to revisit the grotto many a time thereafter.

But Fortune, noting with envious eye a happiness of such
degree and duration, gave to events a dolorous turn, whereby
the joy of the two lovers was converted into bitter lamentation.
'Twas Tancred's custom to come from time to time quite alone
to his daughter's room, and tarry talking with her a while.
Whereby it so befell that he came down there one day after
breakfast, while Ghismonda—such was the lady's name—was in
her garden with her damsels ; so that none saw or heard him
enter ; nor would he call his daughter, for he was minded that
she should not forgo her pleasure. But, finding the windows
closed and the bed-curtains drawn down, he seated himself on
a divan that stood at one of the corners of the bed, rested his
head on the bed, drew the curtain over him, and thus, hidden as
if of set purpose, fell asleep. As he slept Ghismonda, who, as
it happened, had caused Guiscardo to come that day, left her
damsels in the garden, softly entered the room, and having
locked herself in, unwitting that there was another in the room,
opened the door to Guiscardo, who was in waiting. Straightway
they got them to bed, as was their wont ; and, while they there
solaced and disported them together, it so befell that Tancred
awoke, and heard and saw what they did : whereat he was
troubled beyond measure, and at first was minded to upbraid
them ; but on second thoughts he deemed it best to hold his
peace, and avoid discovery, if so he might with greater stealth
and less dishonour carry out the design which was already in
his mind. The two lovers continued long together, as they were
wont, all unwitting of Tancred ; but at length they saw fit to
get out of bed, when Guiscardo went back to the grotto, and
the lady hied her forth of the room. Whereupon Tancred, old
though he was, got out at one of the windows, clambered down
into the garden, and, seen by none, returned sorely troubled
to his room. By his command two men took Guiscardo early
that same night, as he issued forth of the orifice accoutred in

his suit of leather, and brought him privily to Tancred ; who, as he saw him, all but wept, and said :—" Guiscardo, my kindness to thee is ill requited by the outrage and dishonour which thou hast done me in the person of my daughter, as to-day I have seen with my own eyes." To whom Guiscardo could answer nought but ·—" Love is more potent than either you or I." Tancred then gave order to keep him privily under watch and ward in a room within the palace ; and so 'twas done. Next day, while Ghismonda wotted nought of these matters, Tancred, after pondering divers novel expedients, hied him after breakfast, according to his wont, to his daughter's room, where, having called her to him and locked himself in with her, he began, not without tears, to speak on this wise :—" Ghismonda, conceiving that I knew thy virtue and honour, never, though it had been reported to me, would I have credited, had I not seen with my own eyes, that thou wouldst so much as in idea, not to say fact, have ever yielded thyself to any man but thy husband : wherefore, for the brief residue of life that my age has in store for me, the memory of thy fall will ever be grievous to me, And would to God, as thou must needs demean thyself to such dishonour, thou hadst taken a man that matched thy nobility ; but of all the men that frequent my court, thou must needs choose Guiscardo, a young man of the lowest condition, a fellow whom we brought up in charity from his tender years ; for whose sake thou hast plunged me into the abyss of mental tribulation, insomuch that I know not what course to take in regard of thee. As to Guiscardo, whom I caused to be arrested last night as he issued from the orifice, and keep in durance, my course is already taken, but how I am to deal with thee, God knows, I know not. I am distraught between the love which I have ever borne thee, love such as no father ever bare to daughter, and the most just indignation evoked in me by thy signal folly ; my love prompts me to pardon thee, my indignation bids me harden my heart against thee, though I do violence to my nature. But before I decide upon my course, I would fain hear what thou hast to say to this." So saying, he bent his head, and wept as bitterly as any child that had been soundly thrashed.

Her father's words, and the tidings they conveyed that not only was her secret passion discovered, but Guiscardo taken, caused Ghismonda immeasurable grief, which she was again and again on the point of evincing, as most women do, by cries and tears ; but her high spirit triumphed over this weakness ;

by a prodigious effort she composed her countenance, and taking
it for granted that her Guiscardo was no more, she inly devoted
herself to death rather than a single prayer for herself should
escape her lips.   Wherefore, not as a woman stricken with grief
or chidden for a fault, but unconcerned and unabashed, with
tearless eyes, and frank and utterly dauntless mien, thus
answered she her father :—" Tancred, your accusation I shall
not deny, neither will I cry you mercy, for nought should I
gain by denial, nor aught would I gain by supplication : nay
more ; there is nought I will do to conciliate thy humanity and
love ; my only care is to confess the truth, to defend my honour
by words of sound reason, and then by deeds most resolute to
give effect to the promptings of my high soul.   True it is that
I have loved and love Guiscardo, and during the brief while I
have yet to live shall love him, nor after death, so there be then
love, shall I cease to love him ; but that I love him, is not im-
putable to my womanly frailty so much as to the little zeal
thou shewedst for my bestowal in marriage, and to Guiscardo's
own worth.   It should not have escaped thee, Tancred, creature
of flesh and blood as thou art, that thy daughter was also a
creature of flesh and blood, and not of stone or iron ; it was, and
is, thy duty to bear in mind (old though thou art) the nature
and the might of the laws to which youth is subject ; and,
though thou hast spent part of thy best years in martial exercises,
thou shouldst nevertheless have not been ignorant how potent
is the influence even upon the aged—to say nothing of the
young—of ease and luxury.   And not only am I, as being thy
daughter, a creature of flesh and blood, but my life is not so far
spent but that I am still young, and thus doubly fraught with
fleshly appetite, the vehemence whereof is marvellously en-
hanced by reason that, having been married, I have known the
pleasure that ensues upon the satisfaction of such desire.
Which forces being powerless to withstand, I did but act as
was natural in a young woman, when I gave way to them, and
yielded myself to love.   Nor in sooth did I fail to the utmost
of my power so to order the indulgence of my natural propensity
that my sin should bring shame neither upon thee nor upon me.
To which end Love in his pity, and Fortune in a friendly mood,
found and discovered to me a secret way, whereby, none witting,
I attained my desire : this, from whomsoever thou hast learned
it, howsoever thou comest to know it, I deny not.   'Twas not
at random, as many women do, that I loved Guiscardo ; but
by deliberate choice I preferred him before all other men, and

of determinate forethought I lured him to my love, whereof, through his and my discretion and constancy, I have long had joyance. Wherein 'twould seem that thou, following rather the opinion of the vulgar than the dictates of truth, find cause to chide me more severely than in my sinful love, for, as if thou wouldst not have been vexed, had my choice fallen on a nobleman, thou complainest that I have forgathered with a man of low condition ; and dost not see that therein thou censurest not my fault but that of Fortune, which not seldom raises the unworthy to high place and leaves the worthiest in low estate. But leave we this : consider a little the principles of things : thou seest that in regard of our flesh we are all moulded of the same substance, and that all souls are endowed by one and the same Creator with equal faculties, equal powers, equal virtues. 'Twas merit that made the first distinction between us, born as we were, nay, as we are, all equal, and those whose merits were and were approved in act the greatest were called noble, and the rest were not so denoted. Which law, albeit overlaid by the contrary usage of after times, is not yet abrogated, nor so impaired but that it is still traceable in nature and good manners ; for which cause whoso with merit acts, does plainly shew himself a gentleman ; and if any denote him otherwise, the default is his own and not his whom he so denotes. Pass in review all thy nobles, weigh their merits, their manners and bearing, and then compare Guiscardo's qualities with theirs : if thou wilt judge without prejudice, thou wilt pronounce him noble in the highest degree, and thy nobles one and all churls. As to Guiscardo's merits and worth I did but trust the verdict which thou thyself didst utter in words, and which mine own eyes confirmed. Of whom had he such commendation as of thee for all those excellences whereby a good man and true merits commendation ? And in sooth thou didst him but justice ; for, unless mine eyes have played me false, there was nought for which thou didst commend him but I had seen him practise it, and that more admirably than words of thine might express ; and had I been at all deceived in this matter, 'twould have been by thee. Wilt thou say then that I have forgathered with a man of low condition ? If so, thou wilt not say true. Didst thou say with a poor man, the impeachment might be allowed, to thy shame, that thou so ill hast known how to requite a good man and true that is thy servant ; but poverty, though it take away all else, deprives no man of gentilesse. Many kings, many great princes, were once poor, and many a ditcher or

herdsman has been and is very wealthy. As for thy last per-
pended doubt, to wit, how thou shouldst deal with me, banish it
utterly from thy thoughts. If in thy extreme old age thou art
minded to manifest a harshness unwonted in thy youth, wreak
thy harshness on me, resolved as I am to cry thee no mercy,
prime cause as I am that this sin, if sin it be, has been com-
mitted ; for of this I warrant thee, that as thou mayst have
done or shalt do to Guiscardo, if to me thou do not the like, I
with my own hands will do it. Now get thee gone to shed thy
tears with the women, and when thy melting mood is over,
ruthlessly destroy Guiscardo and me, if such thou deem our
merited doom, by one and the same blow."

The loftiness of his daughter's spirit was not unknown to the
Prince ; but still he did not credit her with a resolve quite as
firmly fixed as her words implied, to carry their purport into
effect. So, parting from her without the least intention of
using harshness towards her in her own person, he determined
to quench the heat of her love by wreaking his vengeance on
her lover, and bade the two men that had charge of Guiscardo
to strangle him noiselessly that same night, take the heart out
of the body, and send it to him. The men did his bidding :
and on the morrow the Prince had a large and beautiful cup
of gold brought to him, and having put Guiscardo's heart therein,
sent it by the hand of one of his most trusted servants to his
daughter, charging the servant to say, as he gave it to her :—
" Thy father sends thee this to give thee joy of that which thou
lovest best, even as thou hast given him joy of that which he
loved best."

Now when her father had left her, Ghismonda, wavering not
a jot in her stern resolve, had sent for poisonous herbs and
roots, and therefrom had distilled a water, to have it ready for
use, if that which she apprehended should come to pass. And
when the servant appeared with the Prince's present and
message, she took the cup unblenchingly, and having lifted
the lid, and seen the heart, and apprehended the meaning of
the words, and that the heart was beyond a doubt Guiscardo's,
she raised her head, and looking straight at the servant, said :—
" Sepulture less honourable than of gold had ill befitted heart
such as this : herein has my father done wisely." Which said,
she raised it to her lips, and kissed it, saying :—" In all things
and at all times, even to this last hour of my life, have I found
my father most tender in his love, but now more so than ever
before ; wherefore I now render him the last thanks which will

ever be due from me to him for this goodly present." So she
spoke, and straining the cup to her, bowed her head over it,
and gazing at the heart, said :—" Ah ! sojourn most sweet of
all my joys, accursed be he by whose ruthless act I see thee with
the bodily eye : 'twas enough that to the mind's eye thou wert
hourly present. Thou hast run thy course ; thou hast closed
the span that Fortune allotted thee ; thou hast reached the
goal of all ; thou hast left behind thee the woes and weariness
of the world ; and thy enemy has himself granted thee sepulture
accordant with thy deserts. No circumstance was wanting to
duly celebrate thy obsequies, save the tears of her whom, while
thou livedst, thou didst so dearly love ; which that thou shouldst
not lack, my remorseless father was prompted of God to send
thee to me, and, albeit my resolve was fixed to die with eyes
unmoistened and front all unperturbed by fear, yet will I
accord thee my tears ; which done, my care shall be forthwith
by thy means to join my soul to that most precious soul which
thou didst once enshrine. And is there other company than
hers, in which with more of joy and peace I might fare to the
abodes unknown ? She is yet here within, I doubt not, con-
templating the abodes of her and my delights, and—for sure I
am that she loves me—awaiting my soul that loves her before
all else."

Having thus spoken, she bowed herself low over the cup ;
and, while no womanish cry escaped her, 'twas as if a fountain
of water were unloosed within her head, so wondrous a flood of
tears gushed from her eyes, while times without number she
kissed the dead heart. Her damsels that stood around her
knew not whose the heart might be or what her words might
mean, but melting in sympathy, they all wept, and compassion-
ately, as vainly, enquired the cause of her lamentation, and in
many other ways sought to comfort her to the best of their
understanding and power. When she had wept her fill, she
raised her head, and dried her eyes. Then :—" O heart," said
she, " much cherished heart, discharged is my every duty
towards thee ; nought now remains for me to do but to come
and unite my soul with thine." So saying, she sent for the
vase that held the water which the day before she had distilled,
and emptied it into the cup where lay the heart bathed in her
tears ; then, nowise afraid, she set her mouth to the cup, and
drained it dry, and so with the cup in her hand she got her upon
her bed, and having there disposed her person in guise as
seemly as she might, laid her dead lover's heart upon her own,

and silently awaited death. Meanwhile the damsels, seeing and
hearing what passed, but knowing not what the water was that
she had drunk, had sent word of each particular to Tancred ;
who, apprehensive of that which came to pass, came down with
all haste to his daughter's room, where he arrived just as she
got her upon her bed, and, now too late, addressed himself to
comfort her with soft words, and seeing in what plight she was,
burst into a flood of bitter tears. To whom the lady :—" Re-
serve thy tears, Tancred, till Fortune send thee hap less longed
for than this : waste them not on me who care not for them.
Whoever yet saw any but thee bewail the consummation of his
desire ? But, if of the love thou once didst bear me any spark
still lives in thee, be it thy parting grace to me, that, as thou
brookedst not that I should live with Guiscardo in privity and
seclusion, so wherever thou mayst have caused Guiscardo's
body to be cast, mine may be united with it in the common
view of all." The Prince replied not for excess of grief ; and
the lady, feeling that her end was come, strained the dead
heart to her bosom, saying :—" Fare ye well ; I take my leave
of you ; " and with eyelids drooped and every sense evanished
departed this life of woe. Such was the lamentable end of the
loves of Guiscardo and Ghismonda ; whom Tancred, tardily
repentant of his harshness, mourned not a little, as did also all
the folk of Salerno, and had honourably interred side by side
in the same tomb.

NOVEL II

*Fra Alberto gives a lady to understand that she is beloved of the
Angel Gabriel, in whose shape he lies with her sundry times ;
afterward, for fear of her kinsmen, he flings himself forth of
her house, and finds shelter in the house of a poor man, who
on the morrow leads him in the guise of a wild man into the
piazza, where, being recognized, he is apprehended by his
brethren and imprisoned.*

MORE than once had Fiammetta's story brought tears to the
eyes of her fair companions ; but now that it was ended the
king said with an austere air :—" I should esteem my life but
a paltry price to pay for half the delight that Ghismonda had
with Guiscardo : whereat no lady of you all should marvel,
seeing that each hour that I live I die a thousand deaths ; nor

is there so much as a particle of compensating joy allotted me.
But a truce to my own concerns : I ordain that Pampinea do
next ensue our direful argument, wherewith the tenor of my
life in part accords, and if she follow in Fiammetta's footsteps,
I doubt not I shall presently feel some drops of dew distill
upon my fire." Pampinea received the king's command in a
spirit more accordant with what from her own bent she divined
to be the wishes of her fair gossips than with the king's words ;
wherefore, being minded rather to afford them some diversion,
than, save as in duty bound, to satisfy the king, she made choice
of a story which, without deviating from the prescribed theme,
should move a laugh, and thus began :—

'Tis a proverb current among the vulgar, that :—" Whoso,
being wicked, is righteous reputed, May sin as he will, and
'twill ne'er be imputed." Which proverb furnishes me with
abundant matter of discourse, germane to our theme, besides
occasion to exhibit the quality and degree of the hypocrisy of the
religious, who flaunt it in ample flowing robes, and, with faces
made pallid by art, with voices low and gentle to beg alms,
most loud and haughty to reprove in others their own sins,
would make believe that their way of salvation lies in taking
from us and ours in giving to them ; nay, more, as if they had
not like us Paradise to win, but were already its lords and
masters, assign therein to each that dies a place more or less
exalted according to the amount of the money that he has
bequeathed to them ; which if they believe, 'tis by dint of self-
delusion, and to the effect of deluding all that put faith in their
words. Of whose guile were it lawful for me to make as full
exposure as were fitting, not a few simple folk should soon be
enlightened as to what they cloak within the folds of their
voluminous habits. But would to God all might have the like
reward of their lies as a certain friar minor, no novice, but one
that was reputed among their greatest [1] at Venice ; whose
story, rather than aught else, I am minded to tell you, if so I
may, perchance, by laughter and jollity relieve in some degree
your souls that are heavy laden with pity for the death of
Ghismonda.

Know then, noble ladies, that there was in Imola a man of
evil and corrupt life, Berto della Massa by name, whose pestilent
practices came at length to be so well known to the good folk

1 *de' maggior cassesi.* No such word as *cassesi* is known to the lexi-
cographers or commentators ; and no plausible emendation has yet been
suggested.

of Imola that 'twas all one whether he lied or spoke the truth,
for there was not a soul in Imola that believed a word he said :
wherefore, seeing that his tricks would pass no longer there, he
removed, as in despair, to Venice, that common sink of all
abominations, thinking there to find other means than he had
found elsewhere to the prosecution of his nefarious designs.
And, as if conscience-stricken for his past misdeeds, he assumed
an air of the deepest humility, turned the best Catholic of them
all, and went and made himself a friar minor, taking the name
of Fra Alberto da Imola. With his habit he put on a shew of
austerity, highly commending penitence and abstinence, and
eating or drinking no sort of meat or wine but such as was to
his taste. And scarce a soul was there that wist that the thief,
the pimp, the cheat, the assassin, had not been suddenly con-
verted into a great preacher without continuing in the practice
of the said iniquities,whensoever the same was privily possible.
And withal, having got himself made priest, as often as he
celebrated at the altar, he would weep over the passion of our
Lord, so there were folk in plenty to see, for tears cost him
little enough, when he had a mind to shed them. In short,
what with his sermons and his tears, he duped the folk of
Venice to such a tune that scarce a will was there made but he
was its executor and depositary ; nay, not a few made him
trustee of their moneys, and most, or well-nigh most, men and
women alike, their confessor and counsellor : in short, he had
put off the wolf and put on the shepherd, and the fame of his
holiness was such in those parts that St. Francis himself had
never the like at Assisi.

Now it so befell that among the ladies that came to confess
to this holy friar was one Monna Lisetta of Ca' Quirino, the
young, silly, empty-headed wife of a great merchant, who was
gone with the galleys to Flanders. Like a Venetian—for
unstable are they all—though she placed herself at his feet, she
told him but a part of her sins, and when Fra Alberto asked her
whether she had a lover, she replied with black looks :—" How
now, master friar ? have you not eyes in your head ? See
you no difference between my charms and those of other women ?
Lovers in plenty might I have, so I would : but charms such
as mine must not be cheapened : 'tis not every man that might
presume to love me. How many ladies have you seen whose
beauty is comparable to mine ? I should adorn Paradise
itself." Whereto she added so much more in praise of her
beauty that the friar could scarce hear her with patience.

Howbeit, discerning at a glance that she was none too well
furnished with sense, he deemed the soil meet for his plough,
and fell forthwith inordinately in love with her, though he
deferred his blandishments to a more convenient season, and
by way of supporting his character for holiness began instead
to chide her, telling her (among other novelties) that this was
vainglory : whereto the lady retorted that he was a blockhead,
and could not distinguish one degree of beauty from another.
Wherefore Fra Alberto, lest he should occasion her too much
chagrin, cut short the confession, and suffered her to depart
with the other ladies. Some days after, accompanied by a
single trusty friend, he hied him to Monna Lisetta's house,
and having withdrawn with her alone into a saloon, where
they were safe from observation, he fell on his knees at her
feet, and said :—" Madam, for the love of God I crave your
pardon of that which I said to you on Sunday, when you spoke
to me of your beauty, for so grievously was I chastised therefor
that very night, that 'tis but to-day that I have been able to
quit my bed." " And by whom," quoth my Lady Battledore,
" were you so chastised ? " " I will tell you," returned Fra
Alberto. " That night I was, as is ever my wont, at my orisons,
when suddenly a great light shone in my cell, and before I
could turn me to see what it was, I saw standing over me a
right goodly youth with a stout cudgel in his hand, who seized
me by the habit and threw me at his feet and belaboured me
till I was bruised from head to foot. And when I asked him
why he used me thus, he answered :—' 'Tis because thou didst
to-day presume to speak slightingly of the celestial charms of
Monna Lisetta, whom I love next to God Himself.' Where-
upon I asked :—' And who are you ? ' And he made answer
that he was the Angel Gabriel. Then said I :—' O my lord,
I pray you pardon me.' Whereto he answered :—' I pardon
thee on condition that thou go to her, with what speed thou
mayst, and obtain her pardon, which if she accord thee not, I
shall come back hither and give thee belabourings enough with
my cudgel to make thee a sad man for the rest of thy days.'
What more he said, I dare not tell you, unless you first pardon
me." Whereat our flimsy pumpion-pated Lady Lackbrain
was overjoyed, taking all the friar's words for gospel. So after
a while she said :—" And did I not tell you, Fra Alberto,
that my charms were celestial ? But, so help me God, I am
moved to pity of you, and forthwith I pardon you, lest worse
should befall you, so only you tell me what more the Angel

said." "So will I gladly, Madam," returned Fra Alberto, " now that I have your pardon ; this only I bid you bear in mind, that you have a care that never a soul in the world hear from you a single word of what I shall say to you, if you would not spoil your good fortune, wherein there is not to-day in the whole world a lady that may compare with you. Know then that the Angel Gabriel bade me tell you that you stand so high in his favour that again and again he would have come to pass the night with you, but that he doubted he should affright you. So now he sends you word through me that he would fain come one night, and stay a while with you ; and seeing that, being an angel, if he should visit you in his angelic shape, he might not be touched by you, he would, to pleasure you, present himself in human shape ; and so he bids you send him word, when you would have him come, and in whose shape, and he will come ; for which cause you may deem yourself more blessed than any other lady that lives." My Lady Vanity then said that she was highly flattered to be beloved of the Angel Gabriel ; whom she herself loved so well that she had never grudged four soldi to burn a candle before his picture, wherever she saw it, and that he was welcome to visit her as often as he liked, and would always find her alone in her room ; on the understanding, however, that he should not desert her for the Virgin Mary, whom she had heard he did mightily affect, and indeed 'twould so appear, for, wherever she saw him, he was always on his knees at her feet : for the rest he might even come in what shape he pleased, so that it was not such as to terrify her. Then said Fra Alberto :— " Madam, 'tis wisely spoken ; and I will arrange it all with him just as you say. But 'tis in your power to do me a great favour, which will cost you nothing ; and this favour is that you be consenting that he visit you in my shape. Now hear wherein you will confer this favour : thus will it be : he will disembody my soul, and set it in Paradise, entering himself into my body ; and, as long as he shall be with you, my soul will be in Paradise." Whereto my Lady Slenderwit :—" So be it," she said ; " I am well pleased that you have this solace to salve the bruises that he gives you on my account." "Good," said Fra Alberto ; " then you will see to it that to-night he find, when he comes, your outer door unlatched, that he may have ingress ; for, coming, as he will, in human shape, he will not be able to enter save by the door." "It shall be done," replied the lady. Whereupon Fra Alberto took his leave, and

the lady remained in such a state of exaltation that her nether
end knew not her chemise, and it seemed to her a thousand
years until the Angel Gabriel should come to visit her. Fra
Alberto, bethinking him that 'twas not as an angel, but as a
cavalier that he must acquit himself that night, fell to fortifying
himself with comfits and other dainties, that he might not
lose his saddle for slight cause. Then, leave of absence gotten,
he betook him at nightfall, with a single companion, to the
house of a woman that was his friend, which house had served
on former occasions as his base when he went a-chasing the
fillies ; and having there disguised himself, he hied him, when
he deemed 'twas time, to the house of the lady, where, donning
the gewgaws he had brought with him, he transformed himself
into an angel, and going up, entered the lady's chamber. No
sooner saw she this dazzling apparition than she fell on her knees
before the Angel, who gave her his blessing, raised her to her
feet, and motioned her to go to bed. She, nothing loath,
obeyed forthwith, and the Angel lay down beside his devotee.
Now Fra Alberto was a stout, handsome fellow, whose legs
bore themselves right bravely ; and being bedded with Monna
Lisetta, who was lusty and delicate, he covered her after another
fashion than her husband had been wont, and took many a
flight that night without wings, so that she heartily cried him
content ; and not a little therewithal did he tell her of the glory
celestial. Then towards daybreak, all being ready for his
return, he hied him forth, and repaired, caparisoned as he
was, to his friend, whom, lest he should be affrighted, sleeping
alone, the good woman of the house had solaced with her com-
pany. The lady, so soon as she had breakfasted, betook her
to Fra Alberto, and reported the Angel Gabriel's visit, and what
he had told her of the glory of the life eternal, describing his
appearance, not without some added marvels of her own
invention. Whereto Fra Alberto replied :—" Madam, I know
not how you fared with him ; but this I know, that last night
he came to me, and for that I had done his errand with you,
he suddenly transported my soul among such a multitude of
flowers and roses as was never seen here below, and my soul—
what became of my body I know not—tarried in one of the most
delightful places that ever was from that hour until matins."
" As for your body," said the lady, " do I not tell you whose
it was ? It lay all night long with the Angel Gabriel in my
arms ; and if you believe me not, you have but to look under
your left pap, where I gave the Angel a mighty kiss, of which

the mark will last for some days." "Why then," said Fra
Alberto, "I will even do to-day what 'tis long since I did, to wit,
undress, that I may see if you say sooth." So they fooled it
a long while, and then the lady went home, where Fra Alberto
afterwards paid her many a visit without any let. However,
one day it so befell that while Monna Lisetta was with one
of her gossips canvassing beauties, she, being minded to exalt
her own charms above all others, and having, as we know,
none too much wit in her pumpion-pate, observed :—"Did
you but know by whom my charms are prized, then, for sure,
you would have nought to say of the rest." Her gossip, all
agog to hear, for well she knew her foible, answered :—
"Madam, it may be as you say, but still, while one knows not
who he may be, one cannot alter one's mind so rapidly."
Whereupon my Lady Featherbrain :—"Gossip," said she,
"'tis not for common talk, but he that I wot of is the Angel
Gabriel, who loves me more dearly than himself, for that I
am, so he tells me, the fairest lady in all the world, ay, and in
the Maremma to boot."[1] Whereat her gossip would fain
have laughed, but held herself in, being minded to hear more
from her. Wherefore she said :—"God's faith, Madam, if
'tis the Angel Gabriel, and he tells you so, why, so of course it
must needs be ; but I wist not the angels meddled with such
matters." "There you erred, gossip," said the lady : "zounds,
he does it better than my husband, and he tells me they do it
above there too, but, as he rates my charms above any that
are in heaven, he is enamoured of me, and not seldom visits
me : so now dost see ? " So away went the gossip so agog to
tell the story, that it seemed to her a thousand years till she
was where it might be done ; and being met for recreation with
a great company of ladies, she narrated it all in detail : whereby
it passed to the ladies' husbands, and to other ladies, and
from them to yet other ladies, so that in less than two days all
Venice was full of it. But among others, whose ears it reached,
were Monna Lisetta's brothers-in-law, who, keeping their own
counsel, resolved to find this angel and make out whether he
knew how to fly ; to which end they kept watch for some nights.
Whereof no hint, as it happened, reached Fra Alberto's ears ;
and so, one night when he was come to enjoy the lady once more,
he was scarce undressed when her brothers-in-law, who had
seen him come, were at the door of the room and already

[1] With this ineptitude cf. the friar's "flowers and roses" on the pre-
ceding page.

opening it, when Fra Alberto, hearing the noise and apprehend-
ing the danger, started up, and having no other resource, threw
open a window that looked on to the Grand Canal, and plunged
into the water. The depth was great, and he was an expert
swimmer; so that he took no hurt, but, having reached the
other bank, found a house open, and forthwith entered it,
praying the good man that was within, for God's sake to save
his life, and trumping up a story to account for his being there
at so late an hour, and stripped to the skin. The good man
took pity on him, and having occasion to go out, he put him
in his own bed, bidding him stay there until his return; and
so, having locked him in, he went about his business.

Now when the lady's brothers-in-law entered the room, and
found that the Angel Gabriel had taken flight, leaving his wings
behind him, being baulked of their prey, they roundly rated
the lady, and then, leaving her disconsolate, betook themselves
home with the Angel's spoils. Whereby it befell, that, when
'twas broad day, the good man, being on the Rialto, heard tell
how the Angel Gabriel had come to pass the night with Monna
Lisetta, and, being surprised by her brothers-in-law, had taken
fright, and thrown himself into the Canal, and none knew what
was become of him. The good man guessed in a trice that the
said Angel was no other than the man he had at home, whom
on his return he recognized, and, after much chaffering, brought
him to promise him fifty ducats that he might not be given up
to the lady's brothers-in-law. The bargain struck, Fra Alberto
signified a desire to be going. Whereupon:—" There is no
way," said the good man, " but one, if you are minded to take
it. To-day we hold a revel, wherein folk lead others about in
various disguises; as, one man will present a bear, another a
wild man, and so forth; and then in the piazza of San Marco
there is a hunt, which done, the revel is ended; and then away
they hie them, whither they will, each with the man he has
led about. If you are willing to be led by me in one or another
of these disguises, before it can get wind that you are here,
I can bring you whither you would go; otherwise I see not
how you are to quit this place without being known; and the
lady's brothers-in-law, reckoning that you must be lurking
somewhere in this quarter, have set guards all about to take
you." Loath indeed was Fra Alberto to go in such a guise,
but such was his fear of the lady's relations that he consented,
and told the good man whither he desired to be taken, and that
he was content to leave the choice of the disguise to him.

The good man then smeared him all over with honey, and covered him with down, set a chain on his neck and a vizard on his face, gave him a stout cudgel to carry in one hand, and two huge dogs, which he had brought from the shambles, to lead with the other, and sent a man to the Rialto to announce that whoso would see the Angel Gabriel should hie him to the piazza of San Marco ; in all which he acted as a leal Venetian.   And so, after a while, he led him forth, and then, making him go before, held him by the chain behind, and through a great throng that clamoured :—" What manner of thing is this ? what manner of thing is this ? " he brought him to the piazza, where, what with those that followed them, and those that had come from the Rialto on hearing the announcement, there were folk without end.   Arrived at the piazza, he fastened his wild man to a column in a high and exposed place, making as if he were minded to wait till the hunt should begin ; whereby the flies and gadflies, attracted by the honey with which he was smeared, caused him most grievous distress.   However, the good man waited only until the piazza was thronged, and then, making as if he would unchain his wild man, he tore the vizard from Fra Alberto's face, saying :—" Gentlemen, as the boar comes not to the hunt, and the hunt does not take place, that it be not for nothing that you are come hither, I am minded to give you a view of the Angel Gabriel, who comes down from heaven to earth by night to solace the ladies of Venice."   The vizard was no sooner withdrawn than all recognized Fra Alberto, and greeted him with hootings, rating him in language as offensive and opprobrious as ever rogue was abused withal, and pelting him in the face with every sort of filth that came to hand : in which plight they kept him an exceeding great while, until by chance the bruit thereof reached his brethren, of whom some six thereupon put themselves in motion, and, arrived at the piazza, clapped a habit on his back, and unchained him, and amid an immense uproar led him off to their convent, where, after languishing a while in prison, 'tis believed that he died.

So this man, by reason that, being reputed righteous, he did evil, and 'twas not imputed to him, presumed to counterfeit the Angel Gabriel, and, being transformed into a wild man, was in the end put to shame, as he deserved, and vainly bewailed his misdeeds.   God grant that so it may betide all his likes.

NOVEL III

*Three young men love three sisters, and flee with them to Crete.
The eldest of the sisters slays her lover for jealousy. The
second saves the life of the first by yielding herself to the
Duke of Crete. Her lover slays her, and makes off with
the first : the third sister and her lover are charged with the
murder, are arrested and confess the crime. They escape
death by bribing the guards, flee destitute to Rhodes, and there
in destitution die.*

PAMPINEA'S story ended, Filostrato mused a while, and then
said to her :—" A little good matter there was that pleased me
at the close of your story, but, before 'twas reached, there was
far too much to laugh at, which I could have wished had not
been there." Then, turning to Lauretta, he said :—" Madam,
give us something better to follow, if so it may be." Lauretta
replied with a laugh :—" Harsh beyond measure are you to
the lovers, to desire that their end be always evil ; but, as in
duty bound, I will tell a story of three, who all alike came to
a bad end, having had little joyance of their loves ; " and so
saying, she began.

Well may ye wot, young ladies, for 'tis abundantly manifest,
that there is no vice but most grievous disaster may ensue
thereon to him that practises it, and not seldom to others ;
and of all the vices that which hurries us into peril with loosest
rein is, methinks, anger ; which is nought but a rash and hasty
impulse, prompted by a feeling of pain, which banishes reason,
shrouds the eyes of the mind in thick darkness, and sets the
soul ablaze with a fierce frenzy. Which, though it not seldom
befall men, and one rather than another, has nevertheless
been observed to be fraught in women with more disastrous
consequences, inasmuch as in them the flame is both more
readily kindled, and burns more brightly, and with less impedi-
ment to its vehemence. Wherein is no cause to marvel, for,
if we consider it, we shall see that 'tis of the nature of fire to
lay hold more readily of things light and delicate than of matters
of firmer and more solid substance ; and sure it is that we
(without offence to the men be it spoken) are more delicate than
they, and much more mobile. Wherefore, seeing how prone
we are thereto by nature, and considering also our gentleness
and tenderness, how soothing and consolatory they are to the

men with whom we consort, and that thus this madness of wrath is fraught with grievous annoy and peril ; therefore, that with stouter heart we may defend ourselves against it, I purpose by my story to shew you, how the loves of three young men, and as many ladies, as I said before, were by the anger of one of the ladies changed from a happy to a most woeful complexion.

Marseilles, as you know, is situate on the coast of Provence, a city ancient and most famous, and in old time the seat of many more rich men and great merchants than are to be seen there to-day, among whom was one Narnald Cluada by name, a man of the lowest origin, but a merchant of unsullied probity and integrity, and boundless wealth in lands and goods and money, who had by his lady several children, three of them being daughters, older, each of them, than the other children, who were sons. Two of the daughters, who were twins, were, when my story begins, fifteen years old, and the third was but a year younger, so that in order to their marriage their kinsfolk awaited nothing but the return of Narnald from Spain, whither he was gone with his merchandise. One of the twins was called Ninette, the other Madeleine ; the third daughter's name was Bertelle. A young man, Restagnon by name, who, though poor, was of gentle blood, was in the last degree enamoured of Ninette, and she of him ; and so discreetly had they managed the affair, that, never another soul in the world witting aught of it, they had had joyance of their love, and that for a good while, when it so befell that two young friends of theirs, the one Foulques, the other Hugues by name, whom their fathers, recently dead, had left very wealthy, fell in love, the one with Madeleine, the other with Bertelle. Whereof Restagnon being apprised by Ninette bethought him that in their love he might find a means to the relief of his necessities. He accordingly consorted freely and familiarly with them, accompanying, now one, now the other, and sometimes both of them, when they went to visit their ladies and his ; and when he judged that he had made his footing as friendly and familiar as need was, he bade them one day to his house, and said :—" Comrades most dear, our friendship, perchance, may not have left you without assurance of the great love I bear you, and that for you I would do even as much as for myself : wherefore, loving you thus much, I purpose to impart to you that which is in my mind, that in regard thereof, you and I together may then resolve in such sort as to you shall seem the best. You, if I may trust your words, as also what I seem to have gathered from your demeanour by day and by night, burn with an exceeding great love for the two ladies whom you effect, as I for their sister. For the assuagement whereof, I have good hope that, if you will unite with me, I shall find means most sweet and delightsome ; to wit, on this wise. You possess, as I do not, great wealth : now if you are willing to make of your wealth a common stock with me as third partner therein, and to choose some part of the world where we may live in careless ease upon our substance, without any manner of doubt I trust so to prevail that the three sisters with great part of their father's substance shall come to live with us, wherever we shall see fit to go ; whereby, each with his own lady, we shall live as three brethren, the happiest men in the world. 'Tis now for you to determine whether you will embrace this proffered solace, or let it slip from you." The two young men, whose love was beyond all measure fervent, spared themselves the trouble of deliberation : 'twas enough that they heard that they were to have their ladies : wherefore they answered, that, so this should ensue, they were ready to do as he proposed. Having thus their answer, Restagnon a few days later was closeted with Ninette, to whom 'twas a matter of no small difficulty for him to get access. Nor had he been long with her before he adverted to what had passed between him and the young men, and sought to commend the project to her for reasons not a few. Little need, however, had he to urge her : for to live their life openly together was the very thing she desired, far more than he : wherefore she frankly answered that she would have it so, that her sisters would do, more especially in this matter, just as she wished, and that he should lose no time in making all the needful arrangements. So Restagnon returned to the two young men, who were most urgent that it should be done even as he said, and told them that on the part of the ladies the matter was concluded. And so, having fixed upon Crete for their destination, and sold some estates that they had, giving out that they were minded to go a-trading with the proceeds, they converted all else that they possessed into money, and bought a brigantine, which with all secrecy they handsomely equipped, anxiously expecting the time of their departure, while Ninette on her part, knowing well how her sisters were affected, did so by sweet converse foment their desire that, till it should be accomplished, they accounted their life as nought. The night of their embarcation being come, the three sisters opened a great chest that belonged to their father, and took out therefrom a vast quantity of money and jewels, with which they all three issued forth of the house in dead silence, as they had been charged, and found their three lovers awaiting them ; who, having forthwith brought them aboard the brigantine, bade the rowers give way, and, tarrying nowhere, arrived the next evening at Genoa, where the new lovers had for the first time joyance and solace of their love.

Having taken what they needed of refreshment, they resumed their course, touching at this port and that, and in less than eight days, speeding without impediment, were come to Crete. There they bought them domains both beautiful and broad, whereon, hard by Candia they built them mansions most goodly and delightsome, wherein they lived as barons, keeping a crowd of retainers, with dogs, hawks and horses, and speeding the time with their ladies in feasting and revelling and merry-making, none so light-hearted as they. Such being the tenor of their life, it so befell that (as 'tis matter of daily experience that, however delightsome a thing may be, superabundance thereof will breed disgust) Restagnon, much as he had loved Ninette, being now able to have his joyance of her without stint or restraint, began to weary of her, and by consequence to abate somewhat of his love for her. And being mightily pleased with a fair gentlewoman of the country, whom he met at a merry-making, he set his whole heart upon her, and began to shew himself marvellously courteous and gallant towards her ; which Ninette perceiving grew so jealous that he might not go a step but she knew of it, and resented it to his torment and her own with high words. But as, while superfluity engenders disgust, appetite is but whetted when fruit is forbidden, so Ninette's wrath added fuel to the flame of Restagnon's new love. And whichever was the event, whether in course of time Restagnon had the lady's favour or had it not, Ninette, whoever may have brought her the tidings, firmly believed that he had it ; whereby from the depths of distress she passed into a towering passion, and thus was transported into such a frenzy of rage that all the love she bore to Restagnon was converted into bitter hatred, and, blinded by her wrath, she made up her mind to avenge by Restagnon's death the dishonour which she deemed that he had done her. So she had recourse to an old Greek woman, that was very skilful in compounding poisons, whom by promises and gifts she induced to distill a deadly water, which, keeping her own counsel, she herself gave Restagnon to drink one evening, when he was somewhat heated and quite off his guard : whereby—such was the efficacy of the water—she despatched Restagnon before matins. On learning his death Foulques and Hugues and their ladies, who knew not that he had been poisoned, united their bitter with Ninette's feigned lamentations, and gave him honourable sepulture. But so it befell that, not many days after, the old woman, that had compounded the poison for Ninette, was taken for another crime ; and, being put to the torture, confessed the compounding of the poison among other of her misdeeds, and fully declared what had thereby come to pass. Wherefore the Duke of Crete, breathing no word of his intent, came privily by night, and set a guard around Foulques' palace, where Ninette then was, and quietly, and quite unopposed, took and carried her off ; and without putting her to the torture, learned from her in a trice all that he sought to know touching the death of Restagnon. Foulques and Hugues had learned privily of the Duke, and their ladies of them, for what cause Ninette was taken ; and, being mightily distressed thereby, bestirred themselves with all zeal to save Ninette from the fire, to which they apprehended she would be condemned, as having indeed richly deserved it ; but all their endeavours seemed to avail nothing, for the Duke was unwaveringly resolved that justice should be done. Madeleine, Foulques' fair wife, who had long been courted by the Duke, but had never deigned to shew him the least favour, thinking that by yielding herself to his will she might redeem her sister from the fire, despatched a trusty envoy to him with the intimation that she was entirely at his disposal upon the twofold condition, that in the first place her sister should be restored to her free and scatheless, and, in the second place, the affair should be kept secret. Albeit gratified by this overture, the Duke was long in doubt whether he should accept it ; in the end, however, he made up his mind to do so, and signified his approval to the envoy. Then with the lady's consent he put Foulques and Hugues under arrest for a night, as if he were minded to examine them of the affair, and meanwhile quartered himself privily with Madeleine. Ninette, who, he had made believe, had been set in a sack, and was to be sunk in the sea that same night, he took with him, and presented her to her sister in requital of the night's joyance, which, as he parted from her on the morrow, he prayed her might not be the last, as it was the first, fruit of their love, at the same time enjoining her to send the guilty lady away that she might not bring reproach upon him, nor he be compelled to deal rigorously

with her again. Released the same morning, and told that
Ninette had been cast into the sea, Foulques and Hugues, fully
believing that so it was, came home, thinking how they should
console their ladies for the death of their sister ; but, though
Madeleine was at great pains to conceal Ninette, Foulques
nevertheless, to his no small amazement, discovered that she
was there ; which at once excited his suspicion, for he knew that
the Duke had been enamoured of Madeleine ; and he asked
how it was that Ninette was there. Madeleine made up a long
story by way of explanation, to which his sagacity gave little
credit, and in the end after long parley he constrained her to
tell the truth. Whereupon, overcome with grief, and trans-
ported with rage, he drew his sword, and, deaf to her appeals
for mercy, slew her. Then, fearing the vengeful justice of the
Duke, he left the dead body in the room, and hied him to
Ninette, and with a counterfeit gladsome mien said to her :—
" Go we without delay whither thy sister has appointed that
I escort thee, that thou fall not again into the hands of the
Duke." Ninette believed him, and being fain to go for very
fear, she forewent further leave-taking of her sister, more
particularly as it was now night, and set out with Foulques,
who took with him such little money as he could lay his hands
upon ; and so they made their way to the coast, where they
got aboard a bark, but none ever knew where their voyage
ended.

Madeleine's dead body being discovered next day, certain
evil-disposed folk, that bore a grudge to Hugues, forthwith
apprised the Duke of the fact ; which brought the Duke—
for much he loved Madeleine—in hot haste to the house, where
he arrested Hugues and his lady, who as yet knew nothing of
the departure of Foulques and Ninette, and extorted from them
a confession that they and Foulques were jointly answerable
for Madeleine's death. For which cause being justly appre-
hensive of death, they with great address corrupted the guards
that had charge of them, giving them a sum of money which
they kept concealed in their house against occasions of need ;
and together with the guards fled with all speed, leaving all
that they possessed behind them, and took ship by night for
Rhodes, where, being arrived, they lived in great poverty and
misery no long time. Such then was the issue, to which
Restagnon, by his foolish love, and Ninette by her wrath brought
themselves and others.

NOVEL IV

*Gerbino, in breach of the plighted faith of his grandfather, King
    Guglielmo, attacks a ship of the King of Tunis to rescue
    thence his daughter. She being slain by those aboard the
    ship, he slays them, and afterwards he is beheaded.*

LAURETTA, her story ended, kept silence ; and the king brooded
as in deep thought, while one or another of the company deplored
the sad fate of this or the other of the lovers, or censured
Ninette's wrath, or made some other comment. At length,
however, the king roused himself, and raising his head, made
sign to Elisa that 'twas now for her to speak. So, modestly,
Elisa thus began :—Gracious ladies, not a few there are that
believe that Love looses no shafts save when he is kindled by
the eyes, contemning their opinion that hold that passion may
be engendered by words ; whose error will be abundantly
manifest in a story which I purpose to tell you ; wherein you
may see how mere rumour not only wrought mutual love in
those that had never seen one another, but also brought both
to a miserable death.

Guglielmo, the Second,[1] as the Sicilians compute, King of
Sicily, had two children, a son named Ruggieri, and a daughter
named Gostanza. Ruggieri died before his father, and left a
son named Gerbino ; who, being carefully trained by his grand-
father, grew up a most goodly gallant, and of great renown in
court and camp, and that not only within the borders of Sicily,
but in divers other parts of the world, among them Barbary,
then tributary to the King of Sicily. And among others, to
whose ears was wafted the bruit of Gerbino's magnificent
prowess and courtesy, was a daughter of the King of Tunis,
who, by averment of all that had seen her, was a creature as
fair and debonair, and of as great and noble a spirit as Nature
ever formed. To hear tell of brave men was her delight, and
what she heard, now from one, now from another, of the brave
deeds of Gerbino she treasured in her mind so sedulously, and
pondered them with such pleasure, rehearsing them to herself
in imagination, that she became hotly enamoured of him, and
there was none of whom she talked, or heard others talk, so
gladly. Nor, on the other hand, had the fame of her incom-

---

1 First, according to the now accepted reckoning. He reigned from 1154
to 1166.

parable beauty and other excellences failed to travel, as to
other lands, so also to Sicily, where, falling on Gerbino's ears,
it gave him no small delight, to such effect that he burned for
the lady no less vehemently than she for him. Wherefore,
until such time as he might, upon some worthy occasion,
have his grandfather's leave to go to Tunis, yearning beyond
measure to see her, he charged every friend of his, that went
thither, to give her to know, as best he might, his great and
secret love for her, and to bring him tidings of her. Which
office one of the said friends discharged with no small address ;
for, having obtained access to her, after the manner of
merchants, by bringing jewels for her to look at, he fully
apprised her of Gerbino's passion, and placed him, and all
that he possessed, entirely at her disposal. The lady received
both messenger and message with gladsome mien, made answer
that she loved with equal ardour, and in token thereof sent
Gerbino one of her most precious jewels. Gerbino received the
jewel with extreme delight, and sent her many a letter and
many a most precious gift by the hand of the same messenger ;
and 'twas well understood between them that, should Fortune
accord him opportunity, he should see and know her.

On this footing the affair remained somewhat longer than
was expedient ; and so, while Gerbino and the lady burned with
mutual love, it befell that the King of Tunis gave her in marriage
to the King of Granada ;[1] whereat she was wroth beyond
measure, for that she was not only going into a country remote
from her lover, but, as she deemed, was severed from him
altogether ; and so this might not come to pass, gladly, could
she but have seen how, would she have left her father and
fled to Gerbino. In like manner, Gerbino, on learning of the
marriage, was vexed beyond measure, and was oft-times minded,
could he but find means to win to her husband by sea, to wrest
her from him by force. Some rumour of Gerbino's love, and
of his intent, reached the King of Tunis, who, knowing his
prowess and power, took alarm, and as the time drew nigh for
conveying the lady to Granada, sent word of his purpose to
King Guglielmo, and craved his assurance that it might be
carried into effect without let or hindrance on the part of
Gerbino, or any one else. The old King had heard nothing of
Gerbino's love affair, and never dreaming that 'twas on such
account that the assurance was craved, granted it without

[1] An anachronism ; the Moorish kingdom of Granada not having been
founded until 1238.

demur, and in pledge thereof sent the King of Tunis his glove.
Which received, the King made ready a great and goodly ship
in the port of Carthage, and equipped her with all things meet
for those that were to man her, and with all appointments apt
and seemly for the reception of his daughter, and awaited only
fair weather to send her therein to Granada. All which the
young lady seeing and marking, sent one of her servants privily
to Palermo, bidding him greet the illustrious Gerbino on her
part, and tell him that a few days would see her on her way to
Granada ; wherefore 'twould now appear whether, or no, he
were really as doughty a man as he was reputed, and loved her
as much as he had so often protested. The servant did not
fail to deliver her message exactly, and returned to Tunis,
leaving Gerbino, who knew that his grandfather, King Guglielmo,
had given the King of Tunis the desired assurance, at a loss
how to act. But prompted by love, and goaded by the lady's
words and loath to seem a craven, he hied him to Messina ;
and having there armed two light galleys, and manned them
with good men and true, he put to sea, and stood for Sardinia,
deeming that the lady's ship must pass that way. Nor was he
far out in his reckoning ; for he had not been there many
days, when the ship, sped by a light breeze, hove in sight not
far from the place where he lay in wait for her. Whereupon
Gerbino said to his comrades :—" Gentlemen, if you be as good
men and true as I deem you, there is none of you but must have
felt, if he feel not now, the might of love ; for without love I
deem no mortal capable of true worth or aught that is good ;
and if you are or have been in love, 'twill be easy for you to
understand that which I desire. I love, and 'tis because I
love that I have laid this travail upon you ; and that which I
love is in the ship that you see before you, which is fraught not
only with my beloved, but with immense treasures, which, if
you are good men and true, we, so we but play the man in fight,
may with little trouble make our own ; nor for my share of the
spoils of the victory demand I aught but a lady, whose love it
is that prompts me to take arms : all else I freely cede to you
from this very hour. Forward, then ; attack we this ship ;
success should be ours, for God favours our enterprise, nor
lends her wind to evade us." Fewer words might have sufficed
the illustrious Gerbino ; for the rapacious Messinese that were
with him were already bent heart and soul upon that to which
by his harangue he sought to animate them. So, when he had
done, they raised a mighty shout, so that 'twas as if trumpets

did blare, and caught up their arms, and smiting the water
with their oars, overhauled the ship. The advancing galleys
were observed while they were yet a great way off by the
ship's crew, who, not being able to avoid the combat, put
themselves in a posture of defence. Arrived at close quarters,
the illustrious Gerbino bade send the ship's masters aboard
the galleys, unless they were minded to do battle. Certified
of the challenge, and who they were that made it, the Saracens
answered that 'twas in breach of the faith plighted to them by
their assailants' king that they were thus attacked, and in token
thereof displayed King Guglielmo's glove, averring in set terms
that there should be no surrender either of themselves or of
aught that was aboard the ship without battle. Gerbino, who
had observed the lady standing on the ship's poop, and seen
that she was far more beautiful than he had imagined, burned
with a yet fiercer flame than before, and to the display of the
glove made answer, that, as he had no falcons there just then,
the glove booted him not ; wherefore, so they were not minded
to surrender the lady, let them prepare to receive battle.
Whereupon, without further delay, the battle began on both
sides with a furious discharge of arrows and stones ; on which
wise it was long protracted to their common loss ; until at
last Gerbino, seeing that he gained little advantage, took a
light bark which they had brought from Sardinia, and having
fired her, bore down with her, and both the galleys, upon the
ship. Whereupon the Saracens, seeing that they must perforce
surrender the ship or die, caused the King's daughter, who lay
beneath the deck weeping, to come up on deck, and led her to
the prow, and shouting to Gerbino, while the lady shrieked
alternately " mercy " and " succour," opened her veins before
his eyes, and cast her into the sea, saying :—" Take her ; we
give her to thee on such wise as we can, and as thy faith has
merited." Maddened to witness this deed of barbarism, Gerbino,
as if courting death, recked no more of the arrows and the
stones, but drew alongside the ship, and, despite the resistance
of her crew, boarded her ; and as a famished lion ravens amongst
a herd of oxen, and tearing and rending, now one, now another,
gluts his wrath before he appeases his hunger, so Gerbino,
sword in hand, hacking and hewing on all sides among the
Saracens, did ruthlessly slaughter not a few of them ; till, as
the burning ship began to blaze more fiercely, he bade the sea-
men take thereout all that they might by way of guerdon, which
done, he quitted her, having gained but a rueful victory over

his adversaries. His next care was to recover from the sea the
body of the fair lady, whom long and with many a tear he
mourned : and so he returned to Sicily, and gave the body
honourable sepulture in Ustica, an islet that faces, as it were,
Trapani, and went home the saddest man alive.

When these tidings reached the King of Tunis, he sent to
King Guglielmo ambassadors, habited in black, who made
complaint of the breach of faith and recited the manner of its
occurrence. Which caused King Guglielmo no small chagrin ;
and seeing not how he might refuse the justice they demanded,
he had Gerbino arrested, and he himself, none of his barons
being able by any entreaty to turn him from his purpose,
sentenced him to forfeit his head, and had it severed from his
body in his presence, preferring to suffer the loss of his only
grandson than to gain the reputation of a faithless king. And
so, miserably, within the compass of a few brief days, died the
two lovers by woeful deaths, as I have told you, and without
having known any joyance of their love.

NOVEL V

*Lisabetta's brothers slay her lover : he appears to her in a dream,
and shews her where he is buried : she privily disinters the
head, and sets it in a pot of basil, whereon she daily weeps
a great while. The pot being taken from her by her brothers,
she dies not long after.*

ELISA'S story ended, the king bestowed a few words of praise
upon it, and then laid the burden of discourse upon Filomena,
who, full of compassion for the woes of Gerbino and his lady,
heaved a piteous sigh, and thus began :—My story, gracious
ladies, will not be of folk of so high a rank as those of whom
Elisa has told us, but perchance 'twill not be less touching.
'Tis brought to my mind by the recent mention of Messina,
where the matter befell.

Know then that there were at Messina three young men,
that were brothers and merchants, who were left very rich on
the death of their father, who was of San Gimignano ; and they
had a sister, Lisabetta by name, a girl fair enough, and no less
debonair, but whom, for some reason or another, they had not
as yet bestowed in marriage. The three brothers had also in
their shop a young Pisan, Lorenzo by name, who managed all

their affairs, and who was so goodly of person and gallant, that Lisabetta bestowed many a glance upon him, and began to regard him with extraordinary favour ; which Lorenzo marking from time to time, gave up all his other amours, and in like manner began to affect her, and so, their loves being equal, 'twas not long before they took heart of grace, and did that which each most desired. Wherein continuing to their no small mutual solace and delight, they neglected to order it with due secrecy, whereby one night as Lisabetta was going to Lorenzo's room, she, all unwitting, was observed by the eldest of the brothers, who, albeit much distressed by what he had learnt, yet, being a young man of discretion, was swayed by considerations more seemly, and, allowing no word to escape him, spent the night in turning the affair over in his mind in divers ways. On the morrow he told his brothers that which, touching Lisabetta and Lorenzo, he had observed in the night, which, that no shame might thence ensue either to them or to their sister, they after long consultation determined to pass over in silence, making as if they had seen or heard nought thereof, until such time as they in a safe and convenient manner might banish this disgrace from their sight before it could go further. Adhering to which purpose, they jested and laughed with Lorenzo as they had been wont ; and after a while pretending that they were all three going forth of the city on pleasure, they took Lorenzo with them ; and being come to a remote and very lonely spot, seeing that 'twas apt for their design, they took Lorenzo, who was completely off his guard, and slew him, and buried him on such wise that none was ware of it. On their return to Messina they gave out that they had sent him away on business ; which was readily believed, because 'twas what they had been frequently used to do. But as Lorenzo did not return, and Lisabetta questioned the brothers about him with great frequency and urgency, being sorely grieved by his long absence, it so befell that one day, when she was very pressing in her enquiries, one of the brothers said :— " What means this ? What hast thou to do with Lorenzo, that thou shouldst ask about him so often ? Ask us no more, or we will give thee such answer as thou deservest." So the girl, sick at heart and sorrowful, fearing she knew not what, asked no questions ; but many a time at night she called piteously to him, and besought him to come to her, and bewailed his long tarrying with many a tear, and ever yearning for his return, languished in total dejection.

But so it was that one night, when, after long weeping that her Lorenzo came not back, she had at last fallen asleep, Lorenzo appeared to her in a dream, wan and in utter disarray, his clothes torn to shreds and sodden ; and thus, as she thought, he spoke :—" Lisabetta, thou dost nought but call me, and vex thyself for my long tarrying, and bitterly upbraid me with thy tears ; wherefore be it known to thee that return to thee I may not, because the last day that thou didst see me thy brothers slew me." After which, he described the place where they had buried him, told her to call and expect him no more, and vanished. The girl then awoke, and doubting not that the vision was true, wept bitterly. And when morning came, and she was risen, not daring to say aught to her brothers, she resolved to go to the place indicated in the vision, and see if what she had dreamed were even as it had appeared to her. So, having leave to go a little way out of the city for recreation in company with a maid that had at one time lived with them and knew all that she did, she hied her thither with all speed ; and having removed the dry leaves that were strewn about the place, she began to dig where the earth seemed least hard. Nor had she dug long, before she found the body of her hapless lover, whereon as yet there was no trace of corruption or decay ; and thus she saw without any manner of doubt that her vision was true. And so, saddest of women, knowing that she might not bewail him there, she would gladly, if she could, have carried away the body and given it more honourable sepulture elsewhere ; but as she might not so do, she took a knife, and, as best she could, severed the head from the trunk, and wrapped it in a napkin and laid it in the lap of her maid ; and having covered the rest of the corpse with earth, she left the spot, having been seen by none, and went home. There she shut herself up in her room with the head, and kissed it a thousand times in every part, and wept long and bitterly over it, till she had bathed it in her tears. She then wrapped it in a piece of fine cloth, and set it in a large and beautiful pot of the sort in which marjoram or basil is planted, and covered it with earth, and therein planted some roots of the goodliest basil of Salerno, and drenched them only with her tears, or water perfumed with roses or orange-blossoms. And 'twas her wont ever to sit beside this pot, and, all her soul one yearning, to pore upon it, as that which enshrined her Lorenzo, and when long time she had so done, she would bend over it, and weep a great while, until the basil was quite bathed in her tears.

Fostered with such constant, unremitting care, and nourished by the richness given to the soil by the decaying head that lay therein, the basil burgeoned out in exceeding great beauty and fragrance. And, the girl persevering ever in this way of life, the neighbours from time to time took note of it, and when her brothers marvelled to see her beauty ruined, and her eyes as it were evanished from her head, they told them of it, saying :— "We have observed that such is her daily wont." Whereupon the brothers, marking her behaviour, chid her therefore once or twice, and as she heeded them not, caused the pot to be taken privily from her. Which, so soon as she missed it, she demanded with the utmost instance and insistence, and, as they gave it not back to her, ceased not to wail and weep, insomuch that she fell sick ; nor in her sickness craved she aught but the pot of basil. Whereat the young men, marvelling mightily, resolved to see what the pot might contain ; and having removed the earth they espied the cloth, and therein the head, which was not yet so decayed, but that by the curled locks they knew it for Lorenzo's head. Passing strange they found it, and fearing lest it should be bruited abroad, they buried the head, and, with as little said as might be, took order for their privy departure from Messina, and hied them thence to Naples. The girl ceased not to weep and crave her pot, and, so weeping, died. Such was the end of her disastrous love ; but not a few in course of time coming to know the truth of the affair, there was one that made the song that is still sung : to wit :—

> A thief he was, I swear,
>   A sorry Christian he,
> That took my basil of Salerno fair, etc.[1]

[1] This Sicilian folk-song, of which Boccaccio quotes only the first two lines, is given in extenso from MS. Laurent. 38, plut. 42, by Fanfani in his edition of the *Decameron* (Florence, 1857). The following is a free rendering—

> A thief he was, I swear,
>   A sorry Christian he,
> That took my basil of Salerno fair,
>   That flourished mightily.
> Planted by mine own hands with loving care
>   What time they revelled free :
> To spoil another's goods is churlish spite.

> To spoil another's goods is churlish spite,
>   Ay, and most heinous sin.
> A basil had I (alas ! luckless wight !),

The fairest plant : within
Its shade I slept : 'twas grown to such a height.
But some folk for chagrin
'Reft me thereof, ay, and before my door.

'Reft me thereof, ay, and before my door.
Ah ! dolorous day and drear !
Ah ! woe is me !   Would God I were no more !
My purchase was so dear !
Ah ! why that day did I to watch give o'er ?
For him my cherished fere
With marjoram I bordered it about.

With marjoram I bordered it about
In May-time fresh and fair,
And watered it thrice ere each week was out,
And marked it grow full yare :
But now 'tis stolen.   Ah ! too well 'tis known ! [1]

But now 'tis stolen.   Ah ! too well 'tis known !
That no more may I hide :
But had to me a while before been shewn
What then should me betide,
At night before my door I had laid me down
To watch my plant beside.
Yet God Almighty sure me succour might.

Ay, God Almighty sure me succour might,
So were it but His will,
'Gainst him that me hath done so foul despite,
That in dire torment still
I languish, since the thief reft from my sight
My plant that did me thrill,
And to my inmost soul such comfort lent !

And to my inmost soul such comfort lent !
So fresh its fragrance blew,
That when, what time the sun uprose, I went
My watering to do,
I'd hear the people all in wonderment
Say, whence this perfume new ?
And I for love of it of grief shall die.

And I for love of it of grief shall die,
Of my fair plant for dole.
Would one but shew me how I might it buy !
Ah ! how 'twould me console !
Ounces [2] an hundred of fine gold have I :
Him would I give the whole,
Ay, and a kiss to boot, so he were fain.

[1] This stanza is defective in the original.

[2] The " oncia " was a Sicilian gold coin worth rather more than a
zecchino.

NOVEL VI

*Andreuola loves Gabriotto : she tells him a dream that she has
had ; he tells her a dream of his own, and dies suddenly in
her arms. While she and her maid are carrying his corpse
to his house, they are taken by the Signory. She tells how the
matter stands, is threatened with violence by the Podestà,
but will not brook it. Her father hears how she is bested ;
and, her innocence being established, causes her to be set at
large ; but she, being minded to tarry no longer in the world,
becomes a nun.*

GLAD indeed were the ladies to have heard Filomena's story,
for that, often though they had heard the song sung, they had
never yet, for all their enquiries, been able to learn the occasion
upon which it was made. When 'twas ended, Pamfilo received
the king's command to follow suit, and thus spoke :—By the
dream told in the foregoing story I am prompted to relate one
in which two dreams are told, dreams of that which was to
come, as Lisabetta's was of that which had been, and which
were both fulfilled almost as soon as they were told by those
that had dreamed them. Wherefore, loving ladies, you must
know that 'tis the common experience of mankind to have divers
visions during sleep ; and albeit the sleeper, while he sleeps,
deems all alike most true, but, being awake, judges some of
them to be true, others to be probable, and others again to be
quite devoid of truth, yet not a few are found to have come
to pass. For which cause many are as sure of every dream
as of aught that they see in their waking hours, and so, as their
dreams engender in them fear or hope, are sorrowful or joyous.
And on the other hand there are those that credit no dream, until
they see themselves fallen into the very peril whereof they
were forewarned. Of whom I approve neither sort, for in
sooth neither are all dreams true, nor all alike false. That
they are not all true, there is none of us but may many a time
have proved ; and that they are not all alike false has already
been shewn in Filomena's story, and shall also, as I said before,
be shewn in mine. Wherefore I deem that in a virtuous course
of life and conduct there is no need to fear aught by reason of
any dream that is contrary thereto, or on that account to give
up any just design ; and as for crooked and sinister enterprises,
however dreams may seem to favour them, and flatter the hopes

of the dreamer with auspicious omens, none should trust them :
rather should all give full credence to such as run counter thereto.
But come we to the story.

In the city of Brescia there lived of yore a gentleman named
Messer Negro da Ponte Carraro, who with other children had
a very fair daughter, Andreuola by name, who, being unmarried,
chanced to fall in love with a neighbour, one Gabriotto, a man
of low degree, but goodly of person and debonair, and endowed
with all admirable qualities ; and aided and abetted by the
housemaid, the girl not only brought it to pass that Gabriotto
knew that he was beloved of her, but that many a time to their
mutual delight he came to see her in a fair garden belonging to
her father. And that nought but death might avail to sever
them from this their gladsome love, they became privily man
and wife ; and, while thus they continued their clandestine
intercourse, it happened that one night, while the girl slept, she
saw herself in a dream in her garden with Gabriotto, who to
the exceeding great delight of both held her in his arms ; and
while thus they lay, she saw issue from his body somewhat dark
and frightful, the shape whereof she might not discern ; which,
as she thought, laid hold of Gabriotto, and in her despite with
prodigious force reft him from her embrace, and bore him with
it underground, so that both were lost to her sight for evermore :
whereby stricken with sore and inexpressible grief, she awoke ;
and albeit she was overjoyed to find that 'twas not as she had
dreamed, yet a haunting dread of what she had seen in her
vision entered her soul. Wherefore, Gabriotto being minded
to visit her on the ensuing night, she did her best endeavour
to dissuade him from coming ; but seeing that he was bent
upon it, lest he should suspect somewhat, she received him in
her garden, where, having culled roses many, white and red—
for 'twas summer—she sat herself down with him at the base
of a most fair and lucent fountain. There long and joyously
they dallied, and then Gabriotto asked her wherefore she had
that day forbade his coming. Whereupon the lady told him
her dream of the night before, and the doubt and fear which it
had engendered in her mind. Whereat Gabriotto laughed, and
said that 'twas the height of folly to put any faith in dreams,
for that they were occasioned by too much or too little food,
and were daily seen to be, one and all, things of nought, adding :
—" Were I minded to give heed to dreams, I should not be
here now, for I, too, had a dream last night, which was on this
wise :—Methought I was in a fair and pleasant wood, and there,

a-hunting, caught a she-goat as beautiful and loveable as any that ever was seen, and, as it seemed to me, whiter than snow, which in a little while grew so tame and friendly that she never stirred from my side. All the same so jealous was I lest she should leave me, that, meseemed, I had set a collar of gold around her neck, and held her by a golden chain. And presently meseemed that, while the she-goat lay at rest with her head in my lap, there came forth, I knew not whence, a grey-hound bitch, black as coal, famished, and most fearsome to look upon ; which made straight for me, and for, meseemed, I offered no resistance, set her muzzle to my breast on the left side and gnawed through to the heart, which, meseemed, she tore out to carry away with her. Whereupon ensued so sore a pain that it brake my sleep, and as I awoke I laid my hand to my side to feel if aught were amiss there ; but finding nothing I laughed at myself that I had searched. But what signifies it all ? Visions of the like sort, ay, and far more appalling, have I had in plenty, and nought whatever, great or small, has come of any of them. So let it pass, and think we how we may speed the time merrily."

What she heard immensely enhanced the already great dread which her own dream had inspired in the girl ; but, not to vex Gabriotto, she dissembled her terror as best she might. But, though she made great cheer, embracing and kissing him, and receiving his embraces and kisses, yet she felt a doubt, she knew not why, and many a time, more than her wont, she would gaze upon his face, and ever and anon her glance would stray through the garden to see if any black creature were coming from any quarter. While thus they passed the time, of a sudden Gabriotto heaved a great sigh, and embracing her, said :— " Alas ! my soul, thy succour ! for I die." And so saying, he fell down upon the grassy mead. Whereupon the girl drew him to her, and laid him on her lap, and all but wept, and said : " O sweet my lord, what is't that ails thee ? " But Gabriotto was silent, and gasping sore for breath, and bathed in sweat, in no long time departed this life.

How grievous was the distress of the girl, who loved him more than herself, you, my ladies, may well imagine. With many a tear she mourned him, and many times she vainly called him by his name ; but when, having felt his body all over, and found it cold in every part, she could no longer doubt that he was dead, knowing not what to say or do, she went, tearful and woebegone, to call the maid, to whom she had confided her

love, and shewed her the woeful calamity that had befallen
her. Piteously a while they wept together over the dead face
of Gabriotto, and then the girl said to the maid :—" Now that
God has reft him from me, I have no mind to linger in this life ;
but before I slay myself, I would we might find apt means to
preserve my honour, and the secret of our love, and to bury
the body from which the sweet soul has fled." " My daughter,"
said the maid, " speak not of slaying thyself, for so wouldst
thou lose in the other world, also, him that thou hast lost here ;
seeing that thou wouldst go to hell, whither, sure I am, his soul
is not gone, for a good youth he was ; far better were it to put
on a cheerful courage, and bethink thee to succour his soul with
thy prayers or pious works, if perchance he have need thereof
by reason of any sin that he may have committed. We can
bury him readily enough in this garden, nor will any one ever
know ; for none knows that he ever came hither ; and if thou
wilt not have it so, we can bear him forth of the garden, and
leave him there ; and on the morrow he will be found, and
carried home, and buried by his kinsfolk." The girl, heavy-
laden though she was with anguish, and still weeping, yet gave
ear to the counsels of her maid, and rejecting the former
alternative, made answer to the latter on this wise :—" Now
God forbid that a youth so dear, whom I have so loved and made
my husband, should with my consent be buried like a dog, or
left out there in the street. He has had my tears, and so far
as I may avail, he shall have the tears of his kinsfolk, and
already wot I what we must do." And forthwith she sent the
maid for a piece of silken cloth, which she had in one of her
boxes ; and when the maid returned with it, they spread it on
the ground, and laid Gabriotto's body thereon, resting the
head upon a pillow. She then closed the eyes and mouth,
shedding the while many a tear, wove for him a wreath of roses,
and strewed upon him all the roses that he and she had gathered ;
which done, she said to the maid :—" 'Tis but a short way
hence to the door of his house ; so thither we will bear him,
thou and I, thus as we have dight him, and will lay him at the
door. Day will soon dawn, and they will take him up ; and,
though 'twill be no consolation to them, I, in whose arms he
died, shall be glad of it." So saying, she burst once more into
a torrent of tears, and fell with her face upon the face of the
dead, and so long time she wept. Then, yielding at last to
the urgency of her maid, for day was drawing nigh, she arose,
drew from her finger the ring with which she had been wedded

to Gabriotto, and set it on his finger, saying with tears :—" Dear
my lord, if thy soul be witness of my tears, or if, when the spirit
is fled, aught of intelligence or sense still lurk in the body,
graciously receive the last gift of her whom in life thou didst
so dearly love." Which said, she swooned, and fell upon the
corpse ; but, coming after a while to herself, she arose ; and
then she and her maid took the cloth whereon the body lay,
and so bearing it, quitted the garden, and bent their steps
towards the dead man's house. As thus they went, it chanced
that certain of the Podestà's guard, that for some reason or
another were abroad at that hour, met them, and arrested them
with the corpse. Andreuola, to whom death was more welcome
than life, no sooner knew them for the officers of the Signory
than she frankly said :—" I know you, who you are, and that
flight would avail me nothing : I am ready to come with you
before the Signory, and to tell all there is to tell ; but let none
of you presume to touch me, so long as I obey you, or to take
away aught that is on this body, if he would not that I accuse
him." And so, none venturing to lay hand upon either her
person or the corpse, she entered the palace.

So soon as the Podestà was apprised of the affair, he arose,
had her brought into his room, and there made himself con-
versant with the circumstances : and certain physicians being
charged to inquire whether the good man had met his death
by poison or otherwise, all with one accord averred that 'twas
not by poison, but that he was choked by the bursting of an
imposthume near the heart. Which when the Podestà heard,
perceiving that the girl's guilt could but be slight, he sought
to make a pretence of giving what it was not lawful for him to
sell her, and told her that he would set her at liberty, so she
were consenting to pleasure him ; but finding that he did but
waste his words he cast aside all decency, and would have
used force. Whereupon Andreuola, kindling with scorn,
waxed exceeding brave, and defended herself with a virile
energy, and with high and contumelious words drove him
from her.

When 'twas broad day, the affair reached the ears of Messer
Negro, who, half dead with grief, hied him with not a few of his
friends to the palace ; where, having heard all that the Podestà
had to say, he required him peremptorily to give him back his
daughter. The Podestà, being minded rather to be his own
accuser, than that he should be accused by the girl of the
violence that he had meditated towards her, began by praising

her and her constancy, and in proof thereof went on to tell
what he had done ; he ended by saying, that, marking her
admirable firmness, he had fallen mightily in love with her,
and so, notwithstanding she had been wedded to a man of low
degree, he would, if 'twere agreeable to her and to her father,
Messer Negro, gladly make her his wife. While they thus
spoke, Andreuola made her appearance, and, weeping, threw
herself at her father's feet, saying :—" My father, I wot I need
not tell you the story of my presumption, and the calamity
that has befallen me, for sure I am that you have heard it and
know it ; wherefore, with all possible humility I crave your
pardon of my fault, to wit, that without your knowledge I
took for my husband him that pleased me best. And this I
crave, not that my life may be spared, but that I may die as
your daughter and not as your enemy ; " and so, weeping, she
fell at his feet. Messer Negro, now an old man, and naturally
kindly and affectionate, heard her not without tears, and weeping
raised her tenderly to her feet, saying :—" Daughter mine, I
had much liefer had it that thou hadst had a husband that
I deemed a match for thee ; and in that thou hadst taken one
that pleased thee I too had been pleased ; but thy concealing
thy choice from me is grievous to me by reason of thy distrust
of me, and yet more so, seeing that thou hast lost him before
I have known him. But as 'tis even so, to his remains be paid
the honour which, while he lived for thy contentment, I had
gladly done him as my son-in-law." Then, turning to his sons
and kinsmen, he bade them order Gabriotto's obsequies with
all pomp and honourable circumstance.

Meanwhile the young man's kinsmen and kinswomen, having
heard the news, had flocked thither, bringing with them almost
all the rest of the folk, men and women alike, that were in the
city. And so his body, resting on Andreuola's cloth, and covered
with her roses, was laid out in the middle of the courtyard, and
there was mourned not by her and his kinsfolk alone, but
publicly by well-nigh all the women of the city, and not a few
men ; and shouldered by some of the noblest of the citizens,
as it had been the remains of no plebeian but of a noble, was
borne from the public courtyard to the tomb with exceeding
great pomp.

Some days afterwards, as the Podestà continued to urge his
suit, Messer Negro would have discussed the matter with his
daughter ; but, as she would hear none of it, and he was
minded in this matter to defer to her wishes, she and her maid

entered a religious house of great repute for sanctity, where in just esteem they lived long time thereafter.

NOVEL VII

Simona loves Pasquino ; they are together in a garden ; Pasquino rubs a leaf of sage against his teeth, and dies ; Simona is arrested, and, with intent to shew the judge how Pasquino died, rubs one of the leaves of the same plant against her teeth, and likewise dies.

WHEN Pamfilo had done with his story, the king, betraying no compassion for Andreuola, glancing at Emilia, signified to her his desire that she should now continue the sequence of narration. Emilia made no demur, and thus began :—

Dear gossips, Pamfilo's story puts me upon telling you another in no wise like thereto, save in this, that as Andreuola lost her lover in a garden, so also did she of whom I am to speak, and, being arrested like Andreuola, did also deliver herself from the court, albeit 'twas not by any vigour or firmness of mind, but by a sudden death. And, as 'twas said among us a while ago, albeit Love affects the mansions of the noble, he does not, therefore, disdain the dominion of the dwellings of the poor, nay, does there at times give proof of his might no less signal than when he makes him feared of the wealthiest as a most potent lord. Which, though not fully, will in some degree appear in my story, wherewith I am minded to return to our city, from which to-day's discourse, roving from matter to matter, and one part of the world to another, has carried us so far.

Know then that no great while ago there dwelt in Florence a maid most fair, and, for her rank, debonair—she was but a poor man's daughter—whose name was Simona ; and though she must needs win with her own hands the bread she ate, and maintain herself by spinning wool ; yet was she not, therefore, of so poor a spirit, but that she dared to give harbourage in her mind to Love, who for some time had sought to gain entrance there by means of the gracious deeds and words of a young man of her own order that went about distributing wool to spin for his master, a wool-monger. Love being thus, with the pleasant image of her beloved Pasquino, admitted into her soul, mightily did she yearn, albeit she hazarded no advance, and heaved a

I—*K 845

thousand sighs fiercer than fire with every skein of yarn that
she wound upon her spindle, while she called to mind who
he was that had given her that wool to spin. Pasquino on his
part became, meanwhile, very anxious that his master's wool
should be well spun, and most particularly about that which
Simona span, as if, indeed, it and it alone was to furnish forth
the whole of the cloth. And so, what with the anxiety which
the one evinced, and the gratification that it afforded to the
other, it befell that, the one waxing unusually bold, and the
other casting off not a little of her wonted shyness and reserve,
they came to an understanding for their mutual solace ; which
proved so delightful to both, that neither waited to be bidden
by the other, but 'twas rather which should be the first to make
the overture.

While thus they sped their days in an even tenor of delight,
and ever grew more ardently enamoured of one another,
Pasquino chanced to say to Simona that he wished of all things
she would contrive how she might betake her to a garden,
whither he would bring her, that there they might be more at
their ease, and in greater security. Simona said that she was
agreeable ; and, having given her father to understand that
she was minded to go to San Gallo for the pardoning, she hied
her with one of her gossips, Lagina by name, to the garden of
which Pasquino had told her. Here she found Pasquino
awaiting her with a friend, one Puccino, otherwise Stramba ;
and Stramba and Lagina falling at once to love-making,
Pasquino and Simona left a part of the garden to them, and
withdrew to another part for their own solace.

Now there was in their part of the garden a very fine and
lovely sage-bush, at foot of which they sat them down and
made merry together a great while, and talked much of a
junketing they meant to have in the garden quite at their
ease. By and by Pasquino, turning to the great sage-bush,
plucked therefrom a leaf, and fell to rubbing his teeth and
gums therewith, saying that sage was an excellent detergent
of aught that remained upon them after a meal. Having done
so, he returned to the topic of the junketing of which he had
spoken before. But he had not pursued it far before his
countenance entirely changed, and forthwith he lost sight and
speech, and shortly after died. Whereupon Simona fell a-
weeping and shrieking and calling Stramba and Lagina ; who,
notwithstanding they came up with all speed, found Pasquino
not only dead but already swollen from head to foot, and

covered with black spots both on the face and on the body ;
whereupon Stramba broke forth with :—" Ah ! wicked woman !
thou hast poisoned him ; " and made such a din that 'twas
heard by not a few that dwelt hard by the garden ; who also
hasted to the spot, and seeing Pasquino dead and swollen, and
hearing Stramba bewail himself and accuse Simona of having
maliciously poisoned him, while she, all but beside herself for
grief to be thus suddenly bereft of her lover, knew not how to
defend herself, did all with one accord surmise that 'twas even
as Stramba said. Wherefore they laid hands on her, and
brought her, still weeping bitterly, to the palace of the Podestà :
where at the instant suit of Stramba, backed by Atticciato and
Malagevole, two other newly-arrived friends of Pasquino, a
judge forthwith addressed himself to question her of the matter ;
and being unable to discover that she had used any wicked
practice, or was guilty, he resolved to take her with him and
go see the corpse, and the place, and the manner of the death,
as she had recounted it to him ; for by her words he could not
well understand it. So, taking care that there should be no
disturbance, he had her brought to the place where Pasquino's
corpse lay swollen like a tun, whither he himself presently
came, and marvelling as he examined the corpse, asked her how
the death had come about. Whereupon, standing by the sage-
bush, she told him all that had happened, and that he might
perfectly apprehend the occasion of the death, she did as
Pasquino had done, plucked one of the leaves from the bush,
and rubbed her teeth with it. Whereupon Stramba and
Atticciato, and the rest of the friends and comrades of Pasquino,
making in the presence of the judge open mock of what she
did, as an idle and vain thing, and being more than ever instant
to affirm her guilt, and to demand the fire as the sole condign
penalty, the poor creature, that, between grief for her lost
lover and dread of the doom demanded by Stramba, stood
mute and helpless, was stricken no less suddenly, and in the
same manner, and for the same cause (to wit, that she had rubbed
her teeth with the sage leaf) as Pasquino, to the no small
amazement of all that were present.

Oh ! happy souls for whom one and the same day was the
term of ardent love and earthly life ! Happier still, if to the
same bourn ye fared ! Ay, and even yet more happy, if love
there be in the other world, and there, even as here, ye love !
But happiest above all Simona, so far as we, whom she has left
behind, may judge, in that Fortune brooked not that the

witness of Stramba, Atticciato and Malagevole, carders, per-
chance, or yet viler fellows, should bear down her innocence,
but found a more seemly issue, and, appointing her a like lot
with her lover, gave her at once to clear herself from their foul
accusation, and to follow whither the soul, that she so loved,
of her Pasquino had preceded her !

The judge, and all else that witnessed the event, remained
long time in a sort of stupefaction, knowing not what to say of
it ; but at length recovering his wits, the judge said :—" 'Twould
seem that this sage is poisonous, which the sage is not used to
be. Let it be cut down to the roots and burned, lest another
suffer by it in like sort." Which the gardener proceeding to
do in the judge's presence, no sooner had he brought the great
bush down, than the cause of the deaths of the two lovers plainly
appeared : for underneath it was a toad of prodigious
dimensions, from whose venomous breath, as they conjectured,
the whole of the bush had contracted a poisonous quality.
Around which toad, none venturing to approach it, they set
a stout ring-fence of faggots, and burned it together with the
sage. So ended Master Judge's inquest on the death of hapless
Pasquino, who with his Simona, swollen as they were, were
buried by Stramba, Atticciato, Guccio Imbratta, and Malagevole
in the church of San Paolo, of which, as it so happened, they
were parishioners.

NOVEL VIII

*Girolamo loves Salvestra : yielding to his mother's prayers he
goes to Paris ; he returns to find Salvestra married ; he
enters her house by stealth, lays himself by her side, and
dies ; he is borne to the church, where Salvestra lays herself
by his side, and dies.*

WHEN Emilia's story was done, Neifile at a word from the king
thus began :—Some there are, noble ladies, who, methinks,
deem themselves to be wiser than the rest of the world, and are
in fact less so ; and by consequence presume to measure their
wit against not only the counsels of men but the nature of
things ; which presumption has from time to time been the
occasion of most grievous mishaps ; but nought of good was
ever seen to betide thereof. And as there is nought in nature
that brooks to be schooled or thwarted so ill as love, the quality

of which is such that it is more likely to die out of its own accord than to be done away of set purpose, I am minded to tell you a story of a lady, who, while she sought to be more wise than became her, and than she was, and indeed than the nature of the matter, wherein she studied to shew her wisdom, allowed, thinking to unseat Love from the heart that he had occupied, and wherein perchance the stars had established him, did in the end banish at one and the same time Love and life from the frame of her son.

Know, then, that, as 'tis related by them of old time, there was once in our city a very great and wealthy merchant, Leonardo Sighieri by name, who had by his lady a son named Girolamo, after whose birth he departed this life, leaving his affairs in meet and due order ; and well and faithfully were they afterwards administered in the interest of the boy by his mother and guardians. As he grew up, consorting more frequently with the neighbours' children than any others of the quarter, he made friends with a girl of his own age that was the daughter of a tailor ; and in course of time this friendship ripened into a love so great and vehement, that Girolamo was ever ill at ease when he saw her not ; nor was her love for him a whit less strong than his for her. Which his mother perceiving would not seldom chide him therefor and chastise him. And as Girolamo could not give it up, she confided her distress to his guardians, speaking—for by reason of her boy's great wealth she thought to make, as it were, an orange tree out of a bramble—on this wise :—" This boy of ours, who is now scarce fourteen years old, is so in love with a daughter of one of our neighbours, a tailor—Salvestra is the girl's name— that, if we part them not, he will, peradventure, none else witting, take her to wife some day, and I shall never be happy again ; or, if he see her married to another, he will pine away ; to prevent which, methinks, you would do well to send him away to distant parts on the affairs of the shop ; for so, being out of sight she will come at length to be out of mind, and then we can give him some well-born girl to wife." Whereto the guardians answered, that 'twas well said, and that it should be so done to the best of their power : so they called the boy into the shop, and one of them began talking to him very affectionately on this wise :—" My son, thou art now almost grown up ; 'twere well thou shouldst now begin to learn something for thyself of thy own affairs : wherefore we should be very well pleased if thou wert to go stay at Paris a while, where

thou wilt see how we trade with not a little of thy wealth,
besides which thou wilt there become a much better, finer,
and more complete gentleman than thou couldst here, and when
thou hast seen the lords and barons and seigneurs that are there
in plenty, and hast acquired their manners, thou canst return
hither." The boy listened attentively, and then answered
shortly that he would have none of it, for he supposed he might
remain at Florence as well as another. Whereupon the
worthy men plied him with fresh argument, but were unable
to elicit other answer from him, and told his mother so.
Whereat she was mightily incensed, and gave him a great
scolding, not for his refusing to go to Paris, but for his love ;
which done, she plied him with soft, wheedling words, and
endearing expressions and gentle entreaties that he would be
pleased to do as his guardians would have him ; whereby at
length she prevailed so far, that he consented to go to Paris
for a year and no more ; and so 'twas arranged. To Paris
accordingly our ardent lover went, and there under one pretext
or another was kept for two years. He returned more in love
than ever, to find his Salvestra married to a good youth that
was a tent-maker ; whereat his mortification knew no bounds.
But, seeing that what must be must be, he sought to compose
his mind ; and, having got to know where she lived, he took
to crossing her path, according to the wont of young men in
love, thinking that she could no more have forgotten him than
he her. 'Twas otherwise, however ; she remembered him no
more than if she had never seen him ; or, if she had any recollec-
tion of him, she dissembled it : whereof the young man was
very soon ware, to his extreme sorrow. Nevertheless he did
all that he could to recall himself to her mind ; but, as thereby
he seemed to be nothing advantaged, he made up his mind,
though he should die for it, to speak to her himself. So,
being instructed as to her house by a neighbour, he entered it
privily one evening when she and her husband were gone to
spend the earlier hours with some neighbours, and hid himself
in her room behind some tent-cloths that were stretched there,
and waited till they were come back, and gone to bed, and he
knew the husband to be asleep. Whereupon he got him to
the place where he had seen Salvestra lie down, and said as he
gently laid his hand upon her bosom :—" O my soul, art thou
yet asleep ? " The girl was awake, and was on the point of
uttering a cry, when he forestalled her, saying :—" Hush ! for
God's sake. I am thy Girolamo." Whereupon she, trembling

in every limb :—" Nay, but for God's sake, Girolamo, begone :
'tis past, the time of our childhood, when our love was excusable.
Thou seest I am married ; wherefore 'tis no longer seemly that
I should care for any other man than my husband, and so by
the one God, I pray thee, begone ; for, if my husband were to
know that thou art here, the least evil that could ensue would
be that I should never more be able to live with him in peace
or comfort, whereas, having his love, I now pass my days with
him in tranquil happiness." Which speech caused the young
man grievous distress ; but 'twas in vain that he reminded her
of the past, and of his love that distance had not impaired,
and therewith mingled many a prayer and the mightiest pro-
testations. Wherefore, yearning for death, he besought her
at last that she would suffer him to lie a while beside her till
he got some heat, for he was chilled through and through,
waiting for her, and promised her that he would say never a
word to her, nor touch her, and that as soon as he was a little
warmed he would go away. On which terms Salvestra, being
not without pity for him, granted his request. So the young
man lay down beside her, and touched her not ; but, gathering
up into one thought the love he had so long borne her, the
harshness with which she now requited it, and his ruined hopes,
resolved to live no longer, and in a convulsion, without a word,
and with fists clenched, expired by her side.

After a while the girl, marvelling at his continence, and fearing
lest her husband should awake, broke silence, saying :—" Nay,
but, Girolamo, why goest thou not ?" But, receiving no
answer, she supposed that he slept. Wherefore, reaching forth
her hand to arouse him she touched him and found him to her
great surprise cold as ice ; and touching him again and again
somewhat rudely, and still finding that he did not stir, she
knew that he was dead. Her grief was boundless, and 'twas
long before she could bethink her how to act. But at last she
resolved to sound her husband's mind as to what should be
done in such a case without disclosing that 'twas his own.
So she awakened him, and told him how he was then bested,
as if it were the affair of another, and then asked him, if such a
thing happened to her, what course he would take. The good
man answered that he should deem it best to take the dead
man privily home, and there leave him, bearing no grudge
against the lady, who seemed to have done no wrong. " And
even so," said his wife, " it is for us to do ; " and taking his
hand, she laid it on the corpse. Whereat he started up in

consternation, and struck a light, and without further parley with his wife, clapped the dead man's clothes upon him, and forthwith (confident in his own innocence) raised him on his shoulders, and bore him to the door of his house, where he set him down and left him.

Day came, and the dead man being found before his own door, there was a great stir made, particularly by his mother ; the body was examined with all care from head to foot, and, no wound or trace of violence being found on it, the physicians were on the whole of opinion that, as the fact was, the man had died of grief. So the corpse was borne to a church, and thither came the sorrowing mother and other ladies, her kins-women and neighbours, and began to wail and mourn over it without restraint after our Florentine fashion. And when the wailing had reached its height, the good man, in whose house the death had occurred, said to Salvestra :—" Go wrap a mantle about thy head, and hie thee to the church, whither Girolamo has been taken, and go about among the women and list what they say of this matter, and I will do the like among the men, that we may hear if aught be said to our disadvantage." The girl assented, for with tardy tenderness she now yearned to look on him dead, whom living she would not solace with a single kiss, and so to the church she went. Ah ! how marvellous to whoso ponders it, is the might of Love, and how unsearchable his ways ! That heart, which, while Fortune smiled on Girolamo, had remained sealed to him, opened to him now that he was fordone, and, kindling anew with all its old flame, melted with such compassion that no sooner saw she his dead face, as there she stood wrapped in her mantle, than, edging her way forward through the crowd of women, she stayed not till she was beside the corpse ; and there, uttering a piercing shriek, she threw herself upon the dead youth, and as her face met his, and before she might drench it with her tears, grief that had reft life from him had even so reft it from her.

The women strove to comfort her, and bade her raise herself a little, for as yet they knew her not ; then, as she did not arise, they would have helped her, but found her stiff and stark, and so, raising her up, they in one and the same moment saw her to be Salvestra and dead. Whereat all the women that were there, overborne by a redoubled pity, broke forth in wailing new and louder far than before. From the church the bruit spread itself among the men, and reached the ears of Salvestra's husband, who, deaf to all that offered comfort or consolation, wept a long while ; after which he told to not a few that were there what had passed in the night between the youth and his wife ; and so 'twas known of all how they came to die, to the common sorrow of all.   So they took the dead girl, and arrayed her as they are wont to array the dead, and laid her on the same bed beside the youth, and long time they mourned her : then were they both buried in the same tomb, and thus those, whom love had not been able to wed in life, were wedded by death in indissoluble union.

NOVEL IX

Sieur Guillaume de Roussillon slays his wife's paramour, Sieur Guillaume de Cabestaing, and gives her his heart to eat. She, coming to wit thereof, throws herself from a high window to the ground, and dies, and is buried with her lover.

NEIFILE'S story, which had not failed to move her gossips to no little pity, being ended, none now remained to speak but the king and Dioneo, whose privilege the king was minded not to infringe : wherefore he thus began :—I propose, compassionate my ladies, to tell you a story, which, seeing that you so commiserate ill-starred loves, may claim no less a share of your pity than the last, inasmuch as they were greater folk of whom I shall speak, and that which befell them was more direful.

You are to know, then, that, as the Provençals relate, there were once in Provence two noble knights, each having castles and vassals under him, the one yclept Sieur Guillaume de Roussillon, and the other Sieur Guillaume de Cabestaing ; [1] and being both most doughty warriors, they were as brothers, and went ever together, and bearing the same device, to tournament or joust, or other passage of arms.   And, albeit each dwelt in his own castle, and the castles were ten good miles apart, it nevertheless came to pass that, Sieur Guillaume de Roussillon having a most lovely lady, and amorous withal, to wife, Sieur Guillaume de Cabestaing, for all they were such friends and comrades, became inordinately enamoured of the lady, who, by this, that, and the other sign that he gave, discovered his passion, and knowing him for a most complete knight, was flattered, and

---

[1] Boccaccio writes Guardastagno, but the troubadour, Cabestaing, or Cabestany, is the hero of the story.

returned it, insomuch that she yearned and burned for him
above all else in the world, and waited only till he should make
his suit to her, as before long he did ; and so they met from
time to time, and great was their love. Which intercourse they
ordered with so little discretion that 'twas discovered by the
husband, who was very wroth, insomuch that the great love
which he bore to Cabestaing was changed into mortal enmity ;
and, dissembling it better than the lovers their love, he made
his mind up to kill Cabestaing. Now it came to pass that,
while Roussillon was in this frame, a great tourney was pro-
claimed in France, whereof Roussillon forthwith sent word to
Cabestaing, and bade him to his castle, so he were minded to
come, that there they might discuss whether (or no) to go to
the tourney, and how. Cabestaing was overjoyed, and made
answer that he would come to sup with him next day without
fail. Which message being delivered, Roussillon wist that the
time was come to slay Cabestaing. So next day he armed
himself, and, attended by a few servants, took horse, and about
a mile from his castle lay in ambush in a wood through which
Cabestaing must needs pass. He waited some time, and then
he saw Cabestaing approach unarmed with two servants behind,
also unarmed, for he was without thought of peril on Roussillon's
part. So Cabestaing came on to the place of Roussillon's
choice, and then, fell and vengeful, Roussillon leapt forth
lance in hand, and fell upon him, exclaiming :—" Thou art a
dead man ! " and the words were no sooner spoken than the
lance was through Cabestaing's breast. Powerless either to
defend himself or even utter a cry, Cabestaing fell to the ground,
and soon expired. His servants waited not to see who had
done the deed, but turned their horses' heads and fled with all
speed to their lord's castle. Roussillon dismounted, opened
Cabestaing's breast with a knife, and took out the heart with
his own hands, wrapped it up in a banderole, and gave it to
one of his servants to carry : he then bade none make bold to
breathe a word of the affair, mounted his horse and rode back—
'twas now night—to his castle. The lady, who had been told
that Cabestaing was to come to supper that evening, and was
all impatience till he should come, was greatly surprised to see
her husband arrive without him. Wherefore :—" How is this,
my lord ? " said she. " Why tarries Cabestaing ? " " Madam,"
answered her husband, " I have tidings from him that he can-
not be here until to-morrow : " whereat the lady was somewhat
disconcerted.

Having dismounted, Roussillon called the cook, and said to him :—"Here is a boar's heart ; take it, and make thereof the daintiest and most delicious dish thou canst, and when I am set at table serve it in a silver porringer." So the cook took the heart, and expended all his skill and pains upon it, mincing it and mixing with it plenty of good seasoning, and made thereof an excellent ragout ; and in due time Sieur Guillaume and his lady sat them down to table. The meat was served, but Sieur Guillaume, his mind engrossed with his crime, ate but little. The cook set the ragout before him, but he, feigning that he cared to eat no more that evening, had it passed on to the lady, and highly commended it. The lady, nothing loath, took some of it, and found it so good that she ended by eating the whole. Whereupon :—"Madam," quoth the knight, "how liked you this dish ?" "In good faith, my lord," replied the lady, "not a little." "So help me, God," returned the knight, "I dare be sworn you did ; 'tis no wonder that you should enjoy that dead, which living you enjoyed more than aught else in the world." For a while the lady was silent ; then :—"How say you ?" said she ; "what is this you have caused me to eat ?" "That which you have eaten," replied the knight, "was in good sooth the heart of Sieur Guillaume de Cabestaing, whom you, disloyal woman that you are, did so much love : for assurance whereof I tell you that but a short while before I came back, I plucked it from his breast with my own hands." It boots not to ask if the lady was sorrow-stricken to receive such tidings of her best beloved. But after a while she said :—"'Twas the deed of a disloyal and recreant knight ; for if I, unconstrained by him, made him lord of my love, and thereby did you wrong, 'twas I, not he, should have borne the penalty. But God forbid that fare of such high excellence as the heart of a knight so true and courteous as Sieur Guillaume de Cabestaing be followed by aught else." So saying she started to her feet, and stepping back to a window that was behind her, without a moment's hesitation let herself drop backwards therefrom. The window was at a great height from the ground, so that the lady was not only killed by the fall, but almost reduced to atoms. Stunned and conscience-stricken by the spectacle, and fearing the vengeance of the country folk, and the Count of Provence, Sieur Guillaume had his horses saddled and rode away. On the morrow the whole countryside knew how the affair had come about ; wherefore folk from both of the castles took the two bodies, and bore them with grief and lamentation exceeding great to the church in the lady's castle, and laid them in the same tomb, and caused verses to be inscribed thereon signifying who they were that were there interred, and the manner and occasion of their death.

NOVEL X

The wife of a leech, deeming her lover, who has taken an opiate, to be dead, puts him in a chest, which, with him therein, two usurers carry off to their house. He comes to himself, and is taken for a thief; but, the lady's maid giving the Signory to understand that she had put him in the chest which the usurers stole, he escapes the gallows, and the usurers are mulcted in moneys for the theft of the chest.

Now that the king had told his tale, it only remained for Dioneo to do his part, which he witting, and being thereto bidden by the king, thus began :—Sore have I—to say nought of you, my ladies—been of eyne and heart to hear the woeful histories of ill-starred love, insomuch that I have desired of all things that they might have an end. Wherefore, now that, thank God, ended they are, unless indeed I were minded, which God forbid, to add to such pernicious stuff a supplement of the like evil quality, no such dolorous theme do I purpose to ensue, but to make a fresh start with somewhat of a better and more cheerful sort, which perchance may serve to suggest to-morrow's argument.

You are to know, then, fairest my damsels, that 'tis not long since there dwelt at Salerno a leech most eminent in surgery, his name, Master Mazzeo della Montagna, who in his extreme old age took to wife a fair damsel of the same city, whom he kept in nobler and richer array of dresses and jewels, and all other finery that the sex affects, than any other lady in Salerno. Howbeit, she was none too warm most of her time, being ill covered abed by the doctor ; who gave her to understand— even as Messer Ricciardo di Chinzica, of whom we spoke a while since, taught his lady the feasts—that for once that a man lay with a woman he needed I know not how many days to recover, and the like nonsense : whereby she lived as ill content as might be ; and, lacking neither sense nor spirit, she determined to economize at home, and taking to the street, to live at others'

expense. So, having passed in review divers young men, she
at last found one that was to her mind, on whom she set all her
heart and hopes of happiness. Which the gallant perceiving
was mightily flattered, and in like manner gave her all his love.
Ruggieri da Jeroli—such was the gallant's name—was of noble
birth, but of life and conversation so evil and reprehensible that
kinsman or friend he had none left that wished him well, or
cared to see him ; and all Salerno knew him for a common thief
and rogue of the vilest character. Whereof the lady took little
heed, having a mind to him for another reason ; and so with
the help of her maid she arranged a meeting with him. But
after they had solaced themselves a while, the lady began to
censure his past life, and to implore him for love of her to
depart from such evil ways ; and to afford him the means
thereto, she from time to time furnished him with money.
While thus with all discretion they continued their intercourse,
it chanced that a man halt of one of his legs was placed under
the leech's care. The leech saw what was amiss with him, and
told his kinsfolk, that unless a gangrened bone that he had in
his leg were taken out, he must die, or have the whole leg ampu-
tated ; that if the bone were removed he might recover ; but
that otherwise he would not answer for his life : whereupon the
relatives assented that the bone should be removed, and left
the patient in the hands of the leech ; who, deeming that by
reason of the pain 'twas not possible for him to endure the
treatment without an opiate, caused to be distilled in the
morning a certain water of his own concoction, whereby the
patient, drinking it, might be ensured sleep during such time as
he deemed the operation, which he meant to perform about
vespers, would occupy. In the meantime he had the water
brought into his house, and set it in the window of his room,
telling no one what it was. But when the vesper hour was
come, and the leech was about to visit his patient, a messenger
arrived from some very great friends of his at Amalfi, bearing
tidings of a great riot there had been there, in which not a few
had been wounded, and bidding him on no account omit to hie
him thither forthwith. Wherefore the leech put off the treat-
ment of the leg to the morrow, and took boat to Amalfi ; and
the lady, knowing that he would not return home that night,
did as she was wont in such a case, to wit, brought Ruggieri in
privily, and locked him in her chamber until certain other folk
that were in the house were gone to sleep. Ruggieri, then,
being thus in the chamber, awaiting the lady, and having—

whether it were that he had had a fatiguing day, or eaten something salt, or, perchance, that 'twas his habit of body—a mighty thirst, glancing at the window, caught sight of the bottle containing the water which the leech had prepared for the patient, and taking it to be drinking water, set it to his lips and drank it all, and in no long time fell into a deep sleep.

So soon as she was able the lady hied her to the room, and there finding Ruggieri asleep, touched him and softly told him to get up : to no purpose, however ; he neither answered nor stirred a limb. Wherefore the lady, rather losing patience, applied somewhat more force, and gave him a push, saying :—"Get up, sleepy-head ; if thou hadst a mind to sleep, thou shouldst have gone home, and not have come hither." Thus pushed Ruggieri fell down from a box on which he lay, and, falling, shewed no more sign of animation than if he had been a corpse. The lady, now somewhat alarmed, essayed to lift him, and shook him roughly, and took him by the nose, and pulled him by the beard ; again to no purpose : he had tethered his ass to a stout pin. So the lady began to fear he must be dead : however, she went on to pinch him shrewdly, and singe him with the flame of a candle ; but when these methods also failed she, being, for all she was a leech's wife, no leech herself, believed for sure that he was dead ; and as there was nought in the world that she loved so much, it boots not to ask if she was sore distressed ; wherefore silently, for she dared not lament aloud, she began to weep over him and bewail such a misadventure. But, after a while, fearing lest her loss should not be without a sequel of shame, she bethought her that she must contrive without delay to get the body out of the house ; and standing in need of another's advice, she quietly summoned her maid, shewed her the mishap that had befallen her, and craved her counsel. Whereat the maid marvelled not a little ; and she too fell to pulling Ruggieri this way and that, and pinching him, and, as she found no sign of life in him, concurred with her mistress that he was verily dead, and advised her to remove him from the house. "And where," said the lady, "shall we put him, that to-morrow, when he is discovered, it be not suspected that 'twas hence he was carried ? " "Madam," answered the maid, "late last evening I marked in front of our neighbour the carpenter's shop a chest, not too large, which, if he have not put it back in the house, will come in very handy for our purpose, for we will put him inside, and give him two or three cuts with a knife, and so leave him. When he is found,

I know not why it should be thought that 'twas from this house rather than from any other that he was put there ; nay, as he was an evil-liver, 'twill more likely be supposed, that, as he hied him on some evil errand, some enemy slew him, and then put him in the chest." The lady said there was nought in the world she might so ill brook as that Ruggieri should receive any wound ; but with that exception she approved her maid's proposal, and sent her to see if the chest were still where she had seen it. The maid, returning, reported that there it was, and, being young and strong, got Ruggieri, with the lady's help, upon her shoulders ; and so the lady, going before to espy if any folk came that way, and the maid following, they came to the chest, and having laid Ruggieri therein, closed it and left him there.

Now a few days before, two young men, that were usurers, had taken up their quarters in a house a little further on : they had seen the chest during the day, and being short of furniture, and having a mind to make great gain with little expenditure, they had resolved that, if it were still there at night, they would take it home with them. So at midnight forth they hied them, and finding the chest, were at no pains to examine it closely, but forthwith, though it seemed somewhat heavy, bore it off to their house, and set it down beside a room in which their women slept ; and without being at pains to adjust it too securely they left it there for the time, and went to bed.

Towards matins Ruggieri, having had a long sleep and digested the draught and exhausted its efficacy, awoke, but albeit his slumber was broken, and his senses had recovered their powers, yet his brain remained in a sort of torpor which kept him bemused for some days ; and when he opened his eyes and saw nothing, and stretched his hands hither and thither and found himself in the chest, it was with difficulty that he collected his thoughts. "How is this ? " he said to himself. " Where am I ? Do I sleep or wake ? I remember coming this evening to my lady's chamber ; and now it seems I am in a chest. What means it ? Can the leech have returned, or somewhat else have happened that caused the lady, while I slept, to hide me here ? That was it, I suppose. Without a doubt it must have been so." And having come to this conclusion, he composed himself to listen, if haply he might hear something, and being somewhat ill at ease in the chest, which was none too large, and the side on which he lay paining him, he must needs turn over to the other, and did so with such adroitness that,

bringing his loins smartly against one of the sides of the chest,
which was set on an uneven floor, he caused it to tilt and then
fall ; and such was the noise that it made as it fell that the
women that slept there awoke, albeit for fear they kept silence.
Ruggieri was not a little disconcerted by the fall, but, finding
that thereby the chest was come open, he judged that, happen
what might, he would be better out of it than in it ; and not
knowing where he was, and being otherwise at his wits' end,
he began to grope about the house, if haply he might find a
stair or door whereby he might take himself off.   Hearing him
thus groping his way, the alarmed women gave tongue with :—
" Who is there ? "   Ruggieri, not knowing the voice, made no
answer : wherefore the women fell to calling the two young
men, who, having had a long day, were fast asleep, and heard
nought of what went on.   Which served to increase the fright
of the women, who rose and got them to divers windows, and
raised the cry :—" Take thief, take thief ! "   At which sum-
mons there came running from divers quarters not a few of the
neighbours, who got into the house by the roof or otherwise as
each best might : likewise the young men, aroused by the din,
got up ; and, Ruggieri being now all but beside himself for
sheer amazement, and knowing not whither to turn him to
escape them, they took him and delivered him to the officers
of the Governor of the city, who, hearing the uproar, had hasted
to the spot.   And so he was brought before the Governor, who,
knowing him to be held of all a most arrant evil-doer, put him
forthwith to the torture, and, upon his confessing that he had
entered the house of the usurers with intent to rob, was minded
to make short work of it, and have him hanged by the neck.

In the morning 'twas bruited throughout all Salerno that
Ruggieri had been taken a-thieving in the house of the usurers.
Whereat the lady and her maid were all amazement and
bewilderment, insomuch that they were within an ace of per-
suading themselves that what they had done the night before
they had not done, but had only dreamed it ; besides which,
the peril in which Ruggieri stood caused the lady such anxiety
as brought her to the verge of madness.   Shortly after half
tierce the leech, being returned from Amalfi, and minded now
to treat his patient, called for his water, and finding the bottle
empty made a great commotion, protesting that nought in his
house could be let alone.   The lady, having other cause of annoy,
lost temper, and said :—" What would you say, Master, of an
important matter, when you raise such a din because a bottle

of water has been upset ?   Is there never another to be found
in the world ? "   " Madam," replied the leech, " thou takest
this to have been mere water : 'twas no such thing, but an
artificial water of a soporiferous virtue ; " and he told her for
what purpose he had made it.   Which the lady no sooner heard,
than, guessing that Ruggieri had drunk it, and so had seemed
to them to be dead, she said :—" Master, we knew it not ; where-
fore make you another."   And so the leech, seeing that there
was no help for it, had another made.   Not long after, the maid
who by the lady's command had gone to find out what folk
said of Ruggieri, returned, saying :—" Madam, of Ruggieri they
say nought but evil, nor, by what I have been able to discover,
has he friend or kinsman that has or will come to his aid ; and
'tis held for certain that to-morrow the Stadic [1] will have him
hanged.   Besides which, I have that to tell you which will
surprise you ; for, methinks, I have found out how he came
into the usurers' house.   List, then, how it was : you know the
carpenter in front of whose shop stood the chest we put Ruggieri
into : he had to-day the most violent altercation in the world
with one to whom it would seem the chest belongs, by whom
he was required to make good the value of the chest, to which
he made answer that he had not sold it, but that it had been
stolen from him in the night.   ' Not so,' said the other ; ' thou
soldst it to the two young usurers, as they themselves told me
last night, when I saw it in their house at the time Ruggieri
was taken.'   ' They lie,' replied the carpenter.   ' I never sold
it them, but they must have stolen it from me last night ; go
we to them.'   So with one accord off they went to the usurers'
house, and I came back here.   And so, you see, I make out that
'twas on such wise that Ruggieri was brought where he was
found ; but how he came to life again, I am at a loss to con-
jecture."   The lady now understood exactly how things were,
and accordingly told the maid what she had learned from the
leech, and besought her to aid her to get Ruggieri off, for so
she might, if she would, and at the same time preserve her
honour.   "Madam," said the maid, " do but shew me how ;
and glad shall I be to do just as you wish."   Whereupon the
lady, to whom necessity taught invention, formed her plan on
the spur of the moment, and expounded it in detail to the maid ;
who (as the first step) hied her to the leech, and, weeping, thus
addressed him :—" Sir, it behoves me to ask your pardon of a
great wrong that I have done you."   " And what may that be ? "

[1] The Neapolitan term for the chief of police.

inquired the leech. " Sir," said the maid, who ceased not to
weep, " you know what manner of man is Ruggieri da Jeroli.
Now he took a fancy to me, and partly for fear, partly for love,
I this year agreed to be his mistress ; and knowing yestereve
that you were from home, he coaxed me into bringing him into
your house to sleep with me in my room. Now he was athirst,
and I, having no mind to be seen by your lady, who was in the
hall, and knowing not whither I might sooner betake me for
wine or water, bethought me that I had seen a bottle of water
in your room, and ran and fetched it, and gave it him to drink,
and then put the bottle back in the place whence I had taken it ;
touching which I find that you have made a great stir in the
house. Verily I confess that I did wrong ; but who is there
that does not wrong sometimes ? Sorry indeed am I to have
so done, but 'tis not for such a cause and that which ensued
thereon that Ruggieri should lose his life. Wherefore, I do
most earnestly beseech you, pardon me, and suffer me to go
help him as best I may be able." Wroth though he was at
what he heard, the leech replied in a bantering tone :—" Thy
pardon thou hast by thine own deed ; for, whereas thou didst
last night think to have with thee a gallant that would
thoroughly dust thy pelisse for thee, he was but a sleepy-head ;
wherefore get thee gone, and do what thou mayst for the
deliverance of thy lover, and for the future look thou bring him
not into the house ; else I will pay thee for that turn and this
to boot." The maid, deeming that she had come off well in
the first brush, hied her with all speed to the prison where
Ruggieri lay, and by her cajoleries prevailed upon the warders
to let her speak with him ; and having told him how he must
answer the Stadic if he would get off, she succeeded in obtaining
preaudience of the Stadic ; who, seeing that the baggage was
lusty and mettlesome, was minded before he heard her to grapple
her with the hook, to which she was by no means averse, knowing
that such a preliminary would secure her a better hearing.
When she had undergone the operation and was risen :—" Sir,"
said she, " you have here Ruggieri da Jeroli, apprehended on a
charge of theft ; which charge is false." Whereupon she told
him the whole story from beginning to end, how she, being
Ruggieri's mistress, had brought him into the leech's house and
had given him the opiate, not knowing it for such, and taking
him to be dead, had put him in the chest ; and then recounting
what she had heard pass between the carpenter and the owner
of the chest, she shewed him how Ruggieri came into the house

of the usurers. Seeing that 'twas easy enough to find out
whether the story were true, the Stadic began by questioning
the leech as to the water, and found that 'twas as she had said :
he then summoned the carpenter, the owner of the chest and
the usurers, and after much further parley ascertained that the
usurers had stolen the chest during the night, and brought it
into their house : finally he sent for Ruggieri, and asked him
where he had lodged that night, to which Ruggieri answered
that where he had lodged he knew not, but he well remembered
going to pass the night with Master Mazzeo's maid, in whose
room he had drunk some water by reason of a great thirst that
he had ; but what happened to him afterwards, except that,
when he awoke, he found himself in a chest in the house of the
usurers, he knew not. All which matters the Stadic heard with
great interest, and caused the maid and Ruggieri and the
carpenter and the usurers to rehearse them several times. In
the end, seeing that Ruggieri was innocent, he released him,
and mulcted the usurers in fifteen ounces for the theft of the
chest. How glad Ruggieri was thus to escape, it boots not to
ask ; and glad beyond measure was his lady. And so, many a
time did they laugh and make merry together over the affair
she and he and the dear maid that had proposed to give him
a taste of the knife ; and remaining constant in their love,
they had ever better and better solace thereof. The like
whereof befall me, sans the being put in the chest.

Heartsore as the gentle ladies had been made by the preceding
stories, this last of Dioneo provoked them to such merriment,
more especially the passage about the Stadic and the hook,
that they lacked not relief of the piteous mood engendered by
the others. But the king observing that the sun was now taking
a yellowish tinge, and that the end of his sovereignty was come,
in terms most courtly made his excuse to the fair ladies, that
he had made so direful a theme as lovers' infelicity the topic
of their discourse ; after which, he rose, took the laurel wreath
from his head, and, while the ladies watched to see to whom he
would give it, set it graciously upon the blond head of Fiam-
metta, saying :—" Herewith I crown thee, as deeming that
thou, better than any other, wilt know how to make to-morrow
console our fair companions for the rude trials of to-day."
Fiammetta, whose wavy tresses fell in a flood of gold over her
white and delicate shoulders, whose softly rounded face was all
radiant with the very tints of the white lily blended with the
red of the rose, who carried two eyes in her head that matched

those of a peregrine falcon, while her tiny sweet mouth shewed
a pair of lips that shone as rubies, replied with a smile :—" And
gladly take I the wreath, Filostrato, and that thou mayst more
truly understand what thou hast done, 'tis my present will and
pleasure that each make ready to discourse to-morrow of good
fortune befalling lovers after divers direful or disastrous adven-
tures." The theme propounded was approved by all ; where-
upon the queen called the seneschal, and having made with him
all meet arrangements, rose and gaily dismissed all the company
until the supper hour ; wherefore, some straying about the
garden, the beauties of which were not such as soon to pall,
others bending their steps towards the mills that were grinding
without, each, as and where it seemed best, they took meanwhile
their several pleasures. The supper hour come, they all gath-
ered, in their wonted order, by the fair fountain, and in the
gayest of spirits and well served they supped. Then rising they
addressed them, as was their wont, to dance and song, and while
Filomena led the dance :—" Filostrato," said the queen, " being
minded to follow in the footsteps of our predecessors, and that,
as by their, so by our command a song be sung ; and well
witting that thy songs are even as thy stories, to the end that
no day but this be vexed with thy misfortunes, we ordain that
thou give us one of them, whichever thou mayst prefer."
Filostrato answered that he would gladly do so ; and without
delay began to sing on this wise :—

Full well my tears attest,
   O traitor Love, with what just cause the heart,
   With which thou once hast broken faith, doth smart.

Love, when thou first didst in my heart enshrine
   Her for whom still I sigh, alas ! in vain,
   Nor any hope do know,
   A damsel so complete thou didst me shew,
   That light as air I counted every pain,
   Wherewith behest of thine
   Condemned my soul to pine.
   Ah ! but I gravely erred ; the which to know
   Too late, alas ! doth but enhance my woe.

The cheat I knew not ere she did me leave,
   She, she, in whom alone my hopes were placed :
   For 'twas when I did most
   Flatter myself with hope, and proudly boast
   Myself her vassal lowliest and most graced,
   Nor thought Love might bereave,
   Nor dreamed he e'er might grieve,
   'Twas then I found that she another's worth
   Into her heart had ta'en, and me cast forth.

A plant of pain, alas ! my heart did bear,
  What time my hapless self cast forth I knew ;
And there it doth remain ;
And day and hour I curse and curse again,
When first that front of love shone on my view,
  That front so queenly fair,
  And bright beyond compare !
Wherefore at once my faith, my hope, my fire,
My soul doth imprecate, ere she expire.

My lord, thou knowest how comfortless my woe,
  Thou, Love, my lord, whom thus I supplicate
With many a piteous moan,
Telling thee how in anguish sore I groan,
Yearning for death my pain to mitigate.
  Come death, and with one blow
  Cut short my span, and so
With my curst life me of my frenzy ease ;
For wheresoe'er I go, 'twill sure decrease.

Save death no way of comfort doth remain :
  No anodyne beside for this sore smart.
The boon, then, Love bestow ;
And presently by death annul my woe,
And from this abject life release my heart.
  Since from me joy is ta'en,
  And every solace, deign
My prayer to grant, and let my death the cheer
Complete, that she now hath of her new fere.

Song, it may be that no one shall thee learn :
  Nor do I care ; for none I wot, so well
As I may chant thee ; so,
This one behest I lay upon thee, go
Hie thee to Love, and him in secret tell,
  How I my life do spurn,
  My bitter life, and yearn,
That to a better harbourage he bring
Me, of all might and grace that own him king.

Full well my tears attest, etc.

Filostrato's mood and its cause were made abundantly mani-
fest by the words of this song ; and perchance they had been
made still more so by the looks of a lady that was among the
dancers, had not the shades of night, which had now overtaken
them, concealed the blush that suffused her face.   Other songs
followed until the hour for slumber arrived : whereupon at
the behest of the queen all the ladies sought their several
chambers.

END OF VOL. I